S0-AAZ-906

"The expert handicapper explained that a winner was a sure thing. So I borrowed $200 and handed it over to my bookie. My horse came in second and I lost everything. This scenario taught me several important life lessons. One was that gambling is a lot of fun but you have to be a billionaire or an idiot to do it regularly. The other is that not everything in the world is exactly as it seems—especially the integrity of the racetrack. This revelation made it evident that racetracks and the people who inhabit that world are the perfect background for stories of lying, stealing, cheating, and any other crime you can conjure. Here, then, is the field for MURDER AT THE RACETRACK—that rare field in which everyone is a winner."
—Otto Penzler, from the Introduction

**PRAISE FOR *DANGEROUS WOMEN*,
EDITED BY OTTO PENZLER**

"I'm not usually given to superlatives, but *Dangerous Women* may be the best, most varied, and colorful mystery anthology of all time."
—Janet Evanovich

"A brilliant anthology."
—Robert B. Parker

"Wow, what memorable dames! What terrific short stories! *Dangerous Women* is a winning collection."
—Susan Isaacs

MURDER AT THE RACETRACK

EDITED BY

Otto Penzler

NEW YORK BOSTON

The events and characters in this book are fictitious. Certain real locations and public figures are mentioned, but all other characters and events described in the book are totally imaginary.

Copyright of the collection © 2006 by Otto Penzler
Introduction copyright © 2006 by Otto Penzler
"Keller By a Nose" copyright © 2006 by Lawrence Block; "The Return of the Thin White Dude . . . Screaming" copyright © 2006 by Ken Bruen; "Zuppe Inglese" copyright © 2006 by Jan Burke; "Yellow Mama's Long Weekend" copyright © 2006 by Lorenzo Carcaterra; "That Kind of Nag" copyright © 2006 by Max Allan Collins; "The Odds" copyright © 2006 by Thomas H. Cook; "The Hustle" copyright © 2006 by Pat Jordan; "The Great, the Good and the Not-So-Good" copyright © 2006 by H.R.F. Keating; "The Cover Story Is Always a Lie" copyright © 2006 by John Lescroart; "Raindancer" copyright © 2006 by Michael Malone; "The Long Shot" copyright © 2006 by Michele Rebecca Martinez Campbell; "Meadowlands" copyright © 2006 by Joyce Carol Oates; "Hotwalking" copyright © 2006 by Julie Smith; "Pinwheel" copyright © 2006 by Scott Wolven

Mysterious Press
Warner Books

Time Warner Book Group
1271 Avenue of the Americas, New York, NY 10020
Visit our Web site at www.twbookmark.com.
The Mysterious Press name and logo are registered trademarks of Warner Books.
Book design by Fearn Cutler de Vicq
Cover design by Bradford Foltz
Cover illustration by Stanislaw Fernandes
Printed in the United States of America
Published simultaneously in hardcover by Mysterious Press
First Trade Edition: April 2006
10 9 8 7 6 5 4 3 2 1
LCCN: 2005937259

ISBN-13: 978-0-446-69765-1 (pbk.)
ISBN-10: 0-446-69765-6 (pbk.)

For Elmore Leonard
A great hard-boiled writer
A great soft-boiled friend

CONTENTS

INTRODUCTION

Otto Penzler

What is it about horse racing that makes it seem so out of kilter? Here we have exquisitely beautiful animals upon whom are lavished all the care that most men don't even offer their wives. It's an outdoor sport, mainly reserved for warm sunny days, with bright green lawns in the infield and leafy old trees beyond.

Yet if there's a dirtier sport than horse racing, one with more fixes than Needle Park (and let's get this straight—professional wrestling has as much to do with sports as Dennis Rodman has to do with splitting the atom), I have yet to discover it. Even boxing, which has the reputation of being crooked, is purer than a seven-year-old Pakistani bride compared with "the Sport of Kings."

There are good reasons for an owner to want his horse to lose a race. The more times a big old stallion steps into the gate and comes up short, the longer the odds are for the next race. A sudden victory with long odds can pay off very handsomely if a clever fellow has placed a substantial bet on that very outcome.

It's almost impossible to count the ways in which an owner (or a trainer, not to mention the occasional jockey) can stop a horse from winning. Various chemicals can slow down a horse, and so can the wrong food. A long run in the middle of the night probably won't have a positive effect on a horse's stamina the next afternoon. You don't want to know what a sponge shoved way up a horse's nose will do to the poor critter. There are other methods of killing a racer's chances of a first-place finish, some a bit too uncomfortable to describe here, but trust me—there are a lot of them.

Here's a little story that I promise is true, but I'll have to bypass a name for obvious reasons. About a thousand years ago, shortly after the invention of movable type, I worked in the sports department of the New York *Daily News*. An expert handicapper had a desk in the corner and his picks ran in the paper every day. He was heading off for a vacation and asked me for a favor: Would I handicap the races at Aqueduct for the next two weeks? This way there would be no interruption in the handicapping service, and bettors who relied on his picks wouldn't go into withdrawal.

Well, I explained, I didn't think I could pick the winner of the race if it was Secretariat running against a mule. And all that arcane stuff about mudders (nothing to do with fadders) and maidens (who could also be male) was an alien language, so suggesting that I pass myself off as an expert seemed as far-fetched as my dream of playing centerfield for the New York Yankees. "No problem," he assured me. "I'll teach you all about it tomorrow," he said. Which he did.

He went on vacation and I had a merry old time picking the win-place-show results of every race for the next couple of weeks. When he returned from his fun in the sun, we tabulated the results, and to the amazement of one and all (especially me), I had amassed a better winning percentage than he had. Then again, Ray Charles throwing darts at the *Racing Form* would probably have done better than either of us.

Still, he was delighted and grateful that I hadn't embarrassed him and he decided to thank me by telling me to bet on a certain horse a few days later. Understand, I was making about $75 a week at the time, frequently skipping even simple meals a couple of times a week because I couldn't afford both lunch *and* a book I just had to have. So I bet two bucks on the horse he told me about, and sure enough, I won about eight dollars and was feeling pretty good about the whole thing. When he approached me the next day, beaming, he asked how much I'd won, and I told him. He practically threw me out the window. "I give you a winner," he shouted, "and you bet a lousy two bucks?" Well, I had figured, if I can pick them better than he could, just how much did I want to risk?

He patiently explained that when he gave me a *winner,* it wasn't exactly because he had handicapped it. It was a sure thing. So he told me he'd give me another, but this time I should put down a real bet. A week or so later, he gave me another horse. I scraped together what I could and bet twenty dollars this time. I won nearly ninety dollars (more than a week's pay!) and felt like John D. Rockefeller (or Scrooge McDuck, to make a literary reference).

The next day, we replayed the same scene. He was again outraged at my gutlessness and told me so. After calling me lots of not very nice names, most of which described in colorful and comprehensive detail my lack of brains as well as heart, he told me he'd give me one more, but then that was it. By now I was getting the hang of it, so I borrowed $200 and handed it over to my favorite bookie and advised him to lay it off (pass the bet along to another bookie) since this was a sure thing and I didn't want to see him lose all the money that I was going to rake in. He told me he'd risk it. Naturally, and you saw this coming, my horse came in second and I lost everything I'd previously won and a whole lot more. Next day he shrugged and said you can't win 'em all.

This scenario taught me several important life lessons. One is that gambling is really a lot of fun, but you have to be a billionaire or an idiot to do it regularly. The other is that not everything in the world is exactly as it seems, including—and, perhaps, especially—the integrity of the racetrack.

As a result, this revelation made it evident that racetracks and the people who inhabit that world—most of whom, I'm absolutely certain, are utterly fair, honest and aboveboard (which is my moment of political correctness for the month)—are the perfect background for stories of lying, stealing, cheating and any other crime you can conjure.

Here, then, is the field for *Murder at the Racetrack*—that rare field in which everyone is a winner.

Lawrence Block has received the two greatest honors that the mystery world can bestow: the Grand Master Award from the Mystery Writers of America and the Diamond Dagger from the (British) Crime Writers' Association, both for lifetime achievement.

Ken Bruen's twenty novels are among the darkest in the history of crime fiction. He has been nominated for an Edgar and won the Shamus award from the Private Eye Writers of America for *The Guards,* which introduced his Galway-based P.I., Jack Taylor.

Jan Burke won the Edgar for Best Novel in 2000 for *Bones,*

an Irene Kelly novel. She is the founder of the Crime Lab Project, which aims to give greater support for forensic science in America. She has served on the National Board of Directors of MWA and was the president of the Southern California chapter.

Lorenzo Carcaterra is the author of six books including the controversial *Sleepers,* which became a *New York Times* number one bestseller in hardcover and paperback, as well as a major motion picture starring Brad Pitt, Robert De Niro, Kevin Bacon and Minnie Driver. He is the producer and writer of NBC's *Law and Order.*

Max Allan Collins is the author of more than thirty novels, many featuring Nate Heller, all of whose adventures feature real-life people and some element of actual history. He has made films with Patty McCormack and Mickey Spillane, and wrote the *Dick Tracy* comic strip for many years.

Thomas H. Cook has been nominated for Edgars five times in three different categories (True Crime, Paperback Original and Best Novel), winning the Best Novel of the Year award in 1997 for *The Chatham School Affair.* Several of his novels have been filmed in Japan.

Pat Jordan is the author of more than a thousand stories and articles for such publications as *The New Yorker, GQ, The New York Times Magazine, Playboy* and *Harper's.* He has also written eleven books, one of which, *A False Spring,* was hailed by *Time* as one of "the best and truest books about baseball."

H.R.F. Keating is one of the Grand Old Men of mystery fiction. As one of Britain's leading critics for more than half a century and the author of more than fifty books, he was given the Diamond Dagger by the (British) Crime Writers' Association in 1996 for lifetime achievement.

John Lescroart is the author of sixteen crime novels, the last thirteen featuring Dismas Hardy (beginning with *Dead Irish* in 1989), which have become regulars on the bestseller lists. Hardy is named for Saint Dismas, who is the patron saint of thieves and criminals.

Michael Malone has written three mystery novels featuring the wealthy Justin Savile V and his boss, Police Chief Cuddy R. Mangum, plus the *New York Times* bestselling *The Killing Club,* based on the daytime drama series *One Life to Live,* of which he was the head writer. He won an Edgar for Best Short Story, "Red Clay," in 1997.

Michele Martinez, like Melanie Vargas, the chief protagonist of her novel *Most Wanted* (the first of a series), was a federal prosecutor in New York City, serving as Assistant United States Attorney in the Eastern District, home to the biggest and richest drug gangs in America.

Joyce Carol Oates, a winner of the National Book Award as well as five other nominations, is the author of such best sellers as *We Were the Mulvaneys* and *Blonde.* Arguably the greatest living writer in the world, she is the author of nearly a hundred books, including novels, short story collections, poetry, criticism, children's literature and so forth.

Julie Smith has written twenty mystery novels, including five about a San Francisco lawyer, Rebecca Schwartz, who made her debut in *Death Turns a Trick,* and nine about Skip Langdon, a female New Orleans cop who was the heroine of the 1991 Edgar-winning *New Orleans Mourning.*

Scott Wolven has had stories selected for *Best American Mystery Stories of the Year* for four consecutive years—more appearances than any writer aside from Joyce Carol Oates. His first book, the short story collection *Controlled Burn,* was published in 2004 by Scribner.

Now we're at the post and the bugler is raising the horn to his lips, so get ready for a great ride—and some terrifying moments as *Murder at the Racetrack* awaits.

—Otto Penzler
New York, July 2005

MURDER AT THE RACETRACK

KELLER BY A NOSE

Lawrence Block

So who do you like in the third?"

Keller had to hear the question a second time before he realized it was meant for him. He turned, and a little guy in a Mets warm-up jacket was standing there, a querulous expression on his lumpy face.

Who did he like in the third? He hadn't been paying any attention, and was stuck for a response. This didn't seem to bother the guy, who answered the question himself.

"The Two horse is odds-on, so you can't make any money betting on him. And the Five horse might have an outside chance, but he never finished well on turf. The Three, he's okay at five furlongs, but at this distance? So I got to say I agree with you."

Keller hadn't said a word. What was there to agree with?

"You're like me," the fellow went on. "Not like one of these degenerates, has to bet every race, can't go five minutes without some action. Me, sometimes I'll come here, spend the whole day, not put two dollars down the whole time. I just like to breathe some fresh air and watch those babies run."

Keller, who hadn't intended to say anything, couldn't help himself. He said, "Fresh air?"

"Since they gave the smokers a room of their own," the little man said, "it's not so bad in here. Excuse me, I see somebody I oughta say hello to."

He walked off, and the next time Keller noticed him the guy was at the ticket window, placing a bet. Fresh air, Keller thought. Watch those babies run. It sounded good, until you took note of the fact that those babies were out at Belmont, running around a track in the open air, while Keller and the little man and sixty or eighty other people were jammed into a midtown storefront, watching the whole thing on television.

Keller, holding a copy of the *Racing Form*, looked warily around the OTB parlor. It was on Lexington at Forty-fifth Street, just up from Grand Central, and not much more than a five-minute walk from his First Avenue apartment, but this was his first visit. In fact, as far as he could tell, it was the first time he had ever noticed the place. He must have walked past it hundreds if not thousands of times over the years, but he'd somehow never registered it, which showed the extent of his interest in off-track betting.

Or on-track betting, or any betting at all. Keller had been to the track three times in his entire life. The first time he'd placed a couple of small bets—two dollars here, five dollars there. His horses had run out of the money, and he'd felt stupid. The other times he hadn't even put a bet down.

He'd been to gambling casinos on several occasions, generally work related, and he'd never felt comfortable there. It was clear that a lot of people found the atmosphere exciting, but as far as Keller was concerned it was just sensory overload. All that noise, all those flashing lights, all those people chasing all that money. Keller, feeding a slot machine or playing a hand of blackjack to fit in, just wanted to go to his room and lie down.

Well, he thought, people were different. A lot of them clearly got something out of gambling. What some of them got, to be sure, was the attention of Keller or somebody like him. They'd lost money they couldn't pay, or stolen money to gamble with, or had found some other way to make somebody seriously unhappy with them. Enter Keller, and, sooner rather than later, exit the gambler.

For most gamblers, though, it was a hobby, a harmless pastime. And, just because Keller couldn't figure out what they got out of it, that didn't mean there was nothing there. Keller, looking around the OTB parlor at all those woulda-coulda-shoulda faces, knew there was nothing feigned about their enthusiasm. They were really into it, whatever it was.

And, he thought, who was he to say their enthusiasm was misplaced? One man's meat, after all, was another man's *poisson*. These fellows, all wrapped up in *Racing Form* gibberish, would be hard put to make sense out of his Scott catalog. If they caught a glimpse of Keller, hunched over one of his stamp albums, a magnifying glass in one hand and a pair of tongs in the other, they'd most likely figure he was out of his mind. Why play with little bits of perforated paper when you could bet money on horses?

"They're off!"

And so they were. Keller looked at the wall-mounted television screen and watched those babies run.

• • •

It started with stamps.

He collected worldwide, from the first postage stamp,

Great Britain's Penny Black and Two-Penny Blue of 1840, up to shortly after the end of World War II. (Just when he stopped depended upon the country. He collected most countries through 1949, but his British Empire issues stopped at 1952, with the death of George VI. The most recent stamp in his collection was over fifty years old.)

When you collected the whole world, your albums held spaces for many more stamps than you would ever be able to acquire. Keller knew he would never completely fill any of his albums, and he found this not frustrating but comforting. No matter how long he lived or how much money he got, he would always have more stamps to look for. You tried to fill in the spaces, of course—that was the point—but it was the trying that brought you pleasure, not the accomplishment.

Consequently, he never absolutely had to have any particular stamp. He shopped carefully, and he chose the stamps he liked, and he didn't spend more than he could afford. He'd saved money over the years, he'd even reached a point where he'd been thinking about retiring, but when he got back into stamp collecting, his hobby gradually ate up his retirement fund—which, all things considered, was fine with him. Why would he want to retire? If he retired, he'd have to stop buying stamps.

As it was, he was in a perfect position. He was never desperate for money, but he could always find a use for it. If Dot came up with a whole string of jobs for him, he wound up putting a big chunk of the proceeds into his stamp collection. If business slowed down, no problem—he'd make small purchases from the dealers who shipped him stamps on approval, send some small checks to others who mailed him their monthly lists, but hold off on anything substantial until business picked up.

It worked fine. Until the Bulger & Calthorpe auction catalog came along and complicated everything.

Bulger & Calthorpe were stamp auctioneers based in Omaha. They advertised regularly in *Linn's* and the other stamp publications, and traveled extensively to examine collectors' holdings. Three or four times a year they would rent a hotel suite in downtown Omaha and hold an auction, and for a few years now Keller had been receiving their well-illustrated catalogs. Their catalog featured an extensive collection of France and French colonies, and Keller leafed through it on the off-chance that he might find himself in Omaha around that time. He was thinking of something else when he hit the first page of color photographs, and whatever it was he forgot it forever.

Martinique #2. And, right next to it, Martinique #17.

. . .

On the screen, the Two horse led wire to wire, winning by four and a half lengths. "Look at that," the little man said, once again at Keller's elbow. "What did I tell you? Pays three-fucking-forty for a two-dollar ticket. Where's the sense in that?"

"Did you bet him?"

"I didn't bet on him," the man said, "and I didn't bet against him. What I had, I had the Eight horse to place, which is nothing but a case of getting greedy, because look what he did, will you? He came in third, right behind the Five horse, so if I bet him to show, or if I semi-wheeled the Trifecta, playing a Two-Five-Eight and a Two-Eight-Five . . ."

Woulda-coulda-shoulda, thought Keller.

. . .

He'd spent half an hour with the Bulger & Calthorpe catalog, reading the descriptions of the two Martinique lots, seeing what else was on offer, and returning more than once for a further look at Martinique #2 and Martinique #17. He interrupted himself to check the balance in his bank account, frowned, pulled out the album that ran from Leeward Islands to Netherlands, opened it to Martinique, and looked first at the couple hundred stamps he had and then at the two empty spaces, spaces designed to hold—what else?—Martinique #2 and Martinique #17.

He closed the album but didn't put it away, not yet, and he picked up the phone and called Dot.

"I was wondering," he said, "if anything came in."

"Like what, Keller?"

"Like work," he said.

"Was your phone off the hook?"

"No," he said. "Did you try to call me?"

"If I had," she said, "I'd have reached you, since your phone wasn't off the hook. And if a job came in I'd have called, the way I always do. But instead you called me."

"Right."

"Which leads me to wonder why."

"I could use the work," he said. "That's all."

"You worked when? A month ago?"

"Closer to two."

"You took a little trip, went like clockwork, smooth as silk. Client paid me and I paid you, and if that's not silken clockwork I don't know what is. Say, is there a new woman in the picture, Keller? Are you spending serious money on earrings again?"

"Nothing like that."

"Then why would you . . . Keller, it's stamps, isn't it?"

"I could use a few dollars," he said. "That's all."

"So you decided to be proactive and call me. Well, I'd be proactive myself, but who am I gonna call? We can't go looking for our kind of work, Keller. It has to come to us."

"I know that."

"We ran an ad once, remember? And remember how it worked out?" He remembered, and made a face. "So we'll wait," she said, "until something comes along. You want to help it a little on a metaphysical level, try thinking proactive thoughts."

• • •

There was a horse in the fourth race named Going Postal. That didn't have anything to do with stamps, Keller knew, but was a reference to the propensity of disgruntled postal employees to exercise their Second Amendment rights by bringing a gun to work, often with dramatic results. Still, the name was guaranteed to catch the eye of a philatelist.

"What about the Six horse?" Keller asked the little man, who consulted in turn the *Racing Form* and the tote board on the television.

"Finished in the money three times in his last five starts," he reported, "but now he's moving up in class. Likes to come from behind, and there's early speed here, because the Two horse and the Five horse both like to get out in front." There was more that Keller couldn't follow, and then the man said, "Morning line had him at twelve-to-one, and he's up to eighteen-to-one now, so the good news is he'll pay a nice price, but the bad news is nobody thinks he's got much of a chance."

Keller got in line. When it was his turn, he bet two dollars on Going Postal to win.

• • •

Keller didn't know much about Martinique beyond the fact that it was a French possession in the West Indies, and he knew the postal authorities had stopped issuing special stamps for the place a while ago. It was now officially a department of France, and used regular French stamps. The French did that to avoid being called colonialists. By designating Martinique a part of France, the same as Normandy or Provence, they obscured the fact that the island was full of black people who worked in the fields, fields that were owned by white people who lived in Paris.

Keller had never been to Martinique—or to France, as far as that went—and had no special interest in the place. It was a funny thing about stamps; you didn't need to be interested in a country to be interested in the country's stamps. And he couldn't say what was so special about the stamps of Martinique, except that one way or another he had accumulated quite a few of them, and that made him seek out more, and now, remarkably, he had all but two.

The two he lacked were among the colony's first issues, created by surcharging stamps originally printed for general use in France's overseas empire. The first, #2 in the Scott catalog, was a twenty-centime stamp surcharged "MARTINIQUE" and "5c" in black. The second, #17, was similar: "MARTINIQUE / 15c" on a four-centime stamp.

According to the catalog, #17 was worth $7,500 mint, $7,000 used. #2 was listed at $11,000, mint or used. The listings were in italics, which was the catalog's way of indicating that the value was difficult to determine precisely.

Keller bought most of his stamps at around half the Scott valuation. Stamps with defects went much cheaper, and stamps that were particularly fresh and well centered could command a premium. With a true rarity, however, at a well-publicized auction, it was very hard to guess what price might be realized. Bulger & Calthorpe described #2—it was lot #2144 in their sales catalog—as "mint with part OG, F-VF, the nicest specimen we've seen of this genuine rarity." The description of #17—lot #2153—was almost as glowing. Both stamps were accompanied by Philatelic Foundation certificates attesting that they were indeed what they purported to be. The auctioneers estimated that #2 would bring $15,000, and pegged the other at $10,000.

But those were just estimates. They might wind up selling for quite a bit less, or a good deal more.

Keller wanted them.

• • •

Going Postal got off to a slow start, but Keller knew that was to be expected. The horse liked to come from behind. And in fact he did rally, and was running third at one point, fading in the stretch and finishing seventh in a field of nine. As the little man had predicted, the Two and Five horses had both gone out in front, and had both been overtaken, though not by Going Postal. The winner, a dappled horse named Doggen Katz, paid $19.20.

"Son of a bitch," the little man said. "I almost had him. The only thing I did wrong was decide to bet on a different horse."

• • •

What he needed, Keller decided, was fifty thousand dollars. That way he could go as high as twenty-five for #2 and fifteen for #17 and, after buyer's commission, still have a few dollars left for expenses and other stamps.

Was he out of his mind? How could a little piece of perforated paper less than an inch square be worth $25,000? How could two of them be worth a man's life?

He thought about it and decided it was just a question of degree. Unless you planned to use it to mail a letter, any expenditure for a stamp was basically irrational. If you could swallow a gnat, why gag at a camel? A hobby, he suspected, was irrational by definition. As long as you kept it in proportion, you were all right.

And he was managing that. He could, if he wanted, mortgage his apartment. Bankers would stand in line to lend him fifty grand, since the apartment was worth ten times that figure. They wouldn't ask him what he wanted the money for, either, and he'd be free to spend every dime of it on the two Martinique stamps.

He didn't consider it, not for a moment. It would be nuts, and he knew it. But what he did with a windfall was something else, and it didn't matter, anyway, because there wasn't going to be any windfall. You didn't need a weatherman, he thought, to note that the wind was not blowing. There was no wind, and there would be no windfall, and someone else could mount the Martinique overprints in his album. It was a shame, but—

The phone rang.

Dot said, "Keller, I just made a pitcher of iced tea. Why don't you come up here and help me drink it?"

• • •

In the fifth race, there was a horse named Happy Trigger and another named Hit the Boss. If Going Postal had resonated with his hobby, these seemed to suggest his profession. He mentioned them to the little fellow. "I sort of like these two," he said. "But I don't know which one I like better."

"Wheel them," the man said, and explained that Keller should buy two Exacta tickets, Four-Seven and Seven-Four. That way Keller would only collect if the two horses finished first and second. But, since the tote board indicated long odds on each of them, the potential payoff was a big one.

"What would I have to bet?" Keller asked him. "Four dollars? Because I've only been betting two dollars a race."

"You want to keep it to two dollars," his friend said, "just bet it one way. Thing is, how are you going to feel if you bet the Four-Seven and they finish Seven-Four?"

• • •

"It's right up your alley," Dot told him. "Comes through another broker, so there's a good solid firewall between us and the client. And the broker's reliable, and if the client was a corporate bond he'd be rated triple-A."

"What's the catch?"

"Keller," she said, "what makes you think there's a catch?"

"I don't know," he said. "But there is, isn't there?"

She frowned. "The only catch," she said, "if you want to call it that, is there might not be a job at all."

"I'd call that a catch."

"I suppose."

"If there's no job," he said, "why did the client call the broker, and why did the broker call you, and what am I doing out here?"

Dot pursed her lips, sighed. "There's this horse," she said.

• • •

The fifth race was reasonably exciting. Bunk Bed Betty, a big brown horse with a black mane, led all the way, only to be challenged in the stretch and overtaken at the wire by a thirty-to-one shot named Hypertension.

Hit the Boss was dead last, and which made him the only horse that Happy Trigger beat.

Keller's new friend got very excited toward the end of the race, and showed a ten-dollar Win ticket on Hypertension. "Oh, look at that," he said when they posted the payoff. "Gets me even for the day, plus yesterday and the day before. That was Alvie Jurado on Hypertension, and didn't he ride a gorgeous race there?"

"It was exciting," Keller allowed.

"A lot more exciting with ten bucks on that sweetie's nose. Sorry about your Exacta. I guess it cost you four bucks."

Keller gave a shrug that he hoped was ambiguous. In the end, he'd been uncomfortable betting four dollars, and unable to decide which way to bet his usual two dollars. So he hadn't bet anything. There was nothing wrong with that, as a matter of fact he'd saved himself two dollars, or maybe four, but he'd feel like a piker admitting as much to a man who'd just won over three hundred dollars.

• • •

"The horse's name is Kissimmee Dudley," Dot told him, "and he's running in the seventh race at Belmont Saturday. It's the feature race, and the word is that Dudley hasn't got a prayer."

"I don't know much about horses."

"They've got four legs," she said, "and if the one you bet on comes in ahead of the others, you make money. That's as much as I know about them, but I know something about Kissimmee Dudley. Our client thinks he's going to win."

"I thought you said he didn't have a prayer."

"That's the word. Our client doesn't see it that way."

"Oh?"

"Evidently Dudley's a better horse than anybody realizes," she said, "and they've been holding him back, waiting for the right race. That way they'll get long odds and be able to clean up. And, just so nothing goes wrong, the other jockeys are getting paid to make sure they don't finish ahead of Dudley."

"The race is fixed," Keller said.

"That's the plan."

"But?"

"But a plan is what things don't always go according to, Keller, which is probably a good thing, because otherwise the phone would never ring. You want some more iced tea?"

"No, thanks."

"They'll have the race on Saturday, and Dudley'll run. And if he wins you get two thousand dollars."

"For what?"

"For standing by. For making yourself available."

"I think I get it," he said. "And if Kissimmee Dudley should happen to lose—where'd they come up with a name like that, do you happen to know?"

"Not a clue."

"If he loses," Keller said, "I suppose I have work to do."

She nodded.

"The jockey who beats him?"

"Is toast," she said, "and you're the toaster."

. . .

None of the horses in the sixth race had a name that meant anything to Keller. Then again, picking them by name hadn't done him much good so far. This time he looked at the odds. A long shot wouldn't win, he decided, and a favorite wouldn't pay enough to make it worthwhile, so maybe the answer was to pick something in the middle. The Five horse, Mogadishy, was pegged at six-to-one.

He got in line, thinking. Of course, sometimes a long shot came in. Take the preceding race, for instance, with its big payoff for Keller's OTB buddy. There was a long shot in this race, and it would pay a lot more than the twelve bucks he'd win on his six-to-one shot.

On the other hand, no matter what horse he bet on, the return on his two-dollar bet wasn't going to make any real difference to him. And it would be nice to cash a winning ticket for a change.

"Sir?"

He put down his two dollars and bet the odds-on favorite to show.

. . .

Dot lived in White Plains, in a big old Victorian house on Taunton Place. She gave him a ride to the train station, and a little over an hour later he was back in his apartment, looking once again at the Bulger & Calthorpe catalog.

If Kissimmee Dudley ran and lost, he'd have a job to do. And his fee for the job would be just enough to fill the two spaces in his album. And, since the horse was racing at Belmont, it stood to reason that all of the jockeys lived within easy commuting distance of the Long Island racetrack. Keller wouldn't have to get on a plane to find his man.

If Kissimmee Dudley won, Keller got to keep the two-thousand-dollar standby fee. That was a decent amount of money for not doing a thing, and there were times when he'd have been happy to see it play out that way.

But this wasn't one of those times. He really wanted those stamps. If the horse lost, well, he'd go out and earn them. But what if the damned horse won?

• • •

The sixth race ended with Pass the Gas six lengths ahead of the field. Keller cashed his ticket, and ran into his friend, who'd been talking with a fellow who bore a superficial resemblance to Jerry Orbach.

"Saw you in line to get paid," the little man said. "What did you have, the Exacta or the Trifecta?"

"I don't really understand those fancy bets," Keller admitted. "I just put my money on Pass the Gas."

"Paid even money, didn't he? That's not so bad."

"I had him to show."

"Well, if you had enough of a bet on him—"

"Just two dollars."

"So you got back two-twenty," the man said.

"I just felt like winning," Keller said.

"Well," the man said, "you won."

• • •

He'd put down the catalog, picked up the phone. When Dot answered he said, "I was thinking. If that Dudley horse wins, the client wins his bet and I don't have any work to do."

"Right."

"But if one of the other jockeys crosses him up—"

"It's the last time he'll ever do it."

"Well," he said, "why would he do it? The jockey, I mean. What would be the point?"

"Does it matter?"

"I'm just trying to understand it," he said. "I mean, I could understand if it was boxing. Like in the movies. They want the guy to throw a fight. But he can't do it, something in him recoils at the very idea, and he has to go on and win the fight, even if it means he'll get his legs broken."

"And never play the piano again," Dot said. "I think I saw that movie, Keller."

"All the boxing movies are like that, except the ones with Sylvester Stallone running up flights of steps. But how would that apply with horses?"

"I don't know," she said. "It's been years since I saw *National Velvet*."

"If you were a jockey, and they paid you to throw a race, and you didn't—I mean, where's the percentage in it?"

"You could bet on yourself."

"You'd make more money betting on Kissimmee Dudley. He's the long shot, right?"

"That's a point."

"And that way nobody'd have a reason to take out a contract on you, either."

"Another point," Dot said. "And if the jockeys are all as reasonable as you and I, Keller, you're not going to see a dime beyond the two grand. But they're very small."

"The jockeys?"

"Uh-huh. Short and scrawny little bastards, every last one

of them. Who the hell knows what somebody like that is going to do?"

• • •

Keller's friend was short enough to be a jockey, but a long way from scrawny. Facially, he looked a little like Jerry Orbach. It was beginning to dawn on Keller that everybody in the OTB parlor, even the blacks and the Asians, looked a little like Jerry Orbach. It was a sort of a horseplayer look, and they all had it.

"Kissimmee Dudley," Keller said. "Where'd somebody come up with a name like that?"

The little man consulted his *Racing Form*. "By Florida Cracker out of Dud Avocado," he said. "Kissimmee's in Florida, isn't it?"

"Is it?"

"I think so." The fellow shrugged. "The name's the least of that horse's problems. You take a look at his form?"

The man reeled off a string of sentences, and Keller just let the words wash over him. If he tried to follow it he'd only wind up feeling stupid. Well, so what? How many of these Jerry Orbach clones would know what to do with a perforation gauge?

"Look at the morning line," the man went on. "Hell, look at the tote board. Old Dudley's up there at forty-to-one."

"That means he doesn't have a chance?"

"A long shot'll come in once in a while," the man allowed. "Look at Hypertension. With him, though, his past performance charts showed he had a chance. A slim one, but slim's better than no chance at all."

"And Kissimmee Dudley? No chance at all?"

"He'd need a tailwind and a whole lot of luck," the man said, "before he could rise to the level of no chance at all."

Keller slipped away, and when he came back from the ticket window his friend asked him what horse he'd bet on. Keller's response was mumbled, and the man had to ask him to repeat it.

"Kissimmee Dudley," he said.

"That right?"

"I know what you said, and I suppose you're right, but I just had a feeling."

"A hunch," the man said.

"Sort of, yes."

"And you're a man on a lucky streak, aren't you? I mean, you just won twenty cents betting the favorite to show."

The line was meant to be sarcastic, but something funny happened; by the time the man got to the end of the sentence, his manner had somehow changed. Keller was wondering what to make of it—had he just been insulted or not?

"The trick," the fellow said, "is doing the wrong thing at the right time." He went away and came back, and told Keller he probably ought to have his head examined, but what the hell.

"Kissimmee Dudley," he said, savoring each syllable. "I can't believe I bet on that animal. Only way he's gonna win the seventh race is if he was entered in the sixth, but it'll be some sweet payoff if he does. Not forty-to-one, though. Price is down to thirty-to-one."

"That's too bad," Keller said.

"Except it's a good sign, because it means some late bets are coming in on the horse. You see a horse drop just before post time from, say, five-to-one to three-to-one, that's a good sign." He shrugged. "When you start at forty-to-one, you need more than good signs. You need a rocket up your ass, either that or you need all the other horses to drop dead."

• • •

Keller wasn't sure what to watch for. He knew what you did to get your horse to run faster. You hit him with the whip and dug your heels into his flanks.

But suppose you wanted to slow him down? You could sit back in the saddle and yank on the reins, but wouldn't that be a little on the obvious side? Could you just hold off on the whip and cool it a little with the heel-digging? Would that be enough to keep your mount from edging out Kissimmee Dudley?

The horses were entering the starting gate, and he picked out Dudley and decided he looked like a winner. But then they all looked like winners to Keller, big, well-bred horses, some taking their positions without a fuss, others showing a little spirit and giving their riders a hard time, but all of them sooner or later going where they were supposed to go.

Two of the jockeys were girls, Keller noticed, including the one riding the second favorite. Except you were probably supposed to call them women, you had to stop calling them girls these days around the time they entered kindergarten, from what Keller could tell. Still, when they were jockey-size, it seemed a stretch to call them women. Was he being sexist? Maybe, or maybe he was being sizeist, or heightist. He wasn't sure.

"They're off!"

And so they were, bursting out of the starting gate. Neither of the girl jockeys was riding Kissimmee Dudley, so if one of them won, well, she'd live to regret it, albeit briefly. Some people in Keller's line of work didn't like to take out women, while others were supposed to get a special satisfaction out of it. Keller didn't care one way or the other. He wasn't a sexist when it came to business, although he wasn't sure that was enough to make him a hero in the eyes of the National Organization of Women.

"Will you look at that!"

Keller had been looking at the screen, but without registering what he was seeing. Now he realized that Kissimmee Dudley was out in front, with a good lead on the rest of the field.

Keller's little friend was urging him on. "Oh, you beauty," he said. "Oh run, you son of a bitch. Oh yes. Oh yes!"

Were any of the horses being held back? If so, Keller couldn't see it. If he didn't know better, he'd swear Kissimmee Dudley was simply outrunning all of the other horses, proving himself to be superior to the competition.

But wait a damn minute. That piebald horse—what did he think he was doing? Why was he gaining ground on Dudley?

"No!" cried the little man. "Where'd the Two horse come from? It's that fucking Alvie Jurado. Fade, you cocksucker! Die, will you? Come on, Dudley!"

The guy had liked Jurado well enough when he was making money for him on Hypertension. Now, riding a horse named Steward's Folly, he'd become the enemy. Maybe, Keller thought, the jockey was just trying to make it look good. Maybe he'd ease up at the very end, settling for the place money and avoiding any suspicion that he'd thrown the race.

But it was a hell of a show Jurado was putting on, standing up in the stirrups, flailing away with the whip, apparently doing everything he possibly could to get Steward's Folly to the wire ahead of Kissimmee Dudley.

"It's Kissimmee Dudley and Steward's Folly," the announcer cried. "Steward's Folly and Kissimmee Dudley. They're neck and neck, nose to nose as they hit the wire—"

"Shit on toast," Keller's friend said.

"Who won?"

"Who fucking knows? See? It's a photo finish." And indeed the word *photo* flashed on and off on the television screen. "Son of a *bitch*. Where did that fucking Jurado come from?"

"He gained a lot of ground in a hurry," Keller said.

"The little prick. Now we have to wait for the photo. I wish they'd hurry. See, I really got behind that hunch of yours." He showed a ticket, and Keller leaned over and squinted at it.

"A hundred dollars?"

"On the nose," the little man said, "plus I got him wheeled in the five-dollar Exacta. You got a hunch and I bet a bunch. And he went off at twenty-eight-to-one, and if it's a Six-Two Exacta with him and Steward's Folly, Jesus, I'm rich. I'm fucking rich. And you got two bucks on him yourself, so you'll win yourself fifty-six dollars. Unless you went and played him to show, which would explain why you're so calm, 'cause it'd be the same to you if he comes in first or second. Is that what you went and did?"

"Not exactly," Keller said, and fished out a ticket.

"A hundred bucks to win! Man, when you get a hunch you really back it, don't you?"

Keller didn't say anything. He had nineteen other tickets just like it in his pocket, but the little man didn't have to know about them. If the photo of the two horses crossing the finish line showed Dudley in front, his tickets would be worth $58,000.

If not, well, Alvie Jurado would be worth almost as much.

"I got to hand it to you," the little man said. "All that dough on the line, and you're calm as a cucumber."

• • •

Ten days later, Keller sat at his dining room table. He was holding a pair of stainless steel stamp tongs, and they in turn were holding a little piece of paper worth—

Well, it was hard to say just how much it was worth. The stamp was Martinique #2, and Keller had wound up bidding $18,500 for it. The lot had opened at $9,000, and there was a bidder in the third row on the right who dropped out around the $12,000 mark, and then there was a phone bidder who hung on like grim death. When the auctioneer pounded the gavel and said, "Sold for eighteen five to JPK," Keller's heart was pounding harder than the gavel.

It was still racing eight lots later when the second stamp, Martinique #17, went on the block. It had a lower Scott value than #2, and was estimated lower in the Bulger & Calthorpe sales catalog, and the starting bid was lower, too, at an even $6,000.

And then, remarkably, it had wound up sailing all the way to $21,250 before Keller prevailed over another phone bidder. (Or the same one, irritated at having lost #2 and unwilling to miss out on #17.) That was too much, it was three times the Scott value, but what could you do? He wanted the stamp, and he could afford it, and when would he get a chance at another one like it?

With buyer's commission, the two lots had cost him $43,725.

He admired the stamp through his magnifier. It looked beautiful to him, although he couldn't say why; aesthetically, it wasn't discernibly different from other Martinique overprints worth less than twenty dollars. Carefully, he cut a mount to size, slipped the stamp into it, and secured it in his album.

Not for the first time, he thought of the little man at the OTB parlor. Keller hadn't seen him since that afternoon and doubted he'd ever cross paths with him again. He remembered the fellow's excitement and how impressed he'd been by Keller's own coolness.

Cool? Naturally he'd been cool. Either way he won. If he didn't cash the winning tickets on Kissimmee Dudley, he'd do just about as well when he punched Alvie Jurado's ticket. It was interesting, waiting to see how the photo came out, but he couldn't say it was all that nerve-racking.

Not when you compared it to sitting in a hotel suite in Omaha, waiting for hours while lot after lot was auctioned off, until finally the stamps you'd been waiting for came up for bids. And then sitting there with your pencil lifted to indicate you were bidding, sitting there while the price climbed higher and higher, not knowing where it would stop, not knowing if you had enough cash in the belt around your waist. How high would you have to go for the first lot? And would you have enough left for the other one? And what was the matter with that phone bidder? Would the man never quit?

Now that was excitement, he thought, as he cut a second mount for Martinique #17. That was true edge-of-the-chair tension, unlike anything those Jerry Orbach look-alikes in the OTB parlor would ever know.

He felt sorry for them.

What difference did it make, really, how the photo finish turned out? What did he care who won the race? If Kissimmee Dudley held on to win by a nose or a nose hair, it was up to Keller to work out a tax-free way to cash twenty $100 tickets. If Steward's Folly made it home first, Alvie Jurado moved to the top of Keller's list of Things to Make and Do. Whichever chore Keller wound up with, he had to pull it off in a hurry; he had to have his money in hand—or, more accurately, in belt—when his flight took off for Omaha.

And now it was over, and he'd done what he had to, so did it matter what it was he'd done?

Hell, no. He had the stamps.

THE RETURN OF THE THIN WHITE DUDE . . . SCREAMING

Ken Bruen

I was in love with Joan Baez.

Does it get more fucked than that?

You'll notice I said . . . *was*.

Not anymore; that ship has sailed.

We're about the same age, me and Joanie, racked up the same amount of mileage. Course, she looks a hell of a lot better.

I'm into Bowie again . . . yeah, me and Ziggy, gonna go out on the same stage. Back in the '80s, I was still with the department. The horses were then just a hobby, an expensive one but not yet a jones.

The thin white dude did a concert at the Garden. I pulled point, got to be part of the squad inside.

Man, I'll never forget, on his way from the dressing room, looking like some damned golden angel, he paused, looked at me and said in that Brit accent,

"Ta very much, Guv."

I needed that translated . . . it means, "Thank you very much, Boss."

Fucking A.

Class, you better believe it.

Other concerts I pulled, the cocksuckers wouldn't give you the freaking time of day. Faggots, all of 'em, especially the guys from the West Coast.

Punks?

Yeah, you got that right.

I was a pretty good cop for a time, but what can I tell you? I had a family, kids to feed, a wife who seemed to change the furniture every year, so I began to take a little. Started to spend more and more time at OTB. Days I was on call, I went to the track and fuck, I was hemorrhaging cash. Got involved with a loan shark and the vig . . . murder. When I was trying to deal with the bloodsucker, he said, in a Brooklyn accent, the words leaking out of the side of his mouth,

"You know fuck all about racing. Why don't you just put a Zippo to the money, save you the trip to the track."

Go on . . . trot it out

> Bad cop
> Rotten apple
> Bag man
> On the dime

You're taking twenty bucks here, then, what the hell, it's Franklins, then you stop counting. You're telling yourself,

"No biggie."

It is.

I became a regular at OTB. That shit creeps up on you.

Next thing, the loan shark, he wants, like, a favor and I'm

getting in the hole so bad. Meanwhile, they started cleaning up the department, and I'm asking, like, what about the goddamn streets. No, go after their freaking own. I'd made lieutenant and when the board got through with me, I was real lucky not to do time. Bounced me of course, no pension.

So, my wife takes off—with a CPA. Always hated accountants. Figures, right?

Ended up in a room in Brooklyn, not a rape away from Bed Stuy. Man, those were rough times. I was hitting the sauce and doing a little blow, nothing major, just to clear the cobwebs ... Bowie, Major Tom ...

Still listening to Joan till one night I'm real close to eating my piece. Not my department issue, naw, a piece of shit I bought on the street. You're a cop, you gotta have hardware. I'd blown the last of my savings on a sure thing in the Kentucky Derby.

Got the metal in my mouth, Joanie is doing "Diamonds and Rust," I can taste the oil on my gums and I'm a hair from squeezing when the phone rang. Near pulled the trigger from the start the sound gave me.

I wasn't getting a whole lot of calls then. I put the gun aside, real careful, and snatching the receiver, hear,

"Loot?"

Only one guy in the whole Manhattan area calls me that.

Lenny.

Me and the Lenster go way back. He was with Manhattan South for a while but got busted early on in a scam over hookers.

Said to me one time,

"You got horse fever and me, I got hooker fever. H and H, going to be the death of us, bro."

Got himself a sweet deal with some mob guy and was

pulling down serious change. He'd offered me some of that, but mob guys? I'd gone,

"You fucking nuts? I'm a cop for chrissakes."

Not no more.

He asked,

"How's it hanging, bro?"

I said,

"Been better."

And he laughed. I swear, I think he could see the Saturday Night Special I'd tossed. He went,

"Listen, I'm living out on the Island, got me a real nice pad. What say you hop a cab, get yer ass over here and we sink some brews. How's that sound?"

Sounded better than Baez is what it sounded.

The fare to Long Island was a bitch but Lenny had been waiting, right on the curb, saw the cab pull up. He's over to the driver, palms him a wad, says,

"Take the evening off, buddy."

Lenny's a small guy, comes up to maybe my shoulder, but built like the proverbial shithouse and ferocious with it. He's from Boston but came to New York as his old lady was from the Bronx. Used to box, welterweight, till some spade stopped his clock. His nose is scrunched to the right, gives him an almost comical appearance, but you don't get too many guys laughing about it, least not twice. He has a hair-trigger temper. Made him one ballsy cop but brought him down—that and the mob stuff. He was wearing an Armani suit, not a rip-off but the real deal; you can always tell. The way it hangs? Like attitude.

I get out of the cab and he goes,

"Come here, you big lug."

I'm a tall guy, getting a little stooped but can still measure up, least where it matters. He shoots his cuff and I see the Rolex . . . shining against his Miami tan, "Diamonds and Rust."

He gives me a tight hug. I'm not real comfortable with that shit but what the hell, no one had touched me in a while.

A hooker I had in Bed Stuy, whining,

"Don't touch the hair and no kissing."

Real affectionate broad.

I'm banging away, trying to get it over, get off, and she asked,

"You near done?"

Just like my old lady, if a little better looking, and at least she took the cash up front, not the daily bleeding me useless.

Lenny goes,

"We gonna stay on the curb all evening? Get your sorry ass in here." Christ, what a pad, massive and with white leather furniture, paintings on the wall. I don't know art from shinola but they had little lights above them, so I figure they were expensive. There's a young girl on the couch, dressed in bra and panties, a real beaut, her head nodding like the junkies on Seventh.

Lenny said,

"Say hello to Angie. She's a little outta it but she bangs like a trooper."

Lenny always had a mouth on him. He shouts,

"Yo, babe, get us some cold ones and bring the bottle of Grey Goose."

Took her a time, but eventually we got behind some serious drinks and Lenny said,

"The fuck you standing for? Take the weight off, get your ass on that couch, chill buddy."

I had on a Goodwill sports jacket, and truth to tell, I was a little ashamed of it. Got it off with more than a bit of relief and Lenny asked,

"You're not packing?"

A cop without his piece is like a pimp without rock. I had no answer to that, so chugged my vodka and that shit, it goes down, real smooth. Lenny fills it right up, says,

"No prob, get you fixed up."

He goes out of the room and the girl looks at me, her eyes drooping, asks,

"You a cop?"

I take my time, she's not going to remember in five minutes anyway, then I said,

"Used to be."

She stared at me, then,

"Lenny says you're a compulsive gambler."

Lenny and his mouth. I feel regret that I no longer carry the shield. The regret is more than I expected and I swear I feel my eyes tearing up. Must have been that Grey Goose; sneaks up on you.

Lenny comes back, hands me a Glock, says,

"Lock 'n' load, bro."

It's like a toy in my big hand. Light as hope. Dull sheen that catches the light.

The girl asks,

"What's with you guys and guns?"

Lenny says, real quiet,

"Shut up, bitch."

The steel in his voice, no fucking around with that.

He smiles then, swallows a huge dollop of his drink, the ice clinking against his teeth, freshly capped and gleaming, like a movie star. Set you back three grand. I know; I inquired.

He said,

"October twenty-seventh."

The booze has muddled my head and I don't know what he means, so I go,

"Dunno what you mean."

He's incredulous, then,

"The Sox, man, we became world champions."

He's fucking with me, big time. I've been a Yankee fan all my life—how could I not?—and I'd almost forgotten how Lenny liked to stick it to people. The Glock is still in my hand and for one glorious moment I considered shooting the fucker.

Wish I had.

He's not finished.

"You guys choked—am I right?—got your ass handed to you."

Like I said, I should have shot him.

He busted my chops some more, making a few comments about slow horses and slower ex-cops, then suddenly jumps up, disappears into the bedroom, returns with a suede jacket, still in its plastic, asked,

"You go an XL, right? Try this. That piece of crap you got looks like you got it in Goodwill. No offense, buddy, this will make you look like a player. Next time you hit the ponies, you'll at least look the part."

I wanted to tell him to shove it, but pride had long ago taken a walk. The jacket fits snugly and he sits down, a smirk in place, and I wondered,

"Did I ever like this prick?"

He puts down a line of snow, takes a deep snort, says as he lays down some more,

"Get on the other side of this, bro."

What the hell, I do a few and feel the icy drip down the back of my throat and the instant clear thinking in my brain, like it's been washed in intelligence. Everything is hunky-dory and if I'd a copy of a form sheet, I'd have picked me some sure winners, I know it.

He smiles, says,

"See, you got to lighten up, pal."

Light? I'm floating, on clouds of ease.

I need music and hop up, ask,

"You got any music?"

Dumb, huh?

He's got Sinatra and . . . Sinatra. Sees me hesitate and says,

"There's some other crap over near the wall, the broad picked it up."

I flip through them, lots of names that mean nothing to me, *The Killers, The Streets, Franz Ferdinand,* then at the very end, *Bowie's Greatest Hits.* I grab that, like a prayer, and put it on, the opening of "Aladdin Sane" begins, Lenny snorts,

"That English faggot?"

The coke had mellowed me way low so I let that slide.

Lenny sits forward, wiping at a dribble from his nose, says,

"Time to talk business, buddy."

No free lunch, especially with cops.

His voice changes. He's got the Boston twang in place, sounding like one of the goddamn Kennedys, all fake sincerity, says,

"You want to get behind some serious change, am I right?"

I want to go,

"Take a wild fucking guess."

But just nod, shaking hands with the devil, he shakes . . . a cigarette loose from a pack of Marlboro Lights, and I nearly smile. He's shoving every substance known up his nose and smoking *Lights*?

He cranks a battered Zippo, the flame making his eyes look demented. He drags deep, then,

"We got us a sweet deal. Two lowlifes, they owe my employers a lot of green and they ain't coming up with it. They need a lesson in manners, nothing too major, no biblical stuff, but a wake-up call, you following me?"

Jesus, how complicated is it?

I ask,

"And you need me, why?"

He emits a short laugh, more like a bark, says,

"I need backup, you think I'm gonna trust some guinea in a suit to have my rear and if I remember, you were pretty damn good at shakedown before you got all fucked with that racing gig."

Not something I like to recall.

The gig smells to high heaven but what's my alternative? Joan Baez, and the barrel of a piece I'm not sure even works, so I agree.

Hearing Bowie has made me want things I used to want and haven't been able to get for a long time, like respect.

Am I blaming Ziggy? . . . duh . . . yeah.

Lenny says,

"C'mon, buddy, I'll drive you back to Brooklyn."

He's about to finish the remnants of his drink when the girl comes out of the bathroom. She's obviously been doing some dope, or rather more of it, and she staggers, knocks into

Lenny, his drink spilling on the Armani suit and he loses it, big time, goes,

"The fuck you doing?"

Begins to lay into her, slapping her face with a concentration that is pure, unadulterated hate

> One
> Two
> Three

Slap.

And I grab his arm, say,

"Enough."

Her face is already bruising, he spins, out of control, spits at me,

"You're telling me what to do . . . *Loo-tenant*? Memo to asshole: You don't get to give orders anymore, you take 'em, got that?"

I've got it.

The girl is weeping and one thing I could never take is women weeping. Reminds me of my little girls, bawling as their mother dragged them out the door and out of my life. Her final words:

"Your father is only interested in horses."

And my youngest, said,

"I like Black Beauty."

Words to kill you. Time was I'd read that to her at bedtime but got sucked into the *Racing Post* instead.

Lenny is right in my face, his spittle on my cheek, like acid. I bite down, tell myself,

"Chill, buddy, you need this gig, let it burn, slow, and keep it on simmer."

When he sees I'm not going to muscle, he spins on the girl and screams,

"Take that fucking whining cunt off my stereo."

Calling Bowie that, I add it to the shopping list.

His ride is, of course, a Chevy and I try not to think about the amount of booze and chemicals in his blood, but the rage has cleansed him and he's Mr. Affability. We get to Brooklyn, him extolling the Sox the whole trip and he pulls up, looks around at the hood, says,

"Man, you're almost in Bed Stuy."

Then he gives me a good-natured punch on the shoulder, asks,

"We cool, buddy?"

I give him the yard about letting off steam, and we both act like it's true. He aims a feint blow at my chin, says,

"Try and stay out of the OTB. In a little while, you can go to the track in style. A week from Friday, come to my place, we'll go do our work and after, we'll party hard. Sound good? We do it right, you can buy your own horse."

I agree it sounds great.

In my rathole, I pour a large tumbler of the Stoli, knock a hole in the wall with my fist and throw Baez out the window.

Something had to give, right?

Friday evening, he's wearing a long raincoat and packing a Mossberg in the right cutaway pocket. I ask,

"Shotgun? You expecting up close and personal?"

He's also putting a Nine in his left, says,

"For show, bro, get them focused."

I have the Glock. In the movies, you see them stick it in the waist of their pants, at the back.

Fuck that.

I have it in the new suede jacket, my finger lightly caressing the trigger.

We drive to the East Village, up a flight of stairs and I notice Lenny has a run of sweat on his forehead. He says,

"Follow my lead."

Knocks on a door and I hear a deadbolt drawn, a guy in his early thirties opens, goes,

"Lenny, hey."

And we're in, there's a guy on the couch, watching *The Wire,* box of pizza on the table, Bud longnecks, riding point. He has a sweatshirt with the logo JIMMY'S GYM. And the guy sees me, a look of recognition in his eyes. Lenny has the Mossberg out, blows the first guy's face off and pumps the second load into the guy on the couch, the logo obliterated.

The sound is deafening and the smell of cordite is overpowering, Lenny goes,

"Move. Let's get the fuck out of here."

We don't speak a single word on the ride back to the Island, except for Lenny asking,

"You don't get that rush from horses, am I right?"

He didn't expect a reply and I didn't have one.

We go into the apartment and Lenny shucks off his jacket. He's running on pure adrenaline and me, I'm running on empty.

I'm sitting on the couch, glass of Beam in my hand and Lenny is pacing, mania blowing off him and he stops, asks,

"Gone a little quiet there, buddy?"

I put my glass down, say,

"Jimmy's Gym."

He's staring at me, his eyes wild, snaps,

"So?"

I take my sweet time, get it right, go,

"Guy's from the eighty-fifth, they practically own that place and that kid on the couch, I knew him. Ted Brennan's eldest."

He's reaching in his coat and asks,

"You got a point or you going to sit there, swilling my hooch."

"Cops. Those guys were on the job."

His Nine is in his hand and he sighs,

"Horse players, the bottom feeders, you're still a fuck-up. Course they were cops. You think you get the big bucks for offing some lowlifes? Those guys, they were nosing around where it don't concern them. I try to do a good thing here, get you out of the hole, but gamblers, you wouldn't recognize a winning bet if it bit you on the ass."

The Nine is leveled at me, and the thing is, I don't feel a thing, maybe sadness, he says,

"Ah, you could have been a contender, know? But we handed you your ass at Fenway Park and guess what, you're . . ."

He never got to finish. The bedroom door had opened and the girl was out, swung the bottle of Grey Goose at his head. He went down like a bad song.

After I dumped him in the East River, I muttered,

"You choked, pal, and your horse is disqualified."

Back on the Island, the girl has built me another Jim Beam, is running her hand along my thigh and I ask,

"Why?"

Her head is nodding again, she's way into that coke and she whispers,

"For Ziggy."

The riff unreeling in my head . . . *and where were the spiders?*

I look around the apartment, wondering if I can hold off tomorrow's runners. I'm feeling lucky, figure I'll bet the Nine horse in the last race.

I think Lenny would appreciate the irony. I'd stuffed the Nine in his mouth, not an easy fit. Figured it would be the last time he pulled it and he sure as hell wouldn't be running his mouth no more.

ZUPPA INGLESE

Jan Burke

Eric Halsted ran a hand over his closely cropped hair, sighed, and shifted in the big leather chair. He was being made to wait, and he didn't like it.

Over the past weeks, taking over all the loose ends of his late brother's loosely led life had tried Eric's patience nearly to the limit, and today the delaying tactics of trainer Arnie Shackel just might exceed that limit.

Eric had spent all of yesterday afternoon and evening, as well as an hour or two this morning, rehearsing exactly what he was going to say to Shackel. He would praise the trainer, thank him for his work with Zuppa Inglese, and make it clear to him that his services were no longer required. About that time, Shackel would probably do a little arguing, claim he had a contract saying he must have a certain amount of notice, but Eric would point out that his attorneys had already provided that notice, and mention that certain features of that contract undoubtedly made it null and void in this state.

Donna Freepoint, the new trainer, had also found the contract to be highly unusual. "Downright odd for there to be one. Weirder still for Mark to have signed it," she had said.

Why Mark had signed it without first letting one of Eric's attorneys look it over—as had been Mark's practice with other business deals—was one of a great many questions Eric would ask him if he saw him in the Great Beyond. It would be very far down the list on such a quiz.

Why didn't you call me, talk to me, tell me how much you were troubled? That one would be much higher. Far above that would be, *How could you bear to do this to Jimmy?*

The inevitable images, derived from Eric's imagination and what he had been told about his brother's death, played through his mind, his personal horror film.

Setting: the rolling hills north of this racetrack. A rural road crests near Shackel Horse Farm.

Action: Mark stands outside his vintage Corvette on a hill that overlooks the farm, watching the morning workouts through binoculars. Perhaps he had wanted to watch Zuppa Inglese run one last time but did not want to interact with the people who worked there. Remote, from above.

Another horse owner is the last person to have seen him alive. (*Was she?* His mind never wants to let go of this question.) She drives past him, does not stop to say, "Mark, think of the people who love you," "Mark, there is a way through this, let me help you," or any of the things Eric would have said if he had been the one to have a last chance to talk to his brother.

But Eric is not there, and Mark gets back into his car and drives to a vacant, wooded lot not far away. He has the courtesy, at least, to do this away from the house, in a place where Jimmy is unlikely to discover him. Mark takes the gun he has brought with him and . . . hesitates? Reconsiders? It does not matter. Ultimately, he lifts it to his mouth and fires it.

No note. Detective Delmore, who investigated the suicide for the Osita County Sheriff's Department, said that often was the case. So no note, just the body of a man who couldn't even bring himself to communicate last thoughts to his son or brother. All that he had to say to be said by the act itself.

This is what Eric has to be satisfied with. His questions, his initial denial of the idea that Mark has done this to himself, his insistence that Mark would never kill himself while Jimmy still needed him, Delmore patiently and inexorably, and ultimately pityingly, refutes. Delmore has investigated many deaths. Eric is no more an expert in suicide and homicide than he is in horses.

· · ·

Eric sighed. He knew what would happen if he kept thinking about Mark's death, and he sure as hell didn't want to have Shackel find him in here on a crying jag, so he forced his thoughts in another direction. Rehearsed what he would say again. Tried to envision success. A former girlfriend had been big on the envisioning thing. Although her vision of Eric proposing to her was all for naught, maybe envisioning could work in situations like this one. He tried to picture Shackel taking the news like a grown-up. The horse transport van would arrive and Zuppa Inglese would be moved from Shackel's barn at the Fox River Racetrack to Copper Hills Farms. He didn't really know if that could make a difference in the horse's performance, but it would make his nephew happy.

His attempt to picture Jimmy feeling happy about much of anything caused the vision to evaporate.

So far, nothing had gone according to plan. Shackel was the sort of man Eric thought of as a Forceful Personality, so Eric couldn't help feeling a bit wound up in anticipation of this encounter—after all, Eric came here to fire him. And the truth was, he was doing the firing at the insistence of a twelve-year-old. He trusted Jimmy when it came to horses, but that didn't make this task a pleasant one. He would do it, though. He would stick to what he planned to say and be done with it.

No sooner had he stepped into the trainer's cramped office than he realized that things might not follow his hoped-for script.

Shackel was standing behind his desk, frowning, holding an unopened bottle of a sports drink. Several inches taller than Eric, who was just under six feet tall, right at that moment Shackel appeared to be a broad-shouldered giant. When he saw Eric, his expression suddenly changed, and he looked for all the world as if he were struggling not to weep. He set the drink down and came out from behind the desk to take Eric's hand in a firm grip. "Eric, my God—I'm so sorry. You've had a difficult time of it, haven't you? I can't believe we haven't had a chance to talk since Mark . . ." He let the sentence trail off, then went on in a soft, choked voice. "Since the funeral. I hope you know that if there's anything I can do for you or Jimmy, you just say the word. That kid practically grew up here, you know." Shackel guided him to the oversized guest chair, while Eric tried to quickly figure out a way to go from condolence and reminiscence to telling the man that he was taking a horse away from him.

Shackel moved back behind his desk and said, "You've had a long drive out here. Can I get you anything? Coffee? Bottled water? I've got some cold Pellegrino." He motioned toward a refrigerator behind the desk. He picked up the sports drink and said, "I'd offer you one of these, but they're warm. But anything else . . . ?"

"No, thank you," Eric replied, the only words he managed to speak before Shackel's intercom buzzed.

Shackel excused himself, saying, "Sorry, the vet's here and needs to talk to me. Make yourself at home, this shouldn't take long. And I want to get the times for Zuppa's workout this morning . . ." but he was closing the office door behind him as he said this.

The window air conditioner wasn't keeping up with the late summer afternoon heat. After fifteen minutes of waiting for Shackel's return, Eric's nervousness got the better of him, and he began pacing around the small office, trying to learn a little more about the man he was going to confront.

The desk was cleared of any business papers, so Shackel was apparently neat and private. The other objects on its surface gave few hints: a notebook computer, closed and quiet. A phone, a radio, and a marble and brass penholder. Eric walked around the desk to see the office from Shackel's point of view and nearly tripped over a big case of the sports drinks. It was pulled halfway out from beneath the kneehole. A couple of bottles were missing, and apparently Shackel hadn't pushed it back beneath the desk. No points away from neatness, though—Eric had obviously interrupted him before he had a chance to put them away. A small stack of the *Daily Racing Form* and another of *The Blood-Horse*. A remote control for a television.

He saw a small television set mounted on one wall, cables running from it to a VCR on a long shelf beneath it, the rest of the shelf taken up by a row of videotapes, all marked with what he eventually realized were names of races. A tray atop a little cabinet had a few expensive brands of liquor and some handsome crystal tumblers on it, but either the bottles were new or Shackel didn't drink much. Something for visiting owners as they watched a replay of races?

A short bookcase held thick tomes similar to ones Mark owned, which Jimmy had told him were called "stud books," and were horses' family trees. Eric spent a while studying the spines of Shackel's books. A number were about breeding racehorses; many more seemed to be professional general textbooks on horses and their care; a few were highly specialized titles, mostly about equine medical issues.

Along the other walls of the room were certificates and licenses from the state horse-racing board and various associations for horse racing, horse training, and horse breeding. There was a small, gaudy, red-and-white shirt and cap made of silk, with "SHF" for Shackel Horse Farm worked into the design. Jockey's silks—Eric knew that from seeing something equally gaudy at Mark's house, although the Halsted colors were different, blue and green in a diamond pattern. The wall opposite the bookcase was covered with finish line and winner's circle photographs, and a large painting of a handsome horse who looked down at him with an air of serene self-assurance. A brass plate on the frame identified him as Pete's Cake.

The name was familiar. Eric had been told by Jimmy that this horse's parents were Pete's Bread and Cakewalk. How did they come up with these names? Shouldn't a name sound fast? "Lightning," or something like that? Well, somebody else probably took that name a long time ago. He shrugged and kept pacing.

He did know a little about some of these horses. Mark had once been a part owner of Pete's Cake, he knew, and the horse had won some races. Mark had sold his share to Shackel in a complicated arrangement that Eric could hardly grasp, one that somehow allowed Pete's Cake to have sex with one of Mark's other horses—a mare named Don't Trifle With Me, a fact that Eric found amusing, given her role in the proceedings. The baby of the mother horse—no, no, Jimmy said to call her "the dam" and Pete's Cake was "the sire," and the baby was the foal. That's right. The foal was Zuppa Inglese.

Pete's Cake was in several of the photographs. Eric studied the jockeys' names. Were they famous? Were the races important ones?

He sighed. He might as well have landed on another planet. His nephew's immediate, scornful, but accurate appraisal of Eric's understanding of this milieu ran through his mind in a continuous loop as he paced. *You don't know anything about horse racing. You don't even know what you're looking at when you see a horse.*

One additional part of Jimmy's assessment Eric had deemed going a bit too far: *I'm not sure you can tell a mane from a tail, so if you ever get close to a horse, watch where you put your hands.*

The pacing made him feel a little too warm, so he decided to look for that Pellegrino. He opened the refrigerator and saw beer and a bunch of carrots—well, horses liked carrots. He knew that much, didn't he? Probably some sugar cubes in here, too. There were other vegetables, a couple of apples, some sealed plastic containers, a box of baking soda, what looked to be a wide variety of veterinary medications (perhaps this was the horses' refrigerator, too?), some nondairy creamer, and a bag of coffee beans. He looked at the racks in the refrigerator door: two bottles of fume blanc and at long last, the Pellegrino. He thought of putting away some of the sports drinks, decided he didn't owe Shackel any favors, and shut the refrigerator door. He found a bottle opener at the wet bar, poured himself a crystal tumbler's worth, and sat back down.

He was finishing off the last of it when Shackel returned. For a moment, surprise registered on Shackel's face, and he glanced toward the desk. Eric felt a little bloom of confidence. *Didn't think I'd get out of the chair, eh? No, I didn't go through your desk or computer.*

"I shouldn't have left you in here alone for so long. I'm sorry," Shackel said. "I'm glad to see you made yourself comfortable, though. Good, good."

The bloom faded. Eric suddenly felt criminal for taking even this small bit of water from a man he was about to fire. But he glanced at his watch and regained his resolve. A forty-minute wait!

"Zuppa's a youngster, a two-year-old that hasn't let us really see his stuff yet," Shackel said, "but I've made some changes and—"

"Mr. Shackel, forgive me, I've arranged to have the horse trained elsewhere."

Shackel went pale. "You can't—"

Eric explained that yes, indeed, he could.

"You—you don't blame me for what happened to Mark, do you?"

"For my brother's suicide? No." Was that a lie? Not for the first time, Eric wondered if he did irrationally blame Shackel, and if that were really what lay beneath his willingness to move the horse from this trainer. He chose his words carefully. "Mr. Shackel, this has been a difficult time for everyone, but I assure you my decision is final."

He had no sooner said this than the intercom buzzed again. Shackel answered it, his frown deepening as he listened. "Wait a minute . . ." He looked up at Eric. "Eric, they tell me a transport truck you ordered is here, and that Donna Freepoint followed it in. If she's your new trainer, well—you really couldn't be making a worse mistake. Not just in taking Zuppa from here at this point in his training, but in choosing her."

"I'm sorry you feel that way, but there's nothing more to be said, really."

Eric discovered that from Shackel's perspective, this was not quite true. The trainer treated him to a tirade that included a great many terms that Eric was not familiar with and few that he knew well and seldom used, and ended with, "You don't know anything about horses!"

"On that we agree," Eric said, feeling much better about drinking the Pellegrino now, and walked out of the office.

He stayed on the grounds only long enough to ensure that the horse was actually led into the trailer and that Donna Freepoint did not meet with physical harm. The daughter of a retired trainer, she was a slender, athletic blonde in her early thirties, who had a no-nonsense air about her. Eric found her incredibly attractive and completely out of reach. Not only was he sure the difference of perhaps as much as ten years between their ages would make him seem too old to her, he was certain his ignorance of horses doomed whatever slight chance he might have. And because he was almost always (eventually) honest with himself, he owned up to the fact that she had not shown the slightest degree of romantic interest in him.

He saw her watching as Shackel followed him out of the office, still shouting, and so he did his best to appear completely unruffled. This was not easy, given Shackel's rage, and only the thought that she might need him to defend her kept him from hurrying away from the man.

She managed to silence Shackel with one look, and Eric realized that not even the burly driver of the transport truck, who had just come to her side, was going to need to intervene on her behalf.

Although Eric had seen a number of horses being ridden or walked around the track grounds, when he saw the big dark horse being led toward them, he suddenly felt the hair rise on the back of his neck. There was something . . . some something about this horse that made Zuppa Inglese stand out. He was tall, but not really more of a giant than some of the other big horses in the stables. Well, now that Eric looked around, he wasn't any bigger than average. He just *seemed* taller. He held himself differently, Eric decided. He had an attitude.

Zuppa Inglese let Donna look him over without making a fuss, even letting her pull his lip to take a quick look inside his mouth. "The tattoo checks—he's your colt," she said to Eric, further baffling him. Shackel took offense at this, and tried to come nearer, but the horse flattened his ears and tried to nip at him.

Shackel evaded the colt's teeth and turned to Donna. "The track lip reader not good enough for you?"

"Don't worry, everything will be done by the rule book," she said. She smiled at Shackel in a way that seemed designed to further infuriate him.

A moment later, a pair of Shackel's workers tried to approach to help load the horse, and Zuppa Inglese tossed his head at one and kicked at the other. "I'll do it," Donna said, and led the horse up the ramp without further incident.

"Go on ahead, Mr. Halsted," she told Eric when this operation was completed. "We'll see you at Copper Hills."

Mr. Halsted. He refused to let himself sigh in disappointment.

So he began the long drive to Copper Hills Farms, where Jimmy was waiting. Even before Eric had met Donna Freepoint, he had been pleased with the place. He had visited it twice to make arrangements for Zuppa Inglese's transfer, and he liked it even better now that he had spent time with Shackel. Copper Hills was well equipped—or so Jimmy had said—but it wasn't showy. The grounds were clean and neat, and obviously well-cared-for. The staff was smaller than Shackel's, but they struck Eric as being friendlier. Which was just the sort of observation that would probably make Jimmy roll his eyes.

At twelve, Jimmy was an expert eye-roller and had a repertoire of other facial expressions designed to let Eric know he didn't think much of his uncle's intelligence. This was a novel experience for Eric, who held advanced degrees in engineering. He also held eleven lucrative patents for robotic devices in use in a variety of manufacturing applications. He knew most other people didn't want to hear about his "widgets," as Mark had called them. He had wealth from those widgets, though, and had been generous with his younger brother and his family. Not that they had ever tried to sponge off him. There had been no need.

Mark and Eric's parents had started their family late in life, and both parents had died before Eric reached thirty. Eric— six years older than his brother, and already a successful entrepreneur by his mid-twenties—never questioned that he should support Mark, and took over tuition and room and board payments.

To Eric's dismay, Mark dropped out of school before the end of his sophomore year, his head full of dreams of being a restaurateur. He convinced Eric to loan him enough money to start an upscale eatery, money Eric had little hope of seeing again. But he had been wrong—the restaurant was a hit, and Mark repaid the loan within a year.

That same year, Mark married his pastry chef, a lovely, lively woman named Carlotta, and together they opened four more restaurants—each doing better than the last. Two years after they married, Jimmy was born.

In those years, Eric thought Mark and Carlotta had a near perfect life. They loved each other. They loved their son. They owned a successful business. And they had enough money to pursue their mutual love of racehorses. Jimmy was no less devoted to horses than they were. Eric, running his own business and caught up in the world of invention, was pleased for them, saw them on holidays, and tried not to yawn when the talk turned to horses.

Late one spring evening, not quite two and a half years ago, Mark and Jimmy were at Shackel Horse Farm, where Don't Trifle With Me was in labor with Zuppa Inglese. Carlotta was on her way there from one of the restaurants. Mark became irritated when she was late, then worried. She had been so excited about the foal, had even chosen the name. Mark called her cell phone. No answer. He tried the home phone, wondering if she had misunderstood where they were to meet. No answer there, either.

The birth of the foal occupied their attention for a time, but both Mark and Jimmy were disappointed that Carlotta had missed the event.

An hour later, a deputy sheriff had finally located Mark. He was the one who told them that Carlotta had apparently lost control of the family SUV on a curving stretch of rural road about ten miles away, just over the county line. Another vehicle may have been involved. They were still investigating the cause, he said, but these high-profile vehicles also rolled on their own if the driver took a curve too fast . . . In any case, the SUV had rolled, going over a steep embankment. She had not survived the accident.

Thinking about that night, Eric wondered if Jimmy associated Shackel Horse Farm with his mother's death. It certainly had some association with Mark's death—he had shot himself in a wooded area not far away from it, after watching morning workouts. Was that association why Jimmy was so adamant about changing trainers? Had Mark made some recommendation to Jimmy? And if so, was Mark's judgment impaired by his depression?

Eric shuddered, thinking of how Mark had changed after Carlotta's death. Mark lost weight—too much weight. He looked haggard, and when Eric mentioned this, he simply shrugged and said he wasn't sleeping well. The doctor had given him some pills, but he didn't like taking them, didn't like how groggy they made him feel the next day.

He had seemed listless in any case, Eric thought. It was as if all of Mark's past pleasures had lost meaning. He sold the restaurants, saying his heart was no longer in the business. Within a year, he also sold off all of his horses except Zuppa Inglese. This had all been noted in the investigation of his death by Detective Delmore and seen as indications of his depression and preparation for suicide.

Eric had asked him about the sale of the horses, but Mark had been evasive, saying only that he now wished he had never gotten into the racing business in the first place. When Eric had tried to convince him that he needed to start up another business or at least find a hobby, Mark fobbed him off, saying he was "working on a project or two," but wouldn't say what they were. Eric now doubted their existence and deeply regretted not being more persistent.

Mark was still a wealthy man at the time of his own death, but his income had declined sharply in the past year. Shortly after Carlotta died, Mark made out a will, telling Eric he was finally forced to believe in his own mortality—but Eric knew that Mark was fearful about what might become of his son if anything happened to him, the boy's only surviving parent.

He left almost everything in trust to Jimmy, with Eric as trustee. One notable exception was Zuppa Inglese. A recently added codicil regarding the horse was nearly longer than the original will. He left the horse to both Eric and Jimmy, with instructions to Eric not to sell the horse without Jimmy's permission. He made it clear that Eric was being given part ownership so that the horse could be entered in races, and that Eric should definitely do so, provided the horse was sound. He was to rely on Jimmy's advice to the greatest extent possible.

Eric felt one of those sudden spikes of anger at Mark that seemed to take him unawares these days. *Why leave all your problems to me? Why couldn't you see how much Jimmy still needs you? I don't know anything about being a parent! I don't know anything about horses!*

Eric realized that he had pressed on the accelerator in his fury, and quickly let up on it, telling himself it would do no good to Jimmy if something happened to *him*. He drove in what Jimmy called his "granny gear"—at a nice, sedate pace. Granny gear or no, he'd muddle through somehow.

Jimmy hurried out to meet him, for once not bothering to feign aloofness. Eric realized that this boy, usually so solemn and quiet, was more animated than he had seen him at any time in the past two years. He was standing outside Eric's car door before Eric had time to set the parking brake.

Tall for his age but thin, Jimmy had large dark eyes and black hair, and the sort of strong features that might or might not grow into handsomeness over the next few years—dark brows, long-but-not-too-long lashes, a nice straight nose, a determined chin. Eric could see something of each of Jimmy's parents in that face.

"What happened?" Jimmy asked, the moment Eric stepped out of the car.

Eric smiled. "I fired him, just as you asked me to. Zuppa Inglese should arrive here any time now."

To Eric's surprise, Jimmy let out a loud whoop, punched his fist in the air, and gave his uncle a quick hug. "Oh, Uncle Eric—that is so awesome. Was he all, like, angry and everything?"

"Yes, he certainly was," Eric said, remembering some of Shackel's choicer insults.

Jimmy's brows drew together in worry. "He didn't try to hurt you or anything, did he?"

"No, no, nothing like that. I simply told him that this was the way it was going to be, and he really had no choice in the matter." Feeling that he might be making himself sound too heroic, he added, "Ms. Freepoint didn't allow him to give her any grief. In fact, Zuppa Inglese tried to bite him."

Jimmy laughed. "Did Zuppa act up?"

"A little. Not with Ms. Freepoint, though."

"He's a little head shy sometimes—he doesn't like people to make sudden moves near his face. Freaks him out a little. But if he likes you, he won't mind. He probably likes Donna."

"I guess he doesn't like Shackel. In any case, he is no longer in Mr. Shackel's clutches."

"I'm glad. I'm so glad." Within the next moment, though, he sounded anxious again. "Uncle Eric?"

"Yes?"

"Stay away from Shackel, okay?"

"I have no plans to go near him," Eric said with feeling.

Jimmy grew quiet again.

A new thought occurred to Eric. "Has Shackel ever tried to harm you or scare you?"

"No . . . But I've seen him act mean to the people who work for him. He can get kind of crazy."

"He was a little crazy today," Eric admitted. "But I'm glad to hear he's never bothered you."

"He was only nice to me because he wanted Zuppa." He frowned, and grew quiet again.

"Did you find things to do while you were waiting?" Eric asked.

"Huh?" he said, coming out of whatever thoughts were troubling him. "Oh, yeah. I love it here. Donna lets me help out. And I know the grooms and hotwalkers and everybody else. They're all nice to me." He paused, then added, "Mom told me that Donna pays her grooms better than other people do, and takes good care of the people who work for her."

"I'm glad to hear that," Eric said, thinking of some of the conditions he had seen along the backstretch. "That means they're probably loyal to her, too."

"Yeah," Jimmy said. "And, like, you know—the best people want to work for her." After another silence, he pointed to a property across the road. "See that house over there?"

"Yes. The one with the 'for sale' sign?"

"Exactly!"

"Oh . . ."

"Could you buy it?" he pleaded. "I mean, or could you buy it now and I could pay you later, you know, like . . . when I'm older?"

This was just the kind of ticklish situation he found himself in lately, Eric thought ruefully. "Have you actually been inside that house?"

"No. But it's ten acres, so if you don't like the house, you could build a different one, and you know, live next door to me."

"Are you sure you'd want me for your neighbor?"

"No—what I mean is, I'd like it better if we lived in the same house, but not if you don't like it."

Eric smiled. "Thanks. I'd rather we lived in the same house, too." Eric thought briefly of the beautiful seaside home he had sold in order to move into Mark's home, all with the idea of not causing further disruption in the boy's life. Now Jimmy wanted to move? "Are you unhappy in the house we're in now?"

Jimmy looked away, then said, "Not exactly. It's just . . . it's hard."

"The memories?"

He nodded. "It's like . . . I don't know . . . it's just hard to be there."

Eric had felt it himself He had put most of his possessions in storage, afraid to make too big an impact on Mark and

Carlotta's home, or to risk further upset for Jimmy. He hadn't been able to bear the thought of staying in their bedroom, and had instead taken over a large guestroom. He hadn't been able to make himself sort through the vast majority of Mark's personal belongings, either, and it was clear to him that Mark had not been able to do so with Carlotta's.

"Well," he said now, "we can move if we want to, but let's get more information before we make a decision, all right?"

Jimmy looked up at him, studying his face, as if he wasn't sure if Eric was humoring him or telling the truth. Apparently he decided on the latter, because he nodded agreement.

They heard the truck approaching. Jimmy had been very specific about the transport company and the style in which his horse was to travel, and he seemed relieved that Eric had followed his instructions.

As the truck came to a gentle stop, the horse made a sound that Eric could only think of as a trumpeting of his arrival. "Here I am, Zuppa!" Jimmy called, and the horse repeated his own call. Eric stood back and watched as the horse was unloaded. Jimmy had apparently forgotten his uncle's existence. The big colt obviously recognized Jimmy, and made a series of soft, low sounds as he approached. Eric grew worried when the horse looked as if he might nip at the boy, but then saw that he was just nuzzling him.

Jimmy became a changed being. He was smiling and laughing, talking constantly to the horse, who looked for all the world to be hanging on his every word. As he led Zuppa to his new stall, telling him how much happier he was going to be, Eric could only watch in wonder.

"Amazing, isn't it?" a voice said from behind him.

He turned to see Donna Freepoint standing nearby. "Yes."

"We need to talk, Mr. Halsted. Jimmy will keep busy for a while, and the folks who work here are fond of him—they'll make sure he doesn't come to any harm."

He followed her into her office and she motioned toward a wooden chair. She began talking about the difference between Zuppa's workout times and his race performances. She was talking about morning glories and clockers and airing, and he got nothing more out of this than the fact that she thought Zuppa was not racing as fast as he worked out. She went on to explain several possible reasons for this, and things she wanted to try for starters. Eric found himself watching her mouth move. A really nice mouth. He had just managed to refocus his attention on the business at hand for about one minute when she paused and asked, "Have you understood a word I've said, Mr. Halsted?"

"Please call me Eric."

She rolled her eyes, not all that differently from the way Jimmy rolled his. "All right, *Eric,* same question."

"Yes, although there were parts I will admit I don't really grasp as yet, being new to all this. You were just saying that you doubt blood tests would show anything, but you'd like to have some done just in case, and to have a different vet take over the care of Zuppa."

"Yes." She stayed silent, but a helpless look came over her face, as if she were struggling to come up with a way to explain rocket science to a four-year-old with a head injury.

"Do you have any objection to explaining this again in front of Jimmy?"

The look of frustration vanished. But she hesitated, then said, "Jimmy has had a lot to deal with lately. An awful lot. You sure you want to put this on his shoulders, too?"

"I don't think anything having to do with that horse will be a burden to him."

She smiled. "No."

"How did you meet him?"

She laughed. "At the track, of course. He came up to me and told me that he had been watching the horses I trained and was trying to talk his mom and dad into moving their horses over to my barn. He must have been just shy of ten. I figured, 'cute kid,' and thanked him, but as he kept talking, I thought, 'little genius,' instead. He's sharp, and he knows horses. More than most of the adults I meet—uh, no offense."

"None taken."

"I'm not saying that he doesn't have more to learn. But what amazes me about Jimmy is how *fast* he learns. And he's got the gift, that way of knowing horses—it goes beyond anything anyone can tell you about them, or anything that's just in your head—but horses know who has it and who doesn't. They can tell." She suddenly blushed. "That probably sounds like a lot of nonsense to a science guy like you. It's hard to explain."

Eric thought of the way Zuppa had responded to Jimmy. Maybe someday someone would do a long and careful study that would reveal what signals or cues a horse reads from a person with the "gift." But in the meantime, Eric was willing to call it that. "I'm not a behavioral scientist," he said, "so your explanation is fine. I'm a glorified tinker, a guy who likes to fool around with mechanical things and make them work better."

"Yeah, right." She added with an even mix of skepticism and amazement, "Jimmy said you make robots."

"Not as smart as the ones you've seen in movies. Anyway, I think I have an idea of what you mean about Jimmy's way with horses. Some idea, anyway. So you found a kindred spirit that day?"

"Absolutely. Next thing I know, he's bringing Carlotta around, and he's got her convinced." She paused. "I didn't know your sister-in-law for all that long before she died, but we just hit it off from the start. We were friends—I liked her a lot."

"So did I."

"She thought highly of you. 'Mark's smarter brother,' she used to say. Told me how good you were to them."

He was surprised to hear this, but shook his head. "Not so much, really. And Mark was smart. Just in a different way."

She looked as if she would counter that but must have changed her mind, because she stayed silent.

"I don't think he knew quite how to live without her," Eric said, offering her the same excuse he offered himself. "He changed, after Carlotta died."

She nodded. "Mark used to let Jimmy stay over here sometimes. Jimmy liked it, I think mostly because of the horses, but also because he just needed a change of scenery, if you know what I mean."

"Yes. Yes, I think I do. And thanks for letting him do that."

"He's good company. He is bright and good hearted, and he's had too much bad luck that he didn't deserve. Although I'm not completely convinced that luck . . ."

"What?"

She shook her head. "Nothing. Anyway, he just needs someone to stand by him, you know? I hope you—" She broke off, apparently realizing she was lecturing a client.

He smiled. "I agree. Don't worry, I have no plans to abandon him."

"Of course you don't," she said quickly. "I could tell that, and I'll bet anything he can, too. Anyway—I'll call the barn and get them to send him over here." She used the intercom on her phone to talk to one of her workers. The worker kept her on the line with some questions about another horse. While she talked to him, Eric stood and stretched.

He looked out the window, seeing the house across the way. How much of a risk would it really be to move out here, let Jimmy be close to someone who cared about him so much? Eric doubted the asking price would be outside his ability to meet it. He wouldn't have to sell Mark's place—keep that in case Jimmy decided he wanted it later on. He felt certain that Donna Freepoint viewed him as someone merely to be tolerated, but so what? Couldn't he be an adult about it, for Jimmy's sake?

"Sorry about that," she said, coming out from behind her desk.

"The place across the road that's for sale—know anything about it?"

She studied him for a moment, then said, "Sure. I grew up here, so I know most of my neighbors." Her description of the house was straightforward: built about sixty years ago, modernized about two years ago by new owners, and kept in good repair. Owners were "perfectly nice folks" who had dreamed of country living and then couldn't handle the isolation once they were out here. "They'll take quite a bit less than they're asking for it," she said. "Thinking of moving?"

But Jimmy came in before he could answer. Eric was still amazed at the transformation being around the horse had made in the boy. He was chattering excitedly about how well Zuppa had settled in, telling Donna how happy he was that she was going to be training Zuppa. "Finally," he said in the tone of someone who often has to wait for adults to come to their senses.

"You have your uncle to thank for that, so don't forget it. And if you're going to be advising Eric, you need to listen up, all right? I explained all this to him, but he wanted you in on the decisions."

He looked at Eric with obvious gratitude.

"I don't know manes from tails, remember?" Eric said.

Jimmy looked embarrassed. "I shouldn't have said that. You'll learn. This is just all new to you."

Donna began again, and hearing the information a second time, Eric found he was taking more of it in. Jimmy stopped her every once in a while to explain things in greater depth to Eric or to ask her questions.

"So," he said, "Shackel might have been doping him?"

"I have no proof of that, Jimmy, and it's probably too late to find any trace of it at this point."

"Nobody ever finds proof of anything he does," Jimmy said bitterly. "My mom knew he was crooked, and I think my dad was . . . well, that doesn't matter now."

Eric wasn't exactly sure what to make of this. He turned to Donna. "Did Carlotta mention this to you?"

"Carlotta didn't like Shackel. Said the more she got to know him, the more he gave her the creeps. She wanted Mark to move the horses here. But he didn't agree, and I have to say I totally understand why he didn't. First, that's not the kind of change anyone makes without a lot of thought. Second, not smart to make someone your trainer on the basis of a friendship. Third, I have a famous trainer for a father, but that hasn't won me the trust of horsemen. As long as my dad was still around here to keep an eye on things, people figured he was the real reason the horses I trained won. Once he retired . . ." She shrugged.

"Carlotta always had good business sense," Eric said. "So I doubt she would have made the decision on an emotional basis. Over the years, I noticed she could usually convince Mark to change his mind if she thought he was making a bad decision."

"They got mad at each other about it," Jimmy said.

"I'm sorry to hear that," Donna said. "But when it came to Shackel, your mom didn't have more to go on than a gut feeling. She knew your dad would need more than that to end a long working relationship—and Shackel didn't have a bad record with your dad's horses. They were doing well. You know that, Jimmy."

"I also know that sometimes people are wrong about other people. They get fooled. Shackel fools people." In a quieter voice, he added, "He fooled my dad."

Eric said, "Maybe not, Jimmy. Maybe selling all his other horses was a way for your dad to have less to do with Shackel."

"I don't know. I don't think so. He was just . . . you know, giving up."

Although Eric had thought this same thing, he found he didn't want Jimmy to look at it this way. "Then why keep Zuppa Inglese?"

"Who knows?" he said. "He did all kinds of crazy stuff after Mom died."

"Did he know you didn't like Shackel?"

"Yeah. We used to fight about it, too, before Mom died.

After that—well, we tried not to fight about anything after she died." He pressed his palms to his eyes, then took a deep breath.

"I think maybe he was moving away from Shackel, Jimmy," Eric said. "Think about what he added to his will about Zuppa. He didn't tell me to 'do what Shackel says.' He trusted you, and you just told me he knew you didn't like Shackel. We're here at Copper Hills because he knew you'd have the strength to take Zuppa to the best trainer. I think he knew you'd bring him here."

Jimmy looked up at him and said, "You think so?"

"Sure."

After a moment, Jimmy said, "Maybe people will finally catch on about Shackel."

"If Zuppa Inglese suddenly starts winning races," Donna said, "people are definitely going to have questions about him."

Eric thought about this for a moment, then said, "Excuse me, but why would someone want a horse he was training to lose races?"

"With a juvenile—a two-year-old horse—probably betting odds," she said. "But I don't think it can ever really be worth it."

Horses might not be Eric's specialty, but probability and statistics were not foreign territory. "Oh, I see . . . so, he waits to place a bet when the odds are favorable, when he knows that whatever has been slowing Zuppa down is no longer in the horse's system."

"Yes, and when Zuppa's being put in company that Shackel knows he can beat."

"Hmm. You think he's doing this with drugs?"

"Maybe," Donna said. "Or sponging—putting a sponge far up in the horse's nostril before he races."

"Good God . . ." Eric said, appalled.

"It can kill a horse, but it doesn't show up in a drug test. Even a drug—drug testing is done on a limited basis. Horses can be slowed in a number of ways, and not all of them show up in blood tests."

"Jockeys pull up," Jimmy said. "Or the horse is fed certain kinds of food—"

"Right," said Donna. "So we'll do what we can to figure out what's going on with Zuppa. And remember that all of this is just my guess at a distance. Shackel deserves some credit for bringing Zuppa along as far as he's come, even if Zuppa hasn't finished in the money. Lots of horses never do. I may find out that he's just a morning glory—a horse that can run like the dickens in a workout, but simply isn't a competitor."

"He's a competitor," Jimmy said with confidence.

• • •

They were to test Jimmy's assertion just a few weeks later, when Zuppa was entered to run his first race after being moved to Copper Hills. Zuppa's new vet had pronounced him fit, with no signs of mononucleosis or other health problems that might have slowed him down. "Good news," Donna said. "And we don't need to worry about harming him with some work."

Donna had given Jimmy the task of training Eric while she trained Zuppa. As a result, Eric came to the track much better informed than he had been on the day he walked into Shackel's office.

Eric placed only a few bets on the day's card. He had decided to begin cautiously. Jimmy had taken Donna's assignment seriously. He awakened his night-owl uncle at an ungodly hour each morning to watch Zuppa's workouts. Living in the house across the road—as they did now—allowed Eric to get about forty-five more minutes of sleep, for whatever that was worth. He no longer groused about it, though—grumpiness had been replaced by pure anticipation. He didn't have the connection to Zuppa that Jimmy did—he would have sworn that the horse showed off when he knew the boy was watching. All the same, Eric came to love watching the way the big colt moved. He supposed he took pleasure, too, from seeing how excited Donna and Jimmy were with Zuppa's times and the way the colt was responding to other aspects of his training.

Eric's own lessons didn't end with watching workouts. They watched horse races on television or from videotapes Jimmy had made. Eric was required to study them endlessly. Jimmy gave him stacks of racing publications and taught him how to read past performance data in the *Daily Racing Form*.

Eric was still too overwhelmed by the combination of new information and other changes in his life to suddenly become a heavy bettor, but at least Jimmy no longer worried that his uncle would place a bet based on the color of the horse, or the design of the stable's silks, or the appeal of the horse's name—and knew that he no longer believed completely in the old advice about the relationship of the production of road apples to friskiness in a race.

He placed losing bets on the first two races and decided that since he didn't have any strong preferences in the third, he'd not bet that race. Still, he was off to a bad start and wondered if Jimmy would despair of him. But the boy shrugged and said, "You'll bet right on the fourth race. Let's go visit Zuppa and wish him luck."

The fourth was Zuppa's race—a mile and a sixteenth, a maiden race. ("No, Uncle Eric," Jimmy had said with disgust a few weeks ago, "they don't have to be fillies!")

They went down to see Zuppa, who called to Jimmy the moment he saw him. Donna had other horses running in other races that day, and Eric decided that he would do his best to stay out of her way. She seemed glad to see them, though, and introduced them to the woman she had been talking to, Debbie Arrington, horse-racing writer for the *Sacramento Bee*. The reporter had been interviewing Donna about a favorite she had trained for a stakes race being held later that afternoon. Arrington seemed taken with Zuppa Inglese, and after asking about Jimmy's connection to the horse, she ended up interviewing him as well, and took several photos of Zuppa and Jimmy together.

Not much later, Eric stood in line at a betting window, trying to ignore an insistent thought that if he was betting so poorly today, he would jinx Zuppa Inglese by putting money on him. He was about three people away from the teller when he heard a familiar voice at the window to his right. Shackel. Laying a two-thousand-dollar bet on Zuppa Inglese to win.

Shackel took his slip and turned, and saw Eric as he did.

Shackel's face turned bright red.

"Apparently you don't think I made such a bad decision after all," Eric said.

"I've always believed in the horse," Shackel said. As he moved away he muttered, "No hard feelings."

"What a handsome apology," Eric murmured back, but Shackel was already lost in the crowd behind him.

"Shackel?" a gravelly voice said behind him. "Old sourpuss. Ignore him."

Eric turned to see a man he recognized—easily—as one of the two men who sat in the box next to Donna's. The man wore a blindingly bright green-and-yellow Hawaiian shirt, dark sunglasses, and a twill hat that seemed better suited for a bass-fishing expedition. "Elias Lazarus," the old man said, extending a leathery hand. "You're Jimmy Halsted's uncle Eric, aren't you? Got a colt with Donna Freepoint now, right? Smart move."

Eric had already learned that Jimmy was known to many of the owners and trainers, who had treated his arrival here today as a kind of homecoming. He had also realized the truth of something Donna had said, that it was too bad you couldn't bet on rumor, because it was the fastest thing at the track. He thanked Lazarus and introduced himself. "Do you have a horse in this race, too, Mr. Lazarus?"

"Call me Laz. No, Eric, my horses are in the sixth and eighth today. I'm here with my son-in-law, Dennis. He's just about as big a sourpuss as Shackel. In fact, Shackel introduced him to my daughter, which is enough reason for me to hate Shackel to the end of my days." He laughed. "Good luck to you." He motioned toward the teller window, and Eric turned to see that he was next.

He placed an even larger bet than Shackel's, then, wishing Lazarus luck as well, returned to the box, where Jimmy was waiting. Seeing that Lazarus's son-in-law, Dennis, was away from their box, Eric mentioned meeting the old man to Jimmy.

Jimmy nodded knowingly. "He owns Give Me Room—a two-year-old colt, really good horse. Like, really, really good. Some people say he could take it all next year. But that's dumb, because with juveniles, a lot can happen between now and the Derby."

Eric now knew better than to ask "Which derby?" when he heard Jimmy give it that capital D. He also knew that the combined bets he and Shackel had placed might lower the payoff if Zuppa won, but at least he'd have the satisfaction of knowing that if Shackel indeed had a scheme, it would be less lucrative.

"He doesn't seem to like his son-in-law much."

"Nobody does. I don't think his daughter likes him much, either. She used to come to the races with them, but he was always embarrassing her by saying rude things."

Eric was reminded that not much missed Jimmy's eyes—or ears.

The bugle call of "Boots and Saddles," the post parade—Eric found himself caught up in these rituals in a way he had not been earlier in the day. He felt a strange mixture of pride and nervous anticipation. The blue-and-green silks didn't look gaudy to him now. They were downright handsome.

Zuppa had drawn a good post position, Jimmy said. Zuppa was number four. The horse appeared to be fine, calm, and self-possessed. He looked up into the crowd, and Jimmy yelled, "Here I am, Zuppa!" which caused laughter all around them. Jimmy shrank back into his seat. Eric leaned over and whispered, "Zuppa heard you, and that's all that counts."

Jimmy nodded and sat forward again.

It was a field of seven. From the moment they were off, the other six seemed to be in a different race, scheduled several minutes after the one Zuppa was running. He broke cleanly, shot to the front, and stayed there. "He'll wear himself out," Laz's surly son-in-law loudly predicted, but Laz immediately said, "I wouldn't be so sure, Dennis."

As they entered the final turn, Zuppa still led. The swell of noise from the crowd was infectious. "Go, Zuppa, go!" Jimmy and Eric yelled as the horses came down the homestretch, and soon Laz and some of the others in nearby boxes took up the chant as well.

Zuppa won by four lengths.

Jimmy and Eric hugged and jumped up and down and cheered as if they had just seen him win the Triple Crown.

"Wire-to-wire—congratulations!" Laz said, and then, winking, added loudly, "I don't think that colt of yours is even breathing hard." Dennis glowered at them as they left for the winner's circle.

It wasn't the money he raked in on his first winning bet, it wasn't the winner's circle, it wasn't even seeing Shackel looking unhappy despite the fact that he had made money, too. The best part of the day was listening to Jimmy and Donna talk about the race over and over again on the way home, their enthusiasm never abating. Even when Jimmy said, "Mom and Dad would have loved to watch him today," it was with pride rather than wistfulness, as if something so right had happened, nothing could mar his pleasure in it.

Donna surprised him by knocking on their door the next morning, carrying a stack of copies of the *Sacramento Bee*. "I cleaned out the newsstand at the little market in town," she confessed. "Call Jimmy, he'll want to see this."

She showed them the sports section, the first page of which had a great photo of Jimmy and Zuppa. When the story continued to the inside, there was a photo of Donna, too. The story about the stakes race was smaller than the one about Zuppa Inglese and those around him. Although appropriately cautious about predicting the future of the horse based on this outing, and noting that only time would tell whether racing fans had just seen a fluke or a phenomenon, the reporter said that if the colt continued to show the kind of speed seen yesterday, he shouldn't have trouble against better company.

Pleased and excited, Jimmy was, nevertheless, puzzled by the play the article got. "Our race wasn't as big as the stakes race."

"The local horse in the stakes race didn't win," Donna said, ruffling Jimmy's hair. "And you and Zuppa—human interest. You two are famous, kid. And going to be more famous."

"So are you," he said.

"He's right," Eric said. "This story talks a lot about how well your horses are doing and that maybe owners ought to take notice."

Jimmy suddenly looked at Donna and grinned. "Did your dad call you?"

She blushed, then said, "How do you think I heard about this story?"

She invited Eric and Jimmy over for a celebratory dinner.

As they worked together in her kitchen that evening, Jimmy helping her make a salad, Eric helping to set the table, Eric realized that he was at ease—a novel experience for him. On any given day, he still had the sense of being caught in the orbit of an alien world, and he spent his waking hours wondering if Jimmy would be messed up for the rest of his life because of something his uncle had done or failed to do. But when it was just the three of them—or the three of them and Zuppa—he felt a kind of contentment that he could not recall experiencing at any other time.

"I saw you watching Shackel after the race," Donna said. "He give you any trouble?"

"Not really. Shackel must have made a bundle on Zuppa yesterday, but I don't think he really enjoyed it." He told them about seeing him at the betting window.

Jimmy was angry, but Donna said, "Look, Jimmy, Eric's right. Shackel had another horse he's been working with do surprisingly well for him, and that didn't make him happy either. Nothing is going to make ol' Shack happy, so we've already beaten him."

"Easy Dreamer? Placed in the sixth race?" Eric asked.

"Yes. Another two-year-old. He was in tougher company than Zuppa faced today."

"Easy Dreamer always breaks fast and fades," Jimmy said. "This is the first time I've ever seen him stay in the race. Shackel puts him up against plodders and he loses."

"Give Me Room is no plodder," Donna argued. "He won, but he didn't finish all that far ahead of Easy Dreamer. Admit that Shack might have a good horse in Easy Dreamer."

"You could make Zuppa start a race from the parking lot, pay admission, and get his hoof stamped for the turf club—and he'd still beat Easy Dreamer. And probably Give Me Room, too."

Donna turned to Eric, obviously trying not to let Jimmy see her stifle a laugh. "We're about set now. Get that bottle of fume blanc out of the refrigerator, will you please, Eric?"

"What is it with you trainers," he asked, "and fume blanc in the refrigerator?"

"What do you mean?" she asked.

He had opened the refrigerator door by then, and said sheepishly, "Sorry, of course your refrigerator would be a thousand times different than, uh, ol' Shack's."

"You've checked out his refrigerator?"

He told them the story of nabbing the Pellegrino on the day Shackel had to give up Zuppa.

They laughed, as he intended them to—or did until he started describing the contents of the refrigerator.

"Wait, wait, wait!" Donna said. "Baking soda—and the sports drinks weren't in the fridge?"

"No."

"Milkshake," Jimmy said with authority.

"Milkshake?" Eric made a face. "Who would ever want to make a milkshake out of those ingredients? Tell me they don't add milk to the mixture . . ."

"They don't. They mix baking soda and the sports drink, feed it through a tube into a horse's stomach not long before a race, and it prevents the build up of lactic acid in the horse's muscles as he's running. That means he won't tire out, he'll be able to maintain his pace for a longer period of time. It's cheating."

"Bet that's how Easy Dreamer managed to run in the money yesterday," Jimmy said. "Fits perfectly—all of a sudden, he's got all the energy he needs to finish second."

"Should we notify someone?" Eric asked.

"It would be impossible to prove. You need to take a blood sample within twenty-four hours."

"Is it possible that he had the baking soda in there to make the refrigerator smell better, and the sports drink is for human consumption?"

"I'm sure that would be his story, which is why you have to catch it in blood tests." She paused, gave her head a shake, and said, "No more talk about Shackel. This evening is for us!"

The cheerfulness was only determined cheerfulness for a short while, giving way to the genuine article as they spoke of plans for Zuppa's future.

Those who thought Zuppa was a fluke winner saw that theory demolished over the next two months. He won his next two races—including his first stakes race—against much tougher company, and did so handily. When his times were posted for the stakes race, Laz offered to buy him. The Halsteds declined. "Can't say I blame you," Laz said unhappily.

One evening, as he watched Eric working on a prototype of a robotic arm, Jimmy asked, "What will that robot do?"

"This one? Police will use it to help defuse bombs."

"Shut up! Seriously?"

Eric smiled. "Seriously."

"What else do they do?"

"All kinds of things. Help doctors operate. Weld car parts. Clear land mines. Human beings are still far, far, more complex, but robots can do some work that would be difficult or dangerous for people. They can explore shipwrecks under the ocean, or sample the air and soil of other planets. I just read about a robot that can ride a camel in a camel race—a robot jockey."

"But why not use a person to do that?"

"The danger. In Qatar, where it's being used, they made it because the young boys who usually have the job of racing camels can be hurt or killed."

"They'll never go for that in horse racing."

"Probably not," Eric agreed, thinking that any sport that still hired hornblowers and prided itself on animals bred from only three common ancestors was not likely to do anything so radical.

"Could you, like, you know . . . teach me how to make a robot?"

"Yes, sure."

Eric helped him build a simple radio-controlled one that would fit in the palm of his hand. Dubbed "the wake-up bot" by Jimmy, it could slip under a door and then be activated to beep. Jimmy used it to wake his uncle up in time for the workouts. He later caused havoc in the stables by playing with it there one morning—apparently the horses were spooked by the sight and sound of it. Donna was not amused. After that, all electronic playthings were confined to the house.

School started not long after Zuppa won his first race, and in Jimmy's absence, Eric found himself with more time on his hands. He used some of this to attend to his own business affairs, but by the beginning of November, he knew that he needed to face several tasks he had been avoiding. One was that of sorting through Mark's belongings.

Unsure of whether or not Jimmy would want to continue to live away from his childhood home, Eric had put off making permanent arrangements regarding Mark's house. He had hired a local semiretired couple to keep an eye on it, to do basic housekeeping and gardening, and forward the mail. They were happy to have the added income, but had warned him that they would be away this week. It was as good a time as any to begin making decisions about which of Mark's belongings would stay there, be moved here, or be disposed of in some other way.

He talked this over with Jimmy. With the sort of insight Eric was by now less surprised by, he said, "I think you should start with my mom's stuff. You can give away her dresses and all that kind of stuff—someone else might need them. You didn't know her as well as you knew my dad, so it won't, like, you know, be so hard on you."

"That's thoughtful of you," Eric said quietly. Then he added, "Do you want me to wait until you can come with me?"

"Not for this part. You won't give away anything I'll want."

"How do you know that?"

He shrugged. "I trust you."

And that was that.

. . .

He missed watching the workout that morning, in favor of getting an early start on an unpleasant task. As he drove toward Mark's house just before dawn, he felt a degree of melancholy settling over him. This did not change after he arrived, although the sky had lightened. He had not realized, even in his avoidance, how difficult it would be to come back to Mark's house.

Although he had been away from the house for only a month, there had been some lessening of the intensity of his sense of loss in that time, to a degree he hadn't realized until now. Grief seemed to have waited for him all that while, just on the other side of the front door, right here with the large pile of this week's uncollected mail, some of it addressed to a dead man. He set down the stack of flattened boxes, three large trash bags, and the shipping tape dispenser he had brought with him, and gathered the envelopes, magazines, and brochures, and set them on the dining room table.

Memories and regret followed him as he moved through the house: He could picture Mark, sitting in this chair, just so, in that lazy posture of his, or straddling the back of this one at the kitchen table, his arms folded over the top of it as they talked about—oh, such stupid things. *Here's where I should have asked you what was on your mind, and here's where I should have let you know that I needed you to stay alive, here's where I should have told you that you mattered so much to me.*

He moved to the foot of the stairs but could not make himself climb them. Instead, he walked over to the mantel of the living room fireplace. Photos of Mark and Carlotta, Mark and Jimmy, the family together, and—he took this one from its place—of Mark and Eric. Eric, the taller of the two, his arm around his brother's shoulder. They were smiling at Carlotta as she took the picture—almost laughing, really. What had she said to make them laugh? The joke was gone.

They were gone. He carefully put the photo back.

A house full of memories.

One memory it did not contain, and he again silently thanked Mark for somehow having the presence of mind to kill himself away from the house. He could not prevent himself from imagining Mark, sitting beneath that tree, holding the gun, and feeling so filled with despair that suicide seemed the best choice.

Were you so lonely, in spite of all of us? Were we just not enough for you?

He felt a hard, insistent, rising pressure in his chest—it seemed to make his throat swell. He made a sound somewhere between a shout and a cough, then suddenly he was weeping. He struggled against it and lost, gave into it, glad Jimmy wasn't here to witness him falling apart.

Eventually, he wore down, and sat benumbed, and not a little ashamed of himself.

This is accomplishing exactly nothing.

At least he didn't feel the pressure. He wasn't sure the emptiness was a good trade-off.

He had just washed his face when the doorbell rang.

Jesus. Not now, whoever you are. He stood very still.

It rang again.

Go away.

A loud knocking, and the doorbell again.

He waited.

A muffled voice. "Eric?"

Donna. Useless to hide; she'd have seen his car in the drive. Why would she be here? In the next second, panic took hold of him and he ran to the front door. He yanked it open and shouted his fear. "Jimmy! What's happened to him?"

He wasn't sure what startled her more, his appearance or his manner. Her mouth formed a perfect, silent "O." Then, perhaps putting absolutely everything all together at once, she said very quietly, "Nothing, as far as I know. I saw him catch the bus to school. Should we call there to make sure he made it there okay?"

"No," he said, completely mortified now. God, she was talking to him as if he were a skittish colt. "No," he said again.

She ignored that, pulled out a cell phone, and called the school. She had permission to pick up Jimmy from school, was the emergency contact, and could have handled the call herself. But she handed the phone to him as the office answered.

Yes, Jimmy was there, and did his uncle need to speak to him? No, he told them, thanks all the same. He hung up and handed the phone back, immeasurably relieved.

"Thanks, I guess I did need to make that call."

"He told me what you were doing today," she said. "I thought—well, maybe I'm just butting in where I don't belong and you'd rather not have help."

He sighed. "Help would be wonderful. As you can see, I— I'm not doing so hot on my own."

"You design robots. You aren't one yourself. Okay if I come inside?"

He found himself smiling. "Sure."

She discovered the supplies he'd left near the front door, grabbed the trash bags and tape dispenser, and told him to grab the boxes and bring them upstairs. She led the way, hesitated in the upper hall, until he told her which way to turn. They entered the large master bedroom, which had a walk-in closet and full bath to each side. They set up near the closet and bathroom that were Carlotta's.

"Why don't you build the boxes while I start sorting through the small stuff in the bathroom and dresser drawers?" Donna said.

"Okay."

His part of the project went well until he cut his thumb on the jagged edge of the tape dispenser. He swore and brought it to his mouth to stop the quick flow of blood.

"Are you all right?" Donna asked.

"Yes. Just clumsy."

She came nearer, took his hand, and examined the thumb. She grabbed a tissue from Carlotta's dressing table and pressed it to the cut. "Had a tetanus shot lately?"

"Yes."

"Good. This cut's not too deep, but I'll bet it stings."

"It does," he admitted.

"Good thing it's the left thumb. Better rinse it off and see if Mark's bathroom cabinet holds anything you can put on it. I just looked through Carlotta's bathroom, and there's nothing but makeup and skin-care stuff in there." She barely kept the disdain out of her voice.

He thanked her, tried not to feel too bad when she released his hand, and went into Mark's bathroom. He washed off the cut, opened the cabinet, found a tube of antibiotic cream and a box of Band-Aids.

As he was replacing them, he noticed a yellow-orange plastic pill bottle on a high shelf, nearly full. He took it down and read the prescription label. Valium. Mark's sedatives, prescribed not long after Carlotta's death—the expiration date on the pills was nearing. Judging by the bottle, Mark had hardly taken any of them. Eric put them back and shut the cabinet door. He avoided looking in any of the mirrored surfaces and braced himself against the sink, again filled with an overwhelming sense of having failed his brother.

"Do you have good handwriting?"

He turned to see Donna standing at the open bathroom door. He straightened. "Yes, why?"

"I don't. You should make the list. Unless you want to do it on a laptop or something?"

"What list?"

"Donation list—you'll need it for taxes."

So Carlotta's closet was emptied while he took dictation. Donna's steady calm helped him to level out his own emotions. What he saw as "the outfit Carlotta wore that last Christmas," with attendant memories, she described as "woman's two-piece blue silk suit, size eight."

At the same time, she wasn't cold. Her regard for Carlotta

was evident to him, demonstrated in the way she folded each item with exquisite care and placed it in a box. And because every now and then, she would pause, and leave something hanging by itself. He didn't object. Eventually, she came back to these items. In the end, the only thing remaining in the closet was a box with Carlotta's wedding dress in it. "Let's let Jimmy decide on that one when he's a little older," she advised.

He agreed with this, then said, "I can't thank you enough. I mean that. I don't know how long it would have taken me to do this on my own. I hope I haven't wrecked your day."

"It's a good day for this, as it turns out. Nothing in crisis, and no horses entered in anything until the weekend. I did everything I needed to do and came over here. The rest, my staff can handle. What else do you have to do here?"

He hesitated, then said, "I'm going to need to do it in stages, I think."

"Sensible. Anything you can take with you and work on away from here?"

He nodded. "Papers and lots of mail."

They moved into Mark's upstairs library. "I've gone through the desk in here once, so we could probably pack it up fairly quickly. The books I'll deal with later."

She boxed up the contents of Mark's desk, keeping each drawer separate, as he gathered loose papers from around the room, then went downstairs and gathered the mail. He came back up and was watching her empty the last drawer, when he said, "Hell's bells."

"What's wrong?"

"I can't believe it. Some engineer I am."

She waited.

"The desk. I think it has a secret compartment. I never realized it while I was sitting at it."

"How can you tell now?"

"The drawer is too short." He showed her how the desk's width was greater than the length of the drawer. He looked more closely. "There's a panel at the back."

He set out to find the device that would open the panel. He enjoyed solving this kind of puzzle, but all the while, he found himself equally concerned that this would be where he would find at best something that might overset all the legal work that went into settling Mark's estate, and at worst, some horrible secret that Mark could not bear to be known, perhaps even some other cause for his suicide.

"Maybe I should leave," Donna said.

"Please don't," he said, more vehemently than he intended. He looked up at her and added, "I know I can trust your discretion."

"Thanks."

A few moments later, he heard a satisfying click, and the panel slid back, revealing a large manila envelope. Eric removed it, looked for any other contents, and found none. He tested for other secret compartments and, satisfied that he had discovered the only one, put the panel back in place and then turned his attention to the envelope.

It contained two file folders. He pulled the top one out. The front of the folder was stamped, COPPER COUNTY SHERIFF'S DEPARTMENT. The label had two lines of type: "Halsted, C." and the date of Carlotta's death on the first, and a long unfamiliar number beneath that. He opened it, saw the first horrible photo, and quickly shut it.

"The accident investigation?"

"So it appears," he said shakily. "My God . . ."

"You going to be okay?"

"Yes. Yes. It just—I hadn't ever seen—"

"No, of course not."

He sat in silence for a moment, then placed the folder back in the envelope.

"Probably hid them here so that Jimmy wouldn't go through what you just did," she said.

"Yes, I'm sure that's the case."

"Can you keep that away from him at the house?"

"Yes," he said. "I have a safe."

"Mark must have had a reason for keeping it."

"Beyond his obsession . . ." he broke off.

"I'm just saying, maybe when you aren't so angry with him, you can take a closer look at it."

"I'm not ang—well, okay, maybe I am. I'm not going to throw it away, if that's what you're worried about."

"No, something like this won't frighten you for long. You've got more spine than your brother ever had. More than Carlotta, for that matter."

He thought she was wrong on both counts, but found he didn't have an ounce of energy left for an argument.

"You going to be okay driving home?" she asked. "Maybe we should head back—we'll get home just before Jimmy gets out of school if we leave now."

He agreed. She insisted on following him on the drive, and he found himself glancing into the rearview mirror often, comforted each time he saw her big pickup truck there.

• • •

That evening, after Jimmy had fallen asleep—and after a period of time spent wondering if Donna might really be signaling him that she was receptive to being dated by him, or if that was wishful thinking on his part—Eric began to go through the mail from Mark's house. He was surprised to find it included two envelopes from two separate law enforcement agencies. One was from the sheriff's department in Osita County, the county where Mark had died. That one was addressed to Eric. The second was addressed to Mark, and was from the sheriff's department in this county, Copper County, which shared a border with Osita County.

He opened the one addressed to himself. A "final notice" (Final? When had there been any previous ones?) saying that Mark's Corvette must be picked up from the Osita County Sheriff's Department impound yard within thirty days, or it would be sold at auction. It had been released to Eric as trustee of Mark's estate per a court order. What Eric considered to be outrageously high storage fines must be paid as well. He sighed. All of California's counties were cash strapped, so fines were levied at every possible turn.

Well, now he had something on tomorrow's to-do list as well.

He opened the other one. A letter from Detective Michael Wade, saying he had repeatedly tried to contact Mark without success, and apparently the phone number he had for Mark was no longer in service. Would Mark please give him a call at his earliest convenience? Detective Wade had finally received the lab reports he had been waiting for and had a few questions for Mark. He apologized for taking so long to contact him again, but as he had explained before, the county crime lab had an overwhelming backlog of cases. He wanted to assure Mark that despite these unavoidable delays, the investigation was continuing.

Eric looked at this more closely. Beneath the date was a reference to a case number.

Eric moved to his office safe and, entering the combination on its electronic keypad, unlocked it, and removed the envelope he had placed there earlier in the day. He removed the file folders. The number in the letter was the number on the folder he had so hastily put away this afternoon.

There was an ongoing investigation into Carlotta's death? It wasn't clearly ruled a single-vehicle accident?

He forced himself to open the folder, quickly flipping the photos over and concentrating on what had been written and diagrammed within. That he was looking at photocopies was evident. Did Detective Wade give him a copy of the whole file? No, clearly some pages were missing. He wondered if Mark had sweet-talked someone else into getting the information to him. Entirely possible, knowing his charming brother. How old was this report?

He looked at the last notation in the file. It mentioned that the detective had followed up with the lab about samples of white and red paint, thought to have transferred from the vehicle that struck the SUV, being sent to the lab, along with several pieces of a broken headlamp. Something about the date of the notation nagged at him. He went back to his safe and took out his copy of the will. The codicil about Zuppa Inglese had been added that week.

He went back to the folder and read more carefully.

An hour later, Eric was convinced that at the very least, another vehicle had been involved in the fatal accident, and that in all likelihood someone had intentionally forced Carlotta off the road. Debris found at the apparent point of impact, skid marks, tire impressions. Footwear impressions—of someone who had walked partway down the slope and back, but never called an ambulance or police.

Eric set the folder aside, staring off into the night for a time, wondering if his rage would cool before dawn.

The second folder contained an assortment of loose notes and pieces of paper. One was a map, upon which someone, presumably Mark, had marked three locations: the restaurant from which Carlotta began that last drive; Shackel Horse Farm, where Mark and Jimmy waited; the place where she was killed.

Another was a photocopy of a credit card bill. He had seen a second-generation copy of it in the other folder—presumably, Mark had given the original to the detective. After studying it, Eric saw that it included a charge for gasoline on the date she died.

A bill for Carlotta's cell phone. The others were slips of paper with brief notes made in Mark's handwriting. The time she left the restaurant. The time she bought gas at the gas station. Michael Wade's business card.

But who on earth would want to kill Carlotta? Mark would probably be a suspect, but anyone who looked closely into their lives would learn that he was devoted to her, and would see that her expertise and skill were a key part of the restaurants' success.

The more Eric thought about it, the more likely it seemed that this was a case of hit and run, or road rage. A stranger, not anyone who knew her.

He studied the map again and realized that not only was Mark's home much closer to the Shackel Horse Farm than the restaurant, the three locations were in a triangle and did not lie along the same route. Leaving the restaurant, she took a different road to go to the farm than she would have taken to go home. Unless someone knew that she was on the way to the farm exactly at that time, on just that night—was it possible?

The only people who knew her plans were Mark, Jimmy, Shackel, and perhaps a few of Shackel's workers. Maybe the veterinarian, if there had even been one there, but anyone who was attending the birth of the foal wouldn't have been able to lie in wait for Carlotta. Detective Wade had interviewed the last two people to see her alive. Two restaurant workers, who knew she was excited about the birth of the foal, but who had no idea that she had gone toward the horse farm—both thought she was going home. Neither had any idea where Shackel Horse Farm was located.

Eric finally locked the folders away in his safe again and went to bed.

Sleep eluded him.

Mark changed the will for a reason, did what he did with the sale of his horses for a reason. He must have suspected Shackel or someone connected with Shackel of arranging Carlotta's fatal accident. Did Mark commit suicide?

Again the nagging doubts arose, but this time they were based on something more than his inability to believe that Mark would abandon Jimmy. If Mark was planning suicide, he would not leave those photos of Carlotta's death behind, not if there was any chance that Jimmy might find them. And suicide did not fit in with his apparent drive to discover what happened to Carlotta.

Or did Mark feel guilty about her death?

Not for intentionally causing it, but bringing her closer to someone who did . . . that might have been hard for him to bear, but would he kill himself before seeing her killer brought to justice? Leave Jimmy behind, unaware of what had happened?

Then he wondered if Jimmy were so unaware after all. He remembered the way he had talked about Shackel, warning Eric to be careful.

He dozed off, but awoke well before dawn. He showered and dressed and made a phone call to a security company he had used on other occasions. The regular staff wasn't in yet, but he was promised a call back as soon as possible.

He put on a warm jacket and wrote a note for Jimmy, who would be up soon. He walked across the road to Copper Hills, his breath fogging in the chill air. Despite the cold and the darkness, grooms and others were already at work in the barn area. He found Donna talking to an exercise rider. He waited out of earshot, not wanting to intrude, but she saw him, smiled, and came over to where he stood.

"You're up early this morning," she said.

"Or up late, depending on how you look at it."

"Hmm. That doesn't sound good."

"It's not. I need to talk something over with you—I know this is the worst time of day—"

She waved this off and invited him into her office. He poured out his story. Although her face registered shock, and then sadness, she listened quietly, not interrupting. She stayed quiet for long moments after he stopped talking. He wondered if he sounded crazy to her, but nothing in her manner indicated that she was withdrawing from him. This was simply the way she dealt with any crisis—she stayed calm, reflective, and did not shout out the first thing that came to mind.

"Where's Jimmy?" she asked.

He glanced at his watch. "He'll probably be over here in a few minutes."

"Then let's talk again after he goes to school. I don't want him coming in on the middle of this, do you?"

"No. In fact—let me call this detective. Maybe I've made something out of nothing."

"Maybe, but all of it taken together—I think there might be something to this. And I can understand why it kept you up last night." She paused, then said, "You need help getting Mark's car from the impound yard?"

"Yes, but I've already taken up so much of your time—"

"I wouldn't offer if I couldn't do it. Besides, we'll have a chance to talk on the way over. Bring that envelope with you— maybe I'll recognize some of the numbers in Mark's notes."

Jimmy soon came into the office, holding up his wake-up bot and controller. "Not going to use them here, I promise. Just want Uncle Eric to know I'm amazed. The first morning . . ." He looked more closely at Eric. "What's wrong?"

"Couldn't sleep, that's all."

Jimmy exchanged a quick glance with Donna, then said, "I think you should wait a little while before going back to the other house."

"Might be a good idea. By the way, I wanted to mention something else to you." He told them he was going to hire security for Zuppa Inglese, and—although they objected—for each of them as well.

"Humor me," he told them. "I can't take any more loss."

That had ended all protest.

After Jimmy got on the school bus, Eric called Detective Wade. He explained that Mark had died.

"Died! He was in his thirties, right?"

"Apparent suicide," Mark said, and explained the circumstances of his brother's death.

There was a pause, then Wade said, "What aren't you telling me, Mr. Halsted?"

He hesitated. "I have absolutely no proof of my suspicions—and those suspicions are not centered on any individual. I'm just less and less certain that my brother committed suicide."

"I'll tell you this, I wouldn't think it of him. Not with the boy to look after. And he was on a mission."

Eric felt an overwhelming sense of relief. "Perhaps we could meet a little later today, Detective?"

Wade agreed to this, and they set an appointment for one o'clock. Wade then asked, "Who handled the case in Osita County?"

Eric recalled the taciturn man who had dealt with him in the "let's get this over with" manner in the days after Mark's death. A heavy-set, gray-haired man who seemed to know his business without demonstrating any real enthusiasm for it. He had not been cruel, he had not been kind. "Detective Delmore," Eric said.

He heard Wade swear softly. "Well, that explains all kinds of things. Your brother's case must have been the last one he handled before he retired. And I'm sorry—I was on vacation around the time your brother died, so I didn't get word."

"Because he died in another county," Eric said.

"That's probably part of it. But I suppose it was in the news here?"

"A small item in the local paper."

"Hmm. Listen, I know a good guy over there in Osita. Fellow by the name of Pearsley. I'll give him a call and see if he'll take another look at it."

On the way to the impound yard, Donna identified the

names on Mark's lists. "If I'm not mistaken, those men all work for Shackel. Jimmy will know for sure, if you can come up with a way of asking him."

"I've been wondering when I should talk to him about this."

"Hard call. I can see why you'd hesitate. But he's a sharp kid, and it would probably be better for you to be up-front with him. I think the worst thing that could happen would be for him to find out about it on his own."

"True."

"He'll also know who was present during the foaling."

She knew only three of the numbers Mark had scribbled down. The number of a veterinarian. The number for the state horse-racing board. "The other is for that attorney who drew up the contract about Zuppa. Shackel likes him. I don't think much of him. We can check those other numbers against my computer records, though."

At the impound yard, he told her not to wait for him, but she insisted on staying. "After all this time sitting here, it may not make it back home. I'd better follow you."

At the front counter they were greeted by a squat, balding sergeant who smiled at Donna and then frowned as he studied his computer records for the car. He scrolled down a bit and whistled. "Long time—oh, I see, it was Delmore's case." He muttered something under his breath about Detective Delmore. He read for a while, his frown deepening. "Your brother?" he asked Eric.

Eric nodded.

"Sorry for your loss . . ." This was said absently as he continued to study the monitor, apparently unable to find something he was looking for. "Tell you what, let me see if I can get the fines lowered, since just between you and me, it was really our detective that caused the thing to sit here all these months."

While they were waiting for him to return, the security company called. Eric told them what he wanted. "Can you get someone to start as early as tomorrow?" he asked. They said they could and gave him the names of the members of the team they would send.

The sergeant came back, pleased to give him the news that all fines were waived. He led them toward the Corvette, rolling a portable battery starter as he went. Seeing the car saddened Eric—he thought of how much Mark had loved riding around in it. Although Eric had never been one for status symbols, he knew Mark was not quite so averse to them. Here was the first status symbol his brother had bought, now covered in dust and bird droppings.

The sergeant released the hood and hooked up the starter, then asked Eric to get in and give it a try. As Eric got into the driver's seat, he found himself in a novel situation—sitting too far back from the wheel and pedals. He started to reach for the seat adjustment, then stopped himself an instant before his hand was on the lever. He got out of the car, much to the sergeant's consternation.

"Pardon me, Sergeant, but can you tell me if the officer who drove the car here from the place where my brother was found is a very tall person?"

"The car wasn't driven here. It was brought here on a flatbed tow truck and lowered right into that space there. Not even the lab guys have been near it, 'cause from all I can tell, Delmore never asked them to take a look. So except for whatever rain and dust and guano might have landed on it over the months, this car is just the way your brother left it, mileage and all."

"That can't be true." He held up a hand as the sergeant bristled. "What I mean is, my brother was shorter than I am. The seat is now so far back, it seems that someone much taller than either of us was the last person to drive the car."

After a moment's pause, he said, "You sure he was shorter than you?"

"Absolutely positive."

The sergeant swore under his breath.

Remembering his conversation with Detective Wade, Eric said, "If you don't mind, Sergeant, would you please contact Detective Pearsley about this? A detective from Copper County was going to try to talk to him about a case that might possibly be related to my brother's death."

"You know Pearsley?" he said, brightening. "Oh sure." He unhooked the charger and lowered the hood. "Let's get in out of this cold."

Within a few minutes, they were introduced to a lean man whom Eric guessed to be in his early forties. Eric liked Pearsley immediately—his manner, his attentiveness, his obvious intelligence all made Eric wish that he had been the one to get Mark's case in the first place. The detective had already spoken to Wade, although he hadn't had time yet to pull the file on the case. Eric showed him the second folder, and Pearsley asked to keep it. Eric was reluctant, until Pearsley agreed to photocopy the materials in it. As he handed the copies to Eric, he smiled and said, "Mind if I have a look at the other folder you have in that envelope?"

"Uh, that might be a little bit ticklish."

Within a matter of minutes, though, Pearsley had not only

reassured him, but managed to talk him into handing the copy of the Copper County investigation over, too. Pearsley won the argument by saying, "Better if Wade hears the explanation about how you got it from me than from you."

He asked if Eric would be willing to leave the car there a little longer. "I don't know what the lab will be able to do at this point, but I'd like to have them take a look at it."

Eric agreed to it.

Pearsley gave him a talk about leaving the investigation to law enforcement.

Eric stayed silent. He understood what Pearsley was saying, but he also couldn't bring himself to promise not to try to find out who killed his brother.

Pearsley tried again.

"I understand," Eric said.

The detective sighed in frustration.

• • •

By the time they finished talking to Pearsley, Eric realized he was nearly late to meet with Wade.

"I'll take you," Donna said. "Easier to go straight there without going back for your car."

"I'm tying up your whole day."

"This is important to me," she said, then added, "Unless you'd rather meet with him alone? I can wait outside—"

"No, no—I like—I mean, I always want . . ." He stopped, took a breath, and said, "I'm glad you're with me today. And not just because of the moral support factor. And I sincerely hope my saying that doesn't make you feel uncomfortable."

She smiled. "No, it doesn't."

"Well . . . good," he said. He looked out the truck window

as they passed rolling pastureland, wondering how three words could make a person feel so relieved, excited, and anxious at the same time.

The meeting with Wade went smoothly—just as he had paved the way with Pearsley, Pearsley had obviously paved the way with Wade. Although Eric wouldn't like to be whatever member of the department had copied the case file once Wade caught up with him or her (a clerical volunteer seemed to be his chief suspect), Wade didn't seem to be inclined to take it out on Eric or Donna.

Wade showed them photographs taken by the lab of a number of fragments of plastic and metal objects, and enlarged views of the microscopic particles of paint.

"When the two vehicles made contact, they damaged each other in ways that caused pieces to fall off each of them. They dented and scraped each other, and each took some of the paint from the other. They tell me the level of impact, and marks on the SUV show that her vehicle was hit from behind, on the left rear side. So we looked at the pieces that this other vehicle might have dropped. It lost most of a headlamp, and our lab guys painstakingly put those pieces together. It's a right-hand side—passenger side—Ford headlamp, could fit either a Ranger or a Bronco, from years 1989 to 1992. So we've got someone in an older truck or Bronco, that limits it somewhat, but then we are still looking at a hell of a lot of vehicles. Rangers are popular. You've got one, right, Ms. Freepoint?"

"An F-250."

"Lotta truck for a gal. But you're a horse trainer, and doing towing. Besides it's blue, and we know that this truck was white."

"I've got a white truck, too," she said, "bigger than this one."

Eric couldn't help smiling.

"An old Ranger?" Wade asked.

"No."

"Well, see, if all we had was white and a truck, or even a Ford truck, you'd be in the pool of possible suspects, along with all the other folks who owned or had access to similar vehicles. But all these little bits of info from the forensic guys add up, and as they add up, they also narrow our pool of possible suspects. White is not an unusual color for trucks, but this one also had paint on it that didn't come from the factory. Now, this is a big break for us, because it was probably custom painted on a vehicle, and we may be able to find the place that did it, if it was done nearby."

"What color?" Eric asked.

"Red," Wade said.

"So the truck was red, not white?"

"It was both, but the red was probably added on later."

"Red and white—those are Shackel Farm's colors."

Wade's brows went up. "Shackel Farm? The place where Mrs. Halsted was going that night?"

"Yes, and the place my brother was watching through field glasses the day he died."

Eric showed him his copies of Mark's notes. "Detective Pearsley has all these as well."

Wade made a set of them, too, muttering something about it being a shame that he hadn't seen him before Pearsley got hold of the originals.

"Detective Wade," Eric said, "I think it's clear that Shackel was involved in both deaths. He was one of a handful of people who knew that Carlotta was on the way to the farm. I'm not saying he forced her off the road himself." He paused, taking a deep breath to try to calm himself. "Well," he added bitterly, "he had a great alibi, didn't he?"

"Mr. Halsted—"

"And while you were on vacation, my brother got copies of your files, and it just confirmed what he had been thinking—that the only people who knew that Carlotta was on that road worked for Shackel—"

Wade tried again. "Mr. Halsted—"

"Mark probably wasn't even watching the horses that day. He was probably spying on Shackel, looking for that truck. And somehow Shackel saw Mark, or maybe Mark confronted him, and then—I don't know, drugged him. Then loaded him into the Corvette and drove him out to the woods and shot him—"

"Mr. Halsted!"

Donna reached over and put a hand on Eric's arm. He fell silent, but he could feel himself shaking with anger.

"Mr. Halsted, you have every reason to be upset, and every reason to let law enforcement professionals handle things from here."

"Like hell. Delmore was a law enforcement professional! He convinced me my brother's death was a suicide! All these months—!" He drew an unsteady breath.

"Let's say," Wade said, his voice low and quiet, "things went just as you theorize—and I must emphasize that it is a *theory,* and *yours,* and at the moment *completely* unproven. But let's say you're right. First, if your brother hadn't tried to play detective, you probably wouldn't be raising his son right now."

Eric looked away.

"Second, as long as Mr. Shackel has no idea you are catching on to him, you're much safer. And Jimmy is safer. Do you understand?"

Eric nodded, miserable.

"Third, if we are going to put this bastard away, we need to build a case that will convince a jury, not just the people who loved Mark and Carlotta. I can't do that if you get in my way. Neither can Detective Pearsley." He paused. "You got a bad deal with Delmore, but he's out of the picture now. Do you trust Pearsley?"

"Yes," Eric said.

Wade's phone rang. He answered it, then said, "Speak of the devil. Yeah, they're still here. You and I need to talk, ol' buddy. Okay, hang on." He handed the phone to Eric. "It's Pearsley."

"Hello?" Eric said.

"Mr. Halsted, I have the autopsy report on your brother here. I'm just wondering, did he have a prescription for Valium?"

"Yes," Eric said, surprised. "I just saw the bottle yesterday."

"Did Detective Delmore ask you that same question?"

Eric thought back. "I think he did ask if Eric was taking any prescription drugs, and I might have mentioned that he had a prescription for sleeping pills, but didn't like taking them. Delmore never said anything more to me about it."

"You saw these yesterday, you said?"

"Yes."

"Remember the prescribing doctor's name?" He did, and gave it to Pearsley, who then asked, "Any idea how many had been taken?"

"The bottle looked full. And the prescription was over two years old. Why do you ask?"

"Your brother had a remarkably high level of diazepam in his system—"

"Of what?" Eric asked, grabbing a pen and paper.

"Diazepam. Another name for Valium. But there's nothing to indicate that they found an empty pill bottle at the scene or in his car." He paused, then said, "I'd like to take a look through the house. Can we meet there tomorrow?"

They made an appointment.

When he hung up, he looked at his watch and said, "Detective Wade, I have to go. My nephew will be home from school soon, and I like to be there."

"Sure."

As they were leaving, Donna turned to Wade and said, "I think you're wrong about something."

"And what would that be, Ms. Freepoint?"

"We aren't safe, and we won't be, no matter how certain Shackel is that he's managed to get away with two murders."

"Believe me, I'm aware that whoever did this has a dangerous amount of confidence right now."

"No, I mean that—we didn't get a chance to talk about motive with you. Shackel's motive has something to do with a horse. Maybe he wanted Zuppa Inglese, or just to be able to control how he races. But that's what this is about."

• • •

"He'll never get him," Eric said as they drove back.

"No, but haven't you ever been around spoiled people? They sometimes wreck what they can't have for themselves. I'm glad you're hiring security for Zuppa. In fact, let me give myself some peace of mind between now and tomorrow morning." She used her cell phone to call one of her workers at the Fox River track. Reassured that Zuppa was doing fine, she then asked that they keep a close watch on him. "There will be extra security there tomorrow morning, but if you see anyone coming near him tonight, don't hesitate to get track security involved."

"Thanks," he said when she ended the call. "And not just for that. For everything. I don't know how I could have managed getting through the last few months without you."

"It's nothing," she said. "And you've done as much or more for me. I don't kid myself about why my phone is ringing more often these days. Training Zuppa has brought me more business. But it's more than that, really. I like spending time with you and Jimmy." She was silent for a time, then asked, "Do you think—do you think Carlotta was killed because she wanted to bring Zuppa to Copper Farms?"

"It's not your fault, if that's what you're asking. Owners removing horses from trainers is part of the business, right?"

"I remember Carlotta talking about how much Shackel pressured Mark, trying to get a percentage of Zuppa before he was born. Mark and Carlotta weren't going to sell, but I'll bet you anything she was the one who told Shackel they wouldn't. Maybe he thought that Mark would sell him a share if the colt wasn't racing well. He couldn't slow Zuppa down if he wasn't the trainer. Not very easily, anyway."

Eric thought this over. "You forget—Carlotta and Jimmy wanted to take *all* their horses from him, not just the foal. Mark sold most of their horses off not long after Carlotta died, and I think that was because he had lost heart. But if she had lived, and they had pulled all those horses away from

Shackel and brought them to you, wouldn't that have done serious damage to his reputation?"

"Yes. Yes, you're right. I guess Mark did eventually figure out Shackel was some kind of rat, or he wouldn't have left Zuppa to you and Jimmy. He would have sold him, too."

"Who knows? Jimmy thinks Zuppa had some kind of look in his eye from the day he was born, one that said he could take on all comers. Maybe Mark saw that, too." He yawned. "Oh, forgive me. Next to no sleep."

"That reminds me—tell your detective friends that diazepam is used as a horse sedative, too."

"What?"

"Valium. I saw you write its generic name—diazepam."

"So Shackel might have had access to a large amount of it?"

"Sure. If a racehorse's behavior becomes dangerous to humans, you want a way to calm him down in a hurry. There are other uses for it, too. Most would have it in injectable form."

. . .

He thanked her again when she dropped him off at the house. He watched her make the turn into her own drive, wondering if he had ever before in his life experienced so many warring emotions in a twenty-four-hour period.

He went inside and sat on the big leather sofa, exhausted, but thinking that Jimmy would be home any minute now, and he needed to come up with some way to tell him—well, whatever it was he should tell him.

He dozed lightly, awakening with a start. "Jimmy?" he called, but the house was silent.

He glanced at his watch. Jimmy should have been home

by now. He had no sooner thought this than the phone rang.

"Uncle Eric?" Jimmy sounded frightened, almost tearful.

"Jimmy? Are you okay? What's wrong?"

But before Jimmy could answer, a man's voice came on the line. "You've had a busy day, haven't you?"

"What's going on? Let me talk to Jimmy!"

"Let's make a trade, then. The boy for a horse. Simple. Zuppa Inglese is going to be stolen and never heard from again, you're going to collect insurance, and life will be beautiful. Leave the sheriff's department out of it. Understood?"

"Yes," said Eric, his mouth dry.

"Grab your cell phone. Get your girlfriend from across the road to go fetch Zuppa Inglese. The two of you are concerned about his health and have decided not to race him. I'll know if you give them any other story, understood?"

"Yes."

"Keep your cell phone on and I'll give you instructions once the horse is out of the gates."

The man hung up. For a brief moment Eric stood still, too horrified to move. Then he grabbed his jacket and keys and ran to Donna's house. As he ran, he tried to place the man's voice. Vaguely familiar, but not Shackel's.

• • •

"What if he's not here?" Eric asked as Fox River Racetrack came within sight. "Maybe my theory is totally wrong."

"I don't think so," Donna said. "It makes sense. Whoever is doing this can't afford to involve too many people. If he's a horse owner or trainer who gets caught at it, all his efforts are for nothing—he'll be run off the track for life. If the voice on the phone had been Shack's, I'd say it may just be him acting alone. So it might be two—we both know he must have had someone helping him on the night Carlotta died." She paused as she negotiated the turn into the track grounds. "Thank God you paid such close attention to what he said on the phone. We know at least one person has to be here, or close enough to see our trailer leave the track, or they couldn't call you when we leave. Jimmy's probably with that person, because they'll want to send us running back here after him when they have the horse."

He had said all of this to her an hour or so ago. Now, repeated back to him, he wasn't sure it was so smart a theory.

"What do you think they've done to him?" Eric asked her as the track security guard opened the gate for them.

"I don't know. We can't think like that."

He swallowed hard. She was right. He had to think about their plans, and not just how wrong they could go. "Your guys are ready?"

"Yes. We all want a piece of these jerks. But they'll only see Paulo and Estefan."

She drove to the farthest barn, the one where Zuppa was stabled.

The men who met them were two grooms who had worked for Donna for many years. Paulo and Estefan were brothers, and the grim expression on Estefan's face made Eric's heart sink. Paulo, the older of the brothers, was Zuppa's groom.

"I looked for him," Estefan whispered, then shook his head. "But others know—Jimmy, he belongs to us all, you understand? They will be looking for him, too. They know to be careful."

Eric knew that an army of about eight hundred worked the backstretch at this track. Not all of them would be here now. But the four of them weren't going to be the only ones with their eyes open tonight.

"You've got people outside?" Donna asked, just as quietly.

"Yes, everything the way you asked, Miss Donna." He gave Eric a quick smile. "We had a lot of volunteers."

"Let's pray this works, then."

"Jimmy is here," Paulo said. "Zuppa, he knows it."

"What do you mean?" Eric asked.

"Zuppa, you know how he loves Jimmy? When he knows that boy is near, he gets excited. He's been mad at me today, Zuppa—started not long before you called, Miss Donna. He wants out of that stall."

"Maybe that's exactly who we should have searching for Jimmy, then," Donna said.

"What if someone's watching?" Eric asked.

"I think we can make it look good."

When they reached Zuppa's stall, for the first time, Eric found himself feeling afraid of the colt. The horse seemed frustrated—he moved restlessly, tail flicking, and as they approached he snorted and kicked at the walls. Paulo talked to him, and he ceased the kicking, but it took the combined efforts of Donna and Paulo to get him to the point where anyone felt it was safe to take him out.

"Stand back," Donna said, no longer whispering. But once out of his stall, Zuppa seemed calmer. He perked up his ears, then gave a call, one Eric had heard him make often—his greeting when Jimmy came to see him. He stretched his head out toward Eric, who came nearer. Zuppa made a loud sighing sound.

"If I load him in the trailer while he's in a mood like this," Donna said, "he'll get hurt—if we manage to load him in at all. We made good time getting here, so I think I'll take a minute to walk him around a little, calm him down." Estefan and Paulo said they would walk with her, just to help out if need be, and all three looked expectantly at Eric.

Realizing this was being said for any potential eavesdropper's sake, he said, "Oh yes, I'm coming, too."

As they began to walk down the row of stalls, some open, some closed up for the night, he noticed that Zuppa had tensed again, head high.

"Where's Jimmy, Zuppa?" Donna whispered to him.

The horse's ears flicked, and he called again.

Something or someone seemed to be disturbing other horses in a nearby barn. They turned down that row. Two workers appeared from the other end and began going down the row from there, looking in stalls as if checking on unsettled horses, then made slight shrugging gestures.

Suddenly Eric heard a familiar noise. "The wake-up bot!"

"Shh," Donna said, but she was just as excited. "Where?"

Eric couldn't quite figure out where the sound was coming from, but Zuppa could. He began to strain against the halter, trying to reach one of the closed stalls.

Eric hurried toward it. Someone had placed a lock on it, illegal if a horse occupied it. Estefan was soon beside him, and before long, the lock was off. Erie pulled open the stall door and saw Jimmy lying on the cement floor, duct tape binding his wrists and ankles, a wide silver strip of it across his mouth. On the ground nearby was the controller for the wake-up bot. Eric ran to him, apologized for the pain that came with removal of the tape gag, and quickly cut his hands and feet free, too. They hugged each other and cried their relief, and Donna soon joined them. "Are you okay?" Eric asked, and Jimmy nodded. From the stall door, Paulo said, "You better come see Zuppa, Jimmy, he's the one who told us you were here."

Eric helped him stand and he moved stiffly to where Zuppa waited. The horse butted Jimmy's chest and whickered, lipping at Jimmy's neck and ears as the boy held on to him and praised him.

"Don't give him away to them, Uncle Eric. Don't."

"Not a chance. Who did this, Jimmy?"

"That guy Dennis—Laz's son-in-law."

Eric was stunned. "Laz? Laz wants Zuppa Inglese?"

"Dennis may not be doing this on Laz's orders," Donna said. "Let's call the sheriff and let him sort it out."

"Let's call him from outside," Eric said, feeling his fists clench.

She looked at him in surprise, then smiled. "All right."

• • •

There was a good chance it wouldn't work, Eric knew, but there was also a good chance that Dennis would go into the wind and never be caught by police. Laz was wealthy and might help his daughter's husband escape punishment.

They put Zuppa into the horse trailer and tucked Jimmy safely into the backseat of the truck's extended cab, where he couldn't be seen through the dark-tinted windows. They had given him blankets, and Donna had the foresight to bring a couple of bottles of water. Jimmy was downing one of them. When his thirst was slaked, he told them that Dennis had been waiting for him near the place where the school bus dropped him off, and overpowered him. After restraining and gagging him, Dennis had put him in a large empty feed sack in the backseat of his car, then covered him with feed sacks and blankets and tack. It was stifling there, and at first, Jimmy was just happy when some of the layers were taken off. Dennis carried him and other supplies into the empty stall, took the gag off only long enough to let Jimmy say Eric's name on the phone call, then left him there. He had been scared that Dennis would kill him. As the night grew colder, he worried that Zuppa would be killed, and Eric and Donna. He'd be left alone, with no one. He managed to get the wake-up bot out of his pocket, and used his chin to try to operate the controls.

"I wasn't very good at it," he said.

"You were terrific," Eric said. "It was a smart and brave thing to do."

Jimmy was still very shaken, Eric could see, and that infuriated him. Eric knew he had to control what seemed at the moment to be a perfectly reasonable impulse to beat the living hell out of Dennis.

He asked Jimmy for a description of the car. A black Mercedes-Benz. Jimmy didn't get a chance to see the license plate.

They pulled out of the backstretch area and checked with the guard, saying just what they had been ordered to say, not knowing how close to the guard shed Dennis might be waiting and watching.

They moved the truck and trailer down the street a short distance and parked.

"Why would Laz do this?" Eric asked in a low voice. "Was he just trying to make sure Give Me Room had less competition?"

"I can't believe it is Laz," Donna said. "I've known him a long time. He'd see, I'm sure, that he just couldn't kidnap every horse that might be able to beat Give Me Room."

"Zuppa hasn't even faced Give Me Room yet. Not until the Fox River Juvenile Stakes next week, right?"

"That race is worth a lot," Jimmy said. "But Donna's right. I—I thought about this a lot when I was tied up. Laz would never hurt anyone."

"I wish they would call," Eric said, looking at his cell phone.

As if he had willed it to do so, it began to vibrate.

"You turned the ringer off?" Jimmy said.

"Yes. I want him to think my phone isn't working."

"You sure this is a good idea?" Donna asked.

"No," he answered, feeling his palms sweat.

Within seconds, the phone rang again. He waited a few moments, then got out of the truck, hearing Donna whisper, "Be careful, Eric!" as he closed the door. He paced anxiously, telling himself that he had to look as if he didn't know where Jimmy was right now and was waiting for a call. He kept looking at the phone. The track workers were well hidden, but he avoided looking at the shrubs where they were concealed.

The cell phone vibrated again, and he did not react to it. He didn't have to pretend to be anxious now.

After a few moments, he heard a car coming. He moved to stand near the driver's side window of the truck. When he was sure the approaching car was a dark Mercedes, he said, "Call the sheriff now, Donna."

Dennis pulled up behind the trailer, and Eric approached with his hands out to his side. Dennis got out of the car, obviously ready to yell, but Eric beat him to it. "You said you would call!"

"I did, damn it!"

"Where's Jimmy? What have you done to him?!"

"He'll be just fine if you do what you're told. We're not off to a good start here. How am I supposed to give you instructions if your damned phone isn't working?"

Eric might have pointed out that no plan should be wholly reliant on technology, but Dennis had moved closer to him, within striking range, and Eric could see movement in the shadows nearby. He gave into selfish desire for the first time in months and landed a hard punch in the middle of Dennis's face.

Before Dennis could cry out more than "You crazy bastard!" he was brought to the ground by a group of a dozen track workers. Estefan and Paulo were among them.

"Here—he has a gun!" someone cried, and wrestled it out of Dennis's hand before he could fire it.

At that moment, the sheriff's department arrived.

The confusion was not easily sorted out, but within the hour Dennis was in custody. Several hours later, and after Dennis, Eric, Jimmy, and Donna had spent time talking to Detective Pearsley, Shackel was arrested. Detective Wade appeared not long after. He did not seem happy with Eric, but Eric had all he cared about. Donna and Jimmy were safe. Paulo and Estefan had taken Zuppa back to his stall, promising Jimmy to give him extra apples and carrots.

Laz, informed of his son-in-law's arrest, was both appalled and embarrassed when he learned why, and told his daughter he would disinherit her if she posted bail. Dennis remained in custody.

After lecturing him briefly on all the things that might have gone wrong as a result of their amateurish plans, Pearsley told Eric that Donna and Jimmy were waiting for him and he could go home.

"You're not going to tell me what you've learned?"

He sighed. "You figured out most of it already. We've got Dennis singing his heart out, or it might have taken us longer to figure it out. Dennis and Shackel go way back—back to when Dennis was using another name and had a record for assault and other crimes. In exchange for not telling his new rich wife about his criminal past, Dennis did some favors for Shackel. Running your sister-in-law off the road was one of them, I'm afraid."

Eric nodded, but didn't say anything. It was one thing to think something was possible, another to have it laid out as cold fact.

"He said Shackel manipulated your brother, and Carlotta was interfering in that. Shackel had big plans and none of them were going to happen if Carlotta got her way. He arranged for Dennis to wait for her car to reach a certain point on the road to Shackel Horse Farm and then run her off it. Dennis would have killed her if the accident didn't. He was paid well for that.

"Shackel was shocked to learn that your brother was less cooperative after she died. More shocked when your brother seemed to figure out that he had something to do with her death. Your brother learned which barn was hiding the damaged truck—the truck Shackel knew better than to take in for repair anywhere nearby. Shackel told Dennis he caught your brother trying to look in the barn that day, and shot him full of horse tranquilizer. He drove him out to the nearby woods and made it look like suicide. We're still working on that part of the case."

"And tonight?" Eric said after a while.

"That horse has become an obsession of Shackel's, according to Dennis. Blames it and you for his troubles. They had a plan to have you take the horse to Laz's property, where they would injure him. He knew that with Zuppa out of contention, and Laz discredited, Easy Dreamer was the most likely winner of the Juvenile Stakes."

"Easy Dreamer. You know what, Detective Pearsley? You can probably get his grooms to talk about all kinds of methods Shackel used to get to his dreams the easy way."

• • •

Donna came to the house with them. She stayed with him while he explained to Jimmy what he knew about how Jimmy's parents died. There were tears and anger, but in the end he hugged Eric and Donna together and said, "You caught him. You caught him! Thank you so much!"

When Jimmy had finally fallen into an exhausted sleep, Eric took Donna by the hand and led her to his bedroom.

Just before they fell into their own exhausted sleep, she said, "Zuppa is going to win the Fox River Juvenile Stakes."

• • •

It was a sure thing.

YELLOW MAMA'S LONG WEEKEND

Lorenzo Carcaterra

This was not the way it was supposed to have played out. At least not the way I had it all figured. I had been behind the financial eight ball lots of times and lots of ways in my fifty-six years, and I always managed to squeeze my way out of the juice. This last time shouldn't have been any different. But this last time was the first time I thought to make Yellow Mama the solution to my fix, and from that second on, every move I made that could go wrong did.

I'm a horse trainer by trade and a degenerate gambler by choice. I'll bet on anything with anybody, doesn't matter what. I'll lay you odds on what time the sun's gonna come up and double down on that when it rolls around to dusk. I once turned a $400 early afternoon daily double winning into a $1,200 *Monday Night Football* loss, with a 3 percent vig tossed in on top. I'm so lost when it comes down to a gambling jones, I'll even lay a few dollars on a pro wrestling match. I've made hundreds of thousands of dollars in my years at the track. Trouble is, I've lost thousands more layin' down bets and side action. My addiction has cost me everything. Besides the money, I lost the only woman I'll ever love, or even better, that would ever love me. Helen stuck around long enough to show me she cared, but gave up the ghost the night Denny Miller laid a knife across her throat and swore he would leave her head on the living room floor if I didn't come across with the six thousand, five hundred I owed his crew. I owned a house for about a year, maybe a little longer, small three-bedroom in the Bronx, on a dead-end street just off Ely Avenue. Now, some bookie from Pakistan lives in it with his family, my payoff to him for the Diamondbacks taking down the Yankees in the 2001 World Series, winning run coming home off the cheapest hit any batter could ever hope to hit. I used to drive nice cars, but gave up that habit when I got tired of signing over each one to some loan shark that I was in with too deep. Not bad enough they peel out with my car, leaving me behind with the monthly payments. They also have to break one of my arms, usually the right one, just so their boss knows they tried to get the cash and settled for the car.

Don't get me wrong. I've had some good nights in this run, too. Won my share of bets and collected as fast as legs or wheels could get me to the payoff drop. I once hit on a number, 213, and a horse race at Saratoga and a baseball game at Fenway Park all in the same day. By midmorning of the next, I had partied away all my winnings, had just enough in my pockets for the cab ride back to the stables. I've won as much as $42,650 in one day and lost twice that much after a bad run at the tables in Atlantic City. It's my life and after fifty-six years of living it, I'm not about to change my ways. Probably couldn't even if I would want to, and I would lay 6-1 odds that for what I got there is no cure.

But, now I got Yellow Mama in the middle of my jackpot, her life at risk, and that's been gnawing away at my insides something fierce. I love that horse, love her more than anything or anybody that's ever walked into and out of my life. And if I don't figure a way out of this mess I got us both in by Sunday night, she's gonna end up legs to the wind and I'll be a springtime floater in the East River sure as there's a Monday coming the next morning.

In fairness, none of this was my idea, I was just dumb enough to agree to it. To ask Yellow Mama to do the one thing she would never do, could never do, and that's lose a race on purpose. That horse has got a heart on her big as a stable and she'll run until her legs are numb. She's lost some races in her years going around the tracks with me, but never without a fight and never on a lay-down or a pull-up. I first laid eyes on Mama at an auction at a farm in Delaware, making my way east for the startup there of racing season. She was a tiny little thing, just barely past eighteen months, legs thin as piano wire, and even if she were soaking wet I could think of dogs that would come in at a higher weight. But she had magic eyes, the kind of eyes a horse trainer spends his entire life lookin' to spot, the dark, round eyes that tell you in an instant that there's no quit in this filly, no give, only guts and guile and a courage a knock-around like me could never hope to have.

I paid her owner, Jack Spinell of Raintop Farms, $1,100 cash for her, watching him sign over her papers on the hood of my Ford F-150 truck. Spinell was a shrewd old-timer and he smiled as I counted out the cash and laid it in his stubby hands, figuring he took me for a ride and made money the easiest way a man knows, getting rid of something he doesn't want in return for something he does. But even I knew, a guy with hundreds more losses than wins tagged to my name, that I had latched on to the one thing I thought I'd never have in my racing career—a winner.

Up till then, I'd had my share of horses, usually training them for owners I never met. There were some good horses through the years and a few special victories, including a stakes race down at Gulfstream Park with a horse named Full Pockets that netted the owners a $75,000 purse. I left the track that day with my $7,500 cut in my back pocket and a smile on my face wide as a starter's gate. Came back to work the next day, still holding the smile, not remembering how or where I spent all that money. Another time, a horse named Spring Thaw, tough little fighter out of Virginia, was leading the Florida Derby from wire to wire. She would have won that race, should have won it, but luck wasn't with her and she pulled up lame less than a sixteenth of a mile to the finish line. Instead of a string of roses around her neck and a walk in the winner's circle, me by her side, she was laid out in her stall, half a dozen men surrounding her, one holding the needle that would pierce a vein and end her misery.

I had just about lost hope and was all but ready to make that season up north my last as a trainer when I came upon Mama. As I walked her up the ramp to my trailer, setting her up for the ride to New York, I asked Spinell why he went and named her Yellow Mama. "She was born old and she was born scared," he said, eyeing both me and the horse with disdain. "Only horse I've ever seen run from a loud fly. I don't know what you expect to get out of her, Bobby. But if you're looking for more than grief, you're in for a big let-down."

I looked back at Spinell and shrugged. "Wouldn't care to bet on that, would you?" I asked.

Old Man Spinell laughed, tossed his cigarette to the dirt and walked away. "On that horse?" he said over his shoulder. "You'd have to pay me off with jars of glue."

Spinell was wrong and I was always sorry he didn't live long enough for me to tell him so. I worked Mama up at the Big A, threw a chunk of my winnings, both on and off the track, her way, and watched her grow bigger and stronger. She was never going to be a large horse, wasn't bred that way. And she never impressed in her training, running alone early in the mornings, me clocking her time. That wasn't her style, either. There wasn't any reason for her to go fast in training, she wasn't going up against other horses. Mama didn't love to run. Never did and never will.

Yellow Mama just loved to win.

I picked Blue Randolph to be her jockey. Would have been easier to latch on to one of the Spanish jockeys, Lord knows there were plenty to pick from around the tracks. But I wanted someone from the States, guy knew his way around stables and horses, guy with a feel for what made them run and some-times not run. And that was Blue. He was tall for a jockey, running about five foot six inches, but he rode atop a horse light as a feather, held the reins as if they were an extension of his hands and only went to the whip when he had to, not just because he felt it was something that had to be done. He was in his late thirties and years past his prime, if he ever had one to begin with, when I signed him on to ride Yellow Mama.

"She got some spunk to her," he said to me after his first few turns around the track with Mama. "How she handles the nasty part of a race we won't know until she's in one, but I'm thinkin' of running her on the inside. You need speed to survive on the outside and I don't think off the one ride she's got enough of that."

"She doesn't look all that strong, either," I said. "And strength is what she'll need to make her way through the inside of a race."

"Sometimes guts gives you more than strength can," Blue said. "If she's got enough of that, she'll win more than her share of races."

I looked away from Blue and at Yellow Mama, running my hands along her slender back, and nodded. "She's got more than enough," I said.

Yellow Mama started off slow, losing her first four claim races, running out of the money each time. But she got better with every race, her time improved, her charge up the inside, Blue keeping her on a steady pace, growing stronger, more daring, her confidence slowly emerging after each start. She won her first race at a small track on Long Island, me and Blue splitting the $400 pay-out. And from there on, the races got bigger and so did the purses and the winning soon turned into a habit. I ran her eleven times in her second year on the tracks and she never finished lower than third in any one of those races.

We lived pretty well for the next couple of years. Yellow Mama's winnings sometimes were even enough to cover my gambling losses. I knew I couldn't run her forever and if I loved her as much as I'm always saying I do, I would have sold her last year to Albie Toney, who wanted to put her out to pasture, have her roam with the studs at his West Virginia farm. Albie was set to hand me $25,000 for the chance to see if Yellow Mama's offspring would inherit her heart and grit. Instead, I turned him down and I have nothing to show for it but empty pockets and a $50,000 debt to pay in less than forty-eight hours.

"You decide yet how you gonna play your way out of this one?" Blue asked. He was standing above me, outside Mama's stable, the setting sun gleaming off the shine on his shaved black head. I looked up at him and saw the sadness in his eyes, not over me, he had learned long ago not to expect much back from trainers, but over Yellow Mama. I may have trained her, but Blue was the one who rode her and if anybody knew how special a horse she was, it was the jockey who saw her fight and flight her way to wins she had no right to expect to take. They rode as one, both of them unheralded, both bred to lose, both, somehow, finding ways to win.

It was early on a Saturday morning and the stables were busy with trainers and jockeys getting ready for the afternoon's card. "This horse they want Mama to race," I asked Blue, "she any good? I'm asking can Mama take her?"

"Blindfolded and with me riding her side saddle," Blue said.

"But if you held her back she would lose, am I right on that?"

"Much as I would hate to do that to her, I would," Blue said, a pained expression crossing his face. "Not to get you out of the hole you're in. I don't care about that. But just to keep her alive."

"What's the risk in that?" I asked, lacking the nerve to look Blue in the face.

"She might buck on me," Blue said. "I've never held her back, especially that deep into a race. If anything, I give her a bit of a nudge, let her know this is where she airs it out. Never need to go to the whip there, either. She has a feel for the finish line and she can taste the win. Pulling on her at that point be like slamming the brakes on the last lap of a car race. Anything can happen and none of it would be good."

"I guess that's why they want me to hit her with the needle before the race," I said. "Make sure she starts the race with no chance of a win."

"Damn you, Bobby," Blue said. "You know the kind of people they are, the kind of crew Touchdown has working for him. You go and put yourself in a fifty-grand hole to them? What did you expect? Getting money back from losers like you is how they make their living."

"You ever give a horse a shot like the one they got for Mama?"

"Not me, no," Blue said, his anger doing a slow simmer. "But I seen it done, too many times not to forget it."

"What's it do to the horse?"

"What it's supposed to do," Blue said. "Slows them down, makes them a little dizzy, the legs tight and weak. They can race but barely, just enough strength in them to get around the track a couple of times. You've seen it, too, don't lie and tell me different. They're never the same horse after a shot like that. Take a good look at Mama now. See the life in her eyes. After that shot makes its way through her body, those eyes will be as dead as any junkie's. But what do you care? You'll be all square on your bet with Touchdown, free to gamble away until another day."

Blue picked up his gear and walked away, heading toward the jockey's lounge. I sat there, my arms resting on a pile of hay, Yellow Mama's breath warming the top of my neck. As much as I had gambled through the years, I had always managed to steer clear of the heavy-hitters, connected guys like Touchdown and his Manhattan gang. I had heard there was a poker game in town, somewhere on the Upper West Side, a brownstone in the 80s. I had five hundred in my pocket and hadn't played much poker since my Florida days and went in search of the game. I didn't plan on losing big, certainly not more than what I had on me. But then again, I never plan on losing big. No gambler does.

I was three hours into the game, playing against six players who seemed born with five cards in their hands, and found myself staring down at six thousand dollars in winnings. That was the moment. That was when I should have thanked the table, tipped the kid bringing over drinks and sandwiches, and walked out into the warm night air, my wallet filled with money. I was going to play one last hand and then bow out. But then I get dealt three Jacks out of five cards and this feeling comes over me, just like it does anyone as hooked on gambling as me. It's the feeling that this is it, your night, your time, and any hand you get is going to be a winning one. That deal lifted my winnings up to eleven thousand and I just kept right on rolling, deep into the night and into the early morning, the drinks and sandwiches replaced by coffee and scrambled eggs.

I was up twenty-two thousand and on my second cup of coffee, black, no sugar, when I spotted Touchdown sitting in the corner, crooked smile on his face, hard look in his eyes. He was dressed in a Brioni suit and held a glass of warm milk in his hands. He didn't play, never gambled, is what I had always heard. At least not on cards or horses. His gamble was on players like me. His bet was that we would end up on the short side of the field, leave the table or the room owing instead of carrying. And Touchdown was almost never wrong and he had the wad in his pocket and the cash in the bank to prove it. I did my best to ignore him and given the lucky run I was on that wasn't all that hard to do. By noon, I had been at the game little less than eighteen hours and could have cashed in my winnings if I pushed my chair away from the table. It was the hot streak of a lifetime, the kind a born loser never lands. I knew it would end, all streaks end, I just didn't know when or how and figured I'd play it out until I lost a few hands, and still walk away with the biggest haul I'd ever see. But it never works out that way.

At least not for guys like me.

I lost eight big hands in a row, betting heavier with each draw, knowing in my gut the luck would turn back my way, ignoring the reality that all the chips were now stacked in front of the other players. I should have pushed back and walked out of that apartment, found an open diner and grabbed myself a bite. But, we were heading toward that last big pot, the one that's won with a dream hand and I needed to be there for that. I couldn't walk away, not until I saw the cards and made the grab for it all. I was so deep into my gambler's haze that I couldn't see the game for what it was, never saw the setup coming my way. One of the rules a gambler learns early on is never to go into a situation blind. Know who you're up against and what their angle is before the game even starts. Don't be blinded by easy wins and great draws and cards coming your way that never would or should. Don't ignore the losing streak that leaves winning that last hand, the biggest pot, as the only way out of the hole. If I was halfway close to smart, I would have remembered all that and not painted myself into a corner, sitting across from five other players, with a hard-ass gangster off to my left, looking as calm and as relaxed as if he were taking the sun at the Jersey shore.

The pot was Las Vegas large, fifty thousand dollars, winner take it all. And I had no choice but to win it, going into the late hours of the game down by twenty-five thousand, my winnings gone after a soiled streak of cold hands. The table had to get the okay from Touchdown in order for me to stay in. I looked over and saw a beefy man with the girth of an old Chevy whisper into Touchdown's ear. Touchdown didn't say a word, glanced at me, stared out with vacant eyes for a handful of seconds and then nodded. He would stake me the twenty-five thousand I needed to stay in the game. If I won the pot, he would get back the money he put out, plus half of my winning cut. It was worth the gamble. Touchdown would see a profit, I would get out from under and we'd both leave the table with smiles. I knew it had to play out that way, there was no choice, it was the only way the game could end. I was lost in the grip of the gambler's reality, my mind clouded by visions of the big win. And when I saw my hand, holding two Queens and two Aces in a game of five-card stud, I knew luck was back at my end and I would walk away a winner.

That's a brutal hand to beat under any circumstance, I don't care who you are or how bad a run you're in. But coming off my hot roll earlier in the game, I knew I had the feel back, sitting there as I was with a calm look and a Shaq slam-dunk hand. I could toss away one of the Queens and still take the pot, that's how strong I felt going to the final draw.

"Make your call, Chief," the young man in the granny glasses and short-cropped hair sitting straight across from me said. It was down to the two of us, last hand of the game, a fifty-grand pot destined to find its way to my hands in less time than it takes to pour a glass of scotch.

I sat up in my chair and laid down my cards, not bothering to hide the smile on my face. I knew I was home clear, a winning hand if there ever was one, until I glanced over at Touchdown and saw an even bigger smile on his face. And guys like Touchdown never smile unless they won the night and that's when I knew I'd been taken. I didn't even need to see the four Kings the guy in the granny glasses laid down on his end of the table to know. I was on the short end of a fifty-thousand-dollar tab and had to wait as the room emptied for Touchdown to explain to me how it was I was expected to pay it back.

"Let's get air," he told me, watching as I could do nothing more than stare at the now empty table where only minutes earlier my surefire score was all spread out, waiting for me to grab. "We can talk while we walk."

I was feeling pretty numb as we slowly made our way up toward Columbus Avenue, crossing against traffic and heading toward the Museum of Natural History. "They tell me you train horses," Touchdown said. "You any good?"

"Depends more on the horse than on me," I said, being honest and hoping it wouldn't come across as flip.

"You got this one horse, Yellow Mama, she seems to be pretty good," Touchdown said. "You would stand by that, am I right?"

"Yeah," I said. "You'd be right about her. She's the best horse I ever worked with or been around."

"Let me get to the point, then," Touchdown said. He was tall, with a solid daily-workout build, even walked like an athlete. That wasn't why they called him Touchdown, though.

That came from the fact that in all his years in the New York rackets, he never failed to make a score. Not for himself and not for the people he worked with. With Touchdown around, everybody cashed out. "You're fifty large in the hole to me. That was my game in there and your debts are now mine as well. I'm guessing you don't have that kind of cash sitting around any local bank branch. And odds are better than good you don't have either a friend or a relative willing to front you that kind of money. You with me so far?"

I nodded and kept my head lowered. I wasn't sure which way this was going, but I knew wherever it was, it wouldn't be a good place. Not for me and not for Yellow Mama. I took a deep breath and tried hard to ignore the uneasy feeling in my stomach.

"Figured as much," Touchdown said. "I don't know how much you know about me or how I do business, so let me fill you in on just the important points. I don't waste time. I'm owed money, I want it back fast. In your case, we're talking the end of the weekend, Sunday afternoon, no later."

"That's in two days," I managed to say. "Barely two days."

"At least you can add," Touchdown said, staring at me with eyes the color of black rock. "The faster we get this done, the better. There's a match race your horse is running this Sunday at one. She figures to win the race in a walk. From what I hear about the other horse, an old goat could outrun her if she got enough of a head of steam. But that's not what's gonna happen. Your horse, Yellow Mama, is gonna tank the race and you and me, we're gonna make sure she does."

"How are we going to do that?" I asked.

"Simple as laying down a bet," Touchdown said. "First you talk to your jockey. Tell him not to go crazy. Run her slow and hold her back if he has to. He gives you any lip, explain to him a jockey needs legs in order to saddle a horse and he'll be missing those if he screws this up."

"What else?"

"Just to cover all our bases," Touchdown said, "you give your horse a shot. Something to slow her down, make her want to nap and not look to break any track records. I'll have someone bring it around the day before the race. Takes about an hour or so to kick in, so give it to her just as you're getting ready to gear her up. Any part of this not clear to you?"

"And if Yellow Mama throws the race, I don't owe you any money," I said. "That how it works?"

"First of all, it's not if but when she throws the race," Touchdown said. "And second, you get out from under me by betting $100,000 on the other horse, what's her name?"

"Valley Girl," I said.

"Cute," Touchdown said with a slow smile. "You lay a hundred big on Valley Girl and she wins the race. I pick up your winnings. The fifty thousand you owe is cleared. The rest is the price of doing business with a guy like me."

"What if I don't agree to it," I said, the question sounding as foolish as I felt.

Touchdown stopped walking and turned to face me. He had me in inches and girth and his body language was just a tick shy of lashing out and leaving me for dead only a few feet from the museum steps.

"Then I kill you, your jockey and your horse," Touchdown said in a calm, even voice. "One after the other. You can bet on that happening and that's a bet you'd be sure to win."

Touchdown gave me a hard pat on the shoulder, turned and walked away, heading uptown on Central Park West.

That was yesterday and since then I haven't come up with any answers that would get me out of this fix. I ran the whole scheme past Blue and got nothing back but a sad and angry look filled with hate and distrust. "I knew you would always risk tossing away your own life," he said to me. "And not give any more of a damn about mine. But I never for once thought you would do anything to hurt Mama."

"It's only a race, Blue," I said in a meek defense.

"To you," Blue said. "And a way out. But it's more than that to me. I'm never going to be confused with the great jockeys of this business, but Mama made me into a winner and I'll always love her for that. And racing and winning is all that horse is about. You shoot her up and make her lose, be just like cutting out her heart."

I stood and opened the door to the stall and stepped in. Mama, as she always did, walked up to my left side and nudged me with her head. I stroked her thick brown mane and gazed into her eyes. They were warm and watery, large dark ovals that made me feel as if she understood everything that went on around her. I reached into my pocket and pulled out a handful of chestnuts and put them near her mouth, watching as she gobbled up each one, careful not to nip at my skin as she did. "You deserved better, Mama," I whispered. "Better than what I've given you. You should have had a trainer who geared you for the big races, not in cash grab stakes. A trainer that would have made you the champion you were born to be."

Behind us, the starter's horn blared for the start of the day's first race. I walked toward the rear of the stall, next to the pile of hay, and picked up a little black box, the one with the needle and the fluid in it. It had been left there by one of

Touchdown's crew, primed and ready to slow the beats of Yellow Mama's runner's heart, make her welcome a loss instead of dying for the taste of the win. I put the box back in its resting place and turned around. Yellow Mama half-turned and stared, her eyes seeing right through me. I stared back for several minutes and then smiled. It suddenly became all so clear. I could get out from under Touchdown's grasp, get away from the hustle of having to score fifty thousand dollars I didn't have and even walk away with some dough for Blue and Yellow Mama, see them live and work the right way, the way they should have been all these years. I checked my watch and turned to walk out of the stall. I stopped and leaned my head against Mama's neck. "You get some rest," I told her. "You got a race in the morning."

I turned and left Mama in her stall, knowing she would lean her head out and stare after me until I was long out of sight.

I started the rest of my day meeting with Blue before placing bets with every bookie in town I knew and then heading uptown to meet with a man I had only read about. Blue sat on the small cot in his tiny apartment and listened to what I came to tell him, his body still as a statue. When I was done, he gazed up at me and, barely moving his lips, asked, "You sure about all this? This the way you want it to go?"

"It's the only way it can go," I told him. "Don't worry. You have to learn to trust me on this one, Blue. Maybe for the only time in your life. But this is one hand I know how to play and come out ahead of the game."

Uptown, the room was dark when I walked in and stayed that way through my stay. The small figure sat straight up on a thick deep couch, at ease in his surroundings, a hot cup of espresso resting on the coffee table by his side. He was in his eighties, his hair white as a cloud and thick, his hands holding a pair of reading glasses, the paper next to him open to the racing pages. "Say what it is you came here to say," he told me, speaking in a low, gentle voice, still coated with traces of his Italian childhood.

I had arranged the meeting through an East Harlem bookie I knew. At first, he wouldn't agree to make the call, but after some prodding and giving him just the slightest hints to my plan, he agreed. "You better make good on this," the bookie warned. "You mess this up, they'll break my fingers just for dialing their number and wasting their time."

"Just get me in the room," I said with all the confidence in the world. "I'll handle the rest."

The old man sipped his coffee and crossed one leg over the other. He had the air of someone who had lived his life on his own set of rules, refusing to allow the words and actions of others to dictate the moments of his day. At an age when most men are either in retirement homes or tending to small gardens out back, he still reigned supreme over a vast criminal enterprise that controlled much of the New York and New Jersey area. I took a deep breath and then broke the silence. "I've laid down close to five hundred thousand dollars in bets on tomorrow's match race at Belmont," I said. "I did that with less than fifty dollars to my name and no chance in hell of paying it back if the horse I bet on loses."

"And what do you want from me?"

"I want you to lay down double my action," I told him. "Bet a million dollars on one race with the horse I tell you to bet."

"And who's going to cover such action?" he asked, more

curious than anything else. "I know the answer isn't you. So who then?"

"You lay your bet down with Touchdown," I said to the old man. "He'll take your action, believe me."

"I don't like to bet," the old man said. "Especially not off the word of a man I only know as a second-rate horse trainer who already owes more than he can pay. And I'm not looking to put any of my money in Touchdown's pockets."

"But you wouldn't mind seeing Touchdown taken out of business," I said, knowing I was about to cross into turf that was unfamiliar to me. "And between my action and yours, he'll finish the day close to two million in the hole and that's a bad place for him to be."

"You owe Touchdown money," the old man said. "Why not pay him and forget about it. You're not made for a play like this one."

"I haven't been given much of a choice," I said.

"Guys like you never are," the old man said.

"This goes the right way and Touchdown belongs to you," I said. "I get out from under his weight and he gets tossed on top of yours. I don't see where either one of us has anything to lose."

"From what I heard of your plan, I have a million dollars to lose," the old man said.

"You're not going to lose," I said, staring at him through the darkness of the room.

"My coffee's cold and your time is up," the old man said. "Time for me to find my way to the kitchen and you to the door. Our time together is over."

"There is just one more thing before I go," I said. "It won't take very long. It has nothing to do with me. But it's something I think you'll want to hear."

"What is it?"

"I'd like to tell you about my horse," I said. "Her name is Yellow Mama and I think it's a story you'll like."

The morning of the race, I was led into Yellow Mama's stall by two of Touchdown's goons. They waited and watched as I opened the black box, pulled out the hypodermic and reached for the small bottle of clear fluid. Blue waited outside the stall, his head down, arms folded across his chest. I turned and walked over toward Yellow Mama, the needle in my right hand. "Where do you shoot it?" one of the goons asked.

"Back of her leg," I told him. "The veins are thick there and it makes anything you inject run through her system faster."

"Get it done then," the goon said.

I leaned on one knee and rubbed Mama's right front leg. I jabbed the needle into the middle of a thick vein and watched as the fluid flowed into her body. Mama didn't even flinch, took the shot and kept her gaze on the two strangers in her stall. I stood and handed the box and the needle to one of the two goons. "Tell your boss that if this stuff works half as good as advertised, she should be pretty much out it by the time the race starts."

"I got a better idea," the bigger of the two goons said. "Why don't you tell him? He's expecting you to watch the race with him. You know, just in case not everything goes off without a hitch."

I glanced over at Blue and nodded. Then, I turned to Yellow Mama and held my hand against a side of her face. "I'm counting on you, champ," I whispered. "Don't let me down now."

I watched the race from the paddock area, surrounded by Touchdown and his crew. They were munching on deli sandwiches and cold beer, waiting for the start of the race. "Don't look so glum," Touchdown said. "You did the right thing. It was the only move you could make and, for once in your life, it was a smart one."

"That's how I feel," I said. "I just hate that it had to come down to this."

"Maybe it'll make you give up the gamble," Touchdown said. "But I wouldn't bet on that. Guys like me live off guys like you. Always have and always will."

"I might just take you up on that bet," I said.

The bell sounded and the two horses shot out of the starting gate. Valley Girl jumped to a three-length lead, with Mama laying back, getting a feel of the track, Blue gently easing her from the outside rail to the inside. Valley Girl was a pace horse, the kind that runs a great race until she hears the pounding hoofs of a horse that's closing in. Then, she either takes off or gives up the chase. I leaned against the railing and watched Yellow Mama move up a length, getting the measure both of the track and of her opponent.

"She doesn't look doped up to me," Touchdown said, ignoring me and throwing the question to one of his goons.

"He pumped the shot into her," the goon said. "Me and Jimmy both saw it for ourselves. Gave it to her right in the leg."

"Then why isn't she running at half-mast?" Now Touchdown was looking at me, the veins in his neck throbbing with anger.

"Could be you got your hands on a sour batch of dope," I

said. "Or it could be it was just sugar water I shot into her veins and that does nothing but make her thirsty. And she'll get plenty to drink once the race is over."

"She wins this race, the only thing that horse is going to be drinking is her own blood," Touchdown said. "I'll chop her up with my own hands."

"Oh, she'll win this race," I assured him. I turned to glance at the track and Mama was now up by two lengths with Valley Girl fading fast. "But you won't be cutting her up or bothering Blue either for that matter."

Touchdown managed a laugh, reached out and grabbed on to my shirt. "And why's that, gambler?"

"Old Man Tomasino has a soft spot for animals, especially horses," I said. "You know he had one in Sicily when he was a boy, raised it as his own. Just so happens his old man got into a gang war and during one of the battles their barn caught fire and Tomasino's horse died in the flames."

Touchdown slammed a fist against the hard edge of a guardrail as Yellow Mama crossed the finish line.

"What the hell has Tomasino's bullshit Sicily story got to do with what just happened here?" he asked through clenched teeth.

"I told him about Yellow Mama and by the end of the story he did two amazing things," I said. "Two things I never in my wildest dreams would ever imagine him doing."

"Spill," Touchdown said, his tough veneer starting to wilt under the hot sun.

"First, he offered me a hundred grand for the horse," I said. "On top of which he included a nice salary for me and Blue to keep taking care of her. All I had to promise him was never to lay down another bet in my life. On anything."

"What's the second thing?" Touchdown asked.

"He laid a million-dollar bet on Yellow Mama to win," I said. "Hard for me to believe a nice old man like that has that kind of cash sitting around, but he does. He covered his action with your bookies. I did, too. Not as much, only five hundred thousand, but then me and Old Man Tomasino don't play ball in the same league."

Touchdown lifted me off the ground and tossed me against the railing, hard, the pain in my back shooting down to my legs. "What are you so pissed about?" I asked. "I got the fifty thousand I owe you, back in my office near the stables. You can have one of your boys pick it up, if you want. Or, you can just subtract it from the dough your bookies need to come across with early tomorrow morning. I'm sure Old Man Tomasino will be first in line looking to collect a million-plus winnings. But, I'll be there right behind him."

"You're not going to be around to collect anything," Touchdown said. "You'll be dead by morning."

"I work for Old Man Tomasino now and he wants me to train Yellow Mama," I said. "Just like he expects Blue to race her. You step into that and you're in bigger trouble than you already are. So go ahead and kill me. But if I were you, Touchdown, I'd be looking to raise that million plus that needs to be paid out come sunup."

I stared over at Touchdown, savored his defeat, then surveyed his silent crew. I fixed my jacket, ignored the pain in my back and started to walk away.

"Who the hell you think you are, walking away from me?" Touchdown asked. "A small-time loser like you."

I turned to Touchdown and smiled for the first time that weekend. "I'm not a loser," I said, my arms stretched out.

"You're looking at a winner. Across the board. At least for today."

I left Touchdown and his crew in the paddock area and walked at a steady pace toward the stables. I reached into my left jacket pocket and pulled out a paper bag filled with roasted chestnuts.

A warm gift for Yellow Mama.

THAT KIND OF NAG
A Nathan Heller Story
Max Allan Collins

When the cute high school girl, screaming bloody murder, came running down the steps from the porch of the brown-brick two-story, I was sitting in a parked Buick reading *The Racing News.*

At ten after eleven in the a.m., Chicago neighborhoods didn't get much quieter than Englewood, and South Elizabeth Street on this sunny day in May 1945 ran to bird chirps, muffled radio programs and El rattle. A banshee teenager was enough to attract the attention of just about anybody, even a drowsy detective who was supposed to be watching the very house in question.

A guy in T-shirt and suspenders, mowing the lawn next door, got to her just before me.

"Sally, honey, calm down," the guy said.

"Bob, Bob, Bob," she said to her neighbor.

His name, apparently, was Bob. Like I said, I'm a detective.

"What's wrong, honey?" I asked the girl.

She was probably sixteen. Blonde hair bounced off her shoulders, and with those blue eyes and that heart-shaped face, she would have been a knockout if she hadn't been devoid of makeup and wearing a navy jumper that stopped mid-calf, abetted by a white blouse buttoned to her throat.

"It's . . . it's *Mother*," she said, and in slow motion she turned toward the narrow front of the brick house and pointed, like the Ghost of Christmas Future indicating Scrooge's gravestone.

"Look at me," I said, and she did, mouth and eyes twitching. "I'm a policeman. Tell me what happened."

"Something . . . something *terrible*."

Then she pushed past me, and sat on the curb and buried her face in her hands and sobbed.

Bob, who was bald and round-faced and about forty, said, "You're a cop?"

"Actually, private. Is that kid named Vinicky?"

"Yes. Sally Vinicky—she goes to Visitation High. Probably home for lunch."

That explained the prim getup: Visitation was a Catholic all-girl's school.

Another neighbor was wandering up, a housewife in an apron, hair in a net, eyes wide; she had flecks of soapsuds on her red hands. I brought her into my little group.

"My name is Heller," I said. "I'm an investigator doing a job for that girl's father. I need one of you to look after Sally . . . ma'am? Would you?"

The woman nodded, then asked, "Why, what's wrong?"

"I'm going in that house and find out. Bob, call the Englewood Station and ask them to send a man over."

"What should I tell them?"

"What you saw."

As the housewife sat beside the girl on the curb and slipped an arm around her, and Bob headed toward the neighboring house, a frame bungalow, I headed up the steps to the covered porch. The girl had left the door open and I went on in.

The living room was off to the left, a dining room to the right; but the living room got my attention, because of the woman's body sprawled on the floor.

A willowy dame in her mid-thirties and blue-and-white floral dress, Rose Vinicky—I recognized her from the photos her husband had provided—lay on her side on the multicolor braided rug between an easy chair and a spinet piano, from which Bing Crosby smiled at me off a sheet music cover, "I Can't Begin to Tell You." Not smiling back, I knelt to check her wrist for a pulse, but judging by the dark pool of blood her head rested in, I was on a fool's errand.

Beyond the corpse stood a small table next to the easy chair with a couple of magazines on it, *Look, Life.* On the floor nearby was a cut-glass ashtray, which the woman presumably had knocked off the table when she fell forward, struck by a fatal blow from behind. A lipstick-tipped cigarette had burned itself out, making a black hole in the braiding of the rug. I wasn't sure whether she'd been reaching for the smoke when the killer clubbed her, or whether she'd gone for the table to brace her fall.

With her brains showing like that, though, she was probably already unconscious or even dead on the way down.

She looked a little like her daughter, though the hair was darker, almost brunette, short, tight curls. Not pretty, but attractive, handsome; and no midlength skirt for Rose: She had liked to show off those long, slender, shapely legs, which mimed in death the act of running away.

She'd been a looker, or enough of one, anyway, to make her husband suspect her of cheating.

I didn't spend a lot of time with Rose—she wasn't going anywhere, and it was always possible her killer was still around.

But the house—nicely appointed with older, in some cases antique, furniture—was clear, including the basement. I did note that the windows were all closed and locked, and the backdoor was locked, too—with no signs of break-in. The killer had apparently come in the front door.

That meant the murder took place before I'd pulled up in front of the Vinicky home around ten. I'd seen no one approach the house in the little more than an hour my car and ass had been parked across the way. It would've been embarrassing finding out a murder had been committed inside a home while I was watching it.

On the other hand, I'd been surveilling the place to see with whom the woman might be cheating when here she was, already dead. Somehow that didn't seem gold-star worthy, either.

I had another, closer look at the corpse. Maybe she hadn't been dead when she fell, at that—looked like she'd suffered multiple blows. One knocked her down, the others finished her off and opened up her skull. Blood was spattered on the nearby spinet, but also on the little table and even the easy chair.

Whoever did this would had to have walked away covered in blood . . .

Her right hand seemed to be reaching out, and I could discern the pale circle on her fourth finger that indicated a ring, probably a wedding ring, had been there until recently. Was this a robbery, then?

Something winked at me from the pooled blood, something floating there. I leaned forward, got a better look: a brown button, the four-eyed variety common to a man's suit—or sportcoat.

I did not collect it, leaving that to . . .

"*Stand up!* Get away from that body."

Sighing, I got to my feet and put my hands in the air and the young patrolman—as fresh-faced as that Catholic schoolgirl—rushed up and frisked me, finding no weapon.

I let him get that out of his system and told him who I was, and what had happened, including what I'd seen. I left the button out, and the missing wedding ring; that could wait for the detectives.

The next hour was one cop after another. Four or five uniformed men showed, a trio of detectives from Englewood Station, a couple of dicks from the bureau downtown, a photographer, a coroner's man. I went through the story many times.

In the kitchen, a yellow-and white affair with a door on to the alley, Captain Patrick Cullen tried to make a meal out of me. We sat at a small wooden table and began by him sharing what he knew about me.

"I don't remember ever meeting you, Captain," I said.

"I know you all too well, Heller—by reputation."

"Ah. That kind of thing plays swell in court."

"You're an ex-cop and you ratted out two of your own. You're a publicity hound, and a cooze hound, too, I hear."

"Interesting approach to detective work—everything strictly hearsay."

A half hour of repartee, at least that scintillating, followed. He wanted to know what I was doing there, and I told him "a job for Sylvester Vinicky," the husband. He wanted to know what kind of job, and I said I couldn't tell him, because attorney/client privilege pertained. He accused me of not being an attorney, and I pled guilty.

"But certain of my cases," I said, "come through lawyers. As it happens, I'm working for an attorney in this matter."

He asked the attorney's name and I gave it to him.

"I heard of that guy . . . divorce shyster, right?"

"Captain, I'd hate to spoil any of your assumptions with a fact."

He had a face so Irish it could turn bright red without a drop of alcohol, as it did now, while he shook a finger at me. "I'll tell you what happened, Heller. You got hired to shadow this dame, and she was a looker, and you decided to put the make on her yourself. It got out of hand, and you grabbed the nearest blunt instrument and—"

"I like that. The nearest blunt instrument. How the hell did you get to be a captain? What are you, Jake Arvey's nephew?"

He came half out of his chair and threw a punch at me.

I slipped it, staying seated, and batted his hat off his head, like I was slapping a child, and the fedora fluttered to the floor.

"You get *one*," I said.

The red in his face was fading, as he plucked the hat from the linoleum, and the embarrassment in his eyes was almost as good as punching him would've been.

"Is that a threat, Heller?"

"This reputation of mine you've heard so much about—

did you hear the part about my Outfit ties? Maybe you want to wake up in a fucking ditch in Indiana, Captain . . . *That* was a threat, by the way."

Into this Noël Coward playlet came another cop, a guy I did know, from the Detective Bureau in the Loop: Inspector Charles Mullaney, a big fleshy guy who always wore mortician black; he had a spade-shaped face, bright dark eyes and smiled a lot. Unlike many Chicago cops who do that, Mullaney actually had a sense of humor.

"What's this, Captain?" Mullaney had a lilting tenor, a small man's voice in the big fat frame. "My friend Nate Heller giving you a hard time?"

Mullaney scooted a chair out and sat between us, Daddy arriving to supervise his two small children. He was grinning at Cullen, but his eyes were hard.

"When you say 'friend,' Inspector, do you mean—"

"Friend. Don't believe what you hear about Heller. He and me and Bill Drury go way back—to the Pickpocket Detail."

Captain Cullen said, defensively, "This guy found the body under suspicious circumstances."

"Oh?"

For the sixth or seventh time, I told my story. For the first time, somebody took notes—Mullaney.

"Charlie," I said to him, "I'm working through an attorney on this. I owe it to my client to talk to him before I tell you about the job I was on."

Frowning, Cullen said, "Yeah, well, *we'll* want to talk to your client, too."

I said, "Might be a good idea. You could inform him his wife is dead. Just as a, you know, courtesy to a taxpayer."

Mullaney gave me a don't-needle-this-prick-anymore look,

then said, "The husband is in the clear. We've already been in touch with him."

Cullen asked, "What's his alibi?"

"Well, a Municipal Court judge, for one. He had a ten-thirty at the court, which is where we found him. A former employee is suing him for back wages."

Sylvester Vinicky ran a small moving company over on nearby South Racine Avenue. He and his wife also ran a small second-hand furniture shop, adjacent.

"Any thoughts, Nate?" Mullaney asked. "Any observations you'd care to share?"

"Did you notice the button?"

"What button?"

So I filled Mullaney in on the sportcoat button, pointed out the possible missing wedding ring, and the inevitability of the killer getting blood spattered.

"She let the bastard in," Mullaney said absently.

"Somebody she knew," I said. "And trusted."

Cullen asked, "Why do you say that? Could have been a salesman or Mormon or—"

"No," I said. "He got close enough to her to strike a blow from behind, in the living room. She was smoking—it was casual. Friendly."

Cullen sighed. "Friendly . . ."

Mullaney said, "We're saying 'he'—but it *could* be a woman."

"I don't think so. Rose Vinicky was tall, and all of those blows landed on the back of her head, struck with a downward swing."

Cullen frowned. "And how do you know this?"

"Well, I'm a trained detective. There are courses available."

Ignoring this twaddle, Mullaney said, "She could have

been on the floor already, when those blows were struck—hell, there were half a dozen of them."

"Right. But at least one of them was struck when she was standing. And the woman was five ten, easy. Big girl. And the force of it . . . skull crushed like an eggshell. And you can see the impressions from multiple blows."

"A man, then," Mullaney said. "A vicious son of a bitch. Well. We'll get him. Captain . . . would you give Mr. Heller and me a moment?"

Cullen heaved a dramatic sigh, but then he nodded, rose, stepped out.

Mullaney said, "I don't suppose you'll stay out of this."

"Of course I'll stay out of it. This is strictly police business."

"I didn't think you would. Okay, I understand—your name is going to be in the papers, it's going to get out that the wife of a client was killed on your watch—"

"Hey, she was already dead when I pulled up!"

"That'll go over big with the newshounds, especially the part where you're twiddling your thumbs in your car while she lay dead . . . Nate, let's work together on this thing."

"Define 'together.'"

He leaned forward; the round face, the dark eyes, held no guile. "I'm not asking you to tag along—I couldn't ask that. You have 'friends' like Captain Cullen all over town. But I'll keep you in the know, you do the same. Agreed?"

"Agreed."

"Why don't we start with a show of good faith."

"Such as?"

"Why were you here? What job were you doing for Sylvester Vinicky?"

Thing was, I'd been lying about this coming through a lawyer, though I had a reasonable expectation the lawyer I'd named would cover for me. Really what I'd hoped for was to talk to my client before I spilled to the cops. But Mullaney wasn't just *any* cop . . .

So I told him.

Told him that Sylvester Vinicky had come to my office on Van Buren, and started crying, not unlike his daughter had at the curb. He loved his wife, he was crazy about her, and he felt so ashamed, suspecting her of cheating.

Vinicky had sat across from me in the client's chair, a working man with a heavy build in baggy trousers, brown jacket and cap. At five nine he was shorter than his wife, and was pudgy where she was slender. Just an average-looking joe named Sylvester.

"She's moody," he said. "When she isn't nagging, she's snapping at me. Sulks. She's distant. Sometimes when I call home, when she's supposed to be home, she ain't at home."

"Mr. Vinicky," I said, "if anything, usually a woman having an affair acts nicer than normal to her husband. She doesn't want to give him a chance to suspect anything's up."

"Not Rose. She's always been more like my sweetheart than my wife. We've never had a cross word, and, hell, we're in business together, and it's been smooth sailing at home and at work . . . where most couples would be at each other's throats, you know?"

In addition to the moving business, the Vinickys bought and sold furniture—Rose had an eye for antiques and found many bargains for resale. She also kept the books and paid off the men.

"Rose, bein' a mother and all, isn't around the office, full-time," Vinicky said. "So maybe I shouldn't be so suspicious about it."

"About what?"

"About coming home and finding Rich Miller sitting in my living room, or my kitchen."

"Who is this Miller?"

"Well, he works for me, or anyway he did till last week. I fired him. I got tired of him flitting and flirting around with Rose."

"What do you know about him?"

A big dumb shrug. "He's just this knockabout guy who moves around a lot—no wife, no family. Goes from one cheap room to another."

"Why would your wife take to some itinerant worker?"

A big dumb sigh. "The guy's handsome, looks like that asshole in the movies—Ronald Reagan? He's got a smooth way, real charmer, and he knows about antiques, which is why he and Rose had something in common."

I frowned. "If he's such a slick customer, why's he living in cheap flops?"

"He has weaknesses, Mr. Heller—liquor, for example, and women. And most of all? A real passion for the horses."

"Horses over booze and broads?"

"Oh yeah. Typical horseplayer—one day he's broke, next day he hits it lucky and's rolling in dough."

I took the job, but when I tried to put one of my men on it, Vinicky insisted I do the work myself.

"I heard about you, Mr. Heller. I read about you."

"That's why my day rate's twice that of my ops."

He was fine with that, and I spent Monday through Thursday dogging the heels of Rich Miller, who indeed resembled Dutch Reagan, only skinny and with a mustache. I picked him up outside the residential hotel at 63rd and Halstead, a big brick rococo structure dating back to the Columbian Exposition. The first day he was wearing a loud sport shirt and loose slacks, plus a black fedora with a pearl band and two-tone shoes; he looked like something out of Damon Runyon, not some bird doing pick-up work at a moving company.

The other days he was dressed much the same, and his destination was always the same, too: a racetrack, Washington Park. The IC train delivered him (and me) right outside the park—just a short walk across the tracks to the front admission gate. High trees, shimmering with spring breeze, were damn near as tall as the grandstand. Worse ways for a detective to spend a sunny day in May, and for four of them, I watched my man play the horses and I played the horses, too, coming out a hundred bucks ahead, not counting the fifty an hour.

Miller meeting up with Rose at the track, laying some bets before he laid her, was of course a possibility. But the only person Miller connected with was a tall, broad-shouldered brown-haired guy with the kind of mug janes call "ruggedly handsome" right down to the sleepy Robert Mitchum eyes. They sat in the stands together on two of the four days, going down to the ground-floor windows beneath to place similar small-time bets—ten bucks at the most, usually to Win.

Still, Miller (and his two-day companion) would bet every race and cheer the horses on with a fist-shaking desperation that spoke of more at stake than just a fun day at the races. Small-time bettor though he was, Miller was an every-day-at-the-track kind of sick gambler—the friend only showed twice, remember—and I came to the conclusion that his hard-on was for horses, and if anybody was riding Rose Vinicky to the finish line when her hubby wasn't home, this joker wasn't the jockey.

"That's why," Mullaney said, nodding, "you decided to stake out the Vinicky home, this morning."

"Yeah."

Mullaney's huge chest heaved a sigh. "Why don't we talk to the girl, together. Little Sally."

Little Sally had a build like Veronica Lake, but I chose not to point that out.

"Sure," I said.

We did it outside, under a shade tree. A light breeze riffled leaves, the world at peace. Of course, so is a corpse.

Sally Vinicky wasn't crying now—partly cried out, partly in shock, and as she stood with her hands figleafed before her, she answered questions as politely and completely as she no doubt did when the nuns questioned her in class.

"I went in the back way," she said. "Used my key."

Which explained why I hadn't seen the girl go in.

"I always come home for lunch at eleven, and Mom always has it ready for me—but when I didn't see anything waiting in the kitchen . . . sometimes soup, sometimes a sandwich, sometimes both, today, nothing . . . I went looking for her. I thought for a minute she'd left early."

"Left early for where?" I asked.

"She had errands to do, downtown, this afternoon."

Mullaney asked, "What sort of mood was your mother in this morning, when you left for school?"

"I didn't see her—Mom sleeps in till nine or sometimes ten. Does some household chores, fixes my lunch and . . ."

"How about your father?"

"He was just getting up as I was leaving—that was maybe a quarter to eight? He said he had to go to the court at ten-thirty. Somebody suing us again."

I asked, "Again?"

"Well, Mom's real strict—if a guy doesn't work a full hour, he doesn't get paid. That starts arguments, and some of the men who work for Mom and Dad sometimes say they've been shorted . . . Oh!"

Mullaney frowned. "What is it?"

"We should check Mom's money!"

The blanketed body had already been carted out, and the crowd of neighbors milling around the house had thinned. So we walked the girl in through the front. Sally made a point of not looking into the living room where a tape outline on the floor provided a ghost of her mother.

In her parents' room, where the bed—a walnut Victorian antique as beautiful as it was wrong for this house and this neighborhood—was neatly made, a pale brown leather wallet lay on the mismatched but also antique dresser. Before anyone could tell the girl not to touch it, she grabbed the wallet and folded it open.

No moths flew out, but they might have: it was that empty.

"Mother had a lot of money in here," Sally said, eyes searching the yawning flaps, as if bills were hiding from her.

I asked, "How much is a lot, Sally?"

"Almost twelve hundred dollars. I'd say that's a lot!"

"So would I. Why would your mother have that kind of money in her wallet?"

"We were going for a trip to California, as soon as my school got out—me, Mother, and my aunt Doris. That was the errand Mother had to do downtown—buy railroad tickets."

Mullaney, eyes tight, said, "Who knew about this money?"

"My dad, of course. My aunt."

"Nobody else?"

"Not that I can think of. Not that I know of. I wish I could be of more help . . ."

I smiled at her. "You're doing fine, Sally."

A uniformed officer stuck his head in. "Inspector, Captain Cullen says Mr. Vinicky is here."

Sally pushed past Mullaney and me, and the uniformed man, and the girl went rattling down the stairs calling, "Daddy, Daddy!"

When we caught up with her, she was in her father's arms in the yellow-and-white kitchen. He held her close. They both cried and patted each other's backs. Cullen, seated at the kitchen table, regarded this with surprising humanity.

"I want you to stay with your aunt tonight," Vinicky said to his daughter.

"Okay. That's okay. I don't want to sleep in this house ever again."

He found a smile. "Well, not tonight, anyway, sweetheart. They let me call your aunt—she's on her way. Do you want to wait in your room?"

"No. No, I'll wait outside, if that's all right."

Vinicky, the girl still in his arms, looked past her for permission, his pudgy face streaked with tears, his eyes webbed red.

Mullaney and Cullen nodded, and a uniformed man walked her out. The father took a seat at the kitchen table. So did Mullaney. So did I.

Seeming to notice me for the first time, Vinicky looked at me, confusion finding its way past the heartbreak. "What . . . what're you doing here, Mr. Heller?"

"I was watching the house, Mr. Vinicky," I said, and told him the circumstances as delicately as possible.

"I take it . . . I take it you told these gentleman why I hired you."

"I did."

"Did you see anyone go in, Mr. Heller? Did you see that bastard Miller?"

"I didn't." I hadn't reported to him yet. "Mr. Vinicky, I spent four days watching Miller, and he always went to the track—that's why I came here. I don't believe he was seeing your wife."

But Vinicky was shaking his head, emphatically. "He did it. I know he did it. You people have to *find* him!"

Cullen said, "We're already on that, Mr. Vinicky."

I asked the captain, "Do you need his address? He's in a residential hotel over on—"

"We know. We sent a detective over there already—next-door neighbor says this guy Miller used to hang around here a lot. Only now Miller's nowhere to be seen—his flop is empty. Ran out on a week's rent."

Vinicky slammed a fist on the table. "I told you! I told you!"

Mullaney said, "We need you to calm down, sir, and tell us about your day."

"My day! Tell you about, what . . . *this*? The worst day of my life! Worst goddamn day of my life. I loved Rose. She was the best wife any man ever had."

Neither cop was nasty enough to mention that the bedroom dick this weeping husband had hired was sitting at the table with them.

Vinicky's story was unremarkable: He'd got up around eight, dressed for the court appearance, stopped at the office first (where he was seen by various employees) and then took breakfast at a restaurant on Halsted. From there he'd gone to the post office, picked up a parcel, and headed downtown by car to Municipal Court. He had littered the South Side and the Loop alike with witnesses who could support his alibi.

"You're being sued, we understand," Mullaney said.

"Yeah—but that's nothing. Kind of standard with us. Rose is . . . was . . . a hard-nosed businesswoman, God love her. She insisted on a full day's work for a full day's pay."

Mullaney was making notes again. "Did Miller ever complain about getting shorted?"

"Yeah. That's probably why he was . . . so friendly with Rose. Trying to get on her good side. Sweet-talk her into giving him the benefit of the doubt on his hours. I was a son of a bitch to ever suspect—"

Cullen asked, "Could you give us a list of employees who've made these complaints, over the last two years?"

"Sure. No problem. I can give you some off the top of my head, then check the records at the office tomorrow for any I missed."

Mullaney wrote down the names.

When that was done, I asked, "Did your wife have a wedding ring?"

"Yes. Of course. Why—wasn't it on her . . . *on* her?"

"No rings."

Vinicky thought about that. "She might've taken it off to

do housework. Was it on her dresser? There's a tray on her dresser . . ."

"No. What was the ring worth?"

"It was a nice-size diamond—three hundred bucks, I paid. Did the bastard steal it?"

Mullaney said, "Apparently. The money in her wallet was missing, too."

"Hell you say! That was a small fortune—Rose was going to buy train tickets with that, and cover hotel and other expenses. She was treating her sister to a trip to California, and Sally was going along . . . It was robbery, then?"

"We're exploring that," Mullaney said.

Vinicky's eyes tightened to slits. "One of these S.O.B.s who claimed they were shorted, you think?"

The inspector closed his notebook. "We're exploring that, too. This list should be very helpful, Mr. Vinicky."

I gave Mullaney the eye, nodding toward the backdoor, and he and I stepped out there for a word away from both the husband and Captain Cullen.

"How long will you boys be here?" I asked.

"Another hour, maybe. Why, Nate?"

"I have a hunch to play."

"You want company?"

"No. But I should be back before you've wrapped up, here."

I tooled the Buick over to 63rd Street, a lively commercial district with all the charm of a junkyard. Not far from here, Englewood's big claim to fame—the multiple murderer H.H. Holmes—had set up his so-called Murder Castle in the late 1880s. The Vinicky case could never hope to compete, so maybe I could make it go away quickly.

In the four days I'd kept an eye on Rich Miller, I'd learned a handful of useful things about the guy, including that when he wasn't betting at Washington Park, he was doing so with a guy in a back booth at a bar called the Lucky Horseshoe (whose only distinction was its lack of a neon horseshoe in the window).

The joint was dim and dreary even for a South Side gin mill, and business was slow, midafternoon. But I still had to wait for a couple of customers to finish up with the friendly bookie in the back booth before I could slide in across from him.

"Do I know you?" he asked, not in a threatening way. He was a small sharp-eyed, sharp-nosed, sharp-chinned sharpie wearing a derby and a bow tie but no jacket—it was warm in the Horseshoe. He was smoking a cigarillo and his sleeves were rolled up, like he was preparing to deal cards. But no cards were laid out on the booth's table.

I laid mine out, anyway: "My name is Heller, Nate Heller. Maybe you've heard of me."

The mouth smiled enough to reveal a glint of gold tooth; the dark blue eyes weren't smiling, though.

"I'm gonna take a wild stab," I said, "and guess they call you Goldie."

"Some do. You the . . . 'Frank Nitti' Heller?"

By that he meant, was I the mobbed-up private eye who had been tight with Capone's late heir, and remained tight with certain of the Outfit hierarchy.

"Yes."

"You wanna place a bet, Nate? My bet is . . . not."

"Your bet is right. I'm not here to muscle you. I'm here to do you a favor."

"What favor would that be?"

"There's a murder a few blocks away—Inspector Mullaney's on it."

"Oh. Shit."

And by that he meant, imagine the luck: one of the *honest* Chicago cops.

"But, Nate," he said, and I got the full benefit of a suspiciously white smile interrupted by that gold eyetooth, "why would Goldie give a damn? I have nothin' to do with murder. *Any* murder. I'm in the entertainment business."

"You help people play the horses."

The tiny shrug conveyed big self-confidence. "It's a noble sport, both the racing and the betting."

I leaned toward him. "One of your clients is shaping up as a suspect. The favor I'm doing you is: *I'm* talking to you, rather than just giving you over to the inspector."

Eyelids fluttered. "Ah. Well, I do appreciate that. What's the client's name?"

"Rich Miller."

The upper lip peeled back and again showed gold, but this was no smile. "That fucking fourflusher. He's into me for five C's!"

"Really. And he's made no move to pay you off? Today, maybe?"

His laughter cut like a blade. "Are you kidding? One of my . . . associates . . . went around to his flop. Miller pulled outa there, owin' a week's back rent."

Which, of course, I already knew.

Goldie was shaking his head, his tone turning philosophical. "You never can tell about people, can you? Miller always paid up on time, before this, whereas that pal of his, who I wouldn't trust far as I could throw him, *that* crumb pays up, just when I was ready to call the legbreakers in."

"What pal of Miller's?"

He gave me a name, but it meant nothing to me. I wondered if it might be the guy Miller had met at Washington Park two of the days, and ran a description by Goldie.

"That sounds like him. Big guy. Six four, easy. Not somebody I could talk to myself."

"Hence the legbreakers."

"Hence. Nate, if you can keep that goody-two-shoes Mullaney off my ass, it would be appreciated. He'll come around, make it an excuse to make my life miserable, and what did I ever do to that fat slob?"

I was already out of the booth. "See what I can do, Goldie."

"And if you ever wanna place a bet, you know where my office is."

When I got back to the brown-brick house on South Elizabeth Street, the Catholic school girl was hugging a tall slender woman, who might have been her mother come to life. On closer look, this gal was younger, and a little less pretty, though that may not have been fair, considering her features were taut with grief.

Sally and the woman who I took to be her aunt were beneath the same shady tree where Mullaney and I had stood with the girl, questioning her, earlier.

I went up and introduced myself, keeping vague about the "investigative job" I'd been doing for Mr. Vinicky.

"I'm Doris Stemmer," she said, Sally easing out of the woman's embrace. The woman wore a pale yellow dress with white flowers that almost didn't show. "I'm Rose's sister."

She extended her hand and I shook it. Sally stayed close to her aunt.

"Sorry for your grief, Mrs. Stemmer," I told her. "Have you spoken to Inspector Mullaney yet?"

"Yes."

"Would you mind if I asked you a few questions?"

"But you're a *private* detective, aren't you? What were you doing for Sylvester?"

"Looking into some of the complaints from his employees."

Her eyes tightened and ice came into her voice. "Those men were a bunch of lazy good-for-nothing whiners. Doris was a good person, fair and with a great heart, wonderful heart. Why, just last year, she loaned Ray three hundred dollars, so we didn't have to wait to get married."

"Ray?"

"Yes, my husband."

"What does he do, if I might ask?"

"He started a new job just last week, at an electrical assembly plant, here on the South Side."

"New job? What was his old one?"

Her strained smile was a signal that I was pushing it. "He worked for Sylvester in the moving business. You can ask him yourself if Rose wasn't an angel. Ask him yourself if she wasn't fair about paying their people."

"But he *did* quit . . ."

"Working as a mover was just temporary, till Ray could get a job in his chosen field." Her expression bordered on glare. "Mr. Heller—if you want to talk to Ray, he's waiting by the car, right over there."

She pointed and I glanced over at a blue Ford coupe parked just behind a squad car. A big, rugged-looking dark-haired guy, leaning against the vehicle, nodded to us. He was in a short-sleeve green sportshirt and brown pants. His tight expression said he was wondering what the hell I was bothering his wife about.

Gently as I could, I said, "I might have a couple questions for him, at that, Mrs. Stemmer. Would you and Sally wait here, just a moment? Don't go anywhere, please . . ."

I went inside and found Mullaney and Cullen in the living room, contemplating the tape outline. Things were obviously winding down; the crime scene boys were packing up their gear, and most of the detectives were already gone.

"Button, button," I said to them. "Who's got the button?"

Cullen glared at me, but Mullaney only smiled. "The brown button, you mean? Cullen, didn't you collect that?"

The captain reached a hand into his suitcoat and came back with the brown button and held out the blood-caked item in his palm.

"You want this, Heller?"

"Yeah," I said, marveling at the evidence-collecting protocol of the Chicago Police Department, "just for a minute . . ."

I returned to Mrs. Stemmer, under the tree, an arm around her niece.

"Couple questions about your husband," I said.

"Why don't you just *talk* to him?" she asked, clearly exasperated.

"I will. I'm sorry. Please be patient. Does your husband have a coat that matches those pants he's wearing?"

"Well . . . yes. Maybe. Why?"

"Isn't wearing it today, though."

"It's warm. Why would he wear it . . . ?"

"Could this button have come off that jacket?"

She looked at it. "I don't know . . . maybe. I guess. That button's filthy, though—what's that caked on there?"

Quietly, I said, "When did you say your husband started his new job?"

"Last week."

"But he didn't have to go to work today?"

"No . . . no. He had some things to do."

"Does he normally get Fridays off?"

"I don't know. He just started, I told you."

"So it's unlikely he'd be given a day off . . ."

"Why don't you ask *him*?"

"Mrs. Stemmer, forgive me, but . . . does your husband have a gambling problem?"

She drew in breath, but said nothing. And spoke volumes.

I ambled over to the tall, broad-shouldered man leaning against the Ford.

"Mr. Stemmer? My name's Heller."

He stood straight now, folded his arms, looked at me suspiciously through sleepy eyes. He'd been out of earshot when I spoke to his wife, but could tell I'd been asking her unpleasant questions.

"Why were you bothering my wife? Are you one of these detectives?"

"Yeah. Private detective."

He batted the air with a big paw. "You're nobody! I don't have to talk to you."

"Private detective," I picked up, "who followed Rich Miller to the track most of this week."

". . . What for?"

"For Rose's husband—he thought she and Miller were playing around."

He snorted a laugh. "Only thing Richie Miller plays is the nags."

"And you'd know, right, Ray? See, I saw you and your buddy Richie hanging out together at Washington Park. You were betting pretty solid, yourself. Not big dough, but you were game, all right."

"So what?"

"Well, for one thing, your wife thinks you started a new job last week."

The sleepy eyes woke up a little. "And I guess in your business, uh . . . Heller, is it? In your business, you never ran across an instance of a guy lying to his wife before, huh?"

"You like the nags, too, don't you, Stemmer? Only you don't like to *get* nagged—and I bet Rose Vinicky nagged the hell out of you to pay back that three hundred. Did she hold back from your paycheck, too?"

He shook his head, smiled, but it was sickly. "Rose was a sweetheart."

"I don't think so. I think she was a hardass who maybe even shorted a guy when he had his hard-earned money coming. Her husband loved her, but anybody working for her? She gladly gave them merry hell. She was that kind of nag."

A sneer formed on his face, like a blister. "I don't have to talk to you. Take a walk."

He shoved me.

I didn't shove back, but I stood my ground; somebody gasped behind me—maybe Doris Stemmer, or the girl.

"You knew about that money, didn't you, Stemmer? The money Rose was going to use to treat your wife to a Hollywood trip. And you could use eleven hundred bucks, couldn't you, pal? Hell, who couldn't!"

He shoved me again. "You don't take a goddamn *hint,* do you, Heller?"

"Here's a hint for you: When a bookie like Goldie gets paid off, right before the legbreakers leave the gate? That means somebody finally had a winner."

His face turned white.

"Sure, she let her brother-in-law in the front door," I said. "She may have had you pegged for the kind of welsher who stiffs his own sister-in-law for a loan, but she probably thought she was at least safe with you, alone in her own house. That should've been a sure bet, right? Only it wasn't. What did you use? A sash weight? A crowbar?"

This time he shoved me with both hands, and he was trying to crawl in on the rider's side of the Ford, to get behind the wheel, when I dragged him out by the leg. On his ass on the grass, he tried to kick me with the other leg, and I kicked him in the balls, and it ended as it had begun, with a scream.

All kinds of people, some of them cops, came running, swarming around us with questions and accusations. But I ignored them, hauling Stemmer to his feet, and jerking an arm around his back, holding the big guy in place, and Cullen believed me when I said, "Brother-in-law did it," taking over for me, and I quickly filled Mullaney in.

They found four hundred and fifteen bucks in cash in Stemmer's wallet—what he had left after paying off the bookie.

"That's a lot of money," Mullaney said. "Where'd you get it?"

"I won it on a horse," Stemmer said.

Only it came out sounding like a question.

• • •

After he failed six lie detector tests, Raymond Stemmer confessed in full. Turned out hard-nosed businesswoman Rose had quietly fired Stemmer when she found out he'd been stealing furniture from their warehouse. Rich Miller had told Rose that Ray was going to the track with him, time to time, so she figured her brother-in-law was selling the furniture on the side to play the horses. She had given him an ultimatum: Pay back the three hundred dollars, and what the furniture was worth, and Rose would not tell her sister about his misdeeds.

Stemmer had stopped by the house around nine-thirty and told Rose he'd brought her the money. Instead, in the living room, as she reached for her already burning cigarette, he had paid her back by striking her in the back of the head with a wrench.

Amazingly, she hadn't gone down. She'd staggered, knocked the ashtray to the floor, only to look over her shoulder at him and say, "You have the nerve to hit *me*?"

And he found the nerve to hit her again, and another ten times, where she lay on the floor.

He removed the woman's diamond wedding ring and went upstairs and emptied the wallet. All of this he admitted in a thirty-page statement. The diamond was found in a toolbox in his basement, the wrench in the Chicago River (after three hours of diving). His guilty plea got him a life sentence.

About a week after I'd found Rose Vinicky's body, her husband called me at my office. He was sending a check for my services—the five days I'd followed Miller—and wanted to thank me for exposing his brother-in-law as the killer. He told me he was taking his daughter to California on the trip her mother had promised; the sister-in-law was too embarrassed and distraught to accept Vinicky's invitation to come along.

"What I don't understand," the pitiful voice over the phone said, "is why Rose was so distant to me, those last weeks. Why she'd acted in a way that made me think—"

"Mr. Vinicky, your wife knew her sister's husband was a lying louse, a degenerate gambler, stealing from the both of you. *That* was what was on her mind."

". . . I hadn't thought of it that way. By God, I think you're right, Mr. Heller . . . You know something funny? Odd. Ironic, I mean?"

"What?"

"I got a long, lovely letter from Rich Miller today. Handwritten. A letter of condolence. He heard about Rose's death and said he was sick about it. That she was a wonderful lady and had been kind to him. After all the people who've said Rose was hard hearted to the people who worked for us? This, this . . . it's a kind of . . . testament to her."

"That's nice, Mr. Vinicky. Really is."

"Postmarked Omaha. Wonder what Miller's doing there?"

Hiding from the legbreakers, I thought.

And, knowing him, doing it at the dog tracks.

Author's Note: My thanks to George Hagenauer, my longtime research associate on the Heller stories, for finding the Vinicky case in an obscure true-detective magazine. I have compressed time and omitted aspects of the investigation; and some of the names in this story have been changed.

THE ODDS

Thomas H. Cook

The paired numbers shot through his mind in quick metallic bursts, the dry slap of bullets hitting beach sand. It is the way he'd lived, like a man under fire, raked by numbers, no trees to shield him, no foxholes, only the endless open beach, with no sun or moon above him, just the melancholy stare of her sea-blue eyes.

"Who is he, anyway?"

"Eddie Spellacy."

He heard his brother Jack's true voice for the first time in almost thirty years, heard it as it actually sounded, not over the phone, but here, beside his bed.

"Eddie the Odds, they called him."

There was a hopeless sorrow in Jack's voice, a yearning for things to have turned out differently, and so he didn't open his eyes because he knew that his brother's long sad face would break his heart.

"He was always figuring the odds."

"The odds on what?"

"Everything, I guess. But he made his living figuring them on horses."

The voices came from a world he could not live in, where men and women moved easily about, heedless of the way things really were, the awesome knowledge that was his, how the odds, no matter what they seemed, could abruptly change. Her sad sweet voice curled through his mind, *What's wrong, Eddie?* Even then, his answer, thrown over his shoulder as he fled from her, had seemed more truth than lie, *I just have to go.*

"They find him on the street?"

"No, he had a room. Nothing more than that. He didn't need anything more. He'd stopped seeing other people years ago. Even me. He said he'd figured the odds that on the way to his place something might happen to me. A car wreck. A plane crash. Too risky, he told me. Anything can happen."

"So how'd he get to the hospital?"

"He had a heart attack. Somebody heard him moaning in his room, I guess. Called 911. I don't know who called. Just someone."

Someone, but not her, Eddie thought. Someone anonymous, a neighbor down the hall who knew only that the guy in Room 603 was Eddie the Odds, one of nature's freaks, a human calculator who never went out, was never seen, never visited, with no dog, no cat, with nothing but his streaming numbers. Eddie the Odds. Eddie the Oddball.

He twisted about violently, the odds streaming through his head, each number an accusation, reminding him of that day, the sudden movement, the heavy fall, the way she'd seen him in the corner of the playground the next day, started toward him, the look in her eyes as he'd risen and walked away. He'd wanted to tell her what had happened, but what were the odds she'd have felt the same about him after that? What were the odds she'd ever laugh with him again, or touch his hand?

"So all these years he just stayed in his room and figured the odds?"

"Yeah."

"On what?"

"On crazy stuff. Whether a tree would fall or a car would jump the curb. Stuff like that. He never got close to anyone. Never married, had kids. He was afraid the odds were against them if he did. That he increased the odds. He said he couldn't help it. It wasn't something he wanted to do. It was something his mind couldn't stop doing. All day, figuring the odds."

"So he's like . . . deranged?"

Yes, Eddie thought. As deranged as a man who washes his hands a hundred times a day, repeats the same phrases over and over and over, turns off the light a thousand times or compulsively opens and reopens the refrigerator before he can withdraw that single bottle of hyper-filtered water. He'd finally turned it into a profession, the only choice he'd had since the fearful results of his compulsion had made it impossible for him to do anything else. He couldn't go to an office, couldn't have a profession.

"So when did this thing start, this thing with the odds?"

"When he was still a kid."

"What did it start with?"

"I don't know."

With a girl, Eddie answered now, though without speaking, keeping his secret safe, the odds now incalculably vast against his ever revealing it. Her sea-blue eyes rose like two lost moons over a turbulent river of rapidly streaming numbers.

She.

The only one he'd ever loved.

He saw her as she looked the morning she'd first come to Holy Cross, Margaret Shaunassey, twelve years old, a new girl in the neighborhood, with a smile like spring rain and sea-blue eyes. What were the odds, he'd asked himself at that first moment, that she would even notice him, a kid from West 47th Street, Eddie the kidder, Eddie the goof, a school-yard prankster, tall for his thirteen years, with a freckled face he could do anything with, shape like dough, turn tragic or comic by turns, hide all his shyness and uncertainty behind.

"So he's been this way his whole life?"

"Not his whole life. But most of it. It came on him when he was thirteen."

Thirteen, Eddie thought as he lay silent and unmoving, save for the backward journey of his mind. Thirteen and in love with Margaret Shaunassey. But what were the odds that he could win her against the likes of handsome boys like Angelo Balderi and smart ones like Herbie Daws? Not very good, he guessed, but in that same instant knew he would shirk off all his fearful lack of confidence, and boldly go where he had never gone, go there with everything on the line, all his chips on this one number, spin the wheel, regardless of the odds.

"And since then?"

"Since then, he's been Eddie the Odds."

Eddie the Odds, alone in a cramped little room in a Brooklyn hotel, staring at Manhattan, but never going there, because he couldn't stop his mind from figuring the odds of a subway accident or a bus collision or the even greater odds against a flooded tunnel or collapsing bridge, odds that were constantly changing, like the flipping numbers on that immense scheduling board he'd once seen in Grand Central, odds forever racing by at an impossible click, turning on him suddenly, throwing endless strings of calculations, odds that exploded all around him, hurling earth and shrapnel, lighting his inner sky with millions of sparks. But worst of all, as he knew too well, they were odds that he increased simply by being on that train or bus, increased by being the carrier of bad luck, misfortune like a virus he could spread to anyone, and so increased the odds that the little girl next to him in the subway or the little boy beside him on a bus would be dead, dead, dead. Dead because of him. Dead because he defied the odds, brought death with him where he stood and where he went, untimely death, against all odds.

He felt his fingers draw into a fist, then the fist thrust outward, the way it had that morning, just a little shove, but one that had finally recoiled and come rushing back toward him, invisibly penetrating the hard bone of his skull, reconfiguring his brain in a freakish and irrevocable way, turning him into what he had become since then, Oddball Eddie, Eddie the Odds.

In a quick vision, he saw the home he might have had, and had so often imagined during the long years he'd lived in his small cramped room. A large house with a large yard, kids playing on the green lawn, and she there, too, the one he'd done it for, Margaret Shaunassey, the girl with the spring-rain smile.

He'd first spotted her in the school playground, and against the odds, approached her.

I'm Eddie Spellacy.

Hi.

You're new, right?

Yes.

After that it had been all jokes, and Eddie the jokester had made her laugh and laugh, laugh until her eyes watered and she fought for breath and clutched her sides and begged him to stop, stop, because it was killing her, this laughter.

And so he'd stopped, fallen silent, then, more in love than anyone in books or movies, revealed the mission of his lovesick heart.

I'll always look out for you.

And he'd meant it, too, meant it as deeply as he'd ever meant anything. He would be her knight, escort her through the mean streets of Hell's Kitchen, fend off the neighborhood dragons, its street toughs and bullies, protect her from catcalls and leering glances, and still later, as they grew older, married and had children, he would protect her from the fear of loss and abandonment, the dread of loneliness and the steady drip of age. He would do all of this. And he would do it forever. He would never cease, until she was safely home.

You can feel safe with me, Margaret.

That was when she'd reached into her lunch box and offered him one of her mother's homemade cookies.

I do feel safe with you, Eddie. I really do.

What else is there but this? he wondered now, the thought cutting through the flaming trails of exploding odds, What else is there for a boy but this offer of protection? If he had ever known nobility, it was then. If he had ever known courage or self-sacrifice, these had come to him through her, fallen cool and sweet upon his shoulders like spring rain. All he had ever wanted was joined with her, his hope for marriage, family, an ordinary life.

And against all odds he had lost it.

A new voice cut through the fireworks of numbers, returning him to the here and now.

"I'm Doctor Patel. Your brother looks agitated."

"Yes, he does."

"I could give him something to help him relax."

His endlessly churning brain immediately figured the odds against just slipping away, quietly and without fuss, a welcomed end to laying odds, and in that instant he tried to imagine the cooling of his brain, its inflamed circuitry finally soothed, the flood of numbers it sent like flaming stones through his mind now little more than a quiet mound of dying embers. If he could just get to that point of rest, that place where his mind could embrace the sleep for which he'd yearned since that day.

That day.

He saw it dawn over the city, a warm glow that slanted through his tenement window and curled around him and seemed almost to lift him from his bed and send him on his way, out into the street and down the avenue to where the sweet and lovely Margaret Shaunassey waited for him each morning, her books in her arms before he drew them from her and together they set off for school. He had during those brief preceding weeks been one of life's winners, the boy who'd won the heart of the kind and beautiful Margaret Shaunassey, she of spring rain and sea-blue eyes. No more Eddie the prankster, with his gapped teeth. No more Eddie the loser, with his indifferent grades. Because of her, because of the love he'd won from her deserving heart, he'd become the waking Miracle of Holy Cross, looked at in wonder by the other boys, the guy who most among them had truly beaten the odds.

"Mr. Spellacy, you're going to feel a slight pinch."

He did, and with its bite he suddenly found himself lifted and carried away on a river of exquisite softness. The eternally cascading numbers slowed and after a time he became pure sensation, beyond the reach of clearly defined thoughts or expressions. Here, levitated, he had no need for devices of any kind, no need for pencils, or racing forms, or the little scraps of paper on which he figured the odds against this horse or that one winning this race or that one. The world of racetrack betting, of starting bells and photo finishes, now lay decidedly in the past, the odds against returning to it increasing with each passing second. He felt only the silent churn of his body drifting delicately forward, as if on a pillow of air, moving steadily and smoothly toward a final endless calm.

Only his thoughts were as weightless as he was. They came and went effortlessly, like small eddies within the gently flowing current. Translucent faces swam in and out as he lay silent and without fret, his bed now a raft gliding peacefully down a misty river. They stayed only a moment, these faces, then faded back into the mist. His mother, her hair pulled back, peering into a steaming kettle of corned beef and cabbage. His father's face, smudged with grease from the mechanic's shop. His older brother, Jack, all spit and polish in his army uniform.

The faces of horses surfaced, too, black or brown, with their huge sad eyes. They had given him more pleasure than any human being, and now, as he floated, they sometimes came rushing out of the engulfing cloud, strong and beautiful, their tails waving like banners in the bright summer air. Holiday Treat appeared, with Concert Master a link behind, noble in their ghostly strides, his only source of awe. They came prancing by the score, these horses upon which he had laid odds without dread. Something he'd never done with human games, baseball, football and the like, least of all on boxing. No, he had laid odds only on horses because though chance might rudely play upon them, it never fell with the dark intent of malicious force, and thus, despite its storied wins and losses, for him the track remained unbloodied ground.

Suddenly, he saw a head slam into a brick wall, a splatter of blood left behind, and closed his already closed eyes more tightly, working to seal off this vision, return it to the darkness.

It worked, and in the blackness, he felt the raft move on, bearing him gently away, down the placid, mist-covered stream. As he drifted, he saw a few friends from his boyhood, but none beyond those early years because his mind's obsessive calculations had figured the odds against ever having friends his evil, odds-defying presence would not harm. He'd done the same with marriage and parenthood, and so no wife or child greeted him from the enfolding mist. The odds, as his eternally fevered brain had so starkly calculated, were against the safe passage of anyone who walked beside him or even passed his way.

A newspaper headline abruptly streamed through his mind, the words carried on a lighted circle, like the zipper on Times Square: LOCAL BOY DIES IN FREAK ACCIDENT.

Freak accident.

It had begun the morning after he'd first heard the news that a local boy had tripped and fallen, slammed his head against a nearby wall, and by freak accident, died as a result. He'd stepped out of his third-floor apartment, on his way to school, when he'd glanced down the flight of stairs that led to the street. What were the chances, his mind had insistently demanded, of someone falling down them, *because they were with him*? He'd frozen in place, with his hand on the banister, briefly unable to move before he'd finally regained some control over his mind's building oddity, then walked slowly, with a disturbing caution, down the uncarpeted steps.

She'd been waiting for him at the corner, just as she'd waited every morning for the last few weeks, her eyes upon him with unimaginably high regard, never noticing his hand-me-down clothes, the gap between his teeth, seeing what no other girl had ever seen, the nobility he craved, tender and eternal, his ragged knighthood. But now she seemed to stand amid a whirl of wildly hurtling traffic, a universe of randomly flying objects, the cement curb no more than a trapdoor over a terrible abyss, a door held in place only because he did not join her there, he, Eddie, against whom the odds were cruelly pitted, Eddie who brought misfortune, imperiling by his own ill luck everyone he loved.

And so he'd turned from her, and walked away, turned from her sea-blue eyes and spring-rain smile, and glimpsed, in his turning, a dimming of those eyes, a winter in the rain.

"I think my brother needs more."

"It's dangerous, Mr. Spellacy."

"How long does he have anyway?"

"Not long."

"Then it doesn't matter. He just wants to rest."

Another pinch and the voices ceased and night fell abruptly within his mind, sweeping everything from view. For a long time he lay, breathing softly in the mahogany blackness. Then from the depths of that impenetrable darkness, he sensed movement, but saw nothing, no relatives, no horses. Seconds passed. Or minutes. Or days. And far, far away, a tiny light emerged, pinpoint small at first, but growing like the dawn, until once again he was on his pillow of silence, drifting down a watery corridor of hazy light.

Still alive, he thought disconsolately, though this knowledge did not come to him as words spoken silently by his mind, but as a sensation mysteriously carried on the subtle beat of his pulse. It was like all his thinking now, composed not of coherent thoughts, but rather the product of unpredictable mental surges, the firings of his brain tapping out codes that seemed to be transmitted, soundlessly and without grammar and syntax, to his decoding heart.

Freak accident.

The repetition of the words struck so resoundingly in his mind that he suddenly felt another, somewhat larger disturbance in the flow. It was not so much a thought as an apprehension, the sense that somewhere far beneath the smoothly drifting raft a malicious creature lurked, huge in body, but largely still, sending ripples upward with its spiked tail.

Freak accident.

Night fell within him again, but not the blackness he sought, the dead calm of oblivion. Instead, it was the mottled darkness of his spare room. Within that room, he saw nothing but the gray-and-white flickering of the small television he kept on the tiny card table where he dined each night on food that required no cooking, since he'd figured the odds that a single match, used to light the single eye of a small gas range, might set his room on fire, then the hotel, then the neighborhood, a whole city ignited because Eddie the Odds defied the odds, Eddie, whose cautiously discarded match, dipped in water, cold to touch, might yet devour millions in whirling storms of flame.

A horn blared in his mind, and the flickering screen resolved into a view of the track, the horses prancing toward the starting gate, Light Bender in sixth place, hustled unwillingly into her stall, the odds against her ten-to-one.

Now a pistol shot rang out, and they were off, Light Bender in tenth place as he'd figured she would be, but moving in ways he'd failed to calculate, her head thrust forward like a battering ram, her stride lengthening, as it seemed, with each forward thrust, her black mane flying as she tore down the track, black hooves chewing up the turf.

From his gently flowing pallet of air, he watched as she rounded the track, eighth, seventh, sixth, now moving within striking distance of a fabled win. Then, suddenly, she began to fall apart, fall into pieces, like a shattered puzzle, her hooves no longer connected to her legs, her haunches no longer connected to her torso, her head thrust out farther than her long neck as if it were trying to outrun the rest of her.

He felt a violent agitation in his drift, and behind closed eyes looked to his right, if it were his right, and there was Light Bender running at full speed beside him, racing the fiercely boiling current, but running without legs, and now without a body, and finally without a head, so that nothing was left but her mane, long and black and shimmering . . . like Margaret Shaunassey's hair.

Without warning she appeared before him as she had so many, many times, come like an incubus to pry open the still unmended rift within him, the cut that bled a crimson stream of numbers, and from which spilled, on each red molecule, the odds against his life.

She stood in front of Holy Cross School on West 43rd Street. He wasn't sure he'd ever actually seen her on the steps of the school, though even if he had, she'd have been standing under the red-brick entrance marked GIRLS, not as she was now, poised between that entrance and the BOYS on the opposite side of the building. She stood silently, with her arms at her sides, dressed in her school uniform of white blouse, checkered skirt, white socks, black shoes. Margaret Shaunassey. How kind she would have been, a wordless impulse told him, to horses.

He felt the flow increase in velocity, make a hard leftward turn, then descend, so that he felt himself sliding down a long metal shoot. As he slid, he sensed the air grow warm around him. A cloud of steam drifted up and blurred his vision of Margaret but not his memory of her, which became all the more vivid as the steam thickened around him. It was as if his experience of her had become even more sharply defined, everything else a blur, the difference, as he conceived it, between a great horse recalled in the moment of its triumph and one recalled as merely another head nodding from the starting gate.

He closed his eyes more tightly and tried to remain in the soothing comfort of darkness, settle back into the flow, move toward death without further delay or interruption. But the lighted string of numbers began to move again, a snake uncoiling in his head, bringing back the odds he'd obsessively figured during all the passing years, the vast eliminations they had cruelly demanded, hopes and pleasures cut from him like strips of skin, all the sensual joys of life, taste and touch, the fierce reprieve of love, odds that had directed his life not according to rules of probability but to the probability of error within those rules, the terrible intrusion of odds-defying chance.

Freak accident.

The speed of the current increased again, and he felt himself racing headlong into an area of shade, the vault of heaven, or wherever he was, turning smoky. Through the smoke, he saw a figure close in upon him, slowly at first, then astonishingly fast, as if he'd traveled the distance between them at warp speed, so that he instantly stood before him, silent in the smoldering air, a kid from Holy Cross, short with pumpkin-colored hair, a rosy-cheeked boy half his size, but the same age.

Mickey Deaver.

Mickey the Clown.

He felt his closed eyes clench, but to no avail, because the vision was inside him, carried toward him on a river of rushing numbers. It faded in and out, hazy at first, but with growing clarity, until at last the mist lifted and Mickey stood in his school uniform, twelve years old, holding a blood-spattered towel against the side of his head. He stared straight ahead. His eyes didn't blink. Not one red hair stirred. The only motion came from his lips, mouthing two unmistakable words:

Freak accident.

Now he was in the school yard, watching from a distance as Mickey sauntered over to Margaret. Within seconds she was laughing. Not very much at first, then harder and harder, as Mickey clowned and made jokes. Her laughter rang through the overhanging trees and spiraled around the monkey bars and curled through the storm fence against which he leaned, watching as Margaret reached into her small lunch box and handed Mickey the Clown one of her mother's cookies.

A siren split the air, and on its desperate keening, he felt a hard jolt in the flow, like a train going off the track, so that he gripped for a hold, now clinging for dear life as he bumped and clattered, the flow rocketing forward at what seemed inhuman speed. The river vanished, and he was on land, his body flat on the hard surface of a metal gurney, wildly jostled as if he were being dragged across rutted ground.

"What's the matter, Doctor?"

"Quick, get the defibrillator!"

The explosion came from the center of his chest, as if he'd lain face down on a land mine. It blasted shards of light in all directions, flashing images of past time through a roiling steam of memory. He saw Mickey emerge, whistling happily, from the rear door of his building, then felt the brutal shove of his hand against Mickey's shoulder, and watched as Mickey tumbled to the side, knees buckling, so that his head struck hard against the side of the building, a geyser of blood spouting from his ear as he fell unconscious onto the cement stairs.

"Give me the paddles!"

A bell tolled, and in its dying echoes he saw Mickey gathered up, placed on a stretcher and wheeled into a waiting ambulance, a local boy, as the paper had described him, dead by freak accident.

"Clear!"

"Okay."

"Hit it!"

He felt the jerk of the gurney like blows to his body, wrenchingly painful punches that sent him into aching spasms each time another jolt rocked the earthbound flow. With each blow a bell tolled and a year passed and logged within those passing years he saw the outcome of his act, Old Man Deaver dead of drink, Margaret confused and shaken, never knowing why he'd turned from her that morning, nor ever approached her again, never knowing that he was still Eddie, her white knight, bent on her protection, and so protecting her from himself, because by his own ill luck, a rift in the laws of chance, a little, half-hearted shove had made of him a murderer.

"Clear!"

"Hit it!"

He jerked in pain, and through the screen of his pain, yearned for the cushion of air, the invisible river, as his defiant brain worked feverishly to figure the odds that he might at least die beyond the reach of odds.

"No good."

But figure as he did, calculate and recalculate, the odds remained the same as long ago, when he'd first begun to lay them, high against stopping yourself in time, getting another chance, high as the odds, he finally concluded, against a peaceful death.

"Too late."

At least a billion to one, he figured on the dying breath of a final calculation.

But for the first time in a long time, he had figured them too low.

THE HUSTLE

Pat Jordan

The shooter rattled the dice in his fist and blew on them. The girl standing behind him massaged his shoulders and whispered in his ear.

The shooter said loudly, "Come *on!* Baby needs a new pair of shoes!" He flung the dice across the green felt table. The other gamblers around the craps table shouted out, too. The dice hit the far end of the table, tumbled back toward the shooter, and came to rest. The other gamblers groaned.

"Craps," the pit boss said. He raked in all the chips and said, "Next shooter."

The young man and the girl moved away from the head of the table. An old man took his place. He was in his eighties, bald, with a friar's tuft of white hair, a brush mustache and a much younger man's pale blue-gray eyes. He wore a double-breasted navy blazer, a rep tie, gray slacks, and he fingered a felt fedora in one hand. The pit boss tossed him the dice and said, "You're the shooter."

Someone around the table called out, "Come on, old man. Show us what you got."

The old man looked embarrassed. He leaned over the table and placed some chips on a number. Then he took the dice in his soft, pink, pudgy fingers, turned his head away from the table, and flung the dice backhanded toward the end of the table. When the dice came to rest the other gamblers cheered.

Someone called out, "Atta boy, old man!"

Someone else called out, "He ain't an old man now. He's a winner."

Five hours later, the old man cashed in his chips. He fingered the bills in his hand. One hundred and seventy-five dollars. He put all the bills into his pants pocket, except one. He folded the bill into a tiny square and went over to the casino coatroom. He got his double-breasted camel hair topcoat from the girl behind the counter and slipped her the folded bill. She flashed him a quick, faint smile that vanished, without looking at the bill. She watched the old man struggle to put on his topcoat as he walked toward the door. She unfolded the bill in her hand, looked at it, a twenty, and then called out, "Thanks, pops! Thanks a lot!"

Without looking back, the old man raised a hand and waved. Then he put on his fedora and pushed open the door.

It was snowing furiously, the snow swirling, blinding him. He stepped back inside the warm casino. He would have to wait it out. He looked around the casino to see where he could rest awhile until the snow let up. There were only a few people in the brightly lighted coffee shop. Losers staring down into their cold cups of coffee. No, that would be too depressing. Then he saw the OTB room, off to his right, with its plush chairs facing the big TV screen relaying the horse races from California and Florida. He had never liked the ponies.

Too many variables. He preferred to be in control. He only bet on things where he could find an edge. He remembered what an old-timer had told him once. You can never beat the race, you can only beat the price, and even that was risky. Better to past-post the bookie, at least that way you were sure of winning. If you didn't get caught.

The old man went into the OTB room and sat down in a plush chair that faced the big-screen TV and the odds board beside it. There were only a few other bettors, looking bored, sitting around him, passing time like those lost souls who passed a Wednesday afternoon in a movie theater in a strange city. A movie theater was where you passed an afternoon if you were in a strange city on the hustle, or a bum who just wanted to sleep, or a degenerate looking for sex.

He took off his hat and coat and tried to relax. A girl in a skimpy hostess costume moved through the room, taking bets and drink orders. When she stopped beside him, she smiled down at him, and said, "Can I get you something, sir?"

"Just a scotch and water, honey," he said. He watched her walk away. Her high-heeled, open-toed shoes were too big for her feet, so she had stuffed cotton in the back.

He sat there, sipping his drink, and watched the races coming from Hialeah. It was a sunny day in Florida. The horses walked between the towering Royal Palms onto the track, and then warmed up with a jog around the track. There was a small lake in the center of the track where a flock of pink flamingos, which didn't look real, nested.

The horses were at the starting gate now for the Flamingo Stakes. A trumpet blew and the flamingos rose up in a whirl of pink wings and flew around the track from the starting line to the finish line and then they floated back down to earth in a cluster around the lake. Then a bell rang and the gates opened and the horses came thundering out . . .

The old man remembered when he was in his twenties he had gone to Hialeah not to bet on the ponies, but on the hustle, he didn't know what hustle, it would come to him, he always did like to improvise, and as a sort of winter vacation where he could rub elbows with the swells from Palm Beach who came down to Hialeah in their own special train. The men wore top hats and cutaway waistcoats and striped pants and spats. Their women wore big, floppy-brimmed hats and pastel-colored chiffon dresses and white gloves to their elbows. They all sat in the reserved dining room at tables set with cut-glass crystal and heavy silverware and china so fine you could see through it. All the napkins were a flamingo pink and the tablecloths a pale green. The old man, in his twenties then, sat with them, after he had slipped the maitre d' a C-note, a lot of money in those days. He was dressed in a creamy cashmere double-breasted suit and brown-and-white spectator shoes. He looked around at the swells, sizing them up for a hustle. He saw Joe Kennedy, with his big eyeglasses and buck teeth, sitting and laughing with Gloria Swanson.

A girl stopped by his table and smiled down at him drinking his scotch and water. She was a beautiful blonde in a pale pink dress, with her floppy-brimmed hat pulled over one eye.

"You shouldn't drink alone," she said, and sat down across from him. He was handsome then, with his slicked-back hair and pale blue eyes, and straight nose. But he had never been much of a ladies' man. Or a drinker. He had a theory, even then, that a man has enough time in his life for only one vice. Booze, broads, gambling. If you're going to do it right, he figured, you had to pick one and stick to it.

He sat with the girl, whose name he couldn't remember now, almost sixty years later. He drank his scotch and she drank her pink lady and they talked. He had taught himself things he knew he would need on the hustle, things he had gotten mostly from books, *The Great Gatsby,* how to dress, the stock market, Ivy League schools, although he could never get over his habit of saying Darthmouth instead of Dartmouth, but they never caught on, although his cronies did, laughing at him, calling him Ivy League. Maybe that was his hustle on that day, just fitting in with the swells, that girl, with no one the wiser. She just assumed he was "one of our crowd," so she chattered away about Palm Beach and how boring it was in-season, all the old fogies, but her mother insisted she spend her spring break from Wellesley with the family during High Season, especially since Daddy had a horse running in the Flamingo Derby.

"It's all so boring," she said as she held up a cigarette in a long mother-of-pearl holder. He lighted her cigarette with a silver lighter he had won in a craps game. She held his hand, looked into his eyes, and blew out the lighter in a way she had seen in a moving picture once.

"Your father has a horse in the Derby?" he said. "Tell me about it."

"Oh, he's just some old horse Daddy bought that nobody wanted. I don't understand any of it. The bloodlines and all that. It seems silly, Daddy keeping his horse out of races until now, like it's some big secret. Who cares?"

But the old man, a young man then, cared, and after a few moments, he excused himself and went to the hundred-dollar window and placed a G-note on the nose of Daddy's horse, which came in first by three lengths. The girl never knew. She was still sitting there, waiting for him to come back, when he collected his winnings, and then walked down the grandstand to the long dirt path that smelled of hay and horseshit, with the sun slanting across his path through the towering Royal Palms that lined the path that led through wrought-iron gates to his car.

The old man smiled to himself. The only time he'd ever scored off the ponies and he owed it to a woman. He checked his watch. It was getting late. He got up and left the OTB room and went outside. It was still snowing, but not so bad now. He hugged himself against the cold and walked carefully through the parking lot so he wouldn't slip. When he got to his old Volkswagen beetle, it was covered with snow. He swept the snow from the roof, and the front and rear windows, with his bare hands that stung from the cold snow. It snapped him alert, heightened his senses after the long hours in the warm casino smelling of smoke and cheap perfume and sweat. It would be a long drive home. Two hours in nice weather. He checked his watch. Five p.m. He'd be lucky to make it home by nine in the snow. If he got home any later, his wife would be worried.

The old man drove slowly on the highway rutted with snow. He put on his windshield wipers to keep the snow from accumulating. He passed a few cars at first, and then none. Cars were pulled off onto the side of the highway, buried in snowdrifts. The old man hunched forward over the steering wheel. He rotated his neck to ease a cramp. It exhausted him to stand for hours at a craps table now that he was an old man. He still wasn't used to it. Old man. When he was younger, in his fifties, he could shoot pool for twenty-four hours straight, pocket his winnings, throw cold water on his face, wash off the baby powder and blue chalk dust on his hands, straighten his rep tie, button his double-breasted navy blazer, and take all his cronies out for a big meal. He smiled to himself. Cronies. An old man's word. Fellow card sharps and shills and past-posters like Tommy the Blonde and Freddie the Welch and Schiamo. Club fighters with scar tissue around their eyes like Billy Bones. Baggy pants vaudeville comics with leering eyes, and their girl-friends, strippers with yellow hair that smelled of peroxide. But they always acted like ladies when he took them out to dinner, especially in front of his wife. She was respectable in their eyes, if for no other reason than that she *was* his wife, now, of sixty years. He always paid for those big dinners. He liked paying. But there was no one to buy dinner for now.

He must have gunned the accelerator in his reverie because the car was slipping sideways. He stabbed at the brake and the car made a full, spinning circle in the snow, disorienting him for a moment, before he managed to straighten it out and continue down the highway.

"For Crissakes!" he said out loud. "Pay attention!" He hunched over the steering wheel again and forced himself to concentrate. That was the thing about getting old. Everyone thought it was about memory, but it was about concentration. It just flew out of his head without warning. He knew he had lost much of his physical stamina, but at least he knew the limits of the stamina he had left. He could adjust to that. But his concentration was something else. He never knew when he'd lose it until it was gone. A hazard in his profession.

It was getting dark so he flipped on the headlights. The bright lights illuminated up ahead in the darkness the falling snow, the passing trees, the abandoned cars, and, in his mind's eye, the faces from his past.

He saw an old Sicilian with elaborately curled and waxed mustaches. Mustache Pete, he called him. Pete sat on a milk crate, reading *Il Progresso* and smoking a crooked Toscano cigar in front of the heavy, bolted door of the Venice Athletic Club. He watched out for the polizia while behind that door, the old man, younger then, forty, dealt hands of poker, from the bottom of the deck. His pink, soft fingers flicked cards around the table faster than a blink.

He saw the face of the French-Canadian logger he had just past-posted in a horse race in a small town outside of Montreal. The logger's face was purple with rage, his features contorted, his breath smelling of whiskey only inches from the old man's face. The old man was in his thirties then. He thought he was invincible. He looked into the Frenchman's eyes and smiled, even as the Frenchman pressed the cold blade of his hunting knife against the old man's throat. "Go ahead," the old man said. "Let's see if you got the moxie."

The old man would never forget that look of open-mouthed disbelief on the Frenchman's face when he realized that even with a hunting knife against his throat, the old man would not pay up.

He saw the faces of the mean, rednecked farmers in a small town pool hall in upstate New York when they finally realized they were being hustled by the old man, in his twenties then. One of the farmers moved toward the front door and another moved to the backdoor. The old man laid his cue stick on the table in the middle of a game, and excused himself. He went to the men's room, hoisted himself up on the sink, pried open a painted-shut window high above his head, climbed out, and walked quickly to his car. That was one of the first lessons the old man learned about hustling in a strange pool hall. Always check the bathroom window before you begin to play.

He saw the faces of the bearded lady and her husband, the Geek, at the county fair, where he'd begun his life on the road at the age of fifteen. The old man was fresh out of the or-phanage where he'd spent most of his early life. He got a job as a roustabout at the fair and then moved up to the shill in the pea-under-the-pod scam. The bearded lady felt sorry for him. She invited him to dinner one night. She roasted a chicken. Hours earlier, her husband, salivating insanely in a cage, had entertained the rubes by biting off the head of that chicken. The old man remembered how he struggled to keep a straight face after dinner when the Geek tossed a head fake toward his wife, washing dishes, and said, "Don't get any ideas about my old lady, kid."

He heard a harsh voice and opened his eyes to see the white, moonlike face of a nun, dressed in her black habit, looming over him in the darkness of the dormitory room where he slept, a child of six, with fifteen other boys in the orphanage. The nun leaned over, her face close to his and smelling of an astringent cleaner. She whispered harshly again, "Come on, Pasquale, time to get up, lazy bones. Get dressed."

He rubbed sleep from his eyes and got out of bed. He did as he was told and dressed.

"Hurry, now," she said. "We don't have much time."

"Where are we going, Sister?"

"To visit your mother."

"But I don't have a mother."

"Don't be silly, boy. Everyone has a mother."

He followed her outside into the early morning darkness

of a muggy, August day. The big yellow school bus was already parked in front of the Gothic stone orphanage, its motor running, its tailpipe spewing smoke. Sister opened the door, hiked up her skirt, revealing her black stockings and the stale smell of her sex, and climbed up and settled into the driver's seat. He climbed up after her and sat behind her as she ground the gearshift into first and the bus lumbered down the long driveway, turned right onto the street, and began moving slowly through the Italian ghetto, past old, three-story houses with three floors of porches, and little gardens in back of tomato plants growing out of Medaglia D'Oro coffee cans. The bus stopped at a red traffic light across from Nanny Goat Park. Old men, smoking crooked Toscano cigars, sat on benches and watched their goats graze on the grass as the sun came up.

When they reached the hospital, the nun held his hand tightly, and hurried down the hallway past doctors and nurses in white, half dragging him behind her, her habit billowing up into his face. When she came to a door, she stopped. She opened the door and pushed him through it. He stopped and turned back to her. "Go on," she said. "I'll stay here."

"But what do I do, Sister?" he said, tears welling up in his eyes.

"Go talk to your mother. She doesn't have much time left. Go on, now."

He turned and saw a shape lying on a cot, a white sheet pulled up to its neck. The shape had thick, wild, black hair spread out on a pillow. He moved closer to see its face. It was a beautiful face, with dark eyebrows, a straight nose, and full lips, except that the face was gaunt, her skin the color of a storm cloud. Her eyes fluttered open. They were as blue as a summer's sky. Her face turned toward him. She studied him with her blue eyes for a long moment and then her lips turned up into a faint smile.

"Pasquale, *meo fillio*," she said, and then gasped for breath. When her gasping subsided, she reached out her hand and touched his cheek with her cold fingers. She smiled and said, "*Te amo*." Then her eyes opened wide in terror and her hand gripped his shoulder so tightly it hurt. He wanted to pull away, but he couldn't. She said loudly, as if pleading, "Pasquale, *me dispiace*! *Me dispiace*!" Then she began gasping for breath again, and her hand fell off his shoulder, dangling beside the cot, and her head fell back onto the pillow.

He heard the nun's harsh voice from the doorway. "That's enough, Pasquale, don't tire the poor girl. Come."

Riding back to the orphanage in the bus, he sat behind the nun and said, "Who was that, Sister?"

"Your mother. Who else?"

He was quiet for a while as the bus moved past Nanny Goat Park in the morning light, now. He saw the young mothers in their summer dresses, sitting on the benches in the park, talking to one another while they held their babies tight to their breasts so they could drink their milk.

Finally, he said, "But I thought I didn't have a mother, Sister."

"Don't be foolish. I told you everyone has a mother."

"Then if she's my mother, why didn't she want me?"

The nun glared at him through the little mirror that hung over the windshield. "Don't you ever say that, understand? *Understand?* Of course she wanted you, but what could she do, a girl, a child, really, fifteen, with no husband.

She had no choice but to give you to us so we could take care of you."

He was quiet again as the bus turned the corner toward the orphanage. Then he said, "What's my mother's name, Sister?"

"Rose."

He said his mother's name out loud. "Rose." He smiled to himself. "What did my mother say to me?"

"She said, she hoped you would forgive her. Then she said, she loved you very much because you were her son."

He sat back in his seat as the bus moved up the long drive toward the orphanage. He remained in the orphanage for nine more years and every night of those years he dreamed for the first time since he could remember. It was always the same dream. He dreamed about his mother, her wild, black hair and her blue eyes. Her name was Rose, he knew that now, and she had loved him, and that was all he would ever know.

• • •

The old man pulled the Volkswagen into a snowdrift in front of his apartment building. He heard the wheels crunch over the snow and then felt them sink deep into the snow. Tomorrow morning he'd have to dig out the car. The snow was still falling in darkness. It was ten. The light was on in their third-floor apartment window. He saw his wife's face pressed to the window. He beeped the horn once. She waved and moved away from the window.

He stamped the snow off his shoes in the hallway. His feet were cold and wet. He held on to the stair rail as he climbed the three flights of stairs. He had to stop at each flight to catch his breath. He was breathing heavily when he reached the third floor. The gambling and the drive had exhausted him. He had never felt so numbingly tired before in his life.

His wife opened the door. "I was worried about you, honey," she said.

He kissed her on the cheek. "It was nothing," he said. "I took my time." He took out the bills from his pocket. "I made almost two bills."

She smiled. "Good," she said. "I kept dinner warm." She hobbled off in her aluminum walker toward their tiny kitchenette.

He brushed off the snow from his fedora and hung it and his overcoat on the coatrack behind the door. He sat down at the dining room table in their threadbare apartment that smelled of things old and worn. Plastic sheeting covered the Mediterranean sofa and easy chair they'd had for years. There were two large sepia-tinted photographs on the dining room wall. The old man in his twenties, balding even then, but handsome. His wife at sixteen, with luxuriant, wavy black hair and dark eyes. A pretty girl then. Now she was just an old woman in a worn housedress, hunched over, with swollen ankles, mottled skin, and a thin puff of white hair. The old man bent over and took off his wet shoes and socks. He looked at his slim, white feet.

His wife returned and put a plate of food down in front of him. Pastina with butter and salt. A child's supper. "Vino?" she said. He nodded. She returned with a grape jelly glass filled with wine she had poured from a gallon jug with no label. She sat down with her husband and watched him eat slowly.

He chewed a few mouthfuls of soft pastina and then had to rest his jaws. "I don't know how much longer I can make that drive," he said.

"I know," his wife said, and looked down at the table. She had watery, red-rimmed eyes and a big nose. She looked up at him, and said, "But what would we do without the extra money?"

"There's always pool. I've been thinking. An old man like me. I could hustle up a nine-ball game downtown."

"Do you still have the stroke?"

"You never lose the stroke. It's the eyes that go."

"There's still my nephew," she said. "We have that money coming in every week."

"A C-note a week isn't enough," he said.

"You could ask him for a raise. You've been driving him to work and home for five years now."

The old man nodded. "I could," he said. "It's about time." He put a mouthful of pastina in his mouth and chewed slowly.

• • •

His wife's younger sister had married a prosperous lawyer. They had only one child, a son, who was born retarded. When the doctor told her her son was born retarded, the sister went into a state of shock. She lost all her hair. After that, she wore an assortment of henna-colored wigs that always made her look much younger than her older sister with her graying, and then white, hair. The younger sister refused to institutionalize her son since he was not severely retarded. She was determined to teach him to function. She trained him like a dog. She was oblivious to his cries and whimpers and even to the pleas of her older sister. She beat him with a belt over the slightest sign of weakness—spilled milk, soiled underpants—until he got his first job at twenty. He became a messenger in the Municipal Courthouse, a job he has held for thirty-five years. His father died when he was forty-five, and his mother got cancer when he was fifty. It took her a year to die. Her older sister visited her every day in the hospital. And every day, the younger sister pleaded with her older sister to watch over her son when she was gone. Then she died. She left her son enough money to remain in their big, old colonial house and to pay for a full-time nurse-housekeeper. The only thing her son needed was someone to drive him to work every morning and drive him home every night.

The old man didn't mind doing that. He looked forward to it even. The only family he had in the world was his wife, who could never have children, and now his retarded nephew. He didn't seem retarded, only odd, childish, talkative in that shrill way of women, which was understandable since he spent all his life close to his mother. He was short, blocky, prone to moods of extreme animation and sullen withdrawal. Sometimes in the morning, he would not stop chattering about a Yankee game he had watched the night before. He kept score of those games on an official scorekeeper's pad. He told his uncle about every pitch, every out. Sometimes, though, nothing his uncle said to him could take him out of his sullen silences. He would spend their morning drive picking at the sleeve of his sweater like a petulant child. The old man tried to understand what put him in such a silent, brooding mood. He studied him for a sign, the oriental cast to his features, the age lines around his slanting eyes, his thick lips, his slack, hairless skin, and then he realized with a shock that his nephew was not a child, but a fifty-year-old man. On such days, the old man felt he more than earned his $100 a week.

• • •

The old man awoke the next morning in the twin bed beside his wife. It was still dark outside. He let his wife sleep. He got out of bed, put on his pot of espresso, and started to get dressed. He picked his clothes with great care. A Gant shirt with a frayed button-down collar. A stained rep tie. No. He put the tie back. He buttoned the shirt at his throat without the tie. He put on a gray cardigan sweater that was unraveling. Gray flannel slacks that had a sheen at the knees. Scuffed wingtip cordovans. All his other shoes were brilliantly polished. He looked at himself in the mirror, and smiled. A defeated old man.

He sat down with his cup of espresso. He rubbed a lemon peel around the lip of the cup and took a sip. He forced himself to remember. The secret was in never losing control. Knowing that one thing the mark didn't know. It was always ego with the mark, not the money. It was all about saving face. The curse of Italians. Saving face. The old man was lucky to be raised in an orphanage by Irish nuns instead of the Italian home of the parents he never knew. It gave him the edge in his profession. He never lost control. He never lost sight of his only goal in the hustle. He always let the mark have his ego while he, the old man, walked out with the money. How you kept score. The cash in the pocket any way you could get it, and then, as you walked out the door the mark would shout after you, "You're one lucky sunuvabitch! But I'll get you tomorrow." Which was the point. If you left him with his ego he'd stay on the string for a lot of tomorrows. Some marks were like his own private bank. He stopped in whenever he wanted to make a withdrawal.

The old man drained his espresso, washed the cup in the sink, and went to the coatrack by the door. His fedora and camel hair topcoat had dried. But not today. He put on a thin raincoat that would make him shiver all day, and a fleece-lined hunter's cap with earmuffs.

It was bitterly cold outside. The snow had already begun to freeze. Ice had frozen to the windows of his Volkswagen. He had to hold a lighted match to the door lock to melt the ice. He got in, started the car, put on the defroster, and then got back out and dug out the snow around the wheels with his bare hands.

He drove slowly up and down hills that were packed down with icy snow. When he got to his nephew's house, he saw him standing outside the front door. He wore a hunter's cap, too, with earmuffs, and an expensive topcoat, and he carried a leather briefcase that contained his tuna fish sandwich and an apple. His nephew got in the car.

"Were you waiting long?" the old man asked.

"The Knicks won last night, uncle," his nephew said. His lips peeled apart like an open wound when he spoke and his eyes were wide and unblinking. The old man drove off. His nephew kept talking in his shrill voice.

"Latrell Sprewell made twenty-four points," his nephew said. He opened his briefcase and pulled out his official NBA scorebook. He traced his finger down the scorebook and began reading. "With two minutes and twenty-eight seconds gone in the first quarter, Latrell Sprewell scored a basket on a . . ." He looked close to the scorebook. ". . . jumpshot from twelve feet away from the basket. Then with four munites and fifty-two seconds gone in the first quarter, he was fouled by . . ." Again he looked close to the scorebook. ". . . Alonzo Mourning. He made his first foul shot and then he missed his second. With six minutes and . . ."

His nephew's droning voice lulled the old man. The endless, meaningless torrent of words let the old man slip into a reverie of what he must do today. He tried to visualize it in his mind's eye. The proper defeated slouch of an old man. Eyes always averted, looking down at the hunter's cap in his hand. The weak shrug. The equivocation. "I don't know." And then, "Maybe just a few games."

His nephew was still talking. He was in the fourth quarter now as they approached the courthouse on Main Street. The street had been plowed at night, but the plowing only packed down the remaining snow like a sheet of ice. The old man stabbed the brakes as they came to the courthouse and the Volkswagen began to slide in the snow. His nephew kept talking as the old man tried to steer the Volkswagen away from a parked car. The Volkswagen began to slow as it slid into the parked car with a jolt. His nephew had stopped talking now. He looked out his window at the crumpled fender of the Volkswagen against the crumpled fender of the parked car.

"Uncle, you hit a car," his nephew said with wide eyes.

"It's nothing," the old man said. "Are you all right?" His nephew nodded with great exaggeration. The old man said, "Hurry. You'll be late for work. I'll leave a note on the windshield so the owner can call me."

He got out of the car and went over to the parked car as his nephew climbed the courthouse steps. The old man called out to him, "I'll pick you up at six." His nephew nodded and disappeared behind the big double doors of the courthouse. The old man looked around to see if anyone had seen him. He took out a piece of paper and a pen and scribbled on it. He stuck it under the parked car's windshield wipers. The note read, "I hit your car. Sorry."

The old man backed his car into the street and drove off. His dented front fender rattled a bit but didn't scrape the tire. He turned down a side street into the warehouse district. Old red-brick buildings long since abandoned. Their windows broken. Rusted machinery in their parking lots. He pulled into one of the warehouses that had a hand-painted sign above the door: SHORTY'S POOL HALL. He parked the car alongside of an Oldsmobile Cutlass painted lime green with gold wheels. "*Melanzana*," the old man said out loud. He sat in his car for a moment until he had calmed himself. Then he got out and went inside. He walked down a narrow, dirty hallway to a pair of frosted glass doors with the words POOL HALL painted on them. He pushed open the doors and stepped inside. It was dark and it smelled of piss and cigarette smoke and spilled beer and b.o. A tall, gaunt man whose face looked like something out of a wax museum—his chalky cheeks had a fake, rosy tint—was sitting hunched over a desk, reading a newspaper. The old man looked around the dimly lit pool hall. All the tables but one were deserted. A *melanzana* in his late thirties was banging the balls around the table by himself. He looked up at the old man and then back to his table. He wore a tight, black silk T-shirt that showed off all the gold chains around his neck, and tight black pants. The old man shuffled over to the bench along the wall behind the *melanzana,* and sat down. He watched him shoot for a few minutes. Banging the balls aimlessly with a touch like a blacksmith.

The *melanzana* was hunched over the table, sighting a shot, when he glanced over his shoulder at the old man watching him. He smiled, flashing his gold teeth. He had processed hair, shimmering with pomade, curling down his cheeks in ringlets.

"You taking a picture, old man, or what?"

The old man looked down at the hunter's hat in his hands, and said softly, "I'm sorry. I was just watching."

"You got nuthin' better to do with your time?" The old man said nothing. The black man said, "No, I guess you don't. An old man with too much time and nuthin' to do, huh?" The black man turned back to his shot, rammed the cue ball hard into a rack of balls, scattering them across the table. He straightened up and turned toward the old man.

"It'll cost you to watch, old man," he said. "I ain't puttin' on a show for free for some old white dude got nuthin' to do but wait to die."

The old man felt his face get hot. "I'm sorry," he said again, and stood up. "I won't bother you anymore."

He began to walk away. The *melanzana* called after him. "Hey, old man. Come on back here. Grab you a stick and we'll play a coupla games."

The old man turned and said, "I don't know. I haven't played in years."

"So what? You're here, ain't you? We'll shoot a coupla games a nine ball for fun. Maybe a dollar or two just to keep score."

The old man looked down at his soft, pink hands fingering his cap. "I don't know," he said again.

"Come on, old man. What else you got to do? I ain't about to hustle no poor old man in some sorry-ass clothes."

"Well . . ." The old man began to take off his raincoat. "Just a few games."

They shot nine ball for hours. The old man won a few games when they shot for a dollar, but then his stroke became erratic, jerky, when they began to shoot for ten dollars a game.

He hit short straight-in shots too hard, and long shots too easily. He blinked repeatedly as he sighted a long shot. The object ball far down the table looked fuzzy, like a tennis ball. He
jabbed his stick at the cue ball and rattled the object ball
around the table. After each game, he dug into his pants
pocket and paid the black man. When he had lost all the
money he had won shooting craps he went over to the rack
against the wall and hung up his cue stick.

"I have to go now," the old man said.

"What? You got an important date? An old man with
nuthin' but time on his hands."

"I have to pick up my nephew from work."

"The good uncle, huh?" The old man put on his raincoat
and cap. He felt tired, but good. A good tiredness. Physical,
not mental. The black man said, "I'll tell you what, old man.
I'll give you a chance to win your money back tomorrow."

The old man shook his head, no. "You're too good for
me."

The black man grimaced. "Aw, I was lucky today. You
shoot a pretty good stick for an old man. Maybe tomorrow
will be your day." The old man shook his head, no. The black
man said, "I'll give you a spot tomorrow. How's that? The
eight and nine. You pocket the seven you win. I gotta go all
the way to the nine."

The old man looked up at his smiling black face and his
gold teeth. "Well," he said. "If you say so. Tomorrow at the
same time."

His nephew was waiting for him on the steps of the
courthouse. He got in the Volkswagen and they drove off.

"How was work today?" the old man said. His nephew did
not respond. The old man looked across at him. He was sit-

ting with his briefcase on his lap, digging at the briefcase with a fingernail. "You're gonna scratch the leather," the old man said. His nephew ignored him and continued scratching at the leather with a brooding concentration. The old man sighed and concentrated on the road.

They drove in silence until they were only a mile from his nephew's house. Finally, the old man said, "Nephew, I've been thinking. It would help me and your aunt if you could pay me one fifty a week instead of one hundred. I've been driving you for five years now." He looked over at his nephew. He was still digging at his briefcase. He had scraped away a spot of dark, shiny leather to reveal the white hide underneath.

"What do you think, nephew?" the old man said.

His nephew just stared at his finger gouging at the leather, but said nothing. The old man shook his head. He turned the corner that led to his nephew's house. When he reached the house, he parked in front and turned to his nephew to ask him again. He had stopped digging at his briefcase now, but he was still staring at it. Finally, his nephew said, "I don't want you to drive me anymore, uncle." He stared at his briefcase as he spoke.

The old man looked at him. "What? But why?"

"You're too old. You got in an accident today. I'm afraid."

"That? That was nothing. The car just skidded on the ice. It could happen to anyone."

"I don't want you to drive me anymore, uncle. You're too old. You got in an accident today. I'm afraid."

Before the old man could respond, his nephew opened the door and got out. He turned his back on his uncle and began walking with quick, prissy steps toward the front door.

The old man called out after him. "Are you sure?" His

nephew did not turn around. He just opened the front door, went inside, and shut the door behind him.

. . .

The old man and his wife ate their dinner in silence. Finally, his wife said, "What will we do?"

The old man, looking down at his food, said, "I'll do what I've always done. I'll find a way."

"What if he's not there tomorrow?"

"He'll be there. He's a greedy *melanzana*."

"But you don't have any money to play with."

"I won't need any. I'll tell him we'll pay up at the end of the day, not after each game."

"Are you sure you can beat him?"

The old man looked up at her. His face was flushed. "That fucking *melanzana*! Laughing at me. It was all I could do not to let him know I was setting him up for a score. I could beat him with one hand."

"Oh no," she said. "That's too dangerous. You can't play him jack up. If you win, he'll know."

The old man smiled at his wife. "Don't worry, honey. All these years, I'm not going to make a mistake. He'll never know what happened. I'll walk out with his money and he'll think he won."

She nodded, but she did not smile.

That night, asleep in bed, the old man dreamed. He tossed and turned and woke up in the middle of the night. His face was flushed with anger. He said, out loud, "Fired by a fucking retard!" His wife groaned in the bed beside him. He whispered to her, "Shhh. Go back to sleep."

. . .

The *melanzana* was waiting for him. He smiled at the old man as he took off his raincoat. The gaunt man with the waxlike face was sitting at his desk, reading a newspaper. All the tables were deserted. The old man noticed another *melanzana,* only younger, leaning against the wall next to a table. He wore a purple satin jogging suit and those fancy *melanzana* sneakers. He had a shaved head and a big earring like a pirate's. He stared at the old man through dark sunglasses.

"I was afraid you wasn't gonna show, old man," the older *melanzana* said.

"I'm here, ain't I?" the old man said. He took a breath and forced himself to smile. "I had to go to the bank to get money."

"Money, eh?" the *melanzana* said. "I don't think you'll be needin' no money today, old man. Today's your lucky day." He smiled and looked over at the younger man. "Ain't that right, brother Reeshaad?" The younger black man gave him a thin smile, but said nothing.

The older *melanzana* racked the balls at the table near the other one while the old man took a cue stick off the rack. He reminded himself not to roll the stick over the green felt tablecloth to make sure it was straight. The older *melanzana* opened a black leather case, took out two pieces of an elaborately carved cue stick, and screwed them together.

"You break 'em first, old man," the older *melanzana* said. "Age before beauty." He laughed.

The old man bent over the table and sighted the cue ball toward the rack of nine balls he would have to pocket in order to the seven, the money ball. The older *melanzana* stood at the other end of the table, grinning. "What say we shoot for twenty a game, old man? Give you a chance to win back your money real quick."

"Make it fifty," the old man said as he rifled the cue ball into the rack, scattering the object balls, and sinking the five. He looked up to see the *melanzana* standing at the end of the table, staring at him. He was not grinning now.

"You ain't hustlin' me, is you, old man?"

The old man said nothing. He studied the layout of balls. He had easy shots on the one and two, and a long straight-in shot on the three. From there on to the seven, it was an easy run.

"If you want to shoot for twenty, that's all right with me," the old man said.

"No. We'll make it fifty, old man."

The old man bent over the table and sighted the one ball. It was a straight shot into the corner pocket. He rammed the cue ball so hard into the one that the one hit the leather back of the pocket and bounced out.

The *melanzana* grinned. "Heh, relax old man. You're too tight." He leaned over the table and pocketed the one, then the two and three. The four was a difficult cut shot into a side pocket. The *melanzana* cut it too much and it bounced off the rail. "Damn!" he said.

The old man made the four, an easy straight-in shot into the side pocket, but his cue ball froze against the rail. The six was across the table against the rail, too. A tough bank shot. The old man hit the six too softly. It bounced off the rail, went to the pocket on the opposite side of the table, and stopped inches from the pocket.

"Either too hard, or too easy, old man," the black man said. "You ain't got your rhythm yet." He pocketed the six but left himself a long shot for the seven. He missed it, sending the seven bouncing off cushions until it came to rest only a few inches from the corner pocket. The cue ball was in the middle of the table.

The black man was shaking his head. "Set it right up for you, old man. A blind man could make that shot."

"You want to give it to me?" the old man said.

The black man laughed, flashing his gold teeth. "No siree, pops. I'm gonna make you earn it."

The old man pointed his stick at the pocket behind the seven. "Straight-in," he said. He bent over and sighted the seven. He hit it hard, slightly off-center, so that the seven hit the corner of the pocket, ricocheted off the opposite corner, came the full length of the table, hit the two far corners and then rolled back toward the pocket the old man had called, and dropped in.

"Damn!" the black man said. "I told you it was your lucky day. Miss you an easy one and turn it into a trick shot." He reached into his pants pocket for his money.

"That's not necessary," the old man said. "We'll pay up at the end of the day."

"Suit yourself, old man."

The old man lost the second and third games, then he won the fourth when he made the seven ball on the break.

"Man, you's lucky today," the black man said.

"Winners are always lucky to losers," the old man said.

The black man blinked, once, twice, then said, "What you say, old man?"

The old man put his head down and chalked the tip of his cue stick. "I said, you got to be lucky to win."

The black man looked at him. "That's what I thought you said."

The old man lost the fourth game when he scratched on an easy shot on the seven. The black man ran out the seven, eight, and nine.

The old man shook his head. "Like I said. Lucky."

"Lucky!" the black man said. "I run three balls to win and you call it luck?"

"Well, you wouldn't have had the chance, if I didn't scratch on the seven."

"Shiiit! Loser like you, old man, that's always your alibi. The other guy was lucky."

The old man bent over the table and racked the balls. He felt his face get hot. Fired by a fucking retard! Condescended to by a fucking *melanzana* asshole! He straightened up and said, "How about we play for a coupla hundred dollars a game. See if my luck can change."

"Hot damn! You hear that, Reeshaad! The old man loses a game and he wants to raise the bet. A real hustler, ain't he? Why not, huh? What you got to lose, old man. Nuthin' but money ain't gonna do you no good, the time you got left. Shit, yeah, we'll play for a hundred." He bent over the table while the old man fumbled with the rack. "You gonna take all day, old man," the black man said. The old man racked the balls loosely, not tight. When the black man fired the cue ball into the rack, only two balls broke loose. The black man straightened up and banged his cue stick on the floor.

"Now you go give me a fuckin' house rack! Or is you just too old to rack the balls tight?"

The old man said nothing. He bent over the table, sank the one ball, and sent the cue ball ricocheting around the table until it landed against the unbroken rack, and split the balls apart.

"Another lucky fuckin' shot," the black man said.

The old man looked up at the grinning black man, his flashing gold teeth, his stupid grin, not getting it. He smiled at the black man, chalked the tip of his cue stick, and bent over the table. The two ball was tight against the rail far from the corner pocket. The old man sighted his cue ball, then cut it into the two ball so delicately that he almost missed it. The two ball began moving slowly down the table, hugging the rail, and fell into the corner pocket. The three ball was only inches from another corner pocket, but the cue ball was behind the four ball, blocking his shot on the three.

"Tough break, old man. You's snookered," the black man said.

The old man didn't hear him. He was standing straight up, aiming the tip of his cue stick down at the cue ball. He stabbed down at the cue ball with a short stroke. The cue ball squirted around the four ball, then curved back toward the three ball and knocked it into the pocket.

Before the black man could say anything, the old man was sighting the four ball. A long straight-in shot. He eased back the cue stick, once, twice, three times, and then with a smooth, maddeningly methodical stroke, sent the cue ball straight into the four. The cue ball stopped on a dime and the four went straight into the pocket. The old man felt his heart beating in his breast now that he was playing the way he used to. Hard and ruthless. He pocketed the five ball in the side pocket, drew the cue ball back off the opposite rail until it was only inches from the six, a short straight-in shot. The seven was against the rail at the far end of the table. The old man hit the cue ball very low, rifling the six into the pocket, and drawing the cue ball back the full length of the table until it, too, was against the rail a few inches away from the seven. A straight-in shot, but very difficult because both balls hugged the rail. The old man sighted his shot. He aimed the tip of his cue stick high and to the right on the cue ball so that it would hug the rail when it hit the seven. Then, before he shot, he looked up at the black man and smiled. He was still smiling at the black man, not even looking at his shot, when his stick swung smoothly forward. The cue ball rolled against the rail, tapped the seven ball, stopped, while the seven ball rolled slowly toward the pocket and dropped in.

The old man straightened up. The black man was staring at him. The old man noticed, for the first time in an hour, the younger black man staring at him, too, through his dark sunglasses.

"You hustlin' me, old man," the older black man said.

The old man looked at him in the eye. "We gonna play, or what?"

The black man began to unscrew his stick. "I don't think so, old man. I ain't no fool."

"Quitting?"

The black man gave him a faint smile and shook his head. "You tryin' to rile me, old man? Damn, you be an old white dude, but you got a young man's balls."

"What about you?"

"What about me?"

"You got balls, or what?"

The black man glared at him. "Yeah, I got balls, old man. But I got me some brains, too. I ain't playin' with you no eight and nine spot."

"I don't need your spot," the old man said. "I'll play you straight up."

"I said, I got brains, old man. I know when I'm in over my head." He put the two pieces of his elaborately carved cue stick into his black leather case, and snapped it shut.

"All right," the old man said. "You win. I'll tell you what I'll do. I'll play you jack up. I'll shoot one-handed. Is that enough of a spot for you?"

The black man shook his head and smiled across at his friend. "You hear that, Reeshaad? Fuckin' old white dude tryin' to embarrass me. Play one-handed, thinks he can still beat me." He looked back at the old man as he opened his case again and began screwing his cue stick together. He went to the end of the table and began racking the balls.

"Your break, old man."

The old man put one hand behind his back and held the end of the cue stick with his other hand. He balanced the cue stick on the edge of the table. He jabbed the stick forward. The cue ball rolled down the table, hit the rack without force, and knocked out only a few balls. One of them was the nine. It stopped in front of the corner pocket. The one ball was only inches in front of it. An easy combination shot.

The black man stepped up to the table, sighted his shot, sent the cue ball into the one which hit the nine which dropped in.

They played in silence now. The black man won two games in a row. Then the old man won a game. The black man won the next three games and then the old man won a game. Neither of them spoke. They moved around the table in silent concentration. The old man felt his arm getting tired. He miscued on an easy straight-in shot on the nine and lost. He scratched on the eight ball in the next game, and lost. He felt his one-handed stroke getting shaky, his arm heavy, numb. He could sustain his stroke for a shot or two but then he could feel his arm tremble with fatigue. He was breathing heavily. His head was swimming. How much was he down? Five hundred, a thousand? He couldn't keep track. He wanted to be home in bed, resting. He was so tired.

The black man was preparing to break the balls again. He looked at the old man, and said, "What say we play for two hundred a game, old man? Give you a chance to win back your money."

The old man nodded. "Fine with me," he said. He laid his cue stick on the table. "Where's the john?"

The black man pointed his stick at a door marked GENTS. The old man shuffled toward the door. Just as he opened it he heard the black man call out from behind him.

"Don't you be takin' too long, old man. I have to be sendin' Reeshaad in there lookin' for you."

The old man sat down on the toilet seat to catch his breath. He felt sick to his stomach, light-headed, dizzy. He couldn't focus. Everything was swimming before his eyes, spinning around him as if he were on the merry-go-round at the fair where he used to work. He tried to force everything to stop spinning. Things began to slow down, the urinals, the mirror, the sink, the old metal steam radiator up against one wall. He stared at the radiator for a long moment until it had stopped moving. He saw, high above the radiator, a window covered with grime. He tried to remember something from his past. He forced himself to remember. Then he stood up. His legs were shaky. He took a few deep breaths until his legs stopped shaking, then he walked over to the radiator. He raised one leg and put his foot on the radiator. He held it there a moment as he looked for something to grab on to so he could hoist himself up. Once he was standing on the radiator he could open the window, crawl out, and get to his car. But there was nothing for the old man to grab on to. And even if he could stand on the radiator, what would he do? Pull himself up to the window with his arms? He was an old man, for Chrissakes. He had no strength left. He took his foot off the radiator and sat down on the toilet seat. He stared into the dirty mirror over the sink. Images began to form in the mirror. Blurry-gray at first, and then more sharply defined. He stared into the mirror at the faces from his past. They were smiling at him. His cronies. Mustache Pete. The French Canadian. The rednecked farmers. The Hialeah blonde. The bearded lady and the Geek. His mother. Rose. He smiled back at them all, long gone, waiting . . .

THE GREAT, THE GOOD AND THE NOT-SO-GOOD

H.R.F. Keating

Goodwood racecourse, set amid the Sussex Downs, which are of course gently rolling hills, Ups rather than Downs, has been in existence since 1801. It was then that the Duke of Richmond, one of the Great of the land, offered the use of his huge park surrounding Goodwood House to the officers of the Sussex Regiment, of which he happened to be colonel, when they needed somewhere to race their horses. As the years went by, successive Dukes improved and improved the course until Glorious Goodwood, as they call it, rose to be one of the most delightful of all England's race meetings. Perhaps, however, jockeys and trainers may secretly think of it as Would-it-were-good because the course, running as it does not on the ideal level but over a distinctly undulating track with some sharp bends in it, can put even the most fancied runner into an ignominious last place.

But back in 1952 the then holder of the dukedom permitted the first public-address race commentary anywhere in

Britain to boom out across his private park. And it was at that time—if the following account is true—that the Not-so-good came on to the scene. Luckily, however, 1952 can also be called the Year of the Seven Old Ladies, who, although they had their faults like all of us, could reasonably be called, too, the Seven Good Old Ladies.

They all lived in a village at some little distance from the racecourse, a flourishing place with its green large enough for games of cricket, two pubs and even, modern miracle tucked away behind the ancient village church, a bright and shiny red telephone box. Whenever the weather was fine enough it was their custom to come out and sit in a row on two benches that were set side by side at the edge of the green almost in the shadow of the church and opposite the pub called the Fox Goes Free, which—if that indeed is the pub in question—was decidedly appropriate because it was thanks to these old ladies that one cunning fox, of the two-legged variety, failed in the end to go free.

Every day that it didn't rain, and sometimes even when it did, well wrapped in macintoshes, the seven of them would sit, morning and afternoon, chattering away, ignoring, when there was a cricket match on the green, any of the red leather balls that occasionally whizzed over their heads and equally ignoring, as they were on this day, the streams of motor cars clattering past in clouds of exhaust fumes on their way to the start of the five-day race meeting in the grounds of their distant ducal neighbor. Nothing disturbed them as they talked and talked.

Three of them, Mrs. Alford, Mrs. Beastock and little Mrs. Capper, had something of the characteristics of those three brass or plastic monkeys you sometimes see perched up on a mantelpiece: one with two little paws blocking its ears, Hear-No-Evil; one with paws blocking its eyes, See-No-Evil; and the third with paws crossed carefully over its mouth, Speak-No-Evil. Certainly no one in the village had ever heard hopping-about, squirrel-like Mrs. Capper say anything unpleasant about anybody, while fat old Mrs. Alford was so deaf she could hear really neither evil nor good, and Mrs. Beastock, who often gropingly wore both her pairs of spectacles at the same time, would, so they said, have missed a murder even if it were committed under her very nose.

The three who habitually sat on the other bench, Mrs. Damworthy, Mrs. Emery and Mrs. Finders, were the very opposite. Mrs. Damworthy was known for somehow getting to discover every little piece of wrongdoing that besmirched the village, whether it was the curious disappearance of a hen or the stuck-together closeness of a girl and a boy. For discovering them and speaking her mind about them, loudly. Mrs. Emery was a thin rake of an old dear whom it was almost impossible not to rub up the wrong way whatever you happened to say to her. And as for bustling-about Mrs. Finders, she was so interested in everything in the village that she was possessed always of a fund of information, some of it sometimes near the truth.

So how did these six very different old ladies, all of them almost completely ignorant about the events that took place in the Duke of Richmond's park every Goodwood Week, contrive to stay together year in year out without any huffy departures? The answer lay in the lady who would seat herself between the two parties, sometimes squeezing onto one bench, sometimes onto the other. Old Lady Bentt, shriveled and thin almost as the ancient crook-handled walking stick without which she could go nowhere, was rumored to be a distant descendant of Lord George Bentinck, the notorious gambler who in 1824 won a race at Goodwood for which, it was jokingly laid down, every rider had to wear a three-cornered hat, a tricorne, commonly called a cocked hat (the Cocked Hat Stakes is, of course, still run at Goodwood today). But aristocratic as she might be, Lady Bentt was certainly a lady in very, very reduced circumstances, poorer most probably than any of the other six on the two benches, widows though they were. However, what she had retained was her ability to say, in a little piping voice, what should and should not be done. And it was this that kept the gossip circle—only it was a straight line—from ever breaking up.

It was this, too, that in the end caused the fox not to go free. As he very nearly did.

• • •

"That chap hasn't shown his face here before," old Mrs. Beastock, sitting with deaf Mrs. Alford and ever-kindly Mrs. Capper, pronounced as a young man with the swept-back greased hair, long sideburns and the tight trousers that marked out the Teddy Boy, the much-fancied look among the 1950s riffraff, brought a noisy motorbike to a halt just behind the two benches. Leaving it propped up, he lifted from the back a big strung-together box or crate and staggered away with it.

"And how would you know he hasn't been here before?" snapped Mrs. Emery from her place among the trio on the other bench. "You've got the wrong pair of spectacles on your nose. As usual."

"What did she say? What did she say?" Mrs. Alford

boomed out. "If you've got anything to say, dear," she added in a voice designed just to be heard on the other bench and which yet carried halfway across the green, "you should say it so people can hear. I'm not deaf, you know."

"I know you're not deaf, dear," Mrs. Finders chipped in from the very other end of the row, "I saw you sitting at your window when I passed by yesterday, nodding away to that little music box you have when I was hardly able to hear it myself."

"Nothing of the kind," Mrs. Damworthy contradicted. "The wretched woman was simply nodding off. She'd sleep away the whole day if she was let."

Now it was time for tiny dried-up Lady Bentt to intervene.

"None of all that," she piped, "alters the fact that a young stranger has just come into the village and gone off carrying a very heavy box of some sort. I can't help wondering what he can want."

Speculation at once united all six of the other old ladies.

"Selling something," suggested Mrs. Alford, to whose unhearing ears Lady Bentt's shrill voice seemed always to penetrate.

"If I'd had my other glasses on," Mrs. Beastock chimed in, "I'd have seen in a jiffy just what it was he was carrying."

"I'm sure it's something nice," Mrs. Capper happily chirped. "A present perhaps for somebody in the village."

"Yes, like one of those nasty bombs," Mrs. Damworthy boomed.

"Oh, I wish you wouldn't talk about bombs," said Mrs. Emery. "It's nothing but bombs, bombs, bombs nowadays, and no one ever tells me what a hydrogen bomb is. If hydrogen's what I mean."

"Ah, I can tell you about that," Mrs. Finders said with unjustified authority. "It's all to do with H-two-O. Hydrogen bombs are just like the water bombs the nasty boys at school used to throw at us."

The young man with the heavy crate had by now vanished in the direction of the village's other proud amenity, the public convenience.

• • •

But only a few minutes later he appeared again with a somewhat younger stranger, equally affecting Teddy Boy garb. He it was now who was clasping to his chest the big box. Talking away together, they began to strap it back on to the rear of the motor bike. But, finding this left no room on the pillion, they eventually set off in the direction of distant, fenced and gated Goodwood House, with the Fox, if that's what he was, in front and his fellow hen-run raider, the Cub, desperately clutching the awkward crate behind him.

"Did you hear what they were talking about?" fat Mrs. Alford asked loudly as they disappeared. "I thought it was something about going for a walk. But I wonder where they're off to for that?"

"Up to no good wherever they're going," Mrs. Damworthy said as loudly.

"You know, I don't think they said *walk*," Mrs. Finders commented. "I think they said *talk*."

"I expect they just want to have a good talk with somebody," Mrs. Capper sweetly suggested.

There were signs of bristling all along the two benches by now. An argument to be settled, or indulged in.

But little Lady Bentt stepped in once more.

"No, no. What they were discussing was one of those new sort of wirelesses," she piped. "You know, all sorts of people have them nowadays, the army, the police, firemen. They're called walkie-talkies, such a vulgar expression. You can use them to exchange messages over quite a distance, I believe."

Perhaps it was as well that the two Teddy Boys had roared noisily away. If they had heard old Lady Bentt they might have decided to shut her up.

• • •

But, as it was, when only some twenty minutes later the pair came roaring back and parked the bike once more on the convenient patch of gravel just behind the benches, neither of them took any notice of the seven old ladies sitting there in the sun. But the old ladies, every one of them, took notice that the crate, whatever had been in it, was no longer with them.

"Nah," the Fox was saying in answer to some question the Cub had asked while the bike engine still thundered away, "can't do nothing till the first race comes on, can we? Gotter see if it's picking up okay, ain't we?"

Fourteen ears stretched to hear meant that, for a time, six or seven mouths, with a lot to say, remained silent.

But soon Fox and Cub had gone far enough away for comment to be possible.

"They can't do something, that's what they said."

"I saw they were worrying enough about it, whatever it was."

"I'm sure it was only some game. You know what boys are like."

"Boys? Youths like those are far from boyish, I'll tell you that."

"I can't abide voices like theirs. Townee voices I call 'em. They'll be from Brighton, I bet a shilling."

"They were saying they were going to pick up some girls. Disgusting."

Only thoughtful Lady Bentt had no comment to make.

• • •

Before long the two visitors came strolling back, still discussing their business, whatever it was.

"Yeah, but weren't you scared?" said Cub.

"Nah."

"But I mean, going into that place, dead o' night an' all."

"Wouldn't be such a fool go in there when that old idiot was behind the counter, taking the bets, would I? Not that 'e takes all that many. Dead-and-alive place like that."

On they strolled.

"The bigger one said someone was an old idiot. I hope he wasn't talking about me."

"I don't think it was the bigger one, dear. I think it was the younger one. I think he was doing most of the talking, the one who looks as if he's only just out of school."

"I could jump up and go after them, and see which one it really was. You know your sight sometimes does let you down, dear."

"Sometimes? Huh."

"They were talking about making bets. I never like to hear anything to do with that sort of thing. It's not right. I'm sure of that."

"No, no. They were talking about cinema films, what the

youngsters call the flicks nowadays. Someone told me that at Midhurst last week they had one called something like *Dead of Night.* You all must have heard them say that, didn't you?"

"Yes," said Lady Bentt before another argument—well, running quarrel really—could break out. "Yes, we all must have heard those words *Dead of Night.*"

. . .

Though none of the old ladies went to the cinema any- more—the village might have two pubs, a public convenience and a telephone box but that was the full extent of its ameni- ties—they all, except Lady Bentt, were full of notions about the films they never saw, whether a dozen miles away in Mid- hurst or in farther-off bright and breezy Brighton, which none of them had visited more than two or three times in their lives.

So, once the subject of the cinema had been brought to the fore, however mistaken Mrs. Finders may have been about those overhead words *dead o' night,* the talk swung this way and that about the comparative entertainment value of films known only by their titles. Fat Mrs. Alford, though she heard less than half of the talk, was firm in her view that all the stories at the cinema were "nice." Mrs. Beastock, who with her failing sight hadn't seen a film since she had sleuthed along with *Charlie Chan at the Opera* fifteen years earlier, was trenchant in her view that everything you saw in the dark of the cinema was "very clever." Mrs. Capper, while modestly admitting she had never been to the cinema, was certain that "nothing nasty" was ever to be seen there.

On the other hand Mrs. Damworthy condemned out of

hand, and in a very loud voice, the whole art of cinematography, while Mrs. Emery recounted at length, and with interruptions, the story of the last film she had seen, *Strangers on a Train,* and how its characters had caused her intense irritation, with Mrs. Finders simultaneously recounting at equal length the story of a film that turned out after all to have been a play on her wireless.

But all that was brought to an abrupt end when Lady Bentt's little pipe of a voice was heard saying, "Listen!"

The command—for, softly spoken though it might be, a command it was—brought a sudden silence all the way along the row. Then, bit by bit, it penetrated to each of the old ladies, even somehow to deaf Mrs. Alford, that they could hear a distant continuous spiel of talk. There was a voice—it was hard to make out—coming from somewhere saying over and over again what a fine time some people were going to have.

Suddenly doubly bespectacled Mrs. Beastock, whose hearing was perhaps more acute than any of the others, broke out in exclamation.

"It's from the Duke's," she said. "It must be. I don't know how we're hearing it, but that's what it is. It's a man telling the people up there for the racing all about what's going to happen, and sounding very excited."

Now all of them were able to make out what was being said by that tiny, tinny, yet somehow plummy, voice that seemed in fact to be coming not from distant Goodwood House but from somewhere in the village.

It was Lady Bentt who had the final explanation.

"It's a walkie-talkie," she said. "Those two young men must have been putting one half of the one in that crate of theirs somewhere just outside the Duke's grounds and have left the other half out of the way here, somewhere near the—"

She balked for an instant at the words, but then brought them out at full pipe. "Somewhere just by the public convenience."

There was general nodding and yes-yessing agreement that this was indeed what had happened, together with a good deal of claiming to have known it all along.

"Well," Mrs. Alford said in her unnecessarily loud deaf-person's voice, "of course I knew all that was coming from a talkie-walkie. It's just that they can't get it as loud as my wireless."

"And that," Mrs. Damworthy announced from the other bench, "is so loud it can be heard all over the village, whether anybody wants to listen or not."

"Yes," Mrs. Beastock put in her pennyworth, "my sight may not be quite as good as it was, but I knew it was a talking-walker that young man was carrying. No doubt about it."

"Walking-talker?" Mrs. Emery snapped, shrill with indignation. "What you mean is a talkie-walkie. Everybody knows it's called that."

"Well, I'm not sure I knew," Mrs. Capper said gently. "I thought what he was carrying was that nice present for somebody."

"And I think I know who's going to be given it," Mrs. Finders contributed. "It's that—"

"Hush," came Mrs. Damworthy's strident voice. "Can't you see the two of them are coming back again?"

But, though the Fox and his Cub could not but have heard, they were so interested in what they themselves were discussing that Mrs. Damworthy might as well have been whispering.

"But weren't it hard to get in there?" the Cub was asking.

"Hard? Nah. Piece o' cake. Screwdriver at the edge o' that rotten old door, an' Bob's yer Uncle."

"An' after that all you 'ad to do was move the hands o' that clock there on for five or six minutes. And now we're all set."

"All set to make damn fools of ourselves it'd be, you berk. The hands on for five minutes? They had ter go back five minutes. Back. Didn't they?"

"Oh. Oh yeah. Yeah, you're right. Back. Back. But what if the old geezer noticed it when he come in this lunchtime?"

"Notice? Old idiot like that wouldn't notice if that big old clock of his fell off the wall right on his daft head."

• • •

Plenty there for the old ladies to discuss, however little they knew what the Fox and his Cub had been talking about.

"Oh yes," Mrs. Finders told Lady Bentt, who had squeezed down beside her today, "the young man said he moved back the minute hand of some clock somewhere. One of the boys at school played that trick once, and we all were let out ten minutes before we should have been. Yes, and I remember now. It was Peter Parker, the little monkey."

"No, it wasn't," Mrs. Alford trumpeted. "It was that Stanley Sillitoe, and wasn't he pleased with himself. Till you told Teacher, Lily Smith."

"I never. I never," Lily Emery (who had) exclaimed indignantly.

"No, it wasn't Stanley," Mrs. Beastock joined in. "I can see him now, climbing up on a desk to do it. It was Jack Parsons. Always in trouble he was."

"I never liked that Jack Parsons," Mrs. Finders announced. "Anything he said to me was dirty. And that's the truth."

"Oh no," Mrs. Capper put in, almost indignantly, "Jack Parsons was the nicest boy in the school, he really was."

"Of course, I was never at the school in the village," Lady Bentt piped in now, perhaps feeling that the subject should be changed. "But I know all about tricks like that, even the girls at the school where I was used to play them."

Her intervention did indeed change the subject. All six of the other ladies on the benches were avidly interested in Lady Bentt's former life.

• • •

So the Fox and the Cub had been standing directly behind the benches for some minutes before Mrs. Alford, happening to turn round to ease her ample form, spotted the pair of them. She promptly issued a huge splashy whisper.

"It's them. I hope they aren't listening to what we're saying."

It was a good thing, however, that the two Teddy Boys were so engrossed in the conversation they had been having that for them the old ladies on the benches might not have existed. Not even, when after Mrs. Alford's sploshed-out warning there had come an abrupt end to the chattering, did the sudden silence attract their attention.

"Yeah, but . . ." the Cub was going on, voice prickly with anxiety.

"But what? You know, pal, you really aggravate me sometimes."

"But— But, well, how can we be sure your brother's waiting on the other side of the street from the place in Kemp Town?"

"How can we? How can we? How d'you think we can? Ain't the whole point of it all that there's a phone box just beside 'im?"

"Oh yeah. Never thought about that. But all the same he might of gone for a cuppa or something."

"Then why don't you bloody go an' ring him up an' ask 'im?"

"Ring up the phone box?"

"That's right, stupid, the phone box. They got a phone in them, ain't they? With a phone number? What you think we took down the number o' that one for? Why d'you think you got a handful o' sixpences in your pocket? Go on, scram."

The Cub walked hurriedly away.

Seven pairs of aged female eyes watched him go.

"Did I hear—I'm getting a bit deaf, you know—that he's going to the phone box round the corner behind the church?"

"Which way did he go? I missed seeing."

"I'm sure it's nice of him to ring up his friend in Kemp Town, wherever that is."

"I tell you one thing, that lad's up to no good. I know about Kemp Town. It's the nastiest place in Brighton. The late Mr. Damworthy told me that once."

"And let me say I don't think much of the way the big one talked to the smaller one. He was rude. Yes, he was."

"No, I think it was the younger one who was rude to the older one."

It was just as well perhaps, as the Fox stood there on his own listening out for the jabbering bursts of encouragement coming occasionally from the walkie-talkie behind the public convenience, that he did not take in any of the exchange of views just in front of him.

In less than five minutes the Cub returned, face flowing with triumph.

"Yeah, yeah," he burst out. "He's there all right. Picked up on the first ring, an' he's all ready to nip across to the place. Soon as we tell 'im."

"All right, keep yer hair on. Keep yer hair on."

"Yeah, but . . ."

"What now, Chris' sake?"

"Well, what if the old geezer somehow gets to know it's finished? Before your brother can . . ."

"'Ow's he gonna do that, stupid? All he got in that hole of a place of his is the *Pink 'Un,* an' all that's got is the lists o' runners an' the starting times. He's not going to know anymore nor that, is he?"

"No. No, 'spose not."

But then the thin trickle of sound from the direction of the public convenience took on a new, altogether more urgent note.

"Cripes, come on," Fox yelled.

The two of them pelted off.

However, scarcely ten minutes later they were back.

"But— But—" Cub was asking, in plain puzzlement. "Why didn't we do it?"

"Berk. You heard him saying the odds. Two-to-one on that winner. What you think we'd have made by that, fifty quid all we got to put on?"

"Oh. Oh, I see."

• • •

So for most of the long afternoon, while the gossips sat in their long row gossiping, the two Teds kept coming back from their trysts at the hidden walkie-talkie, each time looking more disconsolate.

But then—it was when the last race of the day was being run—suddenly from the direction of the public convenience the Cub came belting along fast as he could toward the old ladies' benches, heading for the phone box just round the corner.

"Silver Blaze, Silver Blaze," he was repeating and repeating, as if in mortal fear he would forget the name.

And, as he drew level, "thirty-three-to-one, thirty-three-to-one."

It was at that exact moment that little, shriveled-up old Lady Bentt suddenly leaned forward and shot out the crook-handled walking-stick that she was never without.

It caught the Cub neatly round the ankle of his right foot, and he fell with a jarring crash flat on to the sun-hardened earth in front of the startled old dears, the sixpenny pieces from his crammed pocket spilling out in a silver shower far and wide on the parched ground.

It took him two good sobbing, breath-seeking minutes to recover. Then awkwardly he scrabbled to his feet, took a look at the corner of the church wall behind them, saw the sixpences and started desperately scraping some of them up, brought out chokingly once more the words "Silver Blaze" and began a tottering attempt at a run toward the phone box.

"I'm afraid you'll be too late," old Lady Bentt, who in her day had gone racing at Goodwood with the best of them, called out to him in her little piping voice. "And I think we had better ask the policeman to go and see your friend with that walkie-talkie." She turned away. "Mrs. Capper, if you would . . . ?" Then she had a last word for the Fox's friend, the Cub. "The man in the betting-shop there in Kemp Town will be sure the race is well over now, so he can't take any bets on it, even if his clock is still five minutes slow."

THE COVER STORY IS ALWAYS A LIE

John Lescroart

I swear to God, Cal, it was like he was talkin' to me."

"The dead guy?"

"The dead guy, who else?"

Cal rolled her eyes, but she was faced away from her husband in the bed, and Arnie didn't see it. Since he'd been forced to take early retirement from the police force, she'd been fairly sure she'd recognized a decline that she'd been mostly unwilling to acknowledge. The possibility that Arnie had even the beginnings of any type of dementia was terrifying in itself, but more so because her own father had started down that road at the not very ripe age of fifty-six and she'd nursed him solo until he blessedly passed at sixty-eight.

And now her own husband, also fifty-six, was talking about communicating with the dead. And this after he'd only been off work a few months, during which there had been a proliferating number of other worrying signs. Depression. Too much drinking. Insomnia. General lack of interest in life.

Or—*be honest*—she told herself. The lack of interest showed itself most clearly around *sex*. They'd been married for thirty-three years and if there had been one constant through the ups and downs of a life together and raising a family of two boys and two girls, it was their love life. Even right up until last year, just before he got the word about his pink slip, they were good for two, three, sometimes four times a week. They would privately marvel at the more and more common admissions of their friends over the years, joking about getting it once a month, where they knew there was truth in it.

They couldn't imagine. Once a *month*? How did they live? Kids, fatigue, blah blah blah. What was the matter with them? Cal and Arnie were both appalled—hadn't any of them heard of the nooner?

But since Arnie had been retired, they themselves had only gotten together three times so far, and none of them in Cal's opinion even up to snuff, much less worth remembering. This from the guy who, when they were first together, considered anything above forty-five minutes a critical dry spell.

She scarcely allowed the word *impotence* to cross her brain, but it deeply worried her. He wouldn't talk about it, had flown into a rage when she'd breathed a mention of Viagra. There wasn't anything wrong, goddammit, he was just *tired*.

Always tired, he told her. Tired and re-tired, get it?

And this living at the racetrack. Arnie, who had never shown the slightest interest in horses or gambling or the attendant characters who didn't seem especially savory, now spent at least three afternoons a week at Golden Gate Fields or Bay Meadows and came home trailing the sour smell of beer. Now her highly decorated San Francisco inspector husband was hanging out, she imagined, with many of the very lowlifes he used to arrest.

Her inclination was to ignore this latest frightening admission about communing with the dead, but suddenly her own denial scared her even more. At least he'd started a conversation, something had caught his interest. Cal rolled over, got up on an elbow. "You're scaring me, Arnie. Dead guys don't talk. Please don't tell me you heard him talk."

He humphhed. "I said it was 'like.'"

"What was like it? You've been a cop for thirty years, I never heard you say anything like that. What was like the dead guy talking?"

"His brother. Jason."

"He's got a brother now? Who is this guy again?" When Arnie had started in on the dead guy talking, she had barely heard, didn't want to hear.

"Les Frankel."

"Okay, I've heard the name. I don't remember he died."

"Last week. At the track. Les was my age and died of a heart attack. I told you."

"All right. It's coming back. I'm listening. Jason the brother, I take it, was at the track, too?"

"No." Arnie paused. "At the funeral."

It was Cal's turn to pause, but just for an instant before she sat up completely, pulling the blankets up around her legs. She reached behind herself and flicked on the bedside light. "You were at a funeral today?"

"I told you that, too. You weren't listening. How do you think I got to talking about the dead guy, Les?" He lowered his voice, not really accusing her of anything directly. He might have been talking to himself. But in a bitter and angry tone.

"Naturally. I don't have a job anymore, you still do. So what I do isn't important."

Suddenly, this was getting to something near the nub of it, and her eyes flashed. "That's not fair, Arnie."

"Pretty close, though."

He got up, threw his own blankets off and, wearing his old man's red plaid pajamas, yanked his bathrobe off the peg in the wall and stalked out of the room.

Cal sat there in the dim light for a minute. Could what Arnie was saying be true? Was some of this her doing as well? Maybe, in fact, she wasn't taking him seriously enough anymore, the experience she'd had with her own father making her close up to him. In fact, was she beginning to see his life now and his concerns as not as important as they once were?

Was some part of her giving him the message that she thought that the real work of raising their family was done, and now he was out to pasture, although not put out to stud, but to wither?

She slipped out of the bed, pulled the afghan around her, and went after him.

Like the rest of the downstairs, the television room was in near total darkness. The outlines of things were only visible because of the LED glow of the digital clock on the TV. It was 11:42.

Arnie sat in his chair and she heard his breathing and the ice tinkling in his glass. Pulling the afghan around her shoulders, she settled into the couch across the room.

"I'm sorry. I want to hear," she said. "What was Jason saying at the funeral?"

"Just a story." She heard her husband take a pull at his drink. "Nothing."

"Arn. Come on."

He sighed deeply. She waited him out. Finally he sighed again and spoke. "Probably nothing. Things didn't quite fit, or fit too good. Whatever happened, it didn't seem to have occurred to Jason, or even to Les, for that matter, that anything might have been wrong. It's just my guts."

"And what are they telling you?"

He seemed reluctant to say it, but then it came out. "I was thinking it sounded maybe like it could be a skull case, that's all."

A skull case was a crime that remained unsolved, especially one that had occurred long ago. One way or another, most murders got solved or didn't in under a week, and either way there was a steady enough stream of new ones to keep big-city homicide inspectors busy. The old ones that remained unsolved for too long simply faded into the past and most of them remained technically open, but no one investigated them.

"How old?" Cal asked.

"Twenty-eight years. Jason said Les was twenty-three when it happened, and that was in seventy-four."

"Twenty-eight years," she said. "What was it, the crime?"

"Might have been nothing."

In the dark, she smiled. "You already said that. But pretending for a moment that it wasn't nothing, that your guts are right."

"If it was something, it was a murder."

She realized she'd been holding her breath. Now she let it out, spoke casually. "I hear you used to do those."

"From time to time."

"Used to be pretty good at them."

"I'd win a few, yeah."

For this moment, then, right now, her husband was back. The low-key banter, a voice with no trace of boredom or fatigue. No tiredness. She wanted to keep him here, feed his interest. "I'm getting a glass of wine. Are you good? What are you having?"

"Scotch." He paused. "But I'm fine." It was the first time in months that he'd refused a refresher on his drink. "In fact, you can dump this." He started to roust himself. "I'll get some water."

"I'll get it. I'm up."

"Such service." He turned on the light by his chair and smiled at her when she took his glass, all but untouched. "You sure you want to hear about this? You've got to get up tomorrow."

"Are you kidding?" she asked. "I love a murder story."

When she got back, she gave him his water, walked back to the couch, curled her feet up under her, and wrapped the afghan over her shoulders. She took a sip of her wine. "So talk to me," she said.

"You've got to remember this is all second-hand, so it's hearsay at best."

"All right." He still looked great, she thought. Not just great for fifty-six, but plain old great for anybody. Always strongly built—big shoulders, no fat—and bullet-headed, now his face exuded a natural authority that went well with the buzz cut and the trim waist. He might, she thought, be an aging officer in the active marines. What fools the bureaucrats in the city had been to let him go! No, not just let him go—*force* him to leave. "Hit me with some hearsay."

"Okay. Four guys, pretty good friends, all lived in apartments in the same building on Bush in the city. Les Frankel, Peter Grant, Jose Ropa, Jeff Vaughn."

"You got the names, I notice. No notes."

He shrugged, but she could tell the comment pleased him. "That's who they were. Four friends, all in their early twenties, all struggling financially since they all wanted to be artists of some kind."

"All of them?"

"We're talking early seventies. What are you gonna do? I think they put something in the water back then."

But Cal sat straight up. "Wait a minute. Peter Grant? The TV anchor?"

"Ten points. One of them made it anyway, huh?" He shrugged. "But anyway, Les and the other two had high hopes, too. Ropa and Vaughn were in a band together, evidently close to getting a record deal. Les was painting—he wound up in advertising specialties, selling them—you know, pens with your company's name on 'em, magnets for your refrigerator, calendars . . ." The subject seemed to depress Arnie. "I guess he made a living."

"But not a good one?"

A shrug. "He and his wife live—lived—in a trailer park in Daly City. God knows what's going to happen to her now. Jason sure didn't, and he didn't seem the picture of wealth himself."

"No kids to help?"

Arnie shook his head dejectedly. "No kids. No insurance. Les evidently chose to believe that he and Lora were going to die on the same day. But they didn't. Bad luck for her."

She sipped at her wine. "So was it Vaughn or Ropa? The one that got killed?"

Arnie smiled at her, then nodded. "You're paying attention."

"Always. So what's Jason's story?"

"The four of them went down to Bay Meadows, taking a day off from whatever it was they did. Each of them brought twenty dollars to bet, total, and they decided they'd get more bang for the buck if they pooled their money and bet as a unit. So now they had eighty bucks."

"Big spenders."

Arnie shrugged. "They were starving artists, all of them. But eighty dollars back in the early seventies—you remember—was probably close to five hundred today, maybe more, so it wasn't peanuts. And I guess what made it worse is that this was one of those desperation moves for all of them. No other money, no hopes. Rent was coming due. They had to hit something."

"So they went to the track? Smart."

"They were kids." Arnie sighed. "Anyway, they put together their forty bets for the day and sent Vaughn to the window."

"One guy? Why didn't they all go?"

Arnie shrugged. "Two of them were getting beer, one was holding their seats. Vaughn just happened to be the one."

"Okay."

"Well, as it turns out, Cal, not so okay. They'd all decided, out of their forty two-dollar bets, to bet eight combinations for the Daily Double—high odds, big return if they hit. But while Vaughn was waiting in line, the guy behind him was jawin' about the Six horse in the first race, how he'd heard he'd pulled up lame. He was still on the card, going out at a hundred-and-ten-to-one, but he had no chance. If Vaughn was smart, he'd bet another horse."

"But they—the four of them?—they had decided to bet the Six horse?"

"Right. As half of a major long shot daily double. Jason had heard the story often enough from Les, he even remembered the thoroughbred's name—Steppin' Pretty. Well, long story short, they're watching the first race and Steppin' Pretty comes in first . . ."

"And Vaughn hadn't bet it?"

"You're psychic. He thought he was doing them a favor, saving the two bucks for a better horse. He told them right after the race. Like, 'Uh, hey guys, sorry, but . . .'"

"So they killed him right then."

"No. They waited until the second horse came in at sixty-five-to-one. Then they stomped him to death." He smiled now over his water. "Not really. But it wasn't a pretty moment."

"How much would they have gotten? If Vaughn had bet Steppin' Pretty?"

"You know how a daily double works?"

"No."

"Well, it's what's called a paramutuel bet, so the odds the horses go out at aren't really the crucial element. Like, say, a five-to-one and a three-to-one hit, the amount each winner gets isn't five times three or anything like that. It's the total amount everybody at the track bet on the double, divided by everybody who bet the winning combination, less about twenty percent that the track keeps for expenses. The good news about two long shots winning the double is that fewer people wind up betting the winning combination." Arnie came forward, his eyes alight. "Evidently, this one, there was one winning ticket. So these guys, theirs would have made two."

"How much?" Cal asked.

"Twenty-one thousand, one hundred twenty dollars."

"Oh my God. On a two-dollar bet?"

Arnie nodded. "That's five thousand, two hundred eighty bucks each."

Cal had recovered from her immediate shock and now whistled. "And this was when eighty dollars was a lot of money? That was a fortune, then."

"Yep."

"They must have been devastated."

Arnie had put his glass down now and chewed at the inside of his cheek. His eyes rested on a spot in the air over his wife's head. He came back down to her. "Evidently it hit them all like an act of God. They were all doomed to fail at everything they tried. Jason said Les never really recovered."

"Never?"

"That's what his brother said. He was *this close*. They were all right there. He'd done everything he was supposed to do and fate just came by and screwed him for the fun of it. And it always would."

"Well, maybe that's a little extreme."

"Wait. Maybe not. Listen. In the next couple of weeks, the whole world of these guys went nuts on them and just fell apart. It turns out that Les's wife—Lora?—was six months' pregnant with twins at the time. Couple of days later, she miscarries. And p.s., it turns out her insides get so messed up she can't have kids at all. Ever."

"Not because this boy Vaughn didn't bet Steppin' Pretty."

"No, of course not. But that with the proximity of the betting disaster . . . Jason told me that was why Les was still so hooked on the track to this day. Someday, somehow, it had to give him back some of what he'd lost. And of course he bet long shots over and over and just lost and lost and lost. He also gave up on painting, on his dreams. It wouldn't matter what he did, or how well he did it, fate was going to get him and make him fail."

"The poor man."

"Yeah. But not only him. Listen to this. Not even a week after Lora's miscarriage, and apparently no relation to any of this, Vaughn turns up mugged and dead."

"Dead? Lord!"

"No kidding. So there goes the record contract for Ropa as well, and Grant freaks out, can't handle the vibe, everything in the world going to hell, he splits for LA. Bottom line is a month after the fine day these four guys spent at the track, their lives are ruined. Three of them—Vaughn, Ropa, and Frankel—pretty much forever."

"So what are you thinking?" Cal asked.

"I wouldn't say it was all the way to a thought, yet. Just a little itch. It's all kind of pat, don't you think?"

"What is? Vaughn not making the bet and everything falling apart?"

"Not so much that," Arnie said. "But what if he had made it after all?"

. . .

Mostly out of habit, Arnie had asked Jason for his card at his brother's funeral, and first thing the next morning he called him, trying to pin down the day and year of the original horse race a little more clearly. Arnie still had friends at the Hall of Justice. He got to the building by 9:30 and told them he was working on his memoirs and after giving him ten minutes of pro forma grief, the lieutenant okayed his admission to records in the building's basement—shelves and shelves of evidence and folders on cases going back fifty years and more.

Jeffrey Vaughn had been killed in October 1974. He had gone out to get a six-pack of beer at a convenience store three blocks from his apartment building—a rough three blocks near Fillmore, Arnie knew. Still rough now nearly thirty years later, even with all the gentrification. As Jason had told him, the crime had never been solved.

Arnie read through everything in the pathetically thin folder. What he found provocative, although it didn't surprise him, was that the investigation never came anywhere near focusing on any of Jeff's friends who'd been at the track with him. There were no transcriptions of taped interviews from Frankel, Grant, or Ropa. The only one mentioned in any of the reports was Ropa, who'd been Vaughn's roommate, but who'd been visiting his family in San Diego for several days on either side of the crime.

The investigation's conclusion was clear: Vaughn's murder was one of those tragic, random events that were all too common in big cities. The white boy should have known better than to walk through the ghetto at night. His killer was never caught.

• • •

Ropa was easy to find. He was listed in the phone book in San Jose. His wife, Stella, was home when Arnie called, identifying himself as a policeman. After assuring her that her husband was in no trouble, she told him that he worked as a paralegal for a law firm in Santa Clara, and Arnie could call him directly there.

They met in the Starbucks near his work at 5:15. Ropa was, from Arnie's perspective, a bit of an unusual guy. His gray hair was pulled back off the face of an Aztec chief. Braided, it hung to his belt. A diamond earring gleamed on one earlobe. But he wore a business suit and spoke perfect, educated English. Like Les Frankel, he was probably close to sixty-five, but he was in better shape than Les had been, and much taller.

At Arnie's quizzical glance, he volunteered that he was mostly, still, a musician—a percussionist with Latin bands— but it didn't pay the bills, so he did this law gig in the daytime. Had been doing it for almost twenty years. It beat the constant scraping. He kept up an easy patter until they'd gotten settled over their lattes, then said, "So, this is about Les? I'm sad to hear he died. I haven't heard his name in years."

"Well, to tell you the truth, it's really more about Jeff Vaughn. I understand you two were roommates."

The strong, dark face clouded over immediately. "Stella said I wasn't in trouble. If I am, that's cool, but we don't talk anymore. I go across the street and get a lawyer."

"You think you need a lawyer?"

"Everybody needs a lawyer, inspector. Maybe not all the time, though. That's what I'm wondering about right now."

Arnie held up a palm. "I didn't lie to your wife. The reports indicated you were out of town when it happened. I don't doubt it."

"Way out. I split for a week to chill at the beach. Things were way too heavy up here."

"In what way?"

Ropa's mouth turned, but it wasn't quite a smile. "In what way not? Jeff was my partner back then. Music. We had a band going pretty good, close to a record deal even if you believed the rumors, and we did. But then suddenly all this weird shit started happening, and Jeff and I were getting ready to kill each other—manner of speaking, okay?—so I thought it would be smart to give ourselves some space, you know? So I split."

"Why were you going to kill each other? Over the music?"

"No, the music was always good. Something else."

"The bet he didn't make?"

Ropa met Arnie's eyes, then looked back down. He seemed to notice his coffee for the first time, and blew on it, but still didn't drink. "How do you know about that?"

"Evidently, the day made an impression on Les. We got to be friends at the track."

This almost brought another smile. "He went back to the nags, huh? Me, I haven't been able to bring myself. I figure God told me once loud and clear—keep the fuck out of here. Next time I'll really hurt you. I didn't want to find out how."

"So, it was a bad day, huh?"

"The worst. Really. But that's got nothing to do with Jeff getting killed?"

It was half a question, and Arnie let it hang there.

"I mean, did it?"

"I don't know. I was wondering whether the thought ever crossed your mind. That Jeff got killed on purpose?"

Ropa tugged at his earring, twisted the little diamond a couple of times. "No," he said slowly. "Any real suspicion of anybody, you mean? I can't . . ."

"Who would it have been?" Arnie interrupted on purpose. Talk always flowed more easily than when it started and stopped and he wanted Ropa's impressions as they occurred, before he could reflect on them.

"Who would who have been?" he asked.

"The person you might have suspected."

"Well, no one, really. Except it was just a little strange . . ."

"What was?"

"Well, Peter . . ." Now Ropa sat back, perhaps surprised at what he'd said. He put his palms up in front of him. "I'm not accusing anybody, you understand?"

"Of course. You're talking Peter Grant, though. Right?"

"You've been working this, haven't you?"

"A little bit. What was weird about Grant?"

"I mean . . ." He shifted in his chair, pulled at his earring again. "His leaving. Just like, 'boom,' adios, gone. And never another word."

"Ever?"

"No. Which like isn't the weirdest thing in the world. I mean, we were kids, coming and going where and when the spirit moved. But the four of us . . ." A shrug. "I don't know."

"You were better friends than that?"

Another shrug. "Maybe not. I can't say I've thought a lot about it."

"Not even when Grant started showing up on TV?"

"No. I was happy for him. He wanted success so bad, like we all did."

"And what was his field? What did he want to make it so badly in?"

"Pretty much what he does now, or did when he started out. Now I guess he's mostly a face, huh? But back then he wanted to be the world's greatest investigative reporter. He was good at secrets, finding stuff out." Now Ropa broke a small smile, remembering. "He was such an arrogant son of a bitch, even before he was famous."

"In what way?"

"Well, you know. He had the same motto then that he uses now—'the cover story is *always* some kind of a lie.' He could be a little abrasive about it, which was probably why he couldn't get work in TV early on, but he was right often enough later. As the whole world now knows."

Certainly, Arnie knew it. Peter Grant was the intellectual's Geraldo Rivera. On his weekly magazine show, *Moment of Truth,* he'd broken more big national stories than *60 Minutes.*

"Let me ask you one more question, Jose. Did you, personally, have any doubts about whether your friend Jeff made the bet or not?"

"No," he said without hesitation. "What do you mean? Of course he didn't make it. He . . ." But suddenly, the words ended. Ropa's coffee cup stopped on its way to his mouth, which hung half open.

"I mean," Arnie pressed, "you were living with him. Did he act funny in any way? Beyond being depressed as you all were about the missed opportunity?"

Ropa put his cup down, met the inspector's eyes. "He was a different person," he said. "That's why I had to split for a few days. He was too weird to live with. He didn't sleep for a minute."

"And you thought it was because he'd lost all that money?"

"Right." Then, defensively for his old friend, "He would never have done that."

"What's that, Jose?"

"Made the bet and then lied about it and kept the money."

"I never said he did. I only asked if he acted different than usual."

"He was just strung out," Ropa said. He tipped up his coffee cup, tapped the cardboard side with his fingers. "He didn't make the bet." But something in the man's manner reflected itself in his dark eyes and told Arnie that Mr. Ropa was no longer completely certain about that.

• • •

As a homicide inspector in San Francisco, Arnie was accustomed to gaining admittance when he wanted to talk to someone. Often, if the person held some important position, he would go through the formality of making an appointment, although this wasn't really necessary. One time, he'd had a problem getting with the head of one of the city's biggest advertising firms. He'd called three or four times and Ms. Claire Patchett was always busy—until Arnie got the feeling she'd be busy for him until she retired. So he'd simply walked into her building, flashed his badge and identification, and the next thing Ms. Patchett knew, her *extremely important* presentation to the firm's *biggest client* was interrupted and halted completely in absolutely medias res by Sergeant Arnold Knepp.

No hard feelings, but he was the police, after all. If he needed to talk to you, it would be on his time, thanks.

But now, in the foreign territory of Los Angeles and no longer working in any official capacity, he didn't have the same prerogatives. For most of the first day, identifying himself to the receptionist as more or less himself, he learned that Mr. Grant was at least as busy as Ms. Patchett had been, maybe more so. By about 4:30, Arnie decided to modify his approach and told the receptionist that he was a San Francisco homicide inspector working on the ancient murder of a friend of Mr. Grant's, a musician named Jeff Vaughn.

Mr. Grant called him back within fifteen minutes. Arnie, drinking a club soda and lime at Houston's Bar in Century City, found the prompt return call somewhat instructive. The voice on the telephone sounded as it did on television—relaxed, avuncular, self-assured. "I'd understood that that case had been closed a long time ago," Grant said.

"No. It's still open. The murderer has never been caught."

"I thought it was a random mugging." A sigh. "Whatever, it was a terrible tragedy. So what are you looking into? Is there some new evidence? How can I possibly help? Of course I remember Jeff, but I barely knew him after all."

The hairs stood up on Arnie's arms as they often did when he got conflicting testimony. "Oh," he said, "I had understood from Jose Ropa and Les Frankel that you four were more of a team than that."

"Well," the voice became softer, caressing, almost conspiratorial, "sergeant. It is sergeant, isn't it? What did you say your name was again?"

"Knepp. Inspector Sergeant." Arnie spelled it for him.

"Well, Inspector Sergeant Knepp, you know how that is. I've found as I've become more well known that people you knew when you were younger tend to remember you as closer acquaintances than perhaps you actually were. I don't really see anything wrong with that if it makes them feel somehow a little more important." He chortled. "But if I had a nickel for every girl who said we'd dated, maybe even really believed we had dated in some way, when I was single, I'd be a millionaire."

Arnie forged ahead. "So you weren't friends with Ropa or Frankel?"

"We were acquaintances, that's all. I haven't seen or heard from either of them since I moved down here. Why? Are one of them suspects?"

"In what?"

Grant paused. "Why, in Vaughn's murder, I had supposed. That's what you said you were investigating, wasn't it?"

"Yes, sir. But neither of them are suspects. Les Frankel, in fact, is dead. He died last week." Arnie gave it a beat, then added pointedly. "At the racetrack."

But this brought no clear response. "Well, I'm sorry to hear about that, of course. And don't I seem to remember that Jose Ropa was out of town at the time?"

"Yes, he was."

"Well, then. I'm afraid, inspector, I don't see what all of this might have to do with me. What are you investigating, exactly? What brought this Jeff Vaughn case back up again?"

Arnie realized that he had come to an impasse. In his enthusiasm for the hunt, he realized that he hadn't done enough homework, and didn't really have any kind of workable plan. Embarrassed and frustrated, he mumbled a few platitudes, thanked the great man for his time, and asked permission to call him again if the case heated up.

"Sure." Grant's voice was warm, even friendly, a chuckle at the edge of it. "I'm always looking to catch up with a good story."

• • •

"No wonder they retired me, Cal. I'm a disaster. I was so focused on getting to talk to him that I forgot that I really had nothing to say once I got him."

"So you're out of practice. Figure out what you'll say when you call him next time. Do you really think he might have done it?"

"My guts say yeah."

"Without any proof at all?"

"Yep."

"Do you think you're likely to find any?"

"After twenty-eight years? Doubtful."

Cal hesitated. "I hope you're remembering the upside of not working with the police anymore."

"What's that?"

"You're not going to like how this sounds, but maybe you don't have to follow all the rules so completely. Maybe there's some bend room." She let him live with that forbidden thought for a beat before she continued. "So why are you so sure it's him?"

"That's what I'm trying to get to. I *know* I've got something in the computer up here between my ears. What I'm having trouble with is retrieving the data, which used to come so easy."

It was Cal's turn to chortle. "No, it didn't. You've always gone through this agony where you feel like you know something before you're aware of exactly what it is. You've got the clue and it's tangible, but you can't identify it yet, that's all."

"So what did I do about it, back in the old days when I worked?"

"Well, you'd start by clearing your mind and often, if you recall, I'd play some small role in that."

"There is a vague memory," he said.

"But after *that,* you'd get up and just replay everything, doodling on the kitchen table, until it settled out. Then, often enough, once you had it, you'd come back in with me."

"That would have been twice in one day, which I keep hearing is impossible for a man my age."

"I don't think so. In fact, I'll bet you a hundred dollars it's not."

"Done, the minute I'm back home. But what do I do now with you in San Francisco and me in LA?"

She was silent for a moment. "You know those dirty nine oh oh calls people pay for? We can pretend."

At the desk in his hotel room, he grinned. "You're bad, you know that?"

"I know," she said. "I thought it was why you liked me."

• • •

Late the following afternoon, Arnie placed his next call to the studios of *Moment of Truth.* As soon as he'd identified himself, the receptionist cut him off. "Excuse me" he said, "but Mr. Grant said to tell you if you called that he is a very busy man and he doesn't have time for people who aren't truthful with him. He's a man who puts great stock in the truth."

"As in, 'the cover story is always a lie'?" Arnie asked.

"Exactly."

"And how was I not truthful with him?"

"You told him you were in homicide. But he phoned a friend in the San Francisco police department last night to verify your credentials and discovered that you no longer work for them. Isn't that true?"

Arnie knew that if he answered this question, the telephone call would be over, and so, most likely, his investigation. "I'd just like you to forward a short message to him. Can you do that?"

"No. He's not interested."

"He will be, I promise. Tell him I stole his picture of Steppin' Pretty."

"You what?"

"You heard me. I've just come from his house up in Bel-Air, big old gated thing. Still, his staff seemed very impressed with my badge and let me right in."

"So you stole . . . ?"

"Steppin' Pretty, framed on his office wall. You got that? Write it down."

"All right, but what is it?"

"A horse. Just tell him. He's still got my number, but I'll hold a minute."

This time, when Grant came on feigning a fit of high dudgeon, Arnie demanded that busy or no, he should come out right now, alone and in person, and meet him at the bar at Houston's.

"You've got no business ordering me around," the anchor said in a voice puffed with self-righteous anger. "If you in fact entered my home under false pretenses as you say, I'll bring the police down with me and have you arrested."

"I don't think you'll want to do that, sir. It would be better if we just talked."

• • •

In person, Grant did not appear as imposing as he did on the air, although he was still an instantly recognizable face to everyone in the restaurant. He was shorter, for one thing, and without makeup looked weary and very much older than Arnie, though they were close to the same age. Still, it was cocktail time in LA, and Grant had to run a gauntlet of groupies and well-wishers before Arnie, at the far end of the bar, finally got his attention by holding up his badge. Since he was Peter Grant, there was no problem seating them so early in a far private corner of the main dining room, where no one else had yet been seated.

He began aggressively enough, his usual style. "You've got a hell of a lot of sand trying to pull whatever crap this is. I don't think you fully understand who you're dealing with."

His back to the corner, Arnie faced the humming room. He came forward to within six inches of Grant's face, his elbows on the table. "I'm dealing with a murderer," he said.

Grant threw his head back in histrionic indignation. "That's the most absurd accusation I've ever heard."

"Maybe," Arnie said, "but you wouldn't be here talking to me if it wasn't true. You wouldn't have answered my call yesterday. You wouldn't have checked on my credentials after our completely nonthreatening conversation yesterday." Seeing that Grant was about to respond again, he stabbed a finger into the air between them. "Don't talk. Listen," he said with quiet authority. "I know that Jeff Vaughn lied that day. He placed the bet that he told you he hadn't, the only winning ticket, and decided to keep all the money for himself."

"I don't know what you're talking about," Grant said. But much of the initial bluster was gone and now he was frozen, his eyes locked on the inspector's face.

"Of course you do. What you don't know is that this may in fact be the luckiest day of your life, at least since the day you drove away from San Francisco with no one even suspecting you'd killed Jeff Vaughn."

"Ridiculous," Grant said again. He pushed his chair back, made as if to get up.

"They keep records, you know. I checked."

Grant hesitated, turned in his chair, and looked back behind him at the crowded bar area, the easy escape to freedom.

"You walk out of here," Arnie said, "my next stop is the cops."

The anchor was halfway out of his seat, clearly torn between his impulses. "They'd arrest you before you knew what hit you," he said.

"Okay," Arnie said easily. "Maybe they will. It's your call."

A last look at the tempting exit, then Grant came back to Arnie and lowered himself. "I'm not admitting anything."

Arnie didn't feel he needed to tell him again that by staying, as by his arrival in the first place, he already had. Instead, he leaned back, crossed a leg, drank from his club soda. "Vaughn didn't pick up the money until a week after the race. I'm assuming you didn't believe his cover story, which we know is always a lie. So you went down with him, or followed him. Either way, you were there when he came out with the money. In cash."

Grant said nothing.

"You know," Arnie continued in a conversational, even amiable tone, "it's lucky they didn't have the rule back then that's in effect nowadays where financial transactions over ten thousand dollars in cash have to be reported to the government. And they took the taxes out right at the park, so it was all cash. I'm thinking they took what? About twenty percent?"

"I admire your imagination," Grant said, "but you're out of your mind."

Arnie offered a polite smile. "We'll see. But in the meanwhile, you confronted Vaughn and he probably offered to split the money with you. I don't know what you thought about that—maybe you were just really mad at the deception in the first place, maybe you thought it would be too much of a hassle hiding it from the other two guys, maybe you just needed the money and it was there for the taking. Whatever, you probably kept Vaughn talking and trying to work something out until it was dark, at which time you suggested a walk down to Fillmore to get some beer. I'm thinking you left the cash in your apartment."

Grant focused on him for a beat, then turned his head to check the still-empty room behind him. Coming back to Arnie, he lowered his voice. "You can't prove a word of any of this."

"Ah," Arnie held up a finger, "but that's the beauty of it. Of course I can. It's only a matter of putting in the manpower. No one's even glanced at you for this before and once they start, it's really child's play. They check your bank records when you first arrived here in LA and find a twenty-thousand-dollar deposit, for example, within a month of blowing out of San Francisco where everybody, and certainly Jose Ropa, would testify that to their own personal knowledge, you were poor as a dormouse. No, proving this stuff will be a piece of cake. The minute they turn the fire up under this, you are toast. You really would do well to believe this."

Grant tried a last haughty smile. "And why is that?"

"Because here's the funny truth, *your own* cover story was a lie. That's what I finally realized had been right there in front of me all the time. You *loved* telling all of America every week that the cover story was *always* a lie, didn't you? All the imbeciles out there in TV land who just didn't get it, that you were telling them the deepest truth about yourself."

"And why would I want to do that?"

"Because you, Mister Peter Grant, have always been an arrogant guy. It's why you couldn't resist hanging a photograph of Steppin' Pretty in your office. I never thought I'd find anything that obvious—I was hoping for an old checkbook, maybe, or the race program for the day, and even those were long shots, but I needed something that, if it wasn't actually hard proof, would at least get you to talk to me again. Then, as soon as I saw the picture, of course, it all made perfect sense. Although I must admit that the balls it took to do that surprised even me. That's just who you are." Arnie tipped up his glass, sucked on an ice cube. "Any time you'd like to help me out with any of this, fill in the missing pieces, just jump right in."

"Are you gentlemen all right?" the waiter asked.

"Maybe a refill on the soda, thanks," Arnie said.

"Mr. Grant?"

Grant pointed at his untouched drink. "I'm good," he said. After the waiter withdrew, he leaned forward. "So? What do you want? Is this blackmail? Is that it?"

"Actually, it's a little better than blackmail. Let's wait a minute, here's the waiter again. I love the service here." With a fresh club soda in front of him, Arnie spun the glass with both hands. "Here's the thing, and the reason it's your lucky day. For reasons of my own, I'm not feeling too good about the police myself lately, the way they do things. I'm not particularly inclined to do their work for them and I think it's likely to the point of certainty that if I just forget this whole thing and walk out of here, this whole issue of Jeff Vaughn's murder will never arise again. Of course, that would put me in great jeopardy. You could just have me silenced and that would be the end of it for you. But," Arnie said, "because mama didn't raise a fool, I've taken the precaution of sending your nice photograph of Steppin' Pretty to a friend, along with instructions as to what he might like to do with it in the event of my unfortunate death or disability."

Grant spoke through gritted teeth. "You're actually liking this, aren't you?"

Arnie gave it a serious beat, then broke a smile that would have been positively cheerful if he hadn't realized that that would have struck a wrong note, so he toned it down. "I've had worse days, after all, to be honest," he said soberly. "But the real issue, as you put it, is what do I want?"

"I'm listening."

"Good. Because I want you to understand this very clearly." All trace of the earlier smile was gone. Arnie reached into his shirt pocket and extracted a piece of paper upon which he'd scribbled several columns of numbers. "In nineteen seventy-four, you stole twenty-one thousand, one hundred and twenty dollars from Jeff Vaughn and, really, from your other two friends. Actually, it was less than that because of the taxes, but I already did the figuring and I'm going with the gross amount. Figuring ten percent interest compounded yearly, which is another break I'm giving you since I could also have compounded it daily, that comes to three hundred and four thousand, five hundred seventy-one dollars today. That's the straight settlement amount, if you want to look at it that way. But I think we'll both agree that some punitive damages are called for here as well, since you murdered to get your hands on this money. Punitives usually run three times the settlement amount, as I'm sure you know. So that brings us to nine hundred and thirteen thousand, seven hundred and thirteen dollars, which is ciose enough to a million to round it up, don't you agree?"

"You think I've got a million dollars lying around?"

"Mr. Grant, please don't insult me. I was up at your house today, remember. The cars alone, the art in the living room . . ." Arnie shook his head. "Don't tempt me to ask for more. A million is a reasonable figure."

Grant's weathered face had gone white.

But again, Arnie held up a finger, checking him before he could speak. "If it's a help, you should know that I, personally, don't want the million dollars at all. I want you to send a cashier's check for that amount to Lora Frankel. She lives in a trailer park in Daly City. I've got the address."

"Lora Frankel?"

Arnie nodded. "Les's wife. Who you may recall lost twin babies over this whole thing, and subsequently she and Les could never have children at all. You stole that money from them, and now that Les is gone, she needs it desperately. I think it's only fair that you pay her back."

"Then what?"

"Then I send you your picture of Steppin' Pretty and my notes for the formal police investigation, the whole package. Which if you're smart, you'll destroy."

"The originals, you mean?"

"Right. The one and onlies."

"And this will never come up again?"

"That's right."

"What if I don't believe you?"

"Well, then you'll probably wind up doing a lot of needless worrying in your future life. I wouldn't go there. It won't happen." Arnie raised his chin. "Look, Mr. Grant, this is the deal of a lifetime I'm offering here. You take it, you're out a little money you can easily afford. You don't, you go to jail, maybe even face the death penalty. You're telling me you need to think about this?"

"So this Lora Frankel suddenly gets a check for a million dollars. How do you explain that?"

"I don't. I thought I'd let you come up with some really good cover story."

• • •

Arnie gave Grant three weeks to send the check before he would deliver the package including the photo to the police. He did it with four days to spare. The famous Mr. Peter Grant was sure that Lora wouldn't remember specifically, but the money was a dividend from a penny stock that had been a precursor to a precursor of a company that had finally merged into Cisco. He and his old friend Les had invested in it back in the early seventies when they'd all used to hang out together. He'd come across the original stock certificate, in Grant's name only—ten thousand shares for which they'd pooled their money and spent a hundred dollars—when he'd been going through his old files. On the certificate itself, though, he'd written "half for Les Frankel," and now this payment was his debt of honor repaid. As a personal favor, Grant asked Lora to keep the news of the distribution as quiet as possible. In his position as a serious newsman, he didn't crave publicity for his own sake. Grant was sure she understood.

In the same three weeks, Arnie had rented a small office a few blocks both from their home and from Cal's workplace in the Sunset District. He'd sent a letter out to all the attorneys he knew in the city, advertising his services as a private investigator as soon as his license came through, which should be very shortly. He'd already gotten fourteen calls.

Now he was opening the blinds, letting the sunlight back in after a lunch hour during which he and his wife had broken in—as they put it—the fold-a-bed in the new office digs. Cal was buttoning up her blouse. "Under the circumstances," she told Arnie, "I'll bet he could have told her to super-glue her lips together for six weeks and she would have done it."

"For a million bucks, I might be tempted to do the same thing."

"You do," Cal said, "and I'll kill you."

RAINDANCER

Michael Malone

Please listen, Mr. Jones. Loopy is a hundred percent sure about rain tomorrow. Nobody can beat us on a muddy track."

"Loopy is a hundred percent sure of zero."

"But, Mr. Jones, it's like destiny. I can do it in one-forty-six. Raindancer—" The teenaged Michelle Harlin stood there arguing, small, trim, prettier than she thought, with tight black curls that shook with the vigor of her effort to persuade her trainer of her conviction.

"You've got an occupation, Michelle, not a destiny. And please call that horse by his proper name. His name is Fortune's Child." Tall and thin, Jones, the trainer at Campbell Farms, was an African American in his fifties, fair enough to freckle, with large still hands knobbled by arthritis. His style was so formal that, even in the stables, he wore his dotted tie tucked into a white shirt, the sleeves precisely rolled to sharp elbows; so formal that when asked his name, he replied always, "Mr. Jones."

"Go home, Michelle." His habitual firmness was tempered with a nod on the verge of an affection never made explicit.

"You know what to do. What Mr. Grandors has hired you to do." He locked a metal box on his desk and then placed the box in a drawer that he also locked.

The young woman jumped from atop the tack trunk. "Home? Why? Mama will get off work at the bar and we'll go home to a trailer and watch TV. And the bar will be playing the same dumb songs and the same dumb drunks will be singing along. So . . . oh whatever."

Michelle stepped around a tanned young man, Mr. Grandors's son, here on spring break from college for the races. Saddle over his shoulder, he grinned, waving.

The trainer Jones was already walking away from her, down the long corridor of stalls. Around him dozens of stable hands and grooms hurried back and forth. He nodded at a few men nearby before stopping at the last stall, beyond which stretched perfect meadows of Kentucky bluegrass. At this stall, the sheen of the enameled white wood gleamed and the bright brass hinges on the door flashed in the low slant of sun. On the stall door, a wreath of roses circled a brass plate with the name SPATS.

Jones gave a tap on the door; inside it, a big roan thoroughbred whinnied. When Michelle stepped up beside the trainer, he pointed to the horse. "Spats is going to win tomorrow. Spats is going off the morning-line favorite. Post time Spats will still be the favorite, and a gargantuan sum—"

"What does that mean?"

"Large. A large amount of Mr. Grandors's money—"

"I don't care. I—"

"Spats is the horse can win the Bluegrass. Only horse can beat Spats tomorrow is Windsong. Not you and Fortune's Child, not even on a muddy track. One-forty-six? Not going to happen." Jones felt in his pocket for his car keys; the silver key ring was shaped like a bridle. "So you stick to what we planned, Michelle. You rabbit the Child through the first quarter so fast you wear out Windsong. That's your job." He pointed to a door two stalls back inside the stables where a gray horse stood, craning his neck toward the young jockey. "Fortune's Child's not going to win that race tomorrow. He couldn't win if we wanted him to, which we don't. What's the first thing I told you about Fortune's Child?"

"He couldn't win. You told me he couldn't win."

"That's right." More than a year ago they'd had that conversation here at the Farms. The trainer Mr. Jones was leaning against the paddock fence one dawn, watching while a Costa Rican groom named Loopy legged Michelle up into the tack. She was taking the young thoroughbred Fortune's Child out for a run. Jones said to her then, "The Child's a mornin'-glory of a horse. And that's all he is." In other words, the gray would run like the wind at his morning workout, at least when Michelle Harlin rode him. But in a real race, and real races were in the afternoon, he'd fade away in the backstretch every time.

Now, remembering that, Michelle set her jaw at her boss. "He's not just a morning glory. We did win. You saw. Raindancer will win if I ask him to."

Loopy the groom suddenly popped up behind two exercise boys who were walking their horses back to their stalls. Loopy had a startling habit of appearing and disappearing without notice. He tipped his red cap, which had the name of the champion SPATS spelled on it in white letters. Loopy spoke eagerly. "Raindancer do it for her, that horse, that's true. He come 'round the pole so fast he pull Jesus off the cross."

Mr. Jones held up his hand like a stop signal. "Loopy, stay out of this."

"Yes, señor, all right." Loopy's brown hard-muscled arms crossed protectively over his T-shirt. He backed away.

The trainer motioned the girl to walk with him to his car. "Michelle, you're doing plenty if you push Windsong to the first pole in twenty-two or under. You drew a rotten post, fourteen. You gotta come from way outside. You gotta get over fast."

"I can get over in twenty-one."

"Maybe. You set that pace out of the gate, you're doing your job."

"You say my job is to do the best I . . . You say I have a gift."

"You do have a gift, but you won't have a life. College—"

"I don't want to go to college. I want to win this race."

He shook the bridle key ring at her. "Well, tomorrow you just make sure Windsong doesn't."

The tall man's thin shadow shimmered across the groomed gravel as he moved past a group of tourists visiting the Farms. His car was an unexpectedly sporty one for such a formal man, a blue Chevrolet Corvette Z06 convertible. But Raylan Jones, although himself measured in tempo, was an admirer of speed. He had a high regard for a car that could go 185 mph. As a young exercise boy at Churchill Downs, Jones had watched Secretariat win the Derby in one minute, fifty-nine and two-fifths seconds, and he had then followed Secretariat to Baltimore, where he saw the big red horse set another track record at the Preakness. Then up in New York there'd been another record at the Belmont, thirty-one lengths ahead of the rest of the field. That memorable day, CBS couldn't even get the second horse in the same camera angle with Secretariat at the wire. For the next twenty-five years Mr. Jones had worked as a thoroughbred trainer because in his youth he'd seen Secretariat and had admired his speed. He'd had hopes of training a horse of that caliber (Spats had a little of Secretariat's lineage), but no one had ever come close. Raylan Jones was fairly sure he'd never see anything like that 1973 Triple Crown victory again.

Michelle kept telling him that he was wrong, that right here in Lexington, he could see the gray stallion named Fortune's Child, the gray she called Raindancer, do something just that splendid.

"Well, you like to think so," Jones always replied, not unkindly. "But that horse is not a champion."

Now, the evening before the mile-and-an-eighth race, the Bluegrass Stakes, he was telling her she wouldn't even come in third.

The trainer slid carefully into his Corvette, then turned the motor back off and leaned out. "You want a ride?" He'd never offered Michelle a ride before.

"Thanks, but I need to talk to Raindancer, give him his cookie."

He smiled in his slow way. "Well, just don't eat it yourself. Tomorrow—you weigh in, one-oh-seven, am I right?"

"You're always right, Mr. Jones."

The owner's son came trotting out of the stables on one of the exercise ponies. He gestured a salute to them with his riding stick.

"Eric's a nice kid," said the trainer. "College kid."

"He's okay." The girl shrugged and looked away.

After Jones drove off, Michelle returned to the stables,

where she saw the groom Loopy gesturing furtively with his red cap for her to follow him. To her surprise Loopy led her toward Mr. Jones's small office at the end of the stables.

The other grooms at Campbell Farms called Luis Rojas "Loopy" because, many years ago, a horse panicking in the starting gate had crushed against his leg, ending his career as a jockey. As a result of the injury, he walked at a quick odd off-balance tilt, one that worsened whenever he'd had a few beers, which was often.

There was nobody else around at the far end of the stables. Loopy held a ring of metal picks in his scarred hand, using one of them with a fast furtive motion to open the trainer's office door.

Michelle was shocked. "Loopy, what the F are you doing?"

Silently he moved her brusquely inside, locking the door behind them. In the dusky office, he chose another pick from his ring and used it to open a desk drawer. He took out Jones's metal box and opened it. The box was full of money.

"Jesus, Loopy! You *cabron*! Put that back!"

But the short man shrugged, pouring stacks of bills, neatly bound with rubber bands, onto the seat of an old leather recliner. He whispered to her, "That's ten thousand, eight hundred dollars. Just sitting here."

Michelle grabbed the money from the chair. "That's Mr. Jones's! It's, like, his savings!"

Loopy let her stuff the bills back in the metal box. "Maybe so. Tomorrow, we gonna put it all on Raindancer."

"You can't rob Mr. Jones!"

Nodding, he smiled at her. "He never gonna know. You gonna win the Bluegrass, Michelle. That gray horse love you. Raindancer do anything you ask him. You gonna ask him, come on, big boy, win this thing for me and Loopy's poor little five baby children."

They heard laughter just outside the office. Michelle pressed against the door, listening while two of the exercise boys moved past, talking lewdly about the owner Mr. Grandors's trophy wife, and how she was probably the same age as his son Eric, and how she was probably sleeping with Eric, too. "Assholes," Michelle muttered. Finally the men's voices faded.

Michelle returned to Loopy. "So let me get this straight. You're going to steal Mr. Jones's money and bet it on Raindancer?"

"No, your mama going to bet it for us. Little bit this window, little bit that window. People don't think nothing. Mama just betting her heart."

"No way. You'll get a bonus anyhow if I do win. We'll both get one."

"That bonus is a lousy penny. You and Fortune's Child going off, seventy-to-one, I bet. You and me, this way." He tapped the metal box. "We gonna win about seven hundred thousand dollars. You know how your mama want that house. You can get it. After we win, we put this money back for Mr. Jones. He never know a thing."

"You're loco." But Michelle kept looking at the box the man was holding out to her. ". . . You really think I can beat Spats?"

He pushed the money into her hands. "Girl, I know you can."

• • •

Raindancer and Michelle had met on her birthday, as if the gray colt had been some sort of surprise present. That day in early June, she was hurrying late from school to the roadside tavern where her mother worked as a bartender. A sudden storm caught her as she cut across a Campbell Farms meadow. She went there hoping to see some of the horses that lived at the thousand-acre luxury stables. She'd been watching them for years.

Stung by the hard rain, she raced to the edge of the blue-grass field, where blossoming groves of cherry trees and apple trees grew close together, dark and thick.

It was odd that she felt no fear when the gray colt ran so noisily out of the shadows of the orchard. It was odd because things did scare her then, like when a teacher called her name, or if she suddenly awakened in the trailer in the middle of the night and saw that her mother had not come home.

Rain was beating the apple blossoms into a swirl around the horse as he weaved through the low boughs of the old trees. He looked to her as if he were dancing in the rain, unable to decide what he wanted to do next. Finally, he veered to a stop with a shiver in front of her. They stared at each other, and after a while, she took a cream sandwich cookie from her wet backpack and, stepping toward him, carefully held it out.

There was an arc of wryness in his way of his turning his head a little to the side before accepting the cookie from her outstretched hand. It made her laugh. "You're funny," she said. "You're a Raindancer." He nodded his head as if he liked the name. Then he butted his nose against her backpack. She found a candy bar for him.

When the rain stopped as suddenly as it had begun, the horse galloped away just when a white van with CAMPBELL FARMS written across the side roared up the dirt road beside the orchard. A small Latino man jumped out, holding a lead line, yelling at the gray colt, "Son of a bitch! *Vuelto aquí ahora!*"

That was how Michelle had met Loopy Rojas, who'd immediately started complaining to her about the horse as if he'd known her for years and was certain of her sympathy. "*Híbrido!* That bastard son of a bitch colt, he think he king of the world. Since he's a little baby, he's trying to get me fired. He run off three days one time. They just now break him with the yearlings and he jump the fence!"

Michelle was sympathetic; she'd run away from home herself several times when she was little, taking off to look for her father, although she had no idea where he might be. She tried to strike a deal. "I'll help you catch that horse if you teach me to ride."

"You loca. He got a big buck in him this one, you let him get his head down, you flying to the moon. He's a mess."

"No, he's not." Michelle saw a gray shimmer as the colt moved in the orchard. She gestured for Loopy to look behind a clump of apple trees. "He's watching us. I don't think he likes you."

Loopy laughed loudly. "That's the truth. He don't like me. Mr. Jones gonna fire my ass. I got five babies. Ya ya ya ya ya!" He appeared to realize only now that he was talking to a stranger. "You look like somebody I know. What's your name?"

"Michelle Harlin."

He stared hard at her, then shook his head. "No, I don't know that name." He held out a soiled hand. "I'm Loopy. This horse gonna be my death."

"You stay here." Taking the lead line from him, she started toward the dark trees.

The horse Michelle called Raindancer was officially known as Fortune's Child, the name she saw engraved in brass on his halter when he bent his head to take another cookie and let her snap on the lead line. Foaled and bred in the Kentucky bluegrass, he had been the star weanling at Campbell Farms until his "acting up" turned his trainer Mr. Jones against him. Fortune's Child came from a much better family, far better known, than Michelle's. He was the grandson of the great Fortune, who had never lost a stakes race in his life; his mother was WeepNoMoreMyLady, winner of the Breeders Cup Mile, who'd set a record on a muddy track, who was Filly of the Year. Fortune's Child could trace his ancestry all the way back to Gallant Fox, the 1930 Triple Crown winner.

Michelle's parents were nobodies. Her mother, a foster child, had been for twenty years bartender at the Finish Line, a roadhouse not far from the Keeneland, Kentucky, racetracks. Betsy "Bits" Harlin had one big dream, to own a house you couldn't move. She still lived in a trailer. She had named her daughter for the Beatles' song "Michelle," looking for a little romance in a hard life. It hadn't come. Well, it had come a few times, but it hadn't stayed. Bits had always been, she admitted, a sucker for anyone talking a foreign language. She'd been a sucker for the good-looking jockey from Tijuana, the self-named "El Canon," who'd spent a month in her trailer while racing second-rate mounts at Keeneland. On the best day of his life, he'd finished third. El Canon had left town without knowing that Bits Harlin was pregnant.

"He was a little man, but he was a big mistake," Bits told her daughter years later, when Michelle started asking about her father. "Hey, anyhow, he left me the best thing in my life. You."

It was doubtless because the groom Loopy was from Central America and because he knew all about horses that Michelle had liked him from the first. After he told her that he'd realized that the person she looked like was her father (whom Loopy had met at Keeneland), after he let her hang out at the stables, after he arranged for her to be hired to work in the stalls, after he let her ride Raindancer, she had come to love Luis Rojas.

He lived in a tack room at the Farms, his hot plate and little TV on a shelf, his clothes stored beneath. For years, he had mailed money home to his large family in Costa Rica. He was a good groom. Of all the Campbell Farms thoroughbreds, only Raindancer seemed to distrust him. But Loopy accepted that. And he could see from that first day in the rain that the gray colt had fallen in love with Michelle. A year after they met, watching Michelle hotwalk Raindancer, Loopy told her, "Girl, one day you going to bring your papa back his honor."

By then Michelle was, in her mother's phrase, "horse crazy like your crazy dad." Bits Harlin didn't worry at first. "I guess a lot of girls go through the phase. It won't last." Michelle, however, knew that it would last, that she had inherited a passion from her father El Canon.

Over the next year, Loopy taught her all he knew, and he knew a lot. Grooms, he said, always know the most about thoroughbreds; trainers the next most. Owners know nothing; she should never listen to owners—the thin women wearing hats and pearls, the beefy men in blazers and bright ties. A smart jockey will always avoid owners and listen to grooms. Take Spats in there in the Number One stall, for example. Did his owner, Mr. Grandors, who lived in Naples, Florida, who also owned but cared far less about Fortune's Child, know the difference between those two animals? And did Spats's hotshot jockey really know his mount any more than Mr. Grandors? "Spats in there a little funny, faking how he's sore. Deep down, he don't care, not like Raindancer."

The day that Michelle brought Luis Rojas with her to the Finish Line to "explain" things to her mother, to admit that she'd been working for more than a year at Campbell Farms, sneaking out of the trailer each day before dawn to clean stables, Bits had blamed everything on Loopy.

Betsy "Bits" Harlin took a draw on her long menthol cigarette that day and sighed out the smoke. With a shake of her blonde curls, she pointed her cigarette at the fidgeting Loopy. "I'm looking at you, I'm looking at trouble." Closing the real estate section of the paper that she was always studying, she crossed her arms tightly over her turquoise T-shirt. "Don't let the door hit your backside, Mr. Rojas."

"*Buenos dias*, señora." Loopy smiled, tipping his red cap to the petite woman with hair too big for her thin tired pretty face.

"And, hey, don't try that Latin salsa on me, man." Michelle's mother scrubbed so hard at the bar that she sent a plastic bowl of peanuts spilling down the counter onto a man who didn't notice; a man with the look of someone who'd lost every race he'd bet on for years. Refilling the bowl, Bits Harlin told Loopy, "*No mas,* amigo. Adiós. Been there."

It was then that Loopy told Michelle's mother that he'd known her former lover El Canon and that El Canon's dream while in Lexington had been to win the Bluegrass Stakes at Keeneland. He had not succeeded, although it was that year, the year of his romance with Bits, that the Mexican jockey had come in third in the Bluegrass—the first and last time he'd ever been in the money. It was that year that Michelle had been conceived. (It had been, in fact, that very April day, right after the Bluegrass Stakes, as Bits admitted to herself, but not to Loopy.)

Not that night, but a few weeks later, Loopy told Bits and Michelle that El Canon had died years ago from eleven knife wounds inflicted in a jockey room somewhere abroad, stabbed by a fellow rider who was high on cocaine and certain that his wife was cheating on him. Bits and Michelle hadn't known. The news was no real surprise to Bits.

In the Finish Line bar the night he told them about El Canon's death, Loopy had stood up to Bits Harlin, his arm flung in a paternal way over Michelle's shoulder. "Someday this girl gonna come in first. She gonna make her daddy proud. She gonna give back his honor."

"Give back?" said Bits.

But after a month of pressure, Bits succumbed: As long as Michelle kept her grades high enough to get into college, she was allowed to keep working before and after school at Campbell Farms. It wasn't much of a salary for showing up at five a.m., seven days a week, to help Loopy and the other grooms take off the night bandages, feed and brush the horses, clean out their stalls and tack them up for the morning riders. It wasn't much money, but although she pretended to her mother that she was doing it for money, she wasn't. She was doing it for the chance to race.

One day at first light, Mr. Jones saw Michelle galloping Fortune's Child on the exercise track. His first impulse was to send her packing and to fire Loopy. However, Mr. Jones was not a man who acted on first impulses. Instead he clocked her. The girl and the big gray ran the mile and a quarter in 1:59 and 7/8ths of a second.

The next day in fresh starched shirt and Harris tweed suit, Mr. Jones paid a formal call on Bits Harlin at the Finish Line to discuss Michelle. Two days later he brought Bits a fair and reasonable contract engaging her daughter as a jockey at Campbell Farms. He always called Bits Mrs. Harlin, although Harlin was her maiden name. "I like his style," Bits told Michelle. "He's definitely premier label."

The next week Jones started to train Michelle to ride the horse he kept instructing her, unsuccessfully, to refer to as Fortune's Child instead of Raindancer. The trainer was methodical and repetitive, insisting that she study things she thought she already knew, teaching her to change bad habits for which she'd been compensating unaware.

She worked so hard and on so little sleep that she passed out one day in class. Her mother blamed Loopy, telling him he was "the cheap blend," while Mr. Jones was private barrel single malt.

"Senora," he said, tapping his cap on the bar. "I'm just trying to feed my babies, like you. That's all."

"Yeah, well," she said, "don't use my baby to do it."

When Michelle Harlin ran her first race at Keeneland, Bits told Loopy she wouldn't come to the track, not to watch her daughter "throw her life away." But at the last minute she did so, running down the aisle, leaning over the rail, yelling herself hoarse when Michelle finished fifth. The following Saturday, at the ten-dollar window, Bits bet Fortune's Child to Win. He placed. A week later, on a rainy afternoon, he won for the first time.

Michelle and the gray colt went on to win three of their next four races; the last race again in the rain. Pictures of horse and rider began to show up in the local papers.

GIRL RIDES FORTUNE'S CHILD TO VICTORY

RAIN NO PROBLEM FOR FORTUNE'S CHILD

AND FEMALE JOCKEY

A television reporter sneaked a camera into Campbell Farms; he learned from Michelle that Fortune's Child's barn name was Raindancer and that she herself had been named for a Beatles song. He did a little piece about her on the news that night. Racing papers liked the angle. Soon there were head-lines like RAINDANCING! above a shot of the mud-splattered horse and jockey crossing the finish line, alone. And a full-page front cover: OH, MICHELLE MA BELLE! with a picture of the gray thoroughbred nuzzling the girl's short black curls. The owner's son, Eric Grandors, gave Michelle a copy of the RAINDANCING! photograph in a nice frame.

Michelle rode the gray to victory up and down the Eastern circuit: a mile, a mile-and-an-eighth, a mile-and-a-quarter. Then in Delaware another horse bumped them so hard in the backstretch that Raindancer fell almost to his knees and Michelle was banged against the inside rail. She broke her collarbone, falling after crossing the wire. Publicly, Jones filed a complaint. Privately, he feared Michelle would be too rattled by the accident ever to race again. It was one of the reasons why so many jockeys got addicted to cocaine; they used the drug to fight off fear after a fall.

But three weeks later, back at Keeneland, in the rain on a sloppy track, Raindancer won a mile-and-a-half stakes race by ten lengths. It was the fastest he'd ever run. In the winner's circle, Michelle told Loopy that she had been able to feel the gray stallion move his position beneath her, shifting his weight to favor her strapped left side, speeding so far out in front of the field that no other horse could get anywhere near them. "He protecting you. He love you." Loopy shrugged.

It was there in the winner's circle that day that Mr. Grandors, Raindancer's owner, spoke to her for the first time other than to say, "Hello." He hadn't heard about her collarbone injury. She'd begged Jones not to tell him, fearing he'd replace her as the jockey. "Nice ride," he said without looking at her. "But don't use the Child up; not if you got the lead. One length's as good as ten."

"Yes, sir. I think we can win the Bluegrass, Mr. Grandors."

"Honey, you're not paid to think," said Grandors with a smile that moved his mouth quickly, like a trap. Michelle saw that his son, Eric, standing nearby, didn't like what his father had said.

Then the day before the Bluegrass Stakes race, Mr. Jones called Michelle into his office. As he took a phone call, Michelle, waiting, studied the framed photographs of horses on his walls, in pride of place a picture of Secretariat. Below the pictures were hand-built shelves of paperback books, many of them used textbooks from the college store: *Europe in the Middle Ages, First Year Spanish, My Antonia.*

Jones told her that he had just had a talk with Mr. Grandors. She was not even to try to win the Bluegrass. It was Spats's year to win. Fortune's Child was to serve as a sacrifice; Michelle was to use his speed out of the gate to set so torrid a pace in the first part of the race that the favorite's most serious rival, Windsong, trying to keep up, would fade in the stretch, leaving Spats, a classic closer, to win.

Michelle had been so surprised that she blurted out, "That's not right, Mr. Jones."

His mouth twitched under a peppery mustache that hid a scar from a horse's kick long ago. "Yes, it is. Both these horses belong to Mr. Grandors. His money is on Spats. It's his prerogative."

"I don't know what *prerogative* means."

He nodded. "That's why you're going to college. So you will know." He told her that she had a job, not a destiny.

Michelle understood about sacrificial pacesetters. Mr. Jones had taught her about the kinds of maneuvering that went on in racing. But she'd never thought he'd allow anything that wasn't "right," any more than she could imagine him drunk or having a temper fit. And if Raindancer had a chance to win, wasn't it a cheat to take that chance away from him? Weren't the trainer's stories all moral tales about what happened to cheaters? All right, what Jones was telling her to do was not as bad as bribing a jockey to pull a favorite back, or fraying a cinch, or hiding a dangerous heart stimulant in a carrot. It was not as bad as the way trainers had given Viagra to their horses, even though some of the horses had died from overdoses. "Cheating only cheats the cheater," Jones had often told the girl. "In the short run, you can fix a race, but in the end the best horse is the one with the best record. In the long run, go with the real odds."

In the end, shouldn't Raindancer win if he could? And if he did win . . .

• • •

Loopy Rojas took the money box from her and stuffed the cash into her knapsack. She said nothing as he put the box back in place and locked Mr. Jones's office behind them.

"You can win," he told her at the entrance to the stables. "I don't know much. But I know you. I know Raindancer. I know Spats. I know it's gonna rain. One-forty-six-something, you gonna do it." He pulled her head toward him and kissed her curls, then pushed her away.

Loopy Rojas had his own rules. They were unlike the code by which Michelle had once thought Mr. Jones lived. Loopy appeared to see nothing wrong with fighting or lying, drinking or even stealing. Loopy's rules were practical: Like, "Maybe coke keeps you skinny and maybe it makes you brave. But it makes you crazy, like the loco that stabbed your daddy."

Another rule, the one Loopy now told her to pass along to her mother with the stolen money, was that, starting at 12:30 tomorrow, at Keeneland racetrack, Bits Harlin should place bets at as many different windows as possible, always betting different small amounts, saving her biggest bets to the last possible minute.

Michelle made one more effort to talk Loopy into putting the money back in Jones's desk drawer. "My mom's not going to believe you saved up ten thousand dollars. What if she decides to call the police and get you arrested?"

"Then you phone me quick and I'll be on the road out of this crazy country before the police get the key in their big car. And lose that race? Same thing. Luis Rojas is dust on the road. But you gonna win. Your padre in heaven gonna be proud."

"My dad went to heaven? I doubt it."

"Doubt's a terrible thing, chica. I see you tomorrow." And he was gone in that fast slanting way of his.

Hours later, when Michelle walked into the Finish Line, she still hadn't decided what she was going to say to her mother.

Then, suddenly all that cash burned hot as coals in her backpack. She saw Mr. Jones seated at the smoky bar, talking to Bits Harlin. Mr. Jones, who couldn't bear the smell of cigarettes, sat with his white-shirted elbow leaning on the bar, right next to her mother's ashtray.

Michelle could feel her heart thud as strongly as she felt Raindancer's heart during a race. Did Mr. Jones know that Loopy and she had robbed him that evening? She forced herself to go up to the bar and say hello.

But the trainer treated her the same as always; he just told her to go get some sleep, that she had a big race ahead of her.

He shook hands with Bits. "That's a pretty nice house," he said, and walked out of the Finish Line.

"What's a pretty nice house?" Michelle asked, watching the bar door as he left and the owner's son, Eric Grandors, entered with two young men who looked like fellow college students.

Her mother was showing her a circled photo in the real estate section of the paper. A little Dutch Colonial in a subdivision, a garage and lawn and hedged with new azaleas. "Dream on, right? . . . Michelle?"

"Sure, Mama, right. Dream on . . ." Michelle rubbed her mother's hand. There were cheap rings on each finger. ". . . Mama. Loopy wants you to do him a favor."

"Yeah, I bet."

"He'll pay you."

"Sure he will."

"Just listen."

Bits listened to her daughter's story. Then she looked at the money in the knapsack. Then she took the knapsack to the back corner of the bar and counted the cash. She didn't believe the ten thousand dollars belonged to Loopy Rojas. But she didn't suspect the truth either. Instead she assumed Loopy had given Michelle money pooled by a collection of Latino workers at the Farms who needed someone to place their bets for them. And finally, she agreed to do so; there was nothing illegal in it, was there? If Michelle and Raindancer lost, they lost. If they won, Bits would get a twenty-five-thousand dollar cut out of the winnings.

"But maybe I won't win," the girl added, so nervous about her lies that she felt sweat running down her T-shirt under the red Campbell Farms jacket. "Mr. Grandors doesn't want me to win and Mr. Jones doesn't think I can."

Bits lit a cigarette. "Yeah, Raylan told me tonight how you were a real long shot." She blew a ragged smoke ring at the dirty ceiling. "So, baby, you going to lose? Or you going to show them? Excuse me." Her mother went over to wait on Eric Grandors, who waved at Michelle from the end of the bar.

• • •

Loopy was right that it would rain that afternoon at Keeneland. It was a soft steady rain, and at post time for the Bluegrass Stakes, the track was muddy.

The big crowd cheered as the last horse, Number 14, Fortune's Child, danced into the starting gate.

Bits Harlin held her binoculars tight to her eyes, never taking them from the red number fourteen and the red-and-white clocks of her daughter's satin shirt.

Michelle and Raindancer broke fast and headed inside, catching Windsong by the far turn. To the astonishment of the announcer, Raindancer ran the first quarter mile in twenty-one and three-fifths seconds.

At the half-mile, Raindancer was still right beside Windsong, challenging him to keep up. Windsong couldn't do it.

In the stretch, in the soft rain, in the crowded splatter of mud, Raindancer took the lead.

Michelle felt the gray pulling away from the pack, carrying her with him until there was no mud around them, no noise, only the misty finish line ahead. But then she heard something. And she looked back.

What she saw was Spats coming closer. He wouldn't go away.

Spats brushed past Raindancer, so close that Michelle could feel the leather boot of the champion's jockey. Spats was taking the lead from them. They were only a dozen lengths from the wire. Spats's lead was widening. For one terrible second, doubt rushed through Michelle. They were going to lose. Mud from Spats's hooves splattered on her goggles so she couldn't see; Raindancer faltered as her stick fell from her hand and, losing control, she grabbed at the gray's mane.

She said to him, "Raindancer."

It felt like a moment last summer when Eric Grandors had taken Loopy and her for a motorboat ride on a lake. At a thrust of the throttles, the boat's large engines had lifted them with sudden speed almost out of the water. She felt the horse gather himself beneath her like that, as if he could leave earth behind. She said again, "Raindancer."

The gray caught up with Spats, they raced side by side for an instant, than Spats faded, faded to nothing. There was no one in the world but Raindancer and Michelle at the finish line and the far distant cry of her mother's voice.

Fortune's Child paid fifty-to-one. The odds had dropped

at the last minute when, just before the race, at six-oh-five p.m., Bits Harlin placed the last of her bets to win on Number 14.

Bits collected, before taxes, $540,000. Loopy Rojas darted in and out of the crowd near her as she moved from window to window collecting the money in cash, filling out W2-G forms for the biggest bets. As she left each window, Bits put the money in Michelle's knapsack. Loopy pushed in beside her, leading her to the crowded bar area, taking the money, cramming it in an old duffel bag. But turning around after collecting on her last winning ticket, Bits Harlin couldn't find the groom. She stood there waiting for him, holding seventy-two thousand dollars, the payout on a two-thousand-dollar bet at fifty-to-one, minus the twenty-eight percent deducted then and there for federal taxes.

In the winner's circle, Michelle, muddy-faced, smiled for the cameras. A reporter asked her, "How do you feel?" She shook her head, not wanting to talk. "No," the reporter insisted. "How do you feel, winning this race?"

". . . My horse won the race."

Raindancer pushed his nose at Mr. Jones, as if to say, "I knew I could, too."

Mr. Grandors was red-faced, glaring up at Michelle on the horse, except as the cameras clicked, when he hugged his young handsome wife and tried to look happy. Grinning, his son, Eric, reached out to clasp his hand around the ankle of Michelle's boot. "One-forty-six-point-seventy! Unbelievable!"

Jones bent over, felt the gray stallion's fetlock. "You got a bruise here," he told the horse. But he said nothing to Michelle.

That night, when she looked for Loopy at Campbell

Farms, the groom was nowhere to be found; the shelf empty where his hotplate and TV had once sat. When she called his cell phone, no one answered.

At midnight Michelle took $10,800 of the money her mother had collected to Mr. Jones's office, thinking that she would just leave the cash without explanation on his desk. But she found the trainer standing quietly in the dusky room, waiting for her.

He told her what the official bonus would have been for her as winner. For him as trainer. For Loopy as groom. Loopy wouldn't be getting his bonus though. Loopy was doubtless on his way home to Costa Rica. "Right before the race," he added, "I fired him."

"Because of this?" She handed the trainer the bound stack of hundred-dollar bills.

"Because of this." Mr. Jones showed her a small vial of a drug called Dormosedan that he'd taken from Loopy. It was a powerful tranquilizer, and two cc's of it would drop a horse to the ground. Much less of a dose could slow down a favorite, a closer like the big roan champion Spats, just long enough for a long shot like Fortune's Child to win. Losers in a horse race weren't urine tested. If Loopy drugged Spats, who would ever know?

Michelle felt sick to her heart.

The trainer and the jockey sat there in silence a long while. Finally she couldn't bear it anymore. "What are you going to do?" She pointed at the bound stacks of bills on his desk.

Jones scratched at his grizzled mustache. "Teach you a lesson," he said in his quiet voice and then turned away from her.

Michelle left the office. In Raindancer's stall, she sat on the straw in the dark, quiet, listening to the steady breathing of the gray horse. So they hadn't won. Spats was drugged. Raindancer and she hadn't done the splendid thing after all. True, maybe her mother could now make a down payment on a house that couldn't be moved, but that happiness wouldn't happen because Michelle had won it for her. No, Loopy had hedged his bets, had cheated and slowed down Spats with a drug. And Mr. Jones had caught him cheating. It was true: Cheating only cheated the cheaters. Loopy had cheated them all.

"I'm sorry," she told the gray horse.

Raindancer whinnied at the noise of someone walking toward them. She heard a knock at the stall door. Then a light came on in the corridor and Mr. Jones stood there. "Michelle, come on back to my office." He walked away.

In his office, Jones held out to her a small folded bundle of money. "Five hundred dollars," he said. "That's what I won. Because ten dollars was all I could bet. On Raindancer. Somebody had robbed me."

She said, "I'm sorry." Then, "You bet on Raindancer? You put in your bet before you found Loopy with that tranquilizer?"

He shook his head. "No. I put in my bet afterwards."

The trainer took the vial of tranquilizer from his pocket and handed it to her. The seal on the bottle wasn't broken. Jones said, "Loopy would have used this. But he didn't. I stopped him."

She stared at the tall thin black man. "Spats wasn't drugged?"

"No, he was not."

"And you bet on Raindancer?"

"Well," he said, "you made me a believer. But running that

track in one-forty-six?" He whistled softly. "Young lady, that took my breath away."

"So winning was all right?"

He shook his head. "Winning wasn't your job. Your job was to take out Windsong."

"But I did that, too."

"Yes, you did." Jones held up a framed photograph, the same newspaper clipping Eric Grandors had given her. The trainer stood on a chair and placed the picture on a hook already set in his wall, below but not far from his photo of Secretariat. "Eric gave me this picture." Stepping down carefully, he nodded at her with a regard she'd never before seen in his lined, freckled face.

She smiled back at him. "So Raindancer's not only a morning glory?"

Mr. Jones just held open his office door for her to walk through it. He said, "I'll see you tomorrow at five. Go get some sleep." As they moved into the corridor, Eric Grandors stepped toward them.

"Michelle, you want a ride home?"

"Sure." She shrugged at the young man.

"Tomorrow at five," Jones called after her.

She waved her arm without looking back.

The trainer leaned into Raindancer's stall. "There she goes, Champ."

THE LONG SHOT
Michele Martinez

Lisa Rivera had about twenty minutes left on her shift when the guy walked in and took a seat in a corner booth. She could tell from the way he moved that he was in a hurry, and from his expensive haircut and pinstriped suit that he had money in his pocket, so she brought him ice water and a menu ASAP. She could always spot a high roller, and win or lose they were generous tippers. Especially if she gave them reason to be.

"Specials are on the board. Something to drink?" She smiled just enough to show off her full lips. Lisa had been playing the same game in one form or another since she was twelve years old, and she had the moves down.

"Coffee. Black." He glanced at the menu but didn't bother to open it. "What can you do fast?"

"How long you got?"

He looked at his watch, and so did she. It was a gold Rolex with a diamond bezel, flashy for a man, expensive. "Twenty minutes, max."

"Yeah? Me too. Before my shift ends, I mean." Lisa's tone

was casual, not at all suggestive, but her comment was meant to test the waters. The guy didn't bite. He just looked back at her, waiting for an answer. "It's not real crowded right now, so say five minutes for a sandwich. If you want a burger, maybe a little longer," she said.

"Make it a cheeseburger. Deluxe."

"That'll take around ten."

"No problem. I'm a fast eater." The guy smiled as if this were funny, so Lisa smiled back. He had white teeth and eyes so dark brown that they were almost black. He was good looking in an average sort of way, late forties she guessed, with curly hair, graying and cut short. Lisa held his gaze for an extra beat.

"American, swiss or cheddar?" She glanced down at his hands as she spoke. A wedding ring. That was always good, for her purposes. And manicured nails. This guy must have mad cash.

"American."

She brought the slip back to the kitchen and leaned across the open stainless steel counter. "Hey, Earl, do me a favor. Move this to the front of the line. Customer's in a hurry."

"You see a crowd out there? Lunch is through, ain't no line."

"So move it faster, then. I wanna make him happy." And she pulled her lip gloss out of her apron pocket and slicked the wand over her lips, using the metal napkin holder on the counter for a mirror.

Earl leaned out as far as his big stomach would allow, craning his neck. "Over there in the suit?"

"That's him."

"You got yourself a live one, girl."

"Maybe. We'll see."

"Be good, now."

"*You* be good. Cook the food and mind your own business," she said, and blew him an exaggerated kiss.

Earl chuckled as he turned away, making his belly jiggle. Lisa watched him pick a wan-looking patty off a pile by its square of bloodied paper and slap it down onto the grill. It sizzled, sending up a lick of flame.

She walked back over to the guy, balancing a mug of black coffee and squeeze bottles of ketchup and mustard on a wet plastic tray. He'd been in the middle of a conversation, but he hung up as she approached and slipped his cell phone back into his jacket pocket. Lisa placed the items down before him one by one, leaning over just far enough to give him a flash of cleavage if he cared to look, but not so much that she was shoving her tits in his face. With this one, her instincts said to go slow.

She straightened up and hit him with the look she reserved for the hard cases—nonchalant and yet completely sexual at the same time—and made her voice match her expression. "Can I get you something else?"

She had his attention finally. *Damn,* she was good. She should patent that thing.

"*Lisa,*" he said slowly, reading her name tag. She leaned back on her heel, hand on her hip, and let him take a good look. "What about a horse?" he asked. "You got a horse for me today, Lisa?"

"Sure. Hell's Bells to place in the fifth."

"Yeah? Huh." He looked impressed. "Who says?"

"A guy named Sallie who comes in every day for lunch. Real track rat. Once in a while, I let him play my tip money for me."

"And? Does he win?"

She shrugged. "Mostly. I lost a few times. But one time I hit on long odds and made three hundred bucks off a two-dollar bet."

"Very impressive. Hell's Bells. Okay, I'll remember."

"But you better hurry up. Post time was one, you know."

He was still looking at her, which she took to mean that he didn't mind if she stayed a minute.

"So you play the ponies much? Because I never seen you in here before," she asked idly.

"I work for a living. Can't just spend all day at the track." He was clearly educated, but as he talked, Lisa heard the New Yawk in his voice. Or the Brooklyn, to be more accurate.

"Let me guess. You're, what . . . a stockbroker?"

"Nope. Lawyer."

"Really? We don't get too many lawyers in here. They don't seem to like the horses."

He smiled, those white teeth again. He must've had them done. "We're a cautious bunch of bastards. You could even say boring."

"But not you," she said, widening her doe eyes in faux admiration. As he leaned back against the leatherette of the booth, his gaze lingered on her body. She had him going now.

"Oh, yeah, I'm boring, too. I work all the time, just like the rest of 'em."

"You need to relax, then. A day at the track is just what the doctor ordered."

He frowned. "Who said I'm going to the track?"

"Didn't you just ask me for a horse? Besides, if you lean out the door and spit, you hit Belmont. Why else come to *this* dump?"

"I was making conversation, all right? I never said where I was going."

She'd annoyed him, somehow. But Lisa knew how to backpedal.

"Sure, my mistake. Whatever you say. You're the boss." She raised her dark eyebrows slightly on the last word. She could tell he liked that.

Earl tapped the bell on the counter.

"'Scuse me," she said, breaking off eye contact first. "That's gonna be yours."

"That was fast."

"Just like you wanted."

She could feel the guy's eyes on her ass as she walked away. They were required to wear black pants under their aprons. Hers were low and tight. Lisa had a slamming body, and she worked it.

When she came back with his burger, his eyes followed her the whole way. Whatever she'd done to offend the guy, he'd obviously forgiven her.

"So stay for a minute if nobody else is calling you," he said, glancing around as he took a big bite of the cheese-burger. The diner always cleared out in the middle of the af-ternoon. It was empty now except for two old ladies, virtually indistinguishable from one another, sharing a piece of lemon meringue pie at a table near the window.

Lisa shrugged noncommittally. When the time came to reel them in, it was never good to look eager.

"Seriously," he continued, chewing, then licking some mustard off his hand. "Have a seat. Take a load off."

"We're not allowed to sit down with the customers."

"Who's gonna know?"

"The manager's in the back. Sometimes he comes out."

"If he yells at you, I'll give you a big tip. Promise."

You don't even know the half of it, baby, she thought. "No. I can't, really. But I won't say no to a french fry."

"Help yourself." He nodded at his plate, taking another gigantic bite of the cheeseburger. He was eating like a starving man. Lisa picked up a french fry, dipped it slowly in the ketchup and chewed it. She enjoyed the way he watched her; it made her feel powerful.

"You know my name, but I don't know yours," she said. "That's not fair."

"I'm Bruce. Pleased to meet you." He wiped his hand with the napkin, then put it out for her to shake. Lisa took it, looking into his eyes and squeezing for an extra second, just long enough to turn the handshake into something more. He flushed.

"Bruce," she said. "Nice name. Bruce the Lawyer."

"Bruce the Lawyer," he repeated. "Yup. That sums it up."

"You talk like you don't like it. But that's a good job, being a lawyer, right? You rake in the bucks."

"Yeah, if you're successful at it, it can be very good that way."

"Well, that's what counts, right? Finishing in the money? Just like at the track."

"Can't argue with that," he said, shoving some fries into his mouth, talking through his food.

"And have you? Been successful at it?"

"You cut to the chase, don't you, Lisa?" he said, smiling.

She shrugged, holding his gaze.

"I do very well for myself," he said. "But enough about me. What's a pretty girl like you doing in a shithole like this anyway?"

"Me? I'm between modeling jobs."

"Oh, yeah?" He was chewing.

"Sure. I'd be booked all the time except I'm only five-three."

"Mmm."

"I was in nursing school for a while, too. Nights. But it got to be a lot, with my son and all. And I'm not much for books. So I quit, but I'm definitely going back. Soon. This is only temporary."

"I don't really see you as a nurse."

"No?"

"No." He laughed. "Although you'd look hot in one of those uniforms."

"They don't wear those slutty uniforms no more, you know. It's like, drawstring pants and a smock top. Real serious, like doctors."

His phone rang. "Excuse me," he said, reaching for his pocket and pulling out the phone. "Yeah? Uh, hold on a second." He placed a hand over the mouthpiece, looking up at her. "Can I get a refill on the coffee, please, and the check?"

Shit. And she'd had this guy, too. "Okay, sure," she said, flashing a phony smile.

The thick, burnt liquid in the bottom of the coffeemaker wouldn't even fill half a mug, so Lisa had to make a whole new pot. Fucking Paulette should've been in by now to set up the next shift. Second time she was late this week. Lisa made the fresh coffee, vaguely aware that Bruce was arguing in low tones with whomever was on the other end of his call. By the time she brought the pot over to refill his coffee cup, he'd hung up. She poured, giving him the cleavage view again, but he didn't seem to be checking it out this time. He looked stressed, upset.

"Everything okay?" she asked.

"Ah, just business."

She nodded understandingly, giving a little pout of sympathy. "I'll be right back with your check."

She stowed the coffeepot and wrote up the tab, adding a couple of extra bucks for good measure. He hadn't looked at the menu anyway; he'd never know the difference. All the while, Lisa was trying to figure her next move. Damned if she was gonna let this one slip through her fingers. But when she walked back to his table, it turned out that no further effort was necessary.

She reached out to place the check on the table, and Bruce grabbed her by the wrist. Her heart thumped, part triumph, part lust.

"You're off now?" he asked, looking up at her, his grip tightening. Some guys could surprise you.

"Yeah," she said.

"You have to be anywhere?"

She shrugged. "Not for a few hours."

"Feel like going to the track?"

"Sure. Whatever. I have to get my stuff, though."

"Go ahead. I'll meet you out front. It's a black Porsche Boxster."

A dingy hallway leading out to the trash cans behind the diner served as their locker room. Lisa hung up her apron and checked herself out in the small mirror hanging on the back of the door. She sniffed her underarms, then reached for her handbag, pulling out a purse-size Obsession perfume and spraying it liberally over her wrists and down her shirt. She brushed her long, dark hair and touched up her makeup. When she was satisfied, she took out her cell phone and dialed.

"Yeah?" Manny answered thickly.

"What are you, sleeping?"

"Mmmf."

"Get your lazy ass out of bed. I got a guy."

"What?"

"A guy. Gold Rolex with diamonds. He's on his way to the track. From the looks of him, he's gonna have mad cash."

"Aw, shit, I don't feel like it."

"Just do it, Manny, we need the rent. And take Brandon downstairs so Damarys can watch him, okay? *Don't* leave him alone."

"Yeah, awright."

"I'm gonna try to get the guy in that lot where they keep the trailers. Look for me there. It's a black Porsche."

"Really?"

"Yes, really. What did I *just* say? The guy's loaded. And you wonder why I complain that you don't listen. Now move your ass."

Lisa hung up and headed for the front exit. Outside, the heat and the glare smacked her in the face. Bruce was waiting in a sexy little convertible with the top down. He leaned over and pushed open the door, and she lowered herself into the tan leather seat. It smelled fancy.

"Nice car, Brucie," Lisa said, smiling and letting the wind take her hair as he accelerated. This was fun. It almost made her think she should go back to dancing, meet some guys with real money again. But Manny was crazy jealous, and shit was always getting out of hand. The drama had gotten to be too much for her.

Neither of them spoke. After a minute, they were cruising along a seemingly endless loop through deserted, gravel-topped parking lots. It was a while since Lisa had been here, and she worried momentarily that she'd forgotten which lot they used to use. But closer in toward the clubhouse she spotted it. It was empty except for five or six horse trailers off to one side and a few abandoned-looking cars, and its gravel was dotted with prickly lumps of horse manure.

"You know, if you park out here, you don't have to pay nothing," Lisa remarked.

He glanced over at her. "This is a Porsche. I'm not parking it in the middle of fucking nowhere."

"Suit yourself. Just trying to save you a few bucks."

So much for Plan A. Lisa wasn't worried, though. Manny would find her in the stands if he had to, or else she'd get Bruce to stop here on their way out, after he loosened up a little. All she'd ever had to do was tell a guy the best spot for a blow job was in this lot, behind the horse trailers. Never failed.

They reached the paved lot. Bruce pulled up to the valet stand. He leaned over, his head brushing her chest, and fished around on the floor beneath her feet.

"Could you lift up, please? I need that briefcase," he said.

"Oh. Sorry. I didn't even realize I was stepping on it. Hey, that's *hot*," she said, as he pulled the briefcase onto his lap. It was shiny black alligator, as expensive-looking as everything else Bruce owned.

"Yeah. I don't like to leave it in the car."

"I don't blame you."

They got out. Bruce handed the keys to the valet along with a twenty-dollar bill. "Park it in the shade, and it better be fucking perfect when I get it back."

"Of course, sir."

They rode the long escalator up to the clubhouse level, which was air conditioned to an arctic chill. Smoking was prohibited in here, but the place still reeked with the acrid odor of cigars. A race had just started. Knots of old men—mostly white, a few black—stood shouting in deep outrage at the horses' images on the flat screen TVs.

"Buccaneer, you fucking faggot!"

"Six? Where the fuck is Six? Ah, crap, look at him back there!"

"Fucking disaster!"

Lisa glanced over at Bruce. "So do you wanna—"

"Hold on," he said. His phone was buzzing in his pocket. "Yeah . . . Where? . . . Yeah, okay." He hung up and turned to Lisa. "So listen, I gotta meet some clients."

"Now? We just got here."

"Yeah, they're here, too."

"Oh."

"In a private skybox. Up on the third level."

"Oh." She shrugged. "Okay."

Other people and a private box could screw up her plans, but what could she do except roll with the punches?

Bruce led her to an elevator and pushed the button. They stood waiting. He seemed distracted and made no effort to talk to her. Lisa was starting to get a little confused as to why he'd brought her along. But then they got on, and the second the doors closed Bruce shoved her against the wall and started groping and kissing her, his tongue tasting unpleasantly of the onion from the burger. As his pelvis ground into her, she felt his hard-on. This whole thing was what it looked like, then, she thought with some relief. She reached down to unzip his fly, but he pulled away the second the elevator door opened.

Bruce stepped out, wiping his mouth with the back of his hand. "I like you, Lisa."

"Yeah, I like you, too," she answered automatically.

"Thank you for coming."

"You're welcome," she said, almost thinking she was being dismissed. But then he motioned for her to come along.

This guy was starting to strike her as weird.

She followed him down a deserted hallway lined with doors until he stopped in front of one and knocked. It swung open and they both entered. It was a decent-size room lined with plush movie theater–style armchairs. Its front wall was made of glass, with a door opening directly on to the stands, three tiers above the finish line. There was a fully stocked wet bar in one corner and a door to a private bathroom opposite, which stood open, revealing gleaming white tile within and a toilet with its seat up.

It wasn't until Lisa had finished appreciating the unaccustomed luxury that she looked around and registered the people in the room. Bruce's so-called clients. Then she saw just how badly she'd lost her touch.

Lisa had grown up in Marcy Projects and lived there until she ran away at fifteen. Actually, running away had really improved her life. She made decent money the way she knew how, and lived in better places. But Marcy taught her a few things, things she thought she'd never get soft enough to forget. Like how to take the temperature of an elevator or a stairwell *before* she walked into it, so she didn't realize the guy sharing it with her had a knife when it was already too late to do anything about it. Where the fuck had that knowledge gone? How could it have deserted her at this critical moment? Looking around the room, she felt sick—short of breath, like she might vomit.

There were five men in here, not counting Bruce, but counting the guy who had closed the door behind them when they walked in and now stood blocking it with his massive bulk. That guy was over six feet tall and well over three hundred pounds. *Muscle,* she thought, guys like him were called muscle. She remembered that from the projects. Somebody with his build could count on a long and lucrative career hurting people. The other four were no less fierce looking, but not because of their size. It was their manner, the look in their eyes. From their features, complexions and dress, she made them all to be Puerto Rican or Dominican, local rather than island-born. And from their fade haircuts, tatts and the guns bulging beneath their ghetto-fabulous clothing, guessing their occupation was a no-brainer. They were in the drug trade, to a man.

"Check him for heat," said one of them, a skinny one with an angry scar on his cheek, who lounged in a plush chair with a highball glass full of scotch in his hand.

Muscle threw Bruce up against the wall and patted him down expertly, coming out with two guns—a nine-millimeter from a holster under Bruce's arm, and a small revolver from a complicated-looking holster strapped to his ankle. Lisa was impressed. Who knew Bruce the Lawyer was packing? Muscle stuck Bruce's guns in the waistband of his own pants and looked back at the guy with the scar, who was clearly the boss.

"Her, too?" he asked hopefully, motioning at Lisa.

"Why not?" the guy replied, and Muscle ran his hands all over Lisa's body, paying particular attention to her tits and her crotch. When he was done, he nodded at the guy in the chair and then resumed his position in front of the door.

"So who's your friend, Bruce?" the guy asked.

"She hot," said another one of them, who was youngish and dressed in a white track suit, leaning against the bar.

"This is Lisa," Bruce replied. "Lisa and I are on our way to a bar where a bunch of people are expecting us. So why don't you give me the fucking money you owe me, Orlando," he said, patting his briefcase like he expected the money placed into it immediately, "and we'll get out of your hair."

Lisa felt dizzy with astonishment at the realization that Bruce had gotten over on her. Here she was, thinking *she* was playing *him,* but the whole time she was just his insurance policy. He'd brought her into what he knew would be a major confrontation in the hopes of defusing the ugliness. More specifically, in the hopes that Orlando wouldn't kill him in front of a witness. What a shame, what a *damn* shame, because Lisa could tell with one glance around this room that Bruce's little plan wouldn't work. Orlando looked like he killed when it suited him, and as for witnesses, he didn't seem the type to leave any hanging around.

"I don't even know this guy!" she exclaimed to Orlando. "Really. We just met. I'm a waitress. He picked me up in the diner where I work."

"I knew she too hot to be Bruce woman," said White Track Suit, and several of them laughed.

"Seriously," Lisa said, looking at Orlando, who hadn't cracked a smile. "I don't even know his name, and I don't want to mess in your business. So why don't I go now?"

"You just got here. Don't be disrespectful. Sit down."

"No, look, I gotta be somewhere. I'm late to pick up my kid," she pleaded.

"Sit *down,* bitch." Orlando's voice was so cold that it made her scalp crawl. And before Lisa could move of her own accord, Muscle shoved her into a chair, which she was almost glad of, since her knees were starting to buckle anyway.

"Come on, leave her out of this," Bruce said half-heartedly.

"What the fuck. *You* brought her here. You think this gonna go easier for you 'cause you bring some bitch along, you don't know me," Orlando said, radiating danger.

"Hey, wait a minute. Where do *you* get off being mad at *me*? I got you the name you wanted. I'm risking fucking witness tampering charges, even a murder conspiracy charge, for Chrissakes. You owe me fifty grand, and I expect to be paid."

"Yeah, well, unfortunately, that ain't in the cards right now. I got a few problems with your performance."

"So, fine, tell me. I'm all ears, Orlando. Word of mouth is my stock in trade. I never like to disappoint a client." Bruce's voice dripped sarcasm. He seemed completely unafraid, which dumbfounded Lisa.

Orlando sprang to his feet and got right up in Bruce's face.

"Don't fucking tell me that! We show up to get him, and they all waitin' on us. Explain that to me. The Gomez brothers and their whole crew. I'm lucky to be standing up here breathing right now. You playing both sides, Bruce. You set me up!"

Lisa was shaking uncontrollably, but Bruce was unbowed, staring right back at Orlando.

"Don't look at *me*! I told you before, you got another rat besides Gomez. My guy in Counter-Narcotics says they're looking at doing a wire on you, and they got a real confidential snitch. That can't be Gomez, because everybody and his brother already *knows* Gomez is snitching. If you wanna blame the messenger because you refuse to take care of business, Orlando, *you're* gonna be doing twenty-five to life, not me."

The two men stood eye to eye as everybody else in the room held their collective breath.

"Well? Am I right?" Bruce demanded.

The moment stretched into an eternity. Finally, Orlando's body relaxed, and he asked, "So? Who is it, then?"

Lisa breathed again.

"I don't know," Bruce said. "I told ya, they're playing it real close to the vest. My guy can't get shit on it. I have a couple of other sources I can try to hit up . . ."

"Okay, so do that, then," Orlando said.

"Why the fuck should I? Not only are you holding out on me with the money, but you go and pull a stunt like this. Calling me here to intimidate me. What kind of bullshit is that, Orlando? What kind of trust is that between a lawyer and his client?"

"Come on, son, I was just playing with you."

"Yeah, well, I don't appreciate it. Who else left on Queens Boulevard is gonna do what I do for you? Huh? Tell me that."

"Nobody. Since Del Pietro got got, Bruce Goldman is the man."

"Fucking right, I am."

"No hard feelings, awright, son? Have a drink and let's work this shit out. Alvin, get my man Bruce here a drink, and his lady friend, too."

After that, Lisa started doing tequila shots, lots of them, until her hands stopped shaking and she forgot how scared she'd been. Pizzas were brought in, and eventually someone passed a joint around, a really powerful joint. Somebody else had some Ecstasy. The afternoon ebbed into a delicious, drugged-out haze. Hours seemed to pass, but it might've been minutes, she couldn't be sure and didn't really care. She went outside for a while. The heat of the sun pressed down on her so hard that she was pinned to the chair. She let the unreal emerald green of the oval vibrate on her eyes like a tuning fork and giggled uncontrollably when the blast of trumpets announced a race. At one point, White Track Suit came outside and they made out slowly until Bruce emerged to pull him off her.

"Hey, come on, Alvin, I brought her. Christ, I didn't even do her yet," Bruce said.

They all laughed. Nobody was mad. Lisa's bones were like mush, her face was numb and she felt very pleased with herself that Bruce seemed jealous. He sent one of the guys to buy her a two-dollar ticket for Hell's Bells in the fifth, and when it hit, a forty-to-one long shot, she was so high that she tore the ticket up and threw it in the air just for a laugh.

After a while, Bruce said he had to get to some school thing in Great Neck for one of his kids. He told Lisa he'd drop her back at the diner. As they were leaving, the guys all hugged her like brothers, telling her to come back real soon.

The valet brought the Porsche around. The tan leather seats were almost cool to the touch. Life seemed fat and joyous.

"I got about fifteen minutes," Bruce said, looking at the Rolex.

"Okay. I know a spot. Back behind those horse trailers we passed when we came in."

Later, Lisa would ask herself what she'd been thinking. But part of her was just thinking she felt like blowing this guy. Really.

"So, admit it," she said as they drove. "You brought me there like an insurance policy. You thought Orlando was gonna kill you." And she started giggling again.

"No way."

"Liar. You are such a liar, Bruce," she said, and punched him on the arm.

"Whoa, watch the jacket."

"You definitely thought that. Jesus, *I* thought that. Walking in, I thought we were dead meat."

"No, seriously. You wanna know why I brought you?"

"Yes, I do."

"Because I looked at you and I said, this girl has an unbelievable body and an incredible mouth. And I bet she gives amazing head."

"Really?"

"Yeah, swear to God, that's exactly what I thought when I first saw you."

"Aww. You are so nice."

"It had nothing to do with Orlando. He doesn't scare me, anyway. I figured I'd pick up my money, then you and me would get a room and we'd kill a few hours, have some fun."

He pulled the Porsche around behind the horse trailers and turned off the engine.

"In fact," Bruce continued, turning to face her as he reached for his zipper, "my only regret is, we hung out at the track so long that we don't have much time right now."

"What? Fifteen minutes. That's plenty."

"Yeah?"

"You were right. I *am* good. You won't last long."

Lisa got to her knees, half on and half off the leather seat, and took him in her mouth. Bruce gripped her by her hair and moved her head up and down, slowly at first, then faster, in time to the thrust of his hips. He braced himself against the car door, breathing hard.

"Oh, yeah, that's good. Just like that," he said, moaning.

With the position she was in, Lisa couldn't see anything, so when Bruce's body jerked suddenly, for a second she thought he was starting to come. But then she realized he was shoving her off him, reaching frantically for one of the guns he'd taken back before they left the skybox.

"Shit!" Bruce yelled, looking at something over her shoulder.

"He's got a gun!" Lisa shouted, diving for the floor, and she wasn't exactly sure which guy she was trying to warn.

She saw a flash from behind her, heard a blast and covered her head, screaming.

"Fuck!" Manny said, and Lisa looked up to see Bruce slumped against the driver's side door, dark blood rapidly soaking his white shirt front.

"Manny, you killed him. Shit! Why'd you do that?"

"What the fuck was I supposed to do? He had a gun! Quick, get his wallet before someone comes."

"I don't want to touch him. He's all bloody." And his eyes were staring weird, creeping her out.

"Just get his wallet before I fucking kill *you*! Stupid bitch. I knew this was a bad idea."

She reached for Bruce's pants pocket, shrinking back in momentary horror as her hand touched hot, viscous blood. It was practically pumping out of him now.

"Is his fly open? Were you really blowing him?" Manny demanded.

"You took too long. I got in an awkward situation."

"You slut. You fucking slut."

"Just calm down, okay? We got worse problems than that."

Lisa's mind was suddenly very clear. She steeled herself and reached back into Bruce's pants pocket, pulling out a solid-gold money clip shaped like a dollar sign and stuffed with hundred-dollar bills. Then she swiftly stripped the Rolex from Bruce's wrist and handed both over to Manny.

"Wow, this is like the biggest payday we ever had," Manny said, staring down at them, looking mollified.

Lisa put Bruce's dick back inside his pants and zipped up his fly. He'd gone limp at some point, but she wondered if an autopsy would show that he'd had a hard-on right before he died.

"Help me sit him up and get the seat belt on," she commanded.

"Why?"

"Just do it. I'll explain later."

Manny came around to the driver's side, and they quickly arranged Bruce to make it appear that he'd been driving. Then they got the hell out of there.

For a few days afterward, Lisa bought the newspapers. Everything played out just like she hoped. The cops had it as drug related, with the victim's wallet and watch taken to make it look like a robbery. There was no mention of any girl, or sex, or anything that would make her think the cops were looking for her. Bruce Goldman had been under investigation for acting as "house counsel" to a couple of rival narcotics organizations. It was speculated that he'd gotten caught in the middle of a drug war. The police were following up some leads, but they had no particular suspects at the moment. From the tone of the articles, in fact, it sounded like they weren't looking that hard. It sounded, even, like they figured Bruce Goldman had pretty much gotten what he deserved.

After a while, Lisa thought that, too, and she stopped buying the papers—except to check if the ponies were running. Not that she was necessarily looking for another mark. You couldn't keep robbing and expect never to get caught. Or could you? After all, long shots do come in sometimes. Lisa knew that for a fact.

MEADOWLANDS

Joyce Carol Oates

Bring your driver's license, sweetheart. You're driving."

Fritzi's new car? He was letting her drive?

Smiling his easy smile. Reaching over to squeeze her arm in that way of his, which sent a sensation like a mild electric shock through Katie's body. Even as Katie warned herself, *Don't fall for it. You'll be hurt.*

Fritzi Czechi was known for his upscale but tasteful cars. This new-model steely-silver BMW with the mulberry leather interior and teakwood dash, he'd purchased only two weeks before, he was asking Katie Flanders to drive to the Meadowlands racetrack, handing over the keys to her as if they were husband and wife, not a man and a woman in an undefined if romantic relationship. Katie stared at the keys quivering on the palm of her hand. *Don't! Don't fall for it.*

"Look, Fritzi: Why exactly am I driving, and not you? I missed the reason."

"Because I need to concentrate, sweetheart."

This was so. On the way to Meadowlands, while Katie, always a careful driver, drove the elegant new car at exactly the

• 303

Turnpike speed limit, Fritzi studied what appeared to be racing forms, frowning, making notations with a stubby pencil. After a while he shifted in his seat to stare out the passenger's window, frowning as if painful-size thoughts were working their way through his brain, and Katie glanced over at him wondering, what was Fritzi thinking? (Probably not of what had happened between them the night before, as Katie was. A warm dreamy erotic memory intensified by the smell of the new-car interior.) Fritzi was part-owner of one of the horses scheduled to race this Friday evening at Meadowlands, a three-year-old stallion named Morning Star who was returning to serious racing after being sidelined for months with a hairline fracture of his right front knee. Katie understood that Fritzi was worried about his horse, but also Fritzi was a gambler, which meant he dealt in odds, in numerals, and probably he had a mathematical mind and could "see" figures in his head in a way Katie could only imagine, it was so alien to her way of perceiving the world. Once, when she'd asked Fritzi how much one of his horses had cost, Fritzi had told her, "A racehorse is beyond computation, sweetheart," which had been a mysterious answer yet made sense.

It was a way of telling Katie Flanders, too, that Fritzi's private professional life was beyond her comprehension.

So Katie drove, and liked it that Fritzi so trusted her with his car, which wasn't like Fritzi Czechi in fact, or any man she'd ever known, asking or allowing a woman to drive his car while he sat in the passenger's seat staring out the window. Katie wondered if maybe Fritzi was in one of his moods: captured by the look of the mottled, marbled early-evening sky like the usual sky over northern New Jersey, clouds like chunks of dirty concrete shot with veins of acid-yellow and sulfur-red. This Jersey sky they'd been seeing all their lives, Katie thought. Familiar as a ceiling of some room you could die in.

The last time Fritzi had taken Katie to Meadowlands to see one of his horses race had been a year ago, or more. That year had passed slowly! Fritzi's horse then was Pink Lady, a four-year-old who hadn't won her race but hadn't lost badly, in Katie's opinion. Pink Lady had galloped so hard, Katie's heart had gone out to the shuddering mare, whipped by her scowling little jockey but unable to overtake the lead horses who'd seemed to pull away from the rest immediately out of the gate as if by magic. Pink Lady had come in third, out of nine. That wasn't bad, was it? Katie had seemed to plead with Fritzi, who'd said little about the race, or about Pink Lady, and he hadn't encouraged Katie's encouragement, still less her emotions. Always Katie would remember *A racehorse is beyond computation* and understand it as a rebuke.

A gentle rebuke, though. Not like somebody telling you to shut up and mind your own business, you don't know shit.

Fritzi Czechi was one of those men in Katie's life—Katie didn't want to think how many there were, and that some of them knew one another from Jersey City High where they'd all gone—who'd been in and out of her life since the early 1970s. Now it was 1988 and they were fully grown, no longer high school kids, yet when you looked closely at them, as at yourself in a mirror, frankly, unsparingly, you saw that they were still kids trying to figure what the hell it was all about, and what they were missing out on, they were beginning to realize they'd never get.

Except Fritzi Czechi. But for his broken-up marriages,

Fritzi hadn't done badly. He exuded a certain glamour. He dressed in style. He was a fair-skinned, lean, ropy-muscled man of about five feet nine, not tall, carrying himself with a certain confidence, at least when people were likely to be watching. Fritzi had strangely luminous stone-colored eyes, fair hair thinning at the crown he wore slightly long so that it curled behind his ears; he had a habit of stroking his hair, the back of his head, a medallion ring gleaming on the third finger of his right hand. (Katie recalled Fritzi had once worn a wedding band. But no longer.) Fritzi was a good-looking man, if no longer as good-looking as he'd been six or seven years before when his smiling picture had been printed in Jersey papers as the part-owner of a Thoroughbred that had won $500,000 in the Belmont Stakes. (Katie had saved these clippings. She hadn't been going out with Fritzi at that time, Fritzi had been married then. If he'd been seeing other women, which probably he had been, Katie Flanders wasn't one of these women.)

As well as horses, Fritzi was known to have invested in a number of restaurants, clubs, and bowling alleys in Jersey, though he rarely spoke of his business life; it was part of Fritzi's glamour that he was so reticent, so elusive you might say, keeping his private life to himself, so if you were Katie Flanders you'd have to hear from other sources that things were going well for Fritzi, or not so well. "Investments," horses, marriages. (Three marriages. Children, both boys, from the first, long-ago marriage when Fritzi had thought he'd wanted to be a New Jersey state trooper like his oldest brother. So far as Katie knew, Fritzi was separated from his third wife, not yet legally divorced. But it was only an assumption. She couldn't ask.) Definitely it was part of Fritzi

Czechi's glamour that he did unpredictable things like giving money to bankrupt Jersey City High for new uniforms for both the boys' and the girls' varsity basketball teams, or he'd send boxes of expensive chocolate candies to the mothers of certain of his old friends for their birthdays, or hospitalizations, or a dozen red roses to a woman friend like Katie Flanders he was sorry about not having seen in a while, as a token of his "esteem." Fritzi was known to pick up tabs in restaurants and clubs, and he was known to lend money to friends, if they were old friends, without asking for interest, and often without much hope of getting the money back.

He'd "lent" money to Katie, too. When there'd been a medical crisis in her family. When she'd tried to return it he'd told her, "Someday, sweetheart, you can bail me out. We'll wait."

Katie was a secretary at Drummond Tools, Ltd., in Hackensack. One of those temporary jobs, she'd thought, until she got married, started having babies. But just to be a secretary these days you had to know computers, and computers are always being upgraded, which is scary as hell when you're on the downside of thirty and not getting any younger or smarter while the new girls being hired look like junior high kids. The thought chilled Katie. She reached out to touch Fritzi's arm, needing to touch him, and liking the fact that it was Katie Flanders's privilege to touch Fritzi Czechi in this casual intimate way since they were more than lovers, they were old friends. "This BMW, Fritzi, is *very nice.*"

Fritzi said, "Well, good."

He wasn't listening. He'd put away his racing forms and was staring now at his watch, which he wore turned inward, the flat oval disc of digital numbers against his pulse. As if, with Fritzi Czechi, even the exact time was a secret.

" 'Specially compared to my own." Katie drove a 1985 Ford compact, not a new model when she'd bought it. After this roomy number it would feel about the size of a sardine can.

Katie was suddenly quiet, realizing how she sounded. Like she was hinting that Fritzi give her this car, or another like it. She didn't mean that at all. She only just wanted to talk. She was lonely, and she wanted to talk. After last night, she wanted to be assured that Fritzi cared for her, that he wasn't already forgetting her, his mind flying ahead to the Meadowlands racetrack, to that blur of frantic movement out of the gate and around the dirt track and back to the finish line that would involve less than two minutes, yet could decide so much. She was frightened: If things turned out badly for Morning Star, as, she'd gathered, they hadn't turned out all that wonderfully for Pink Lady, Fritzi would be plunged into one of his moods. If he didn't call her, she could not call him. He'd never exactly said, but that was her understanding. Wanting to tell him, *It's lonely being the only one in love.*

She wondered: Maybe Fritzi wasn't driving because his license had been suspended? Or maybe: nerves?

If they were living together, or married, Katie had to concede, Fritzi would be like this much of the time: distant, distracted. If—why not be extravagant, in fantasy—they had children, he'd never be home. Yet she felt tenderness for him. She wanted to forgive him, for hurting her. Katie's father, now deceased, a machine shop worker in Jersey City through his adult life, had been the same way. Probably most men were. So much to think about, a world of numbers, odds that always eluded them. So much, they couldn't hope to squeeze into their heads.

Lonely? That's life.

The night before, in her apartment, in her bedroom where he'd rarely been, Fritzi had showed Katie snapshots of Morning Star, taken at the Thoroughbred farm where the horse was boarded and trained in rural Hunterdon County. The way Fritzi passed the snapshots to her, Katie could sense that he felt strongly about the horse; the way he pronounced "hairline fracture," with a just-perceptible faintness in his voice, allowed Katie to know that Fritzi felt this injury as painfully as if it had been his own. "Beautiful, eh?" was all Fritzi could say. Katie marveled over the silky russet-red horse with a white starlike mark high on his nose, the high-pricked ears and big shiny black protuberant eyes, for Morning Star was in fact a beauty, and maybe the knowledge that such beauty was fragile, so powerful an animal as a horse can be so easily injured, was a part of that beauty, as pain was part of it: the pain of anticipated loss.

"Oh yes. Oh Fritzi! Beautiful."

Two of the snapshots had been bluntly cropped. A third party, posed with Fritzi and Morning Star, had been scissored out of the picture. Katie wouldn't ask: It had to be the third wife. (Her name was Rosalind. Very beautiful, people said. A former model. And younger than Katie Flanders by several years.) In the snapshots, Fritzi Czechi was smiling a rare wide smile, one of his hard-muscled arms slung around the horse's neck, through the horse's thick chestnut-red mane. Fritzi was wearing a sports shirt open at the throat, his stone-colored eyes gleamed like liquid fire; clearly he'd been happy at that moment, as Katie had to concede she'd never seen him.

Carefully Katie asked, "Was this last summer?"

"Was what last summer?"

". . . These pictures taken."

Fritzi grunted what sounded like yes. Already he'd taken the snapshots back and put them away in his inside coat pocket, with his narrow flat Italian leather wallet that was so sleek and fine.

Later, making love in Katie's darkened bedroom, Fritzi had gotten so carried away he'd almost sobbed, burying his heated face in Katie's neck. She'd been surprised by his emotion, and deeply moved. Katie wasn't the kind of girl who could make love with a man without falling in love with him, or, it was fair to say, she wasn't the kind of girl to make love with a man without preparing beforehand to fall in love with him, and deeply in love with him, like sinking through a thin crust of ice and you discover that, beneath the ice, there's quicksand. She'd been wondering if she would ever hear from Fritzi Czechi since the last time she'd seen him, months before, and now he was with her and in her arms, and he was saying, "You're my good, sweet girl, Katie Flemings, aren't you?" and Katie pretended she hadn't heard the wrong name, or maybe she could pretend she'd heard, but knew that Fritzi was teasing. She said, "I am if you want me, Fritzi." She hadn't meant to say this! It sounded all wrong. Holding Fritzi's warm body, stroking his smooth tight-muscled back, kissing the crown of his head where his hair was thinnest, as, half-consciously, you might kiss an infant at such a spot, to protect it from harm, she teased, "Are you my 'good, sweet guy,' Fritzi Czechi?"

Fritzi was most at ease in banter. The way an eel squirms, so you can't get hold of it.

• • •

Fritzi said, "Exit after next, sweetheart."

The Meadowlands exit was fast approaching. Traffic was becoming congested in the northbound lanes. Katie, who'd been cruising at fifty-five miles an hour, was wakened from her reverie by her lover's terse voice. The BMW handled so easily, you could forget where you were, and why. *Maybe he's testing me. Like a racehorse.*

"Looks like lots of people have the same idea we do." Katie meant the other vehicles, headed for the racetrack. "Coming to see Morning Star win his race!"

Again, this sounded wrong. Childish. Katie knew better. Men who followed the horses, especially men like Fritzi Czechi who were professionally involved in the business, didn't require vapid emotional support from women, probably they resented it. All that they required was winning, which meant good luck, beating the odds, and no woman could provide that for them.

Except for the Meadowlands complex, which covered many acres, this part of Jersey wasn't developed. The land was too marshy. There were dumps, landfills. Long stretches of sere-colored countryside glittering with fingers of water like ice. Toxic water, Katie supposed. All of northeast Jersey was under a toxic cloud. Yet there was a strange beauty to the meadowlands, as it was called. Even the chemical-fermenting smell wasn't so bad, if you were used to it. Katie remembered how once when she'd driven along this northern stretch of the Turnpike, into a wasteland of tall wind-rippled rushes and cattails that stretched for miles on either side of the highway, traffic had been routed into a single, slow lane, for there were scattered fires burning in the area; mysterious fires they'd seemed at the time, which Katie would learn afterward had been caused by lightning. The season had been late summer; much of the marshland was dry, dangerously flammable. Clouds of black, foul-smelling smoke drifted across the highway, making Katie choke, stinging her eyes. There were firetrucks and emergency medical vehicles, teams of fireworkers in high boots in the marsh, Jersey troopers directing traffic. Katie had tried not to panic, forced to drive her small car past fires burning to a height of ten feet, brilliant flamey-orange, some hardly more than a car length from the highway. Like driving through hell, you took a deep breath and held it and followed close behind the vehicle in front of you, hoping the wind (yes, it was windy, out of the northeast) wouldn't blow a spark or a flaming piece of vegetation against your car, and after a mile or so you were out of the fire area and you could see again, and you could breathe again, and you felt the thrill of having come through, a sudden stab of happiness. "I'm alive! I made it."

Fritzi was directing Katie to exit, and where to turn at the top of the ramp. As a horse owner he had a special parking permit. Again Katie wondered why he wasn't driving the BMW and would afterward think, *It was all so deliberate! Like life never is.*

They went to the long open barn behind the racetrack where the horses were stalled before their races. This part of the Meadowlands complex, hidden from view of spectators, was bustling with horse activity. Katie stared: so many horses! A local TV camera crew was filming the noisy disembarkment of a Thoroughbred stallion from his van, led blinkered and whinnying down a ramp by his elderly trainer. Photographs were being taken. Katie was struck, as she'd been at her previous visit, by the number of what you'd call civilians in the barn: families, including young children, hovering about their horses' stalls. And everywhere you looked, horses were the tallest figures: their heads looming above the heads of mere human beings, who appeared weak and inconsequential beside them. Even Fritzi Czechi looked diminished, his face suddenly creased with an expression you wouldn't call worry, more like concern, an intense concern, as he was approaching Morning Star's stall.

For this warm June evening at Meadowlands, Fritzi was wearing designer sports clothes: an Armani jacket, jeans that were fitted to his narrow hips like a cowboy's attire, and dark canvas shoes with crepe soles. The jacket was sleekly tapered, though boxy at the shoulders, with large stylish lapels; the fabric was a soft pale gray, the color of a dove's wings, and only if you looked closely could you see the fine, almost invisible stripes in the cloth. Beneath, Fritzi was wearing a black T-shirt: but a designer T-shirt. Fritzi Czechi always dressed with a certain swagger, unlike most guys from Jersey City of any age or class, and his hair was styled to appear fuller and wavier than it was. Katie saw he wasn't tinting it, though. A fair faded brown beginning to turn nickel-colored, like his eyes.

A photographer for the Newark *Star-Ledger* recognized Fritzi and asked to take his picture with Morning Star, but Fritzi shrugged him off, saying he was too busy. Usually, in public, Fritzi Czechi was smoothly smiling and accommodating, so Katie knew: This race meant a lot to him.

And if to Fritzi, then to Katie Flanders. *My future will be decided tonight.* Suddenly she was scared! On all sides she could feel the excitement of the races, like tension gathering before a thunderstorm, and this evening's Meadowlands races were ordinary events, no large purses at stake. Katie didn't want to imagine what it might be like at the Belmont Stakes, the Kentucky Derby. Millions of dollars at stake. Was this where Fritzi Czechi was headed, or thought he might be headed? Or was Fritzi just a small-time Jersey horse owner, hoping for luck? Katie felt how deeply her life was involved with his, or might be. She wanted him to win, if winning was what he wanted, and if he wanted badly to win, she wanted this badly, too. A man is the sum of his moods, it was moods you had to live with. If he had a soul, a deeper self, that was something else: his secret.

The tips of Katie's fingers were going cold. She clutched at Fritzi's arm, but he was getting away from her, walking so quickly she nearly stumbled in her two-inch cork-heeled sandals with the open toes and tropical-colored plastic straps. Katie was a soft-bodied fleshy girl, and she was wearing a candy-striped halter-top nylon dress that showed her shapely breasts to advantage; the skirt was pleated, to obscure the fullness of her hips and thighs, about which she felt less confidence. Her dark blonde hair was tied back in a gauzy red scarf, and around her neck she wore a tiny jade cross on a gold chain, a gift from Fritzi Czechi on the occasion of some long-ago birthday he hadn't exactly remembered when Katie showed it to him.

Fritzi, see? I love it!

What?

This. That you gave me. This cross.

Quickly Katie had kissed Fritzi, to cover his confusion. She was skilled at such maneuvers with men. Always, you wanted a man to save face: Never did you want a man to be embarrassed by you, still less exposed or humiliated. Unless you were dumping him. But even then, tact was required. You didn't want to end up with a split lip or a blackened eye.

Right now, Ftitzi was practically pushing Katie away. He'd forgotten who she was. At Morning Star's stall, talking in an earnest, lowered voice with a fattish gray-haired man who must have been the horse's trainer, while Katie was left to gaze at the horse, marveling at his beauty, and his size. She would play the wide-eyed admiring glamorously made-up female hiding the fact she'd been rebuffed, and was frightened: "Morning Star! What a beauty. So much depends upon you . . ." Katie was trying to overhear what Fritzi and the trainer were talking about so urgently. This was a side of Fritzi unknown to her: anxious, aggressive, not so friendly. It might have been that he and the other man, who was old enough to be Fritzi's father, were taking up a conversation they'd been having recently, in which the words *she, her, them* were predominant. (Fritzi's wife Rosalind? His ex- or separated wife who was a part-owner of Morning Star? Was Fritzi wanting to know if she was at the track, if the trainer had seen her?) Fritzi had only glanced at his horse, immense and restless in his stall, being groomed by a young Guatemalanlooking stable hand, and must have thought that things looked all right. Morning Star would be racing in a little more than an hour. When she'd visited Pink Lady before her race, Katie had been encouraged to stroke the horse's damp velvety nose, and to stroke her sides and back, astonished at how soft and fine the hair was, but Morning Star was a larger horse, a stallion, and coarser, and when Katie lifted her hand to stroke his head as he drank from a bucket, he raised his head swiftly and made a sharp wickering noise and nipped at her fingers quick as a snake. "Oh! Oh God." Katie stared at her hand, her lacquered fingernails, that throbbed as if they'd been caught in a vise. Within seconds there was a reddened imprint of the horse's teeth across three of her knuckles. Fritzi called over sharply, "Katie, watch it," and the trainer said, with belated concern, "Ma'am, don't touch him, Mister can bite." Katie quickly assured them she was all right. (Later she would realize: The stallion might have severed three of her fingertips, in that split-second. If he'd bitten down a little harder. If he'd been angry. If Katie had been due for some very bad luck.)

Katie was hurt, the young Guatemalan groom hadn't warned her she might be bitten. He was rubbing Morning Star's sides, he'd been combing his mane, must have been aware of Katie putting out her hand so riskily, yet he'd said nothing, and was ignoring her now. And Morning Star was ignoring her, though baring his big yellow teeth, stamping, switching his tail. Ready to race? Did a horse know? Katie supposed yes, the horses must know. But they didn't know how risky their race could be, how they might be injured on the track, break a leg and have to be put down. At one of the races the previous year, a horse and jockey had fallen amid a tangle of horses, and the horse had been "put down," as Fritzi spoke of it, right out on the track beneath a hastily erected little tent. Katie had been appalled, she'd wanted to cry. You came to watch a race and you witnessed an execution. "Morning Star! That won't happen to you."

Fritzi came to inspect his horse. Fritzi dared to stroke the stallion's head, talking to him in a low, cajoling voice, but not pushing it, and not standing too near. Always he was aware of the stallion's mouth. He spoke with the groom, and a short, stunted-looking man who was Morning Star's jockey, not yet in his colorful silk costume. It was a measure of Fritzi's distraction, he hadn't introduced Katie to either the trainer or the jockey. She stood to one side feeling excluded, hurt. Embarrassed! She would make a story of it to amuse her girlfriends, who were eager to hear how things had gone with Fritzi Czechi. *That damned horse!— it almost bit off three of my fingers. And you know Fritzi, all he does is call over, Katie, watch it.*

Or maybe she wouldn't tell that story. It wasn't very flattering to her. Maybe, looking back on this evening at Meadowlands, in Fritzi Czechi's company, Katie Flanders wouldn't carry away with her any story she'd want to recall.

•   •   •

Of the nine races at Meadowlands that evening, Fritzi was interested in betting on the second, third, and fourth. Of the fifth race, in which Morning Star was racing, he seemed not to wish to speak. Maybe it was superstition. Katie knew that gamblers were superstitious, and touchy. She knew that being in a gambler's company when he failed to win could mean you were associated with failing to win. Still she blundered, asking a question she meant to be an intelligent question about Morning Star's jockey, and Fritzi replied in monosyllables, not looking at her. They were in the clubhouse before the first race, having drinks. Katie had a glass of white wine. Fritzi drank vodka on the rocks, and rapidly. He was too nerved up to sit still. Men came over to greet him and shake his hand and he made an effort to be friendly, or to seem friendly, introducing Katie to them by only her first name. Katie smiled, trying not to think what this meant. (She was just a girl for the evening? For the night? Expendable, no last name? Or, Fritzi had forgotten her name?) Many in the clubhouse for drinks were nerved up, Katie saw. Some were able to disguise it better than others. Some were getting frankly drunk. In other circumstances Katie would have asked Fritzi to identify these people, whom he seemed to know, and who knew him, at least by name. Fritzi ordered a second drink. He was looking for someone, Katie knew. *The wife. Ex-wife? Rosalind.* Fritzi was smoking a cigarette in short, rapid puffs like a man sucking oxygen, for purely therapeutic reasons. When forced to speak with someone he smiled a bent grimace of a smile, clearly distracted. Compulsively he stroked the back of his head, his hair curling behind his ears. Katie would have liked to take his nervous hand in hers, as a wife might. In an act of daring, she did take his hand, and laced her fingers through his. She told him she was very happy to be with him. She told him she was very happy about the previous night. "And I won't ask about the future," she said, teasing, "because Fritzi Czechi isn't a man to be pinned down." Fritzi smiled at this, and stroked her hand, as if grateful for the bantering tone. Yet always his gaze drifted to the entrance, as a stream of customers, strikingly dressed women, came inside. Katie asked if he'd stake her at betting, as he had the previous year, and Fritzi said sure. "Not only am I going to stake you, sweetheart, you're going to place bets for me, too." Katie didn't get this. Must be, there was logic to it. She wasn't going to question him. She wished she could take chloroform and wake after the fifth race, when the suspense was over, and Morning Star had either won, or had lost; if he'd lost, had he lost badly; if badly, how badly. Katie had a sudden nightmare vision of the beautiful roan stallion crumpled and broken on the track, medics rushing toward

him, the sinister canvas tent erected over the writhing body . . .
It would be Katie Flanders's broken body, too.

Except Katie wasn't worth as much as Morning Star,
whose bloodlines included Kentucky Derby winners. Katie
had no life insurance, for there was no one for whom her life
was precious.

After his third vodka, Fritzi took Katie to place their bets
at the betting windows. The first race was shortly to begin.
This wasn't a race in which Fritzi was much interested, for
some reason he hadn't explained. Only the next three. And in
each, he was calculating they'd win the exacta, which seemed
to Katie far-fetched as winning a lottery: Not only was your
bet on the winning horse, but on the horse to place. (What
were the odds against the exacta? Katie's brain dissolved into
vapor, thinking of such things.) The money Fritzi gave her to
bet with was in crisp twenty-dollar bills. Katie wasn't paying
much attention to the odds on the horses. How much could
they win, if they won? Especially she didn't want to know the
exact sums of money they'd be losing, if they lost. Of course,
all the money was Fritzi's. Yet, if they won, Katie would win,
too.

She thought, *He does love me. This is proof!*

Fritzi led her to their reserved seats, in a shady section of
the stadium, at the finish line, three rows up. Drinking seemed
to have steadied Fritzi's nerves. He was still smoking, and
looking covertly around. Whoever he was looking for hadn't
arrived yet. Katie was beginning to tremble. (All the money
she'd bet! And the fifth race, Fritzie's race, beyond that.) The
first knuckles of her right hand were reddened, swollen, and
throbbing.

Katie said, "I'm just so—anxious. Gambling makes me nervous."

Fritzi said, "Horse racing isn't gambling, it's an art."

He told her if you knew what you were doing, you didn't risk that much. And if you didn't know what the hell you were doing, you shouldn't be betting.

"My way of betting," Katie said, meaning to be amusing in the little-girl way she'd cultivated since childhood, "would be to bet on the horses' names."

Fritzi let this pass. "A name means nothing. Only the bloodline means anything. At the farm, young horses are identified by their dams' names. Until they demonstrate they're worth something, they don't have any identity."

Katie was grateful that Fritzi was talking to her again. Taking her seriously. She wanted to take his hands in hers and lace their fingers together to comfort him. Horses were at the starting gate, the crowd was expectant. A voice in her head, mellowed by wine, reminisced, *That time at Meadowlands! Remember how nervous we were, Fritzi? I didn't want to tell you how badly my hand was hurting* . . .

Fritzi was saying, as if arguing, "Horse racing isn't a crap shoot. It isn't playing the slots. You figure how the horse has done recently. You figure the horse's history, meaning the bloodline. You figure who the jockey is. You figure who the other horses are, he'll be racing. And the odds. Always, the odds. There's people who believe, and maybe I'm one of them, there's no luck at all. No luck. Only what has to be, that you can figure. Or try to." Katie was silenced by this speech of Fritzi's, which was totally unlike him. He seemed almost to be speaking to someone else. Not the slightest trace of banter here, or irony.

It was during the first race that Fritzi's wife, unless the woman was his ex-wife, came to sit a row down from them, twelve seats to Fritzi's right. Katie saw, and recognized her immediately. Or maybe Katie was reacting to Fritzi's sudden stiffness. Rosalind was with a tall sturdily built man of about Fritzi's age with olive-dark skin and ridged, graying hair. She was a striking young woman, as she'd been described to Katie, stylishly dressed in a lilac pants suit with a loose, low-cut white blouse, and wearing a wide-brimmed straw hat. Her long straight dyed-looking black hair fell past her shoulders. Her skin was geisha-white, and her mouth very red. She was theatrical-looking, eye-catching. Katie felt a pang of jealousy, resentment. Rosalind was said to have been a model even while attending East Orange High School, and at the peak of her brief career she'd appeared in glossy magazines like *Glamour* and *Allure*. She'd married Fritzi Czechi and gotten pregnant and had a miscarriage and within a few years the marriage was over and it was Rosalind who'd sued for divorce. All Fritzi had ever said about this third marriage in Katie's presence was that mistakes were made on both sides: "End of story."

Katie knew better. Not a single guy she'd ever dated, or even heard of, no matter how long divorced, if he hadn't been the one to initiate the divorce, he never forgot. A man never forgets, and never forgives.

Katie wondered what it would be like: a former husband still wanting you, when you didn't want him. A former lover still loving you even as he hated you. A man you'd slept with, and hoped to have children with, fantasizing how he might kill you, for betraying him.

There had to be money involved, too, with Fritzi's marriage. He'd signed over the house to Rosalind, and the house was reputedly worth a half-million dollars. And there was Morning Star, and maybe other horses. Common property. Katie felt how Fritzi was holding himself so still he was almost trembling, as if their seats and the stands and the very earth beneath them were vibrating, shaken by horses' pounding hooves as they galloped around the track. Katie stared, seeing nothing. A blur. People were on their feet, shouting. Katie hadn't bet on any horse in this race, none of the names meant a thing to her. She and Fritzi had no stake in the outcome. She scarcely glanced up when the winner was declared. The time: 1.46.41. The purse was $17,000. (The purse for the fifth race would be $34,000.) Katie brushed her hand against Fritzi's and felt his icy fingertips.

High overhead, drifting across the red-streaked sky, was a lighted dirigible advertising a brand of cigarettes. Katie glanced upward, startled. Though she didn't exactly mean it, she heard herself saying to Fritzi, "These big open stadiums! They scare me. Somebody could drop a bomb. Some sniper could shoot into the stands. On TV I saw this soccer riot somewhere in South America. Think if people panicked, how you could be trampled . . ."

Fritzi said, "There's cops here. Security cops. Things like that don't happen in the U.S." Fritzi was forcing himself to speak in a normal-sounding voice. But still he sat stiffly, turned slightly to the left to prevent him seeing the strikingly dressed young woman who'd been his third wife, and the man who was with her. Katie thought, dismayed, *He loves her. He'll never get over it.* She had a vision of Morning Star winning his race, and Fritzi and Rosalind coming together to hug each other, united in victory. Reconciled. Was that how this evening at Meadowlands would turn out?

Ruefully Katie rubbed her throbbing fingers. She saw, shocked, that one of her meticulously manicured fingernails, lacquered ivory-pink, was broken and jagged. The nail was splitting vertically, into her flesh.

After the first race, in which they had no stake, things would happen swiftly.

• • •

In the second race, Katie had placed bets on Sweet Nougat to win and Iron Man to place. They came through. Katie was on her feet screaming and flailing the air as the horses raced around the track. All of it happening so fast: like a speeded-up dream. The horses' rushing legs, pounding hooves, the jockeys crouched over their backs in colorful silk costumes, little monkey-men wielding whips—"Oh my God! Oh my God we won! We won, Fritzie, we *won*!" Like an overgrown child Katie flailed the air with her arms, hardly able to contain her excitement. The color was up in her face, her pulse beat in a delirium of hope. Fritzi remained seated. With his stub of a pencil he made a check on the racing form. When Katie tried to hug him he stiffened, keeping her at a little distance with his left forearm; not a forcible gesture, and in no way hostile, but Katie would recall it afterward. *Didn't want me to touch him. Oh Fritzi!*

In that first race, clocked at 1.25.01, Katie and Fritzi won $1,336 each.

"Honey, you don't even seem much surprised," Katie said, lightly chiding. She dabbed at her overheated face with a tissue. "*I'm* surprised. I never win things!"

Fritzi shrugged, and smiled. As if to say that, with him, now she would.

In the third race, they'd bet on Hot Ott to win and Angel Fire to place. Another time Katie was on her feet flailing the air and screaming and another time their horses pulled away from the pack, Hot Ott by a length ahead of Angel Fire, the two horses racing head-long and furious in the homestretch, and Angel Fire was overtaking Hot Ott, had almost overtaken Hot Ott, but had not, and so it was Hot Ott to win and Angel Fire to place. "He won! Our picks won!" Perspiration glowed on Katie's skin, her eyes were radiant with innocence and hope. In this race they hadn't won quite so much as they'd won in the first, but it would be $834 apiece. Katie sat close beside Fritzi wanting to hug, hug, hug the man, but content with just nudging knees. She fanned herself with the track program. Tendrils of hair clung to her forehead. She was trying not to glance to the side, to observe the third Mrs. Czechi in her elegant wide-brimmed straw hat, calm and beautiful in profile; though she was wishing she'd worn a straw hat herself, it conferred such class to the wearer. "Some days, they seem to last forever. I mean, you remember them forever. It's like eternity. This is one of them, for me, Fritzi, it *is*." Katie spoke happily, heedlessly. She was one to speak her heart, when she believed she spoke truthfully, and when what she said would be heard, and valued, by another whom she trusted. Stiff and unyielding as a man who has been wounded and is trying not to betray pain, Fritzi was observing Katie with his stone-colored eyes that were oddly moist, sympathetic. That was what Katie believed: sympathetic. Fritzi Czechi was her friend, he'd always be her friend, not only her lover. "It's like at certain times in our lives, rare times, God peers into time out of His place in eternity and it's like a—" Katie paused, blushing, not knowing what she was saying: a flash of lightning? a spotlight in a theater? an eclipse of the sun, as the sun is easing free of the shadow over it? Probably she was making a fool of herself, chattering like this. Fritzi squeezed her hand as if to calm her. "Katie, you're my good, sweet girl, aren't you?" he said, and Katie murmured yes, yes! and Fritzi said, "You and I go 'way back. We're old buddies." Katie shut her eyes to be kissed, and Fritzi did kiss her, but only on the nose, wet and playful as you'd kiss a child.

It was like Fritzi was amused by her, for her caring so much that they'd won a couple of thousand dollars. But Katie was feeling, well—like a winner should. Flying high! Drunk! That happy airy floating kind of drunk before you start to stumble, and find yourself puking into a toilet. She'd had just one glass of dry white wine in the clubhouse but it was as if she'd been drinking champagne all evening. She had a quick warm flash of being married to Fritzi Czechi and the two of them living somewhere suburban; no, they were living in Fair Hills, or was it Far Hills, Jersey horse country, Fritzi could raise Thoroughbreds, champion racehorses. In the barn, she'd liked the smell of the horses. Even the horses' droppings. It was mixed with an overlying smell of hay. And that was sweet. She would learn to ride a horse: It wasn't too late. Tall and elegant in the saddle she would take equestrian lessons, lose eighteen pounds and be slender again, and Fritzi would love her, and possibly he'd be faithful to her. But always, Fritzi Czechi would be her friend.

The fourth race! In the fourth race, Fritzi and Katie won the lottery: the trifecta.

Heavenly Jewel to win, Billy's Best to place, Sam the Ma to show. They'd picked them all.

Another time Katie was on her feet, squealing, radia

with excitement. It was like she was back in high school those frenzied Friday nights cheering for the Jersey City team to win. Except here were nine horses, and of these nine any one could win, all the more triumphant their victory when Heavenly Jewel thundered across the finish line by a nose ahead of Billy's Best, and there came Sam the Man behind, and this time even Fritzi registered a smile, a small smile of surprise, yes Fritzi was surprised to have won the trifecta. (So maybe he did believe in luck, after all.) Katie cried, "Fritzi, it's *magic*. You are *magic*." Magic meant they'd collect $3,799 each.

Still Fritzi seemed not-himself, somehow. Katie nudged his knees. Why wasn't he sexier, funnier? "You don't always win like this, honey, do you?" Katie asked, and Fritzi shrugged, "No. I have to admit." It was like Fritzi that, though he was visibly warm, he wouldn't unbutton the Armani jacket. A film of perspiration gleamed on his fair, flushed skin like miniature jewels. Slowly he stroked his hair behind his ears, a man in a trance.

The next race was the fifth.

Morning Star, and eight others. Katie was so scared, she oped she wouldn't faint. She could see that Fritzi was in ne zoned-out space, very quiet, very still, just staring at the ing gate. Morning Star was second-to-inside, his jockey yellow silks. There was a hush of expectation through ds. Covertly Katie glanced to Fritzi's right and saw the black-haired young woman in the wide-brimmed also sitting very straight, very still, and gripping the man beside her.

trying not to think *hairline fracture, beyond compu-*. Was there a more devastating term than *put* mbered the tangle of horses and jockeys in that race last summer, a horse had balked coming out of the gate, and swerved sideways into another, and horses had fallen, and jockeys, and the race was jinxed from the start though other horses had pulled away in the clear, and Pink Lady had galloped so hard, you could see the filly was running her heart out, yet the evil little monkey-man hunched over her neck continued to use his whip, and shuddering and in a lather she'd galloped over the finish line not first, not second, but third—and wasn't that enough? Wasn't that good enough? Though that evening, Katie had to concede Fritzi had been in an irritable mood, waving away Katie's elation, and the well-intentioned congratulations of others. For third place wasn't good enough. Third place at Meadowlands, a weekday race that's one of nine races, the purse is only $21,000 to win, no: not enough. Not for Fritzi Czechi. Gallop your heart out, it isn't enough.

For a melancholy time then Katie hadn't heard from Fritzi Czechi. He was back with his wife Rosalind. If she'd begun divorce proceedings, these were halted. Temporarily. Katie made inquiries about Pink Lady and learned that the filly had lost races, hadn't qualified for some high-stakes handicap in Florida, and Fritzi had sold her.

What happens then, Katie asked, dreading to know. Whoever it was telling her this, a jokey kind of guy, he'd run his fingers across his throat. "Dog food."

Katie didn't believe that, though. She did not.

Not Pink Lady who'd been so comely, of whom, for a while, Fritzi Czechi had been so proud.

• • •

At the gate, one of the horses was stamping its feet, misbehaving, there was a delay and the horse was led off and an announcement made, Duke II was "scratched." Katie thought: This was good luck, what might have gone wrong in the race went wrong before the race, and Morning Star was safe.

"Morning Star": Katie murmured the name aloud. She squinted to see where he was positioned. The tall horse, beautiful russet-red coat, white starburst high on his nose, was lost amid the others at the starting gate. All nine horses were large, beautiful, powerful beasts with muscled haunches. Each was prized by its owners. Each was worth a lot of money. It was like seeing someone you think you love, unexpectedly in a public place, and you realize he isn't extraordinary, isn't that good-looking, nothing special about him but you've invested your heart in him, you love him and want to love him and to withdraw that love would be to violate your own heart, to turn traitor.

The race began. So fast! Sudden! Katie was on her feet, blinking in confusion. Somehow it was more than the usual confusion of horses' flying hooves, the gaily colored costumes of the jockeys, Katie's eyes were dazzled, hardly could she catch her breath. Morning Star! Where was he? Another horse was in the lead? By a length? Pulling away? She saw the roan stallion thudding along behind, caught in the pack, struggling to break ahead. A horse did break ahead, but it wasn't the roan stallion. On Morning Star, the monkey-man in the yellow silks wielded his whip. All the monkey-men were wielding their cruel little whips. Katie was too frightened to scream, to squeal, to flail her arms this time. For this was the race of her life.

She saw Morning Star, her lover's horse who'd bitten her,

galloping into the turn, straining to pull away from the others. Almost, Katie had an evil thought: wished there would be an upset: a spill: two horses tangled together, three horses, and falling, and Morning Star would pull away, free. In her trance of oblivion she was praying, *God, let him win. God, God, let him win I will never ask another thing of You.* The lead horses were in the backstretch. Morning Star was among the lead horses now. Was Morning Star pulling forward? He was! The lead horse, a big purely black stallion, had begun to wobble, other horses would overtake it. Swift and pitiless other horses would overtake it. There was the yellow-clad jockey easing his horse faster, always faster. Katie was screaming now, unaware. Screaming herself hoarse. She had no awareness of Fritzi, who was on his feet beside her, but very quiet, only just staring, his arms slightly lifted, elbows at his sides. She had no awareness of others in the stands shouting, screaming. There came horses into the homestretch, Morning Star on the inside of the track, in fourth place, now in third place, galloping furiously, now overtaking the front-running horses, in second place close behind the lead horse and edging closer, ever closer, to passing that horse; and if the track had been longer, if only the track had been longer!—the roan stallion would have passed the lead horse, thundering across the finish line only just a half-length behind the winner.

The race was clocked at 1.10.91. It would be the fastest race of the evening. Anchor Bay the winner, Morning Star second, and Blue Eyes third. Katie's cheeks were damp with tears. She had never been so happy. She cried to Fritzi, "Oh, honey, that was good, wasn't it? Wasn't it? His first time back, with his knee hurt? We came in second, we didn't lose, he did real well, didn't he? Honey?" In her excitement Katie was pawing at Fritzi, wanting badly to hug him, and he gripped her elbows to calm her, to steady her; he was himself in a daze though not smiling, not delirious with relief and happiness like Katie, more like a man waking from a dream of heart-stopping intensity not knowing where he was, but knowing what he must do. His face that was usually flushed was ashen, a rivulet of sweat ran down his forehead, his stone-colored eyes were shimmering with moisture. What was wrong with Fritzi Czechi? Telling Katie, with a small fixed smile like a mannequin's smile, "We did real well, sweetheart. Right. This is our lucky day."

. . .

Into Katie's still-shaking hand Fritzi was placing—what? An envelope?

He'd taken it out of his inside coat pocket. It was the size of a greeting card, it was sealed. On the front hand-printed KATIE FLANDERS. Fritzi said, "Don't open this till later. Promise."

"Promise—what?"

"Don't open this till later."

"Later, when?"

But Fritzi was walking away from her. Fritzi was leaving her behind. Like a sleepwalker, she would remember him. Ashen-faced, and sweaty, and his damp hair curling and lank behind his ears. And the back of the sexy Armani jacket sweated through between his shoulder blades. Katie called, "Fritzi? Wait." Tried to follow him but there were too many others in the aisle. Damn, Katie was stumbling in her ridiculous high-heeled shoes. "Fritzi?" Trying to follow the man she loved, and always she would remember: It was one of those nightmares where you are trying, trying desperately, to get somewhere, but can't, like making your way through quicksand, a bog that's sucking at your feet, and she could see Fritzi only a few yards away, quickly descending the steps in the center aisle, for a few confused seconds her vision was blocked, then again she saw, she would be a witness, as Fritzi Czechi made his swift and unerring way to the woman in the wide-brimmed straw hat and eye-catching lilac pants suit, this woman and her male friend who were also on their feet, dazed and exhilarated by the outcome of the race, which for them, too, would seem to have been unexpected, more than they'd hoped, and then Katie was seeing the woman glance around, at Fritzi, her geisha-white face not quite so young as Katie had thought, and frightened, yet she was trying to smile, for a woman's first defense is a smile, and her companion beside her who was just lighting a cigarette turned to see Fritzi, too, and possibly there was a glimmer of recognition here, too, but no time for alarm, for there was a flash of something metallic in Fritzi's upraised right hand, and the man staggered and fell back, and there was a second flash, and the young woman screamed and fell, the straw hat knocked from her head, there came one, two, three more shots and now in the crowd there were isolated screams, shouts, a wave of panic that sucked all the oxygen from Katie's lungs and brain and left her paralyzed unable to believe she'd seen what she had seen, for it had happened too swiftly, nothing like a movie or TV scene for in fact she couldn't see, all was confusion, the backs of strangers, the flailing arms of strangers, a man beside her elbowing her in his desperation to escape, a woman behind her beginning to sob, and Katie was frantic to get to Fritzi, but shoved to the side, her leg bruised against a seat, and now there came another shot, a single shot, and more screams, on all sides strangers were shoving and pushing to escape, while others were ducking down into their seats, and Katie from Jersey City understood it was wisest to imitate these, huddling in her seat with her face pressed against her knees, her arms crossed over the tender nape of her neck, praying to God another time for help, as if in these moments of terror not knowing who the shooter was, and what he'd done, and that, with that last shot, it was probably over.

• • •

He'd killed them with a handgun that would be identified as a .380-caliber semiautomatic pistol with a defaced serial number that would be traced to a shipment of several hundred similar pistols that had been illegally sold in the New York City area in the mid-1980s. He'd killed his estranged wife and her companion with two shots and three shots respectively. From a distance of less than eighteen inches. Both had died within seconds. He'd then turned the gun on himself, as witnesses watched in horror, placing the barrel precisely at the back of his head, aiming upward, and pulling the trigger with no hesitation. It was a stance, it was an act, Fritzi Czechi had clearly rehearsed many times in solitude.

Katie identified herself to police. Katie Flanders, who'd been Fritzi Czechi's companion. Dazed and exhausted yet not hysterical (not yet: that would come later) she'd answered their questions, all that she knew. Suddenly sick to her stomach, vomiting what tasted like hot acid. She was fainting, medics attended her, her blood pressure dangerously low, yet she recovered within a few minutes and was strong enough to refuse to be taken to the hospital. Refused an ambulance. No, no!

She searched for the envelope that had fallen beside her seat. With badly shaking fingers she opened it as police officers looked on. Yet, she opened it. Inside were keys to the BMW, and registration papers, and a document that looked legal, deeding the car to "Katie Flanders." A terse hand-printed note on a stiff white card:

Dear Katie
This is for you. Also the things in the trunk.
A token of my esteem.
    Fritzi C.

Esteem! Fritzi C.! Katie began to laugh shrilly, helplessly, swiping at her eyes. Fritzi Czechi had eluded her, as she'd always known he would. It had not mattered that she loved him. It had not mattered what old, good buddies they were, from Jersey City. Like the roan stallion with the white starburst on its forehead overtaking, passing the other horses, galloping furiously, unstoppable, continuing in his ecstatic head-on plunge away from the dirt track, out of Meadowlands park, out of your vision and into eternity.

HOTWALKING

Julie Smith

I come back to myself around six a.m. one fine December morning. The first thing I'm aware of is that I'm in some kind of institutional cafeteria, my hands clutching one of those generic thick white mugs, this one filled with a murky liquid— undoubtedly coffee, but you couldn't prove it by me. My taste buds aren't working so well, and neither is anything else. I'm still too groggy to even know my name, which is as new as my surroundings. I feel a hand on my shoulder and soft breath at my ear. "Ya feelin' better, baby?"

A black woman is standing behind me, hovering gently. She is the one who brought the coffee. *Better than what?* I wonder. I can't remember feeling anything, ever, but pretty soon I remember too much, and realize that that's because I haven't wanted to. I've been in a state of alcohol-induced numbness for weeks, maybe months. But it comes to me soon that I may be where I want to be.

"I'm fine," I lie. "Thanks for the coffee. Am I at the Fair Grounds, by any chance?"

"Least ya got that right. Ya know what day it is?"

I don't. "But I'm in New Orleans, right?" I ask.

"Oh baby," the woman says. She sits down across from me and I see that she is in her fifties and she has a round, kind face. "Ya need a job? Mr. DeLessep' need a hotwalker. Ya know what hotwalkin' is?"

I do know. And I know the Fair Grounds is a racecourse, and that I am on the backside. I know the backside of a track like my own neighborhood. I know its language, its rhythms, even its secrets—including the fact that it's a good place to hide, that people like me, lost souls who love horses and want a ready-made community, turn up at tracks routinely. No one will think a thing about my being here, will think it odd that I seem to have dropped from the sky, with my Yankee accent and decent grammar. I am Italian by birth, but I can probably pass for Hispanic, like most of the low-level workers at the Fair Grounds. At least till I open my mouth.

"I'm Luz," I say, and I'm acutely aware of the homonym. I must have been feeling self-destructive when I picked it. Big surprise.

"Velvet," she answers, and it takes me a moment to realize that this is her name.

"Good to meet you," I say. "How can I find Mr. De-Lesseps?" I know his name, of course. I've made it my business to know who all the best trainers are, all the important owners, all the big horses. Perhaps I will get to walk Big Easy, which I'd like a lot.

There is more racing in Louisiana than you'd imagine—maybe more than in any other state. Some of the best riders grew up at the cheap tracks in Acadia, sat on the backs of horses while other kids played on seesaws. Still, this is not the land of the Secretariats and the Seabiscuits and the Silky Sullivans. It isn't the big time, but thoroughbreds remind me of that old saying about sex—even the worst is wonderful. There are still some nice animals here, and Big Easy's one of the best—or used to be. He isn't the horse that interests me most, and Jimmy DeLesseps isn't the trainer I came here to meet, but I've still plucked a plum.

In a few hours I've sobered up, and I find that I have an instant family, a ton of new friends, and a half-decent job— walking hots, about all I can handle right now. I also have sunshine, clear blue sky, and the company of horses. Everything I want. I've landed on my feet, though God knows how.

In one way it's a sad day, though. Some horse breaks a leg in the fourth race, and I see his doc put him down, right on the road by the dumpsters. I can't help it, I get tears in my eyes. The vet turns to me. "He didn't suffer," he says, not knowing that I know as much about it as he does. "We used to have to use what they call the Humane Killer." He shakes his head. "How ya like that? the Humane Killer."

"You mean you shot them."

"Yeah, but some of these docs drink a little too much, and they got to missing too many times, and sometimes the wrong horse got shot, or maybe a person. So we switched to strychnine."

"Strychnine." I wince, knowing what that would do to a horse, thinking about the convulsions, how its neck would stretch backward, the agony the drug would cause the animal.

"But then we had to stop that, too. Because they were feedin' the dead horses to the lions at the Audubon Zoo, and the cats were pukin' their guts out."

In spite of myself, I laugh. Because I know I'm really in New Orleans. Where else would you hear a story like that?

I think of my favorite Damon Runyon yarn, "A Story Goes with It," the one about Hot Horse Herbie, the tout whose tips always came with a tale. In New Orleans, a story *always* goes with it—whatever it is—and it usually makes you laugh.

Even though it's early afternoon and a three-year-old colt has just become lion food, I feel okay. I know I can make it. I can stay here and sober up and do what I came here to do.

I get a little apartment in Mid-City, right in the Fair Grounds neighborhood, and I go to meetings when I can, but mostly I work, and that does it by default, almost.

Many of the jobs at the track, like mine, require little or no skill—though some require the nerve of a fighter pilot—but you've got to show up. That's almost the whole job. You have to be there at five a.m. every day, including weekends. *No one gets a day off. Ever.*

• • •

Annalise Marino Finley, the person I was before I morphed into Luz Serrano, used to have her own business, which she ran with her husband, Sam. She has a graduate degree, and people address her as *Dr.* Finley. Annalise is a damn good veterinarian. Luz Serrano walks horses to cool them down.

That's all hotwalking is. They have machines that do it now, but they're awkward and a little dangerous. Most of the good trainers don't use them. Nothing like the human touch, especially with a fractious animal, and thoroughbreds are notoriously fractious.

The backside of the track—the backstage part, if you will—is its own little bustling city. Everybody's got a job to do, but there's a lot of downtime, too, and nobody notices a young Hispanic-looking woman in jeans, as long as she doesn't go where she doesn't work. I pretty much have the run of the place, if I stay out of the big owners' barns. That old-time racetrack secrecy thing is still in force. God forbid somebody should clock your horse, a phrase that means a lot more than time it with a stopwatch. For instance, you might, if you were bold enough, unwrap its bandages to look at its legs. You might discover it had a bowed tendon, which would be disastrous in a claiming race.

Because in a claiming race, you're gambling that the horse you claim is "worth the money," as we say in my village. Claiming is a gamble, like everything else here, and we prefer that word to "bet." If he wants to keep his horse, the owner is gambling that his horse won't get claimed; if he doesn't, he's betting the horse will.

If he gives a horse a drug called etorphine (aka elephant juice), he's betting it'll run like Citation, but not go crazy enough to run into a wall. He's also gambling that it doesn't get tested.

In theory, all the winners get tested after the race, and sometimes—as in a stakes race—so do the other horses who run in the money. But testing is like airport security—some days it doesn't happen the way it's supposed to. The Cajun guys like to roll the dice to see if it's worth it to take a shot. If one guy sends a horse (shoots him up with narcotics, which, oddly enough, stimulate horses), and the horse doesn't test positive, word gets around that the drug he used is passing. And there's suddenly a rash of positives. One weekend, I heard, eighteen winners tested positive at the Fair Grounds.

My friend Bumpy Verrette, who works at the window, takes a philosophical view: "Look, ya got ten horses in a race, half are on the needle, the other half are on the joint. No problem. Ya got a level playing field."

When he says "joint," he's not talking about pot—he means a little battery with two prongs on it that slips in the palm of the rider's hand. Give a horse a jolt of that, he's gonna run his haunches off. It's also called a machine, and it's highly illegal. The old-timers say when they harrow the turf, they turn them up by the dozen.

In a weird way, Bumpy's right—everybody's out for the edge. I should know. My husband, Sam, was a racetrack vet. Here's the simple fact: There's only one injection it's legal to give a horse on race days. That's a diuretic called Lasix, which reduces a horse's blood pressure. Yet ninety percent of the injections given are administered on race days.

So how does it work? Easy. First of all, blood and urine samples can disappear. There's no overseer to watch everyone in the spit barn every minute, and there are plenty of people there to do the dirty. Grooms, for instance. The people who walk the horses in the barn, cooling them out while they're waiting to be tested. The piss catchers themselves. The test barn vet. The secretary in the state vet's office. Nobody else is supposed to be in the barn, but for one reason or another, there's always traffic.

Then, too, lots of drugs don't show up in tests, and they aren't really illegal. They're just against the rules. Simple as that. An owner loses the purse if his horse gets a bad test, but he doesn't go to jail. Most track vets do what they're told, so long as it's not illegal and it doesn't hurt the horse. The vet's got nothing to lose, and certain injections make the animals safer and more comfortable. Calcium and vitamin B1, for instance, which tend to calm the horses. ACTH, a hormone that depletes their stores of adrenaline. Antibiotics to treat infection. Bronchodilators to prevent bleeding in the lungs.

Narcotics *will* test, however, and so will acepromazine, a highly illegal tranquilizer. Commonly given no-nos are morphine, Dilaudid, Ritalin and apomorphine, which Sam and I used to laugh about. When Sam first came to the track, he was so green someone said to him, "Hey, Doc, you gonna give him apo today?" and Sam thought he meant "Alpo."

. . .

Sam and I grew up together in Jersey, in a suburb of New York. We fell in love in high school, mostly, I guess, because of our mutual affinity for animals. I loved the way he talked to his pets, and later to his patients. I'd imagine him talking to our children that way. Maybe the same thing attracted him to me—if I may brag for a moment, back home I had a reputation as a bit of a horse-whisperer.

We got married after college, went through vet school together and opened a small animal hospital. But Sam's first love was always horses. It wasn't long before he began working for first one trainer, then another. Though we both hated the schedule, he was hooked—and not only on the seamy romance of the track. He wanted to make a lot of money in a hurry, so we never had to worry about things like sending our kids to college—the kids we didn't yet have. "Just a few years," he'd say, "and I'll come home to the puppies and kitties and guinea pigs. And we'll have three beautiful children and live in style." A track vet can make as much as $400,000 a season.

Problem was, Sam, poor baby, was so naïve he ended up involved with a small-time mobster. And didn't even know it.

At the time, he was working for a trainer named Clancy Forest. Clancy, in turn, was employed by an owner named Claire Brent, whose "big horse" was a dazzling colt named Satan's Moon. Sam never met Mrs. Brent, and it wouldn't have mattered if he had. She didn't own that horse, or any of the others under her name.

One day Sam reported for work, and the foreman said, "Hey, Doc, got a job for you. The horse in Stall Eighteen got a positive on his Coggins. Clancy said take him outside and put him down." He meant the horse had come down with swamp fever, equine infectious anemia.

Sam did as he was told. Afterward, he covered the dead horse with a tarp and went on to his other duties. An hour later, he heard shouting, to which he paid no attention, and then Clancy hunted him down, car keys in his hand. He rattled them like a weapon, like he was going to go for Sam's eyes. "Doc, you put the wrong goddam horse down."

"No, I didn't. The foreman said Stall Eighteen."

"Stall Eight, dammit. Loose Lady was in Eighteen."

The way Sam told it, sweat popped out on his brow and the back of his neck prickled. Loose Lady had just won a stakes race. She wasn't as fast as Moon, but she was a damned valuable filly.

"Know who that horse's owner is? Burt the goddam Hatch! You know who that is? And you know what they mean by Hatch? Or do I have to spell it out for you?

Poor Sam. He said, "Claire Brent owns that horse."

"You ever heard of a program owner, you little rube? Burt the fuckin' *Hatch* owns the goddam horse. The same Burt the *Hatch* who's got so many fuckin' felonies he couldn't run a horse on a cheap track in fuckin' Kansas.

Know what you just cost me, asshole? My right tibia, if he finds me. I'm outta here *now*." He held up his keys and rattled them some more, for emphasis. "You got any sense, you get on the next plane leaves the airport." He whirled, marched out on the two legs he intended to keep, and Sam never saw him again.

He never met Burt the Hatch either, but it wasn't ten minutes before some Mexican with a tire iron came in and applied it to Sam—all over, but with special emphasis, as Clancy'd predicted, on his legs. Leg-breaking is still very big among the horsy set, and it's not confined to humans—an owner wants to get rid of a rival horse, he sends someone to break the animal's cannon bone.

How can he do this? Easy. Hardly any of the barns have night watchmen, and anyway, a lot of track people get blind and deaf around guys with tire irons.

Sam's left leg healed all right, but the right one never did. He can walk, but barely. He's too shaky to handle large animals anymore, which might not be so bad—he could always go back to the guinea pigs—but he got addicted to painkillers, whether because of the pain, or because he was so goddam depressed he couldn't face anything anymore. He's never come out of it.

He said he wasn't fit to be a husband anymore and moved to a cabin in Maine. Technically we're still married; I have his address for emergencies, and he has my cell number. We even e-mail now and then.

But he took my heart to Maine with him. When he left, I started drinking.

And planning.

Fortunately, I had the sense to sell the hospital before I

started operating drunk and losing people's golden retrievers. It didn't yield much, but I had enough to live on for a while, and enough to carry out the plan. I hired a P.I. to find the Hatch, who'd disappeared soon after Sam was attacked.

For one reason or another (my P.I. never got the details) things had gotten too hot for him, and he'd moved to Louisiana, taking his horses with him—including Satan's Moon. It's a state with a reputation. Guess he figured he'd feel at home there.

Luz Serrano's happy to be there, too. The weather's great and the folks are real friendly.

. . .

Big Easy isn't doing too well this season, and I think I know why. DeLesseps is having his rider hold him, waiting for the odds to go up. But one of the friends I make is Wally Michaels, Big Easy's doc; I hang around Wally and watch what he gives him. Nothing on race days, not even Lasix. Big Easy's an honest horse, I could swear it. And why not? He's a good little horse, I know that from his past record. All he needs is a rider who wants him to win. I don't think he has one.

Another of my new friends is Satan's Moon's trainer, Rayford Burke.

These are two people I need to know. It's not hard for me—track folks are friendly, and so am I. And I look good in jeans.

When the odds are ten-to-one, I start hearing scuttlebutt, and I watch Wally pretty closely, but I still don't see anything funny.

Moon runs a hell of a race, but he only comes in second.

Big Easy wins.

Rayford Burke's way the hell down in the dumps. He tells me the owner, who he doesn't name, is gonna be furious. "He loves that horse more than his own wife. Wants him for stud," he says.

Right. Stud. All these coonass owners have extravagant dreams about stud. For one thing, there's money in it; for another, they all want to think they've got another Seattle Slew.

I tell him Moon's a great horse (which is something of a lie, because Sam has told me things about Moon) but I know they're sending Big Easy (which is a bald-faced lie). And I offer to bet Rayf Big Easy'll win again if he goes off against Moon. I even say I saw Wally shoot him up.

Rayf beetles up his brow and gives me a glare. "Why the hell are you telling me this?"

"If Big Easy wins, I'll be the one walking him," I say. "Jimmy always wants me to walk the big horse."

Rayf nods, getting what I'm saying. The walker in the paddock is on public view and I make a point of being better groomed than most of the others. Realizing that seems to rouse Rayf's suspicions. "Who are you?" he asks suddenly.

At first I panic, thinking he knows something, but then he says, "You're no Mexican hotwalker. You talk like a debutante."

So I give him some cock-and-bull story about being once being an M.D. and going on the skids, and losing my marriage, and taking riding lessons as a kid and loving horses. He buys it, and I'm glad he asked—it puts us on more of an equal footing. I go on with my story.

"Point is," I say, "I've got access to Big Easy's water."

"You could drug his water if he wins, that what you're saying? I don't get it. If he's already drugged, what's the point?"

I shrug. "Maybe I'm wrong. Maybe they're just holding him. Or maybe they're giving him something that doesn't test. I'm just saying I can make sure."

"You want to fix the race for some reason of your own, why the hell tell me about it?" He's trying to sound bored and a little outraged, but I know he's hooked.

"Because I'm looking for a sure thing, Rayf. Why should I be different from anyone else? I need to make a big score in the New Orleans Handicap, and let's face it, it's a two-horse race. If they start holding Big Easy again, the odds get longer and longer. So Big Easy wins, I win big. But Moon wins, I don't, even if I bet it both ways. Because the favorite's not going to pay much."

"I'm losing you."

"I'm offering insurance here—for you, and for me. If Moon comes in second and Big Easy tests positive, Moon takes the purse, right? Big fat $500,000 purse."

"Right."

"Well, the owner's share of that's sixty percent. Three hundred grand's a hell of a lot of money. Half of that ought to be enough for anybody. I make it happen, I want the other half. Then the owner and I both know in advance who's going to win and we each know we're going to walk away with a hundred and fifty grand. We're both happy."

"You want half the purse?" Rayf laughs in my face. "You think the owner's just gonna fork over a hundred and fifty grand?"

"No," I say. "But it's a good place to start."

"Suppose Moon wins. You think you should still get paid?"

"What does insurance mean to you?" I say, and the question isn't exactly rhetorical. "By the way, I'm gonna need half up front."

Rayf laughs his head off, but I don't care. It's not the money I'm after. I don't honestly think Burt the Hatch is going to make a deal with me, I just want Rayf to bring it up with him, if only for laughs. Because when it's all over, I want the Hatch to know he's been scammed by a hotwalker.

Big Easy's rider starts holding him again, and the odds shoot up, so I can see I'm right. DeLesseps is waiting for the Handicap.

Meanwhile, Moon's winning all his races—Rayf wants him to be the favorite because Burt doesn't care about gambling, he doesn't care about anything but Moon's reputation and his future as a daddy. He's evidently not worried about Big Easy at all—who would be?

I put the whole thing out of my head. I have other things to think about. One of them is to open an account with the track, so I can make phone bets whenever I want.

But a couple of days before the race, Rayf hunts me down. "You know what we were talking about that time?" He's being circumspect for fear of being overheard. "I think I might be able to do something for you."

"Ah. Getting nervous, are you? Did you talk to the owner?"

Rayf bites his lip, looking like a little kid. Maybe he's suddenly realized what I meant when I said, *"What does insurance mean to you?"* Because as long as Big Easy runs in the money, he's going to get sent to the test barn, and I'll be walking him. Moon's water'll be there too. My poisoning opportunities will be almost unlimited.

"Look, we need Moon to win this thing the worst kind of way. But I gotta tell ya, the owner's not all that worried about Big Easy. How about ten? Just for insurance."

Ten thousand dollars. I'm drunk with power. "Twenty," I say coolly, thinking maybe I know what's coming.

Sure enough, Rayf starts hemming and hawing. I make it easy for him. "You know as well as I do we've gotta have twenty—my half up front, you keep the back end."

He gives me a smug little nod.

Just before the race, he brings me a thousand dollars. "The owner wouldn't give me the whole ten," he says, "but don't worry, it's coming."

I give him a hurt look, but inwardly, I'm feeling smug myself. Burt probably figures a grand is about right for insurance money. To him, it's pocket change, and he probably thinks it's the most money a hotwalker's ever seen at one time, more than enough to prevent a double-cross. I smile to myself, imagining the Hatch playing the big man in his box up in the clubhouse, secure in the knowledge the bitch is so stupid she really thinks she's going to get the rest of her money.

When the odds are as good as they're ever going to get, I make a phone bet, wagering Burt's entire payment, plus four grand of my own. Satan's Moon goes off at two-to-one and Big Easy, who's all but forgotten by now, at thirty-five-to-one.

And Big Easy wins! *Not* Moon, although he runs his heart out, tail spinning like the devil's chasing him.

Burt and Rayf are probably already high-fiving each other, congratulating themselves on their paltry insurance payment. No way I'm ever gonna see the nineteen large they owe me, but that's nickel-and-dime stuff to me now. I just won $175,000.

Because I bet on Big Easy.

The Hatch doesn't know it, but I stopped his horse that morning. If Satan's Moon tests positive, Burt doesn't even get the twenty percent of the purse the owner of the second-place winner's entitled to. And he *will* test positive. I know because I've already drugged him.

Remember I mentioned most barns don't have night watchmen? And they're never locked, because of the risk of fire. I slipped into Moon's at four-thirty that morning, before anyone else was at work, and dropped acepromazine into his water.

I'm about to follow up with some insurance of my own. I figure Rayf will have someone watching me in the test barn.

I pick up Big Easy in the paddock and lead him there, to walk in circles while he cools down. The way they work the water, they attach buckets to posts and designate one for each horse. Big Easy's has a great big "W" on it, for Winner. As I pass, I open my hand over his bucket, as if I'm dropping something in—which I'm not—and I make sure Big Easy drinks.

It's a near-perfect scam—I win, the Hatch loses, and I've had the pleasure of rubbing his nose in it.

But it's not good enough.

We're still not even, the Hatch and me. He broke my heart; I'm going to break his.

After I take Big Easy back to his own barn, I make myself extremely scarce. I've already moved out of my apartment and into a hotel, to which I return to wait till after midnight, when I know Moon's barn will be good and deserted.

When I think it's late enough, I grab my doctor's bag and go to the Fair Grounds to see my boy Moon. Satan's Moon and I go back a long way. I wonder if he'll be glad to see me. I hope so, because I have his best interests at heart. I'd never harm an animal, and what I'm about to do won't hurt Moon for more than a minute or two.

I know something about Moon, or at least I suspect something. Sam pointed it out to me. "See how his tail makes circles when he runs?" It does, and then it stops, and then it starts up again, maybe two or three times during a race. But this doesn't happen when he's exercising. I know what people say about those circles, but nobody can prove it.

"You're saying Moon's a machine horse?" I asked.

Sam nodded. "Hey, the old-timers say Seabiscuit was. He was still a great horse."

"But everybody says Moon'll be a great stud."

"Oh sure. And maybe all his colts'll run on the machine too. It's cruel, Annalise. These horses love to run, you notice that? They get the best of everything. The whip doesn't even hurt 'em. But shocking them like that. That's gotta scare the shit out of 'em. Best thing for that horse is brain surgery—be a lot happier animal."

Sam is a great believer in brain surgery, by which he does not mean a frontal lobotomy. He means Moon needs to be gelded, to calm him down. But he thinks that'll never happen because of Burt's grandiose stud plan. That they'll keep shocking him and making his life miserable, and then they'll sell his worthless sperm to a new crop of unsuspecting owners. I'm about to prove him wrong.

Normally, no one would dare try what I'm about to do without a helper, but I know better than to try and recruit one: There are no secrets on the backside. I'm going to have to work alone, but I'm running on adrenaline—I'm furious and I'm determined, and Moon knows me, from Jersey. I really think I can do it.

It all depends whether Moon will stand for me. If he won't, I could get killed.

First, Moon and I get reacquainted—we didn't really get a chance that morning. Yep—he's glad to see me. I've got a shot at this.

I set out a sterile surgical pack, put on a pair of gloves, and give him a couple of quick injections. First, some tetanus toxoid. Then, in the jugular furrow, Dormosedan, a sedative, and a painkiller we call bute. Whether he'll stand depends on how he reacts to the sedative, and I've given Moon a little more than the normal dose. I wait to see if his head drops.

Yes! Moon's calm and drowsy, but he's still not going to like what's coming. I move around to his left, inch him up against the wall with my body. I'm tense and sweating, wondering if I can really pull this off. I've done it before, but not on a racehorse—and certainly never alone. I can hear Sam's voice the first time I tried. "You've got to move like a cat, Annalise. If you're fast enough, he won't react."

I reach under Moon's belly and inject him with lidocaine, quick as a cat. Sam's right. It goes smoothly. Then I step back to my surgical pack for a scalpel.

The procedure requires that, and an instrument rather baldly called an emasculator, which resembles large gardening clippers held together with a wing nut.

I make the necessary incision, and the horse cow-kicks, to the side. I duck and give him some love words, which seem to help. I pick up the emasculator, heart pounding like hooves on the turf. My hands are sweaty, and so's my forehead. This is the dangerous part—dangerous for Moon, that is. Over and over to myself, I say the mantra they teach you in veterinary school: "Nut to nut. Nut to nut. Nut to nut." I keep saying it to calm myself and also as a reminder. If I do it wrong—hold the emasculator nut-side up—Moon could bleed to death. It sounds like a hard mistake to make but given the tension of the procedure, it isn't.

I place the instrument properly, nut to nut, and squeeze, crushing Moon's left spermatic chord. After a moment, the horse's testicle drops into my hand. Just like that.

I put it on a glove wrapper on the ground. Then I repeat the procedure on the right. Moon tries another cow-kick, but his heart's not in it. I place the right nut on the wrapper, knowing I've lucked out with this horse—he's very susceptible to the drug.

Normally, I'd throw the testicles up on the roof for luck. This is the backside custom, and it's the vet's job to get them up there. But I've got a plan for this particular pair.

Quickly, I transfer them into two little velvet-lined boxes I've brought along. I say good-bye to Moon and tell him I hope we meet again.

And on the way out of town, I mail one of his nuts to Burt the Hatch (care of Rayford Burke) and the other to Sam with a note that says, "Moon's right moon enclosed herein. Guess who got the left one?" I sign it and add a postscript: "A story goes with it."

I am on the road by the time Sam phones. "Burt didn't hurt him, did he?"

"Hell, no," I answer. "He told Rayf to put him in a claiming race—you want him? I came into some money."

Sam sighs with relief, but he ignores my offer. "Forget the money," he says. "Let me hear the story."

Give you odds he'll be home in a week.

PINWHEEL

Scott Wolven

Every night that June, from my cell window at Orofino, I watched the fireworks color-burn the midnight sky over the Indian reservation across the road. The colors lit up fields and sometimes the sparks would drift to earth and the old horses the Indians kept would scatter, faster than you would think they were capable of. Speed left from races they never ran, I told myself. I knew horses when I was a kid near Saratoga, in upstate New York. Whole worlds had happened since then. Those horses and fireworks were my only friends at the beginning of that summer.

I wasn't in the race to win anymore. I'd fallen on some hard times in Eastern Washington and a gang that was a branch of the Posse made a deal with me. They'd pay me to finish off another man's time in Idaho. I don't know how they rigged it up, who they paid off. But one day they brought me into a hospital room in Spokane and the deputies that shackled me and took me to Orofino called me by a different name. I was inside under a new name and eight years stood between me and the door.

The Idaho State Correctional Facility at Orofino was an old brick campus, housing twice as many men as it was built for. It was a mixed classification facility, which is the worst, because the killers are in with the guys who forgot a child support payment. The guys doing a decade don't look very kindly on the guy who gets to go home in three months. I was a maximum classification at that time, because the guy I was pretending to be had a record that began in the womb.

The guards came for me early one morning and cuffed me and shackled me for transport. I knew it couldn't be good. Someone had filed a writ with the Federal Circuit Court and the federal judge had ordered that I be brought to his temporary chambers, in Boise. They were being forced to produce me, except I wasn't anyone—I wasn't the man they wanted incarcerated and I certainly wasn't going to tell anyone I was working for the Posse. In my own mind, they may as well have been driving a mute to Boise. We passed south through the beautiful Idaho mountains and trees and blue sky. The deputies driving me didn't say a word, just stopped once for coffee and then drove on. We drove into the streets and city of Boise. I slept on a bench overnight in a holding cell and they brought me upstairs into chambers in the morning.

The judge was in robes and seated behind a large desk, with an older woman stenographer in front of the desk. My brother and an Asian man, both impeccably dressed in gray suits, stood in the back of the room. The judge addressed me.

"The court has been made aware of some unusual circumstances surrounding your case." He pointed at my brother and the Asian man. I nodded and the judge continued. "We're convinced . . . the court has been convinced . . ." He paused. "The court is convinced that a sealed record and immediate release is the only way you'll be alive at the end of the week. The State of Idaho didn't seem inclined to let you go—so the appeal was passed up to me."

I didn't say anything. The court bailiff came over and unlocked my cuffs and shackles. I rubbed my wrists.

The judge stood. "I'm instructing one of my marshals to escort you to the Nevada border so we don't have a problem. I can't help you if you re-enter this state. And you're on your own with other problems—but we won't hold you here as a stationary target." He handed me some paperwork. "You're free to go, as long as you're leaving the state."

I looked at my brother, who spoke to the judge. "He'll ride with us to Nevada, Your Honor."

"Keep your head down," the judge said. He looked directly at me. "And watch behind you."

My brother shook hands with me, but we didn't say anything, not a word. He drove the new sedan behind the marshal's car, with Mr. Osaka in the back and me in the passenger's seat. It was a long ride, but finally we saw a sign for the Nevada state line. We crossed it and the marshal pulled a U-turn and headed north, back into Idaho.

Mr. Osaka mumbled something and my brother spoke to me.

"I'm sorry we couldn't warn you, but we had a heck of a time finding you. You got yourself in pretty deep."

"What's going on?" I asked.

My brother nodded as he drove. "We'd been looking for you, to come help with Mr. Osaka's operation. In looking for you, we found out that the man you went as, the real man, just got arrested in Montana. It was only a matter of time before the Posse tried to get to you on the inside."

Mr. Osaka mumbled to my brother.

"What'd he say?" I said.

"Mr. Osaka doesn't speak," my brother said. "He understands English perfectly well and he probably speaks it, although I've never heard him. I speak for him. Always, for the past five years. He talks in a kind of yakuza dialect—he and I speak it to each other and that's it. Nobody else."

"Handy," I said. I hadn't seen my brother much at the beginning of the last decade and not at all in the past five years, but years didn't come between us. I just figured he had his own job going on, somewhere, and when my plans started to fail, I didn't want to bring him down with me. He was a couple years younger than me and maybe I felt responsible. He'd gotten bigger since I'd seen him last.

"Do you want to work for Mr. Osaka?" my brother asked.

"What are we doing?" I said.

"Watching whales," my brother said. And as we drove, he detailed the operation to me. In the end, I agreed.

Whales are a select group of Japanese businessmen, probably only two hundred worldwide, who come to the United States to gamble. They're called whales because they bet huge—they're up seven million, they're down thirty million. If one of these guys walks into a small casino on a good night, he can bankrupt the place, or lose enough to let the casino build another club and a hotel.

Whales like bets that other gamblers can't get their hands on and sometimes it can be exotic—betting on street fights, illegal car racing. But the yakuza control the horse racing and that means that the yakuza can sometimes control the whales.

Mr. Osaka bought seven hundred acres of land outside Reno, flattened it all out, put in a private horse-racing track and was getting set to lay in a private airfield when some of his contractors thought they'd muscle him for more money. Those contractors are gone and now my brother and I are in charge of the operation.

A private racetrack, with all the barns and stables. The whales own stuff all over the world and pretty soon, the private jets are coming in, with the stallions and racehorses the whales have accumulated. A horseman's field of dreams. We've got the compound gated off and the whales pull up, with their limos and their drivers and their party girls. Every morning—the races start at eleven and they walk around, drinking, looking at the horses.

Mr. Osaka has only two betting windows open, run by Asian men the same as him. Tattoos on their hands, one guy with a Japanese character right on his throat. These are the honest men, bound to count the money, to take the verbal bets and always pay. No slips, no tickets. These guys are taking bets in the hundreds of thousands and never sweating.

Mr. Osaka walks the compound with us and mumbles to my brother as we pass the honest men by the bet windows.

"As children, they are not taught about wanting. Then, when they learn about money, they are taught it is filthy. The combination makes them honest," my brother translates.

The favorite bet for the whales is the pinwheel. The pinwheel lets the whale run his horse on Mr. Osaka's track, but bet against other horses running at other tracks that come in by satellite feed. Your horse can finish second here but if you've matched it up against the right combo, say from Saratoga, or Pimlico, or Yonkers, you can double or triple your take. Or you can throw your money in a bigger hole.

Money is green paper, to these people. They give more money to the party girls to keep them quiet than I've ever earned in my life. But that ended, too, once I got on Mr. Osaka's payroll.

The horses thundered around the track every day, a different group. Sired by names you'd recognize. The track stayed hard for the rest of the summer and there were winners—Jack Rabbit Fast, Sun Comet, The Last Laugh. Some of the names didn't translate into English.

One morning, my brother and I had to take pistols out to the building where the stable hands slept and escort someone to the gate. We came back by the track and Mr. Osaka stood at the rail, watching the horses take their morning exercise. He mumbled and my brother spoke.

"Do you know the secret of a fast horse?" my brother translated.

"No," I said.

Mr. Osaka mumbled at length and my brother fed me bits and pieces.

"When horses run fast, all four feet leave the ground. They fly. They like to fly. It's their fantasy. But they have to push themselves back down to the ground, so their hooves can touch the track again. So when you look at a horse, or watch him in a race, see the look on his face and the jockey's. If they like to fly, that is no good. They must like to push themselves back to ground, to run."

"Do you bet?" I asked.

Mr. Osaka mumbled. My brother spoke.

"I swore a vow in the beginning never to bet on horses and I have kept that vow. Once, a horse had to be shot in front of me and my father told me, You can see someone's life in the pattern of their death-blood. The horse's blood stopped at my feet and it was a sign to me that I should not bet on horses."

I nodded. Mr. Osaka moved his lips and my brother continued.

"If you were shot right now, and we saw your death blood, where would it go?"

I looked at the ground, which sloped slightly onto the track, and Mr. Osaka followed my gaze.

My brother finished. "Stay close to horses then, maybe that is your life."

We watched Mr. Osaka walk back to the white clubhouse and he disappeared inside.

• • •

They slammed out of the starting gates all summer and soon my brother and I had to make a bank trip to Reno. We didn't go to a bank. It was just a house on the outskirts of the city; it looked like a regular white-and-blue ranch-style. We put the money in the suitcase on the kitchen table and left, as we'd been told to do by Mr. Osaka. I think I saw the blue sedan following us that day, but I'm not sure. We went to the house later in the week, twice, and the second time, I'm sure I saw it. My brother saw it, too.

• • •

We had dropped the money off an hour before and were a mile away from the racetrack when the blue sedan pulled in front of us and cut us off. I knew as soon as they got out of the car they were cops. Two cops, undercover. My brother opened the passenger side door and ran up over the bank, as they pulled their guns. I slammed them both out of the way with my car and took off. There were shots behind me, and as

I looked in the rearview mirror, my brother was getting into the blue sedan, following me.

. . .

You've never seen so many people in such a hurry from anything. Mexican stable boys running into the desert, limos pulling around with half-dressed women, and the whales, sunglasses falling off, waving for them to hurry. Planes taking off. My brother watched the gate. Running an illegal racetrack, illegal gambling operation, weapons, now shot cops. We needed to leave.

A fire started near the horse barn. I was still looking for Mr. Osaka, but he was nowhere. There was a bulldozer next to the airfield, left from the contractors. I started it, bulldozed the fence down, got off the rig and opened the stall doors as the flames licked the wood. The horses took off across the field, into the heat. I watched them, shining, maybe three hundred million dollars of property on hooves, running like they wanted to. The owners wouldn't be happy, but I had done it. My brother and I climbed into a new truck and cut the corner of Idaho, before slipping into Montana and up into Canada. We took our pay with us, nothing more—maybe we hoped that honorable thing would calm Mr. Osaka. The yakuza were like an ocean, deep and violent, and I knew and my brother knew we would live small lives from now on. If we wanted to live life at all.

. . .

It was Saratoga that finally called us back. We were there in August on a Sunday, walked down Main Street, bought a racing paper and then made our way over to the track. Years had passed, we had different names and we'd just done a big deal in Manhattan. One stop at the track before returning to north of the border. We settled in, examined the sheet with golf pencils and went to the window.

In the third race, we were by the clubhouse rail. There was a tremendous field coming around, the crowd was cheering. It was close. The brown blur of the pack slammed past us to the finish.

A young Asian boy stood in front of us. He'd come out of the crowd; I hadn't seen him till now. He mumbled to my brother and I almost felt bullets piercing my back. Nothing happened. My brother spoke.

"Mr. Osaka says we did the right thing and that we should look for a particular horse in the next race."

The boy bowed and walked into the clubhouse crowd. Sweat ran down my ribs. My brother held up the racing sheet and I looked at it.

It was the maiden race for Komodo Dragon, blinders on, Lasix, and we checked the tote board. Leading off at 85-1. None of the other names could be it. We went to the window and put it all, over seven thousand dollars—that was the lucky limit we'd agreed to bet—on Komodo Dragon. On the nose.

They brought the horses into the starting gate and bang, ring, they're off. Komodo Dragon is at the back of the pack and as they come around the first turn, it can't be. Komodo Dragon is dead last and drifting to the outside. Then it starts. Komodo Dragon passes one, passes two, passes Two-Time Loser, passes Long Johnny. Now it's Komodo Dragon on the outside and the horse starts to fly, to push itself back to the ground, to fly, to push, passing as though the other horses are standing still. You can feel it in the ground and now they're headed for the final turn, it's Komodo Dragon and Rummy, the favorite, Komodo Dragon, Rummy, and the final stretch, Komodo Dragon is flying and pushing and the whip gets him back down on the ground, Komodo Dragon is ahead and further, by a length, Komodo Dragon.

We're walking up to the window with the ticket and we're not saying anything. But it's there in my head and as soon as we're in the car, safe, moving, back in our own race, we'll talk about it. Beautiful houses in Vancouver and the chance to start over again, a little safer. To run under another name, in a different city, with better chances, another day.